UNDER
SUSPICION

RACHEL LEE

UNDER SUSPICION

WHEELER
PUBLISHING, INC.
ROCKLAND, MA

★ AN AMERICAN COMPANY ★

Published in Large Print by arrangement with Warner Books, Inc. in the
United States and Canada

Wheeler Large Print Book Series.

Set in 16 pt Plantin.

Library of Congress Cataloging-in-Publication Data

Lee, Rachel.
    Under suspicion / Rachel Lee.
        p. (large print) cm.(Wheeler large print book series)
    ISBN 1-58724-145-5 (softcover)
    1. Large type books. I. Title. II. Series

CIP information available

                                                    2001055789
                                                            CIP

CHAPTER ONE

At last! The night was at hand. Hiding in plain sight, the watcher saw the head curator come into the lobby of the Museum of Antiquities. Anna Lundgren was tall, slender, redheaded; dressed more like a woman than he'd ever seen, in her clinging black evening sheath and black high heels. She paused to share a few words with the security guard, then scanned the room.

She looked nervous. He wasn't surprised. As her green eyes scraped over him, noticing but not noticing him, he saw the uneasiness there. It was supposed to be her night of triumph, and he thought she must be afraid that something would go wrong. She had absolutely no idea just how wrong it was going to go.

He hugged the knowledge to himself, watching as she circulated among the early arrivals. Tonight was the big night, the private showing of the museum's new visiting exhibit: *Mysteries of the Maya.* Museum benefactors and university officials were arriving steadily and beginning to partake of the sumptuous hors d'oeuvres and open bar.

1

Docents in dark green blazers with gold crests milled around, looking nervous in anticipation of their first public performance.

Moving slowly, with apparent lack of direction, he eased himself steadily closer to Anna Lundgren. She was talking to Mike Armbruster, one of the museum's board of directors.

He got close enough to eavesdrop in time to hear Armbruster tell her, "Sammy Doe walked me through a little while ago." Sammy was one of the student docents, a reliable, intelligent young man. "I'm impressed. You deserve every star in your crown tonight. Enjoy the triumph."

Anna looked delighted. A smile sparkled on her face. He savored her delight. It would accentuate her fall.

"You ought to wear black more often," Armbruster remarked as he turned away. "Brings out all the fire in your red hair."

Anna's face fell, and the watcher figured she didn't like the remark. It seemed to threaten her. Well, she didn't know what threat was.

Anna turned, her eyes grazing over him. A faint smile came to her mouth, acknowledging him, but the watcher knew she didn't really see him. People rarely saw him clearly, unless he made a point of getting their attention, and he liked it that way. Carefully, he followed her across the increasingly crowded room.

Several state senators and legislators graced the crowd now, as well as the high muckety-mucks from the university and museum. The watcher barely saw them. He wasn't interested in them at all. They made an annoying background buzz, a series of elegantly clad obstacles in his path.

Anna's hair made her easy to follow. The color of polished, new copper. She would make a beautiful sacrifice to end the curse, the watcher thought. Perfect. Exquisite. Fire to end fire. How appropriate.

Elegant, too, he thought, as he continued to follow her, listening as she exchanged meaningless pleasantries with people she didn't know. Gracious. They should only know her as he knew her. They'd never imagine her grubby with sweat and grime over the past months as they'd struggled to build the exhibit's framework. They couldn't imagine how she looked with her hair in her eyes as she unpacked the artifacts when they arrived, or the way she swore when she nicked a finger or made a mistake on a catalogue entry.

But he knew. He'd been watching her for months, tucked away among the crews that had labored so mightily to bring vistas of the Yucatán to the museum. He saw a great deal to admire in her, much to respect. Otherwise, she would have been a poor sacrifice.

The watcher was a smart man, though, and he knew he had to set things up in a way that would let *her* know what was happening, but conceal his part in it. Toward that end he was patient, and tonight would only start the ball rolling.

He saw Anna try to slip past Reed Howell, a reporter from the *Sentinel,* but she didn't make it. He snagged her, and looked at her with those opaque shark's eyes of his. The watcher nodded; Howell was just another of his tools. He made sure he was close enough to overhear.

"Hi, Anna," Howell said. "Exciting night, yes?"

"Very," she agreed, smiling sweetly. The watcher knew she was faking it. "We're all *thrilled* to see our dreams come to fruition."

But Howell was looking at Anna as if she were bait in the water. Good. It would begin.

"I can imagine," the reporter said pleasantly enough. He pulled a notebook and pen out of his pocket, but he didn't write down what she'd already said. Instead he looked at her, his pen poised. "I was wondering how you feel professionally about hyping the Pocal Curse to increase public interest in this exhibit."

Her face stiffened, but the smile remained. "The Pocal Curse is part of the story of some of the items we're exhibiting, Reed. I don't have any qualms about exciting the public's imagination. Times have changed; museums can no longer rely on dusty exhibits and neatly typed little cards. As I see it, we're merely enhancing the educational process."

He nodded, and this time scribbled at least part of her remark on his pad. She waited with apparent patience, but the watcher could see she was dying to escape.

Reed looked up from his notes. "That's the standard explanation for this kind of showmanship," he said.

"Yes, and it's a good one. We'd like to share these exciting artifacts and all this wonderful history with a broader audience. And that's why we're highlighting the curse in our promotional materials."

"And not to make money?"

The watcher thought he detected tension in her face, as if she were holding in irritation. "Money? We're a nonprofit organization. What we hope to get out of this is enough public interest to pay the cost of the exhibit. If we do, we'll be able to bring other exciting exhibits here."

"And you have no professional qualms about touting a curse. You don't find it the least bit unscientific?"

"What's unscientific about it? We're reporting a fact. It is part of Mayan lore that there is a curse on Pocal's burial site. And we state quite clearly that it is folk legend that says there is a curse on the jade dagger." She paused, taking a breath and visibly relaxing. "You *will* tour the exhibit tonight, won't you? You can see for yourself how we've handled it, rather than take my word for it."

He smiled, but his eyes were still opaque. "I've seen how you handled it all right. Pictures on every local TV station showing how the staff unpacked some of the items without touching them, supposedly because of the curse. Pure hype. Great promo, though."

Her tone grew faintly defensive. "I'm not responsible for how the media choose to portray things."

"No." Howell kept smiling. "Don't you feel at least a *personal* qualm about hyping this curse?"

Her smile slipped, and she looked dubiously at him. "I already told you how I feel. The curse is simply a tool to get attention. A little showmanship *has* to be part of the modern museum."

"I know, I know. But I'm talking about you, personally, not Anna Lundgren, curator. Don't you feel at least a little trepidation or disgust about using the curse?"

"Why should I?"

"Because it killed your father sixteen years ago."

At that Anna clearly gave up all pretense of pleasantness. She took a quick step away, her face red and her mouth tight. But it seemed her anger wouldn't let her leave without having the last word.

Pausing, she fixed him with an icy glare. "Stick to the facts, Reed. An *earthquake* killed my father."

Soon. The thought kept him going through the endless hour of cocktail-party banter. The watcher waited for Anna to go to her office, where he knew the index cards for her speech were waiting, but she kept right on smiling and talking to everyone who had come. It was her job, of course, to keep the money people happy, but the watcher was growing just a little impatient as the minutes ticked by.

Finally, he settled near a hallway marked EMPLOYEES ONLY. That was when he realized he might have made a mistake.

A small, odd-looking man wearing a dark,

6

out-of-date suit with a polka-dotted burgundy bow tie, wandered over and stood on the other side of the hallway entrance, leaning back and folding his arms.

The watcher observed him surreptitiously, wondering where this relic had come from. The man's dark hair was slicked back, and his moustache, stiffened with wax, curled at the ends. It was an odd thing to see on someone who couldn't be over forty, if that.

Not only was the man odd-looking, but he didn't fit the current crowd at all. In a room aswirl with evening gowns and tuxedos, he looked like a man who'd lost his way. Maybe he was some faculty member. The watcher had noticed that a surprising number of professors seemed to eschew fashion of any kind and take pride in dowdiness.

It was then that the man, who seemed to feel the watcher's gaze on him, turned and looked at him. The watcher wanted to draw back, but forced himself to remain outwardly indifferent. Unlike most people, however, the little man's gaze didn't glide over him without seeing him. Instead those two dark eyes fixed on him, measured him, acknowledged him.

"Quite a squeeze, isn't it," the little man said.

"Uh, yes."

"This isn't the kind of thing I ordinarily like to do."

The man seemed to expect some response and waited until the watcher gave it to him.

"Why not?"

The man shrugged. "Just not my cup of tea. Oh, I'd come to see the exhibit as a regular visitor, but these society splashes... Well, I wouldn't be here except for my aunt. She wanted an escort."

The watcher nodded as if he understood, then looked out toward the crowd, pretending to have lost interest. He wondered if he should move away, then decided that was unnecessary. The silly little man didn't know what he was thinking, and would have forgotten him five minutes after he left tonight.

Where was Anna? For an instant he feared he'd lost sight of her, but then her copper-colored hair emerged from behind an extremely tall man, and she began to head toward the office. Good, she was coming to get her notes for her speech. And there she would find the gift he'd left for her.

Anticipation filled him, drying his mouth and moistening his palms. This was it. Unfortunately, he thought with a sidelong glace at the little man, he wasn't going to be able to dart down the hallway and listen to her reaction. Not with that guy watching...

Anna breezed past, glancing at neither of them. She was looking really nervous now. It was nearly time to give her speech. He'd heard her say several times over the last week that she *hated* to give speeches. The watcher enjoyed knowing that. He enjoyed knowing her every weakness, and figured over the next days he would learn many more of them.

"Beautiful woman," remarked the odd little man.

The watcher nodded, then returned his

attention to the gathering. *Go away,* he silently ordered his unwelcome companion.

But just then, from down the hallway, he heard Anna's cry. He hesitated, unwilling to dash back there when the man would notice. But then, strangely enough, he was rescued by his companion, who rushed down the hallway.

As soon as the footsteps stopped, the watcher peered around the corner. The man was in Anna's office, the way was clear. Soundless in his rubber-soled shoes, he made his way back there. Beside Anna's office there was an alcove, meant to hold vending machines that had not yet been installed. It gave him a perfect cave from which to listen.

"It's nothing," he heard her say. "I was just surprised."

"What is it?"

"It's nothing," she said more firmly. "A joke."

A joke? The watcher didn't want her to think it was a joke. It was meant to frighten her. Annoyance pricked him.

"Is that a dagger?" the little man asked. "It must be old. From the exhibit?"

"It's a replica. I cried out because for an instant I thought it was the real one."

"Ahh."

Unfortunately, to the watcher it sounded as if the little man grew even more interested, not less.

"It's probably just a gift from someone," Anna said firmly. "A memento. Or a joke.

Here's an envelope. I'm sure the card inside says who sent it."

"Don't open it," the stranger said sharply. "There might be prints on it."

The watcher smiled to himself. He had taken great care not to leave any fingerprints.

"Prints?" Anna sounded startled. "Why would anyone be worried about that? Are you crazy?"

"Oh. I forgot." The little man paused, and there was a rustling sound. Pulling out his wallet? Opening his coat? "Clarence Tebbins, Tampa PD."

The watcher started a bit, and felt his heart slam. He hadn't expected the police to get involved this soon.

"Oh, for heaven's sake," Anna said a little sharply. "This isn't a police matter. It's just a...gift or a joke."

Unfortunately, the cop seemed to disagree. "You look pretty pale to me. My guess is that you don't really think it's that innocent."

"Look, I don't have time for this. I have to give a speech."

A chair creaked. Tebbins sitting? Then the little man spoke again, ignoring Anna's objection. "Do you have any idea who sent this?"

"I could open the envelope," Anna said acidly. "Or I could speculate that it's a gag gift from the staff."

"Why a gag gift?"

"Well, there's supposedly a curse attached to the real dagger. Anyone who touches it will die a horrible death."

"I see. Not a very friendly joke," Tebbins remarked after a moment.

"Or possibly a juvenile one." Tissue paper rustled. Was she handling the dagger or was he? Or was she just rewrapping it?

Tebbins spoke. "You're sure it's a copy?"

"Of course. The blade isn't even real jade. It's glass. And the handle appears to be electroplated. The carvings aren't exactly the same. Someone worked hard on it, but not hard enough." She said it emphatically. "I'm sure it's nothing you need to worry yourself about, Officer."

"Detective," he corrected her. "Well, if you're going to insist on handling all the packing materials, you might as well open the envelope. But let me do it for you. No sense smudging more prints than we need to."

"I told you, it's just a prank."

"Then the card will say so, yes?"

Anna sighed audibly. "Be my guest."

"Do you have a letter opener?" he asked.

There was the sound of a drawer opening, and the watcher knew she was pulling out the ivory-handled letter opener that was her family heirloom.

"Lovely," Tebbins remarked. There were some other sounds, too faint to make out. "There is no card—the envelope is empty," he announced with the air of one who is smugly satisfied that he was correct.

"Empty?" The watcher heard the doubt, and the faint undercurrent of fear in Anna's voice. Most others wouldn't have heard it, but he knew Anna well. The almost inaudible note of fear was there. Good. He hadn't failed.

"Generally," Tebbins said, "when people intend no harm, they don't hide."

"But this *is* harmless," she said, still protesting the whole idea.

"In and of itself," he agreed.

There was a silence. The watcher strained his ears, wondering if they might be whispering. But no, the way the hall echoed and amplified sounds, he would have been able to tell.

"Well," Anna said suddenly, her voice brisk, "I've got a speech to give. I just came in here to get my index cards."

"A moment," Tebbins said.

The tapping of her heels on the tile floor stopped and she said, "Are you always so persistent?"

"Of course," the cop answered, sounding surprised that anyone would doubt it. "I want to take the package and its contents to be examined."

The watcher's heart stopped, and he had to grind his teeth to keep from crying out. This was not part of the plan.

"But it's nothing. A prank. There's no evidence of anything criminal. Why do the police need to be involved?"

"One never knows," Tebbins said.

"Sure," said Anna, impatiently. "Take it. What harm could it do?"

"Thank you. Can I leave it here until after the presentation?"

"No problem. Let me lock up."

The watcher shrank backward into a small L at the rear of the alcove and listened to their footsteps fade away. He had time. He had time to rescue the dagger. But for long moments he just stood, shaking and shaken, waiting for his strength to return. He could get the dagger. He *would* get it.

Nothing could be allowed to interfere with his plan.

Narrow jungle paths opened into nooks and crannies containing objects of stone and gold. Tangled vines cloaked a doorway, giving way to a vista of stone pyramids rising amidst vegetation, beneath a concealing canopy of trees. Later, a climb down into the depths of a pyramid, into a small, dark chamber where beautiful artifacts lay carefully arranged around an ornately carved stone sarcophagus. And always in the background, the distant call of exotic birds, even the rumble of faraway thunder...

The exhibit was an unqualified success. As the guests emerged in groups at the end of the manufactured trail, they congratulated Anna and other museum personnel enthusiastically.

The watcher nodded approval. Anna *had* worked hard on the exhibit, as hard as anyone. And it *was* a masterpiece. He himself had felt as if he were back in the jungles of the Yucatán, although the exhibit was not nearly as threatening. She deserved the kudos. He hoped she enjoyed them, since they would probably be her last.

But at an opportune moment, while the crowd swirled and attention seemed to be focused on Anna, he slipped down the now-darkened hallway to her office. Weeks ago he had stolen a master key from the janitor and duplicated it, returning the original before the lazy janitor had even noticed it was missing. Now, as easily as he had earlier in the evening, he let himself into Anna's office.

It was dark, but not nearly as dark as the hallway. Light filtered through the closed horizontal blinds from the parking lot outside. It was enough to see the replica dagger, the box and tissue in which it had come, and the gift-card envelope on which he'd typed Anna's name. Slipping on gloves, he scooped them all up.

The box and tissue were a problem, he realized. He couldn't conceal them. Dropping them back on the desk, he tucked the dagger inside his slacks, slipping his hand into his pocket to hold it until he could find somewhere else to stash it until he needed it.

Even through the fabric of his slacks, the glass blade felt warm to his hand. The original was a ceremonial dagger, about fourteen inches long, with a sharp jade blade and an ornately carved gold hilt. The Mayan king, Pocal, had probably worn it for important occasions. No one was certain if it had ever tasted blood, but the watcher thought it probably had.

The thought gave him a thrill, and he clutched the dagger tighter, crumpling his slacks somewhat. No good, he reminded himself. It had to remain invisible.

Sneaking farther down the hallway, he used the master key to get into a musty storage room and tuck the dagger into a file box. It needed to be concealed there for only a couple of hours. This would work.

Then, slipping back down the hallway, he took up his post again. All that mattered, he reminded himself, was that he accomplish his mission. If the dagger were found...well, it wouldn't be a total loss. It would just muddy the message a little. He could live with that.

It was just a little kink, and if he couldn't handle kinks, then what kind of a mastermind was he?

The crowd began to thin out. He kept his gaze on Anna's coppery hair but didn't follow her. It might become too obvious as the guests left. But when he saw her speaking to Reed Howell again, he eased his way over there. This he didn't want to miss. The duel had begun.

Even Reed Howell seemed to have mellowed, but the watcher put that down to the fact that the reporter had availed himself of some of the liquid refreshment.

"Not bad, Anna," Howell said. "Not bad at all. I'd pay the fourteen bucks to come see it. One thing though...those stairs down into the underground chamber. What about the disabled?"

"There's an elevator, Reed. Handicapped only."

He nodded, appearing satisfied. Just as the watcher thought he was going to move on and leave her unscathed, Howell said, "Someday you gotta tell me about the curse and how your father died."

Anna's face deadened. "It's a matter of public record, Reed. He died in an earthquake."

"Yeah, but the curse says..."

She shook her head. "No. It wasn't a curse. It was an earthquake. They happen all the time down there."

"But don't you ever wonder?"

"I'm a woman of science. I don't believe in curses."

"Thanks," he said, and strode away.

Moments later, Anna turned to a nearby woman, and said, "Oh my God, I walked right into it."

Janine Mason, the art director, moved closer to Anna. "Uh-oh," she said. "You shouldn't have said that."

"I know. I know. But I can explain it."

"Sure." Janine shook her head. "If anyone gives you the opportunity. Look, I'll go chase the asshole down. Maybe I can clear up the problem."

"I should do that."

"Hell no. The guy's a demon, and he wants to skewer you on his little red pitchfork. Let me."

Janine started to move away, then paused and leaned toward Anna. The watcher could barely hear her. "Who's that little guy with the greasy hair and weird moustache? He keeps staring at you."

Anna glanced over. "Oh, don't mind him. That's Clarence Tebbins of the Tampa PD. He's a Hercule Poirot wanna-be."

The watcher shifted his attention to the little man. A Hercule Poirot wanna-be? The idea tickled him, although he wasn't sure why Anna had said that. This mission could be more fun than he'd thought.

He shifted his attention to Janine, who had caught up with Reed Howell near the door. *Damage control.* He hoped it wouldn't work. He'd spent plenty of time and effort to prime Reed's pump so that Anna's story would come out in the papers. He wanted the whole world to understand what had happened. And Reed Howell was his mouthpiece.

It was time, though, to hide himself. He retreated to the musty storage room and sat in the pitch-dark, holding the dagger in his hands, fancying that the real one would glow in the dark, ever so faintly, with the power of the curse. He wished he could hear Anna's reaction, or Tebbins's, when they found the dagger was gone as mysteriously as it had appeared. The images that ran through his brain forced him to stifle a giggle of delight.

Time passed slowly. He checked his Indiglo watch every few minutes, but 1 A.M. seemed to take a long time arriving.

At last, though, he picked up the Thermos bottle he'd stashed there earlier, tucked the dagger safely away, and headed out to greet the curse's first victim.

"Hi, Eddy," he said to the security guard at the front desk. "I brought you some coffee again. How ya doin' tonight?"

CHAPTER TWO

The phone dragged Gil Garcia out of sleep around nine-thirty. It sounded like a slothfully late hour, but considering he'd been working a murder scene until 3 A.M., it felt early to him.

"What now?" he muttered at the telephone. Oh hell, the pager was going off, too. Next it would be his cell phone playing that damn cheery tune he'd never bothered to figure out how to turn off.

"Want me to get it, Dad?" His fifteen-year-old daughter's bright voice called through the door. What was she doing up? She was a teenager, for cripes sake, and she was on spring break besides. How could she possibly sound so chipper?

"I'll get it," he groaned back, his voice raspy from sleep. The phone and pager beeped again, and the c-phone started playing a mad melody from the closet.

"Okay," Trina called back. "I'm making breakfast. Sausage, eggs, grits."

Oh, God, Gil thought, sitting up and rubbing the sleep from his eyes. She wanted something. Something she didn't think he'd agree to.

Then he grabbed the receiver, tucked it to his ear, and switched the pager off. "Garcia," he grumbled.

"Good morning, sleepyhead," said the too-happy voice of Louise Obern. "They're playing tag, and you're it."

"Shit. Louise, I was out on a case until after three this morning."

"Sorry, big boy, but you're all we got. DB near Sixth Avenue and Forty-third. Girl-friend came home this A.M., found the vic dead on the couch. Criminologists to arrive shortly. Uniforms are on the scene. They say it looks like an O.D. She says he never did drugs."

"Jesus."

"Hey, don't blame me. I didn't arrange for all the murders this week."

"Give me a few, will you? My daughter made me a special breakfast, so I at least need to make a quick run at it, and hear what it is she wants this time."

"Sounds heavy. I pity you. Take your time, you poor schmuck. The vic isn't in a hurry, and the scene is secure."

That kind of sympathy he could do without, Gil thought. Rubbing his eyes again, he hung up the phone. Shower fast. Dress faster. Eat quickly. Say no. Soothe tears. Get back to work. Ah, the life of a homicide cop and part-time dad.

The shower helped wake him, though, and by the time he emerged from his bedroom to the smells of a good breakfast, he figured a half gallon of coffee would finish the job.

He was a tall, lean man, with the dark hair and eyes of his Hispanic heritage. He also had a great smile, one which he wasn't ashamed to use to his advantage in his work. But basically he thought of himself as totally ordinary.

19

Trina, however, was a lovely, blossoming dark-haired beauty who was already attracting too much male attention. This morning she was wearing a frilly apron he'd never seen before as she stood at the stove stirring the grits in the pot. Homemade-from-scratch grits. Man, she knew the way to his heart.

"Morning, Dad."

"Morning, honey." He dropped a peck on her smooth cheek, then pulled out a chair at the breakfast table. "I'm afraid I've got to run. There's been another murder. Just time to eat."

"That's okay," she said brightly. A moment later she was filling a plate for him with eggs, sausage patties, and a heaping mound of buttery grits.

"Where on earth did you find the grits?" he asked. His cupboard held only the instant variety.

She shrugged. "I went by the grocery store yesterday and used some of my allowance. They're better this way."

He smiled at her. "I couldn't agree more." Then he tucked in, wondering how long he'd have to wait for the other shoe to drop.

"Oh," Trina said suddenly, just as she was about to join him, "I forgot to bring in the newspaper."

"It's okay, don't worry about it. I won't have time to read it this morning." He glanced pointedly at his watch. "Gotta run in a couple of minutes." He waited, but still she said nothing. "This is a fabulous breakfast, honey. Thanks so much for making it. How come you went to all this trouble?"

He glanced up in time to see her bite her lip, and he found himself mentally ordering her to just tell him what was going on.

"Oh..." she said after a moment, "I just felt like doing something nice."

Shit. It was more than wanting to go to the beach with her boyfriend...of whom he didn't completely approve. A thought suddenly grabbed him by the throat. She couldn't be pregnant, could she? Oh, God...

But she didn't say any more, and he couldn't exactly press her without making her angry by implying that he thought the breakfast was a ploy. Even if it was. Time had taught him such a conversation would go nowhere.

Finally, he asked, "What are your plans for the day?"

Her eyes shifted in a way that made him feel even more uneasy. "I'm just going to hang out."

"With your boyfriend?"

"I don't know. I was thinking about meeting Sally at the mall."

He hoped. But he couldn't be sure. Damn it. In fact, it sounded entirely too innocent. "Do you have bus fare?"

She smiled. "Sure. Don't worry about me."

The problem was, he worried entirely too much, even though she was only with him on school breaks and holidays, and alternate weekends. His ex-wife doled out time with Trina according to her convenience. He was well aware that if he upset Trina too much, she might complain to her mother, and thus not come stay with him for the summer.

On the other hand...

21

He was still thinking about the other hand when he walked through the humid air to his car. It was going to be a hot one. There was a certain feeling in the air that warned him. Not that he much cared. He'd lived in Florida all his life, and heat didn't scare him.

It just wilted him a little.

Unfortunately, just as he was opening his car door, Zoe Fenster, also known as "the widow next door," came trotting over. This morning she wore a fuchsia muumuu and flip-flops, but she'd managed to comb her ash gray hair and put on her lipstick before she attacked. Worse, she was bearing a plastic-wrap-covered plate.

"I just made you some cookies, Gil," she trilled.

He was already drowning in her baked goods, most of which were less than stellar. "Thanks, Zoe," he said, in his official voice. "Just give them to Trina, will you? I've got to get to a murder scene."

She looked suitably impressed, thank God, and merely nodded without looking crushed. Standing there like a lost bird of paradise, she waved after him as he backed out of the driveway and headed down the quiet, tree-lined street.

Good escape. He mentally patted himself on the back, but stopped as soon as he remembered Trina. There was trouble brewing there, and he didn't really know what to do about it. And there was nothing in the world like a teenager to make a parent feel like an utterly incompetent idiot.

The scene was taped off, the requisite neighborhood gawkers had appeared, and the crime-scene van was just jockeying into position. Gil pulled in behind a patrol car and found himself wishing that his partner, Seamus Rourke, wasn't on vacation. He could have used some of the nonsensical patter he and Seamus used to get through these scenes.

Oh well.

He climbed out of the car and pushed everything out of his head except his concern with the job. The always unpleasant job of examining a possible murder scene. Of course this one shouldn't be too bad, unless the vic hadn't been discovered quickly.

He nodded to the uniforms who were keeping an eye on things outside, two guys he didn't know very well. A heavy young woman sat in the backseat of one of the patrol cars, her eyes red and puffy. Probably the girlfriend. But first things first.

He stepped into the house and found Frank Delgado just inside the door. He knew Frank from way back and trusted his judgment. Right now he was just making sure nobody muddied the scene. He'd even already arranged for a taped-off pathway, to confine walkthroughs to a limited area until the criminologists finished. Good man.

"How's it going, Frank?"

"Another day, another dollar." Frank's stock reply. He was a short man, his belly stretching his white uniform shirt more and more as he approached fifty. Lately his favorite topic of conversation was retirement. But other than his sun-lined face and salt-and-pepper hair, Frank was still a young man. If he retired, it would be for mental reasons, not physical ones.

"And another O.D. they tell me."

"Looks like it." Frank stabbed a stubby finger toward the couch. "Went out as peaceful as a baby. I should be so lucky."

Gil took in the scene, a fit young man lying sprawled on the couch, wearing a T-shirt and briefs. Around him lay scattered the detritus of a drug user. The needle lay on the floor as if it had fallen from his right hand, which drooped over the edge. A belt was looped around his upper left arm, a makeshift tourniquet. On the coffee table were a guttered candle in a brass holder, a spoon, and a bag of white powder. What a fucking waste.

"Pretty obvious," Frank remarked. "No rigor yet, so it must have happened in the wee hours."

"Log me in, Frank. I want to take a closer look."

Everyone who entered a potential crime scene was logged in so that anything they left behind unintentionally, from fingerprints to stray hairs, could be ruled out as evidence.

The first thing he did was scan the carpet. Vacuumed frequently, but not recently enough to tell anything. Footprints were all over it. Making his way across the living room, he bent down to peer at the man's left arm. A drop of congealed blood clearly marked the needle site at the vein.

"Told ya," Frank said.

"Maybe."

"What do you mean, *maybe*?"

"Well, there's only one *fresh* needle track." Gil turned a little and checked the other arm. "More tracks on the right arm, but they're old, and there's only a few. Like he's maybe had blood tests a couple of times."

"So maybe he's an occasional user."

"Possible. It wouldn't be the first time somebody's checked out on the first try."

But he looked at the man's left arm again and was troubled. The setup looked experienced. The arm didn't show any practice jabs, the kind you often saw when somebody wanted to test how it felt before doing the whole thing. Very skilled. And why were the rest of the needle marks, as old as they were, on the right arm?

He straightened. "Was he right-handed or left-handed?"

"I don't know. I don't think anybody asked."

"Okay. I'm gonna walk through the rest of the house."

"Nothin' to see. The guy came home, jabbed himself, and died. Plain and simple."

It should only be so easy, Gil thought as he wandered through the rest of the tiny house. Two bedrooms, one turned into a study or office with two messy desks and stacks of textbooks. The guy was either a student or a teacher. Same with the girlfriend, he'd bet.

The bedroom showed only a freshly made

bed. So, whenever he'd decided to juice up last night, he hadn't slept first. All-night worker, maybe?

The kitchen was a little messier. Dishes in the sink, holding the remains of a fast-food burger and cereal. A coffeemaker, nearly empty, turned off. And a pan on the floor. Judging by its location, the girl had knocked it down when she'd reached for the phone to call 9-1-1. No sign anywhere of a real disturbance.

Put a fork in it, Gil, he told himself. It's done.

But he wasn't really sure of that. He stepped out just as the crime-scene team came up the walk with their boxes, cameras, and vacuums.

"Be extra careful," he told them, knowing how they'd brush over things if they thought the case was self-evident and no trial was going to be involved. "It's not as simple as it looks."

"Sure," Henry Beaudry replied. "Not an O.D.?"

Gil shrugged. "Something isn't right."

"Gotcha. We're on it."

He trusted Beaudry.

The woman was still sitting in the back of the cruiser, crying again. This was the part Gil hated most of all, but there was no way around it. He needed information only this woman could provide, and he couldn't wait for her memory to cloud.

He opened the door of the car and squatted. "Hi," he said gently. "I'm Detective Gil Garcia."

A pretty young woman with wavy chestnut hair and brown eyes sat hunched on the seat. Even though she was heavy, youth helped her carry the extra weight beautifully. She dashed a hand over her eyes and glared at him. "He *didn't* do drugs. Eddy never touched the stuff. He said it was stupid."

"I believe you."

"You're just saying that."

"No, I'm serious. But you're going to have to help me figure it all out. You need to tell me everything you can so I can find out what happened."

"I know what happened," she wailed. "Somebody killed him!"

She dissolved into sobs, and Gil straightened, leaning against the side of the car while he waited for her to calm down. The day was growing warmer by the minute, and he began to think of chucking his jacket. The two uniforms had retreated to the shade of an old oak tree, but he wasn't so lucky. The car sat in the sun, and he stood there with it, waiting.

His thoughts flitted back to Trina, and he wondered what the hell was going on with her. With each passing day, his daughter was turning into a bigger mystery to him. She had thoughts and dreams behind her snapping dark eyes that were shut off to him. He found himself wishing she were seven again, and every thought in her head would come tumbling out on her next breath. Perhaps because he wasn't with her all the time, this growing wall between them seemed ominous to him.

He told himself it was natural for a teenager

to behave this way. Of course she would want a more private life now. But he couldn't help thinking of all the dangers she could get into, especially since he was a cop and intimately acquainted with all the possibilities.

His ex had used to complain about that. That he thought too much, worried too much, that he couldn't live a normal life because he spent too much time in the underbelly of society. Maybe she'd been right. Certainly *she* didn't seem to be worried about Trina.

The sobs coming from the car were beginning to slow down, and he leaned over to look in at the woman. "How are you doing?"

She nodded and dashed more tears away. "I'm sorry."

Gil squatted again so he was nearly at her eye level. "It's okay. You've had a terrible shock and a terrible loss. But I need to talk to you to find out what really happened. And the sooner we talk, the better."

She nodded again and sniffled once more.

"I'll just ask you a few questions now, okay? We can talk more at the station later. At least it's air-conditioned."

A bleary smile tugged at the corners of her mouth. "You look awful hot."

"Nah, I'm used to it." *Liar.* Nobody got used to this, dressed the way he was dressed. It was T-shirt and shorts weather. He pulled a pad and pen from his pocket.

"What's your name?"

"Carole Efrem." She spelled it for him.

"And your boyfriend?"

She squeezed her eyes shut and her mouth

28

trembled. After a moment, she quavered, "Eddy Malacek."

"Was Eddy right-handed or left-handed?"

Her eyes popped open. "What difference does it make? He was left-handed though."

Gil made a note of that, keeping his outward cool as inwardly a nervous twitch started in his stomach. He recognized the feeling. The hunt was on. "And you say Eddy never did drugs?"

"Never, not ever. Jeez, I tried them a couple of times. Everybody does. It's no big deal. But Eddy didn't even want to hear about the stuff. He said it was a waste of time and money, and dangerous besides."

"Did he have any friends who used drugs?"

"Not around Eddy. At least as far as I know." She turned her face toward him, tears hanging on her lower lashes. "Eddy was a dweeb. He liked to hang out with a local *Star Trek* group all dressed up like Mr. Spock. A Vulcan wouldn't use drugs."

"Of course not." He knew something of the mythology, having been a bit of a fan back in high school. However, that argument wouldn't stand up in court. "What else did he like to do?"

"Oh, he loved to play *Dungeons & Dragons* with some people who meet on Saturdays at a hobby shop over in Tampa. And sometimes he played Warhammer."

An escapist, Gil thought. That might fit in with drug use. Or not. Eddy, after all, was relatively young. "Later," he said gently, "I'll need all the details about who he hung out with, okay?"

"Sure. But I don't think any of them would...would...*kill* him!" The last words came out on a wail, and he waited for her to settle down again.

"Probably not," he said to soothe her. "But they might know about some people you don't know about."

She nodded and wiped away her tears with her hands. "He's a sweet guy. Nobody'd want to hurt him."

"What did he do?"

"He's a student, and he works nights as a security guard on campus. Just two or three nights a week."

Gil scribbled some more down. "Which campus?"

"USF."

"Okay. And you were away last night?"

"I was away for two days." She sniffled. "I went to see my dad. He lives in Melbourne. Anyway, I left way early so I could be here when Eddy got home this morning. He gets off at 8 A.M., you know?"

He nodded encouragingly.

"But I was late and I got here at nine and there...there he was...and I couldn't wake him up..."

Gil patted her shoulder as she started sobbing again, then straightened and signaled to one of the uniforms. Some new guy he'd seen around a couple of times.

R. Ortiz. Ramon. Yeah.

"Hey, Ramon, could you see that Ms. Efrem gets down to the station? I need to talk to her more, and we might as well be comfortable.

30

And get her someone to sit with her, will you? This is rough."

"Sure," Ortiz said readily enough.

Gil leaned down to Carole Efrem again. "If you have any family or a friend you want to be with you, tell Officer Ortiz here. He'll help you call them, okay?"

Carole reached out and grabbed Gil's hand. "He didn't kill himself. He *didn't*."

"I believe you." And he did. Because no left-handed person was going to use his right hand to stick a needle into his left arm. No fucking way.

Looking back at the house he could almost hear his absent partner say, "What foul deed's afoot?"

"Verily," he heard himself mutter in response, "I haven't a goddamn clue."

CHAPTER THREE

◈◈◈

Anna awoke late, feeling almost as good as she had in childhood, waking on the first day of summer vacation. Stretching luxuriously, she loved the way her muscles felt, the way the smooth percale sheet touched her skin. It was great to be alive.

Last night's success had left her glowing. Her first exhibit as head curator, and it had been a smashing success. At least as far as the benefactors were concerned. The next months might tell a different story.

But she didn't want to think about that now, didn't want to think about the financial risk the museum was taking with this expensive visiting exhibit. She'd suggested it, yes, but the board of directors had conducted long studies into the feasibility, and had concluded the show would at the very least break even.

But who would remember that if it didn't?

She brushed the troubling thought aside and savored the memory of all the congratulations she had received last night. It had been good.

Sitting up, she hugged her knees tightly and grinned into the dim bedroom. A few pale streamers of sunlight found their way around the wood blinds like a blessing.

Thirty-two and her first major triumph. Until a few months ago, as an assistant curator, she'd been little more than a gofer, handling the minutiae of the museum's permanent exhibit.

The Museum of Antiquities had been founded by a university professor who had discovered a sunken Spanish treasure ship off of Key West. Professor Veronica Coleridge, who was an independently wealthy archaeologist, had endowed the museum as part of the university, providing a trust fund sufficient to construct the building in which it was now housed. She had also provided all the original artifacts from her discoveries. Other benefactors had joined the rolls over the past few years, since the founding, and two years ago they had moved into their new home on land provided by the university.

As items were brought to the surface and cleaned, they were shipped to the new museum for storage or display. Anna had handled a lot of the cataloging and arranging, and had even once managed to break through the density of her predecessor by suggesting a major display to show visitors just what was involved in the discovery of these artifacts.

The additions she had suggested had been so successful that, when her boss retired, the board had without hesitation made her head curator. Which meant she was in charge of all the exhibits. And now there were two.

But only temporarily. And today another shipment was coming in from Key West, so she'd probably spend her day overseeing the unpacking and cataloging. But that was okay. The Pocal exhibit wouldn't need her constant oversight anymore. It was up, it was running, and it was fantastic.

Now she needed to focus on the permanent exhibit, and come up with ways to bring the same magic to it. Excitement bubbled inside her as she considered some of the possibilities. For now she could dream. Later, when she went to work, she'd face the reality, which was that making any of these changes would be a lengthy process, starting with persuading the board of directors. But now was the time to start pressing, while they were all glowing about their success.

For a few moments her hand hovered over the telephone as she thought about calling her identical twin sister Nancy to share the good news. Nancy lived out in Austin, working as a computer geek for some high-tech company. She was weird, but she was also wonderful, and the two of them could share their deepest secrets, and their greatest joys.

After their father's death in the earthquake when they were sixteen, their mother's twin sister had moved in with them to help out, a situation which had only added to the craziness level around the house. Nancy, who took after their mother and aunt, had thrived in the atmosphere. Anna, who had more of her father's serious nature, had grown more serious in compensation. Not that it mattered; there had been a level of warmth and affection in the household that nothing could dim.

But...no, she shouldn't call. Nancy would already be at work, and it was getting time for Anna to leave, too. Tonight they could talk longer, unfettered by time restraints and bosses.

When she arrived at the museum an hour later, she was pleased to see visitors entering in a small stream. The morning papers must have published a good review of the exhibit. Part of her wondered what Reed Howell had said—he was good at making jabs—but the rest of her didn't want to know. This was a time to savor. She'd worry about critics later.

Inside, the lobby was busier than usual, and up a flight of steps to the mezzanine she could see a group waiting for the next screening of the introductory film. The seats were about half-full, pretty good for a Wednesday morning. Over the next few months would come the busloads of schoolchildren, and the private organizations that had made reservations, but she was most interested in the walk-ins. Only time would tell if this level of interest would remain steady or grow.

Humming quietly under her breath, she waved to other museum employees as she passed them and made her way to her office. Her door was open, but that didn't surprise her. Her assistant, a tiny dark-haired student name Vicki Leong, usually arrived just before her and opened it. As usual, the mail was sitting on her desk, envelopes neatly sliced open. Unexpectedly, however, there was a large, colorful flower arrangement beside it.

But what hit her, as she stepped through her doorway, wasn't the mail or the flowers; it was the memory of the dagger she had found last night and how it had disappeared sometime during the evening.

Then she had dismissed it as a poor joke, and put the whole thing from her mind, easy enough to do when she was as busy as she'd been, and as high on success. But with the bright morning light pouring through the slats of her blinds, she found it wasn't as easy to shrug off.

Last night, when they'd found the dagger missing, Detective Tebbins had collected all the wrappings and taken them with him, but she'd gotten the distinct impression he didn't expect to learn a thing. In retrospect, it bothered her even more this morning that he'd seemed disturbed by the dagger's disappearance.

Up to that point, she had thought he was merely an intrusive cop who was making more of the dagger than was warranted because he had nothing better to do. But then something in his manner had changed and she sensed that he'd become much more concerned. She'd felt it, but had ignored it. Every time she looked at that waxed moustache of his, all she could think of was Hercule Poirot, and it was hard to take him seriously.

Except that really wasn't fair. Moustache or not, he was a *real* detective, and this morning, without any champagne in her system, she could feel uneasiness creeping coldly along her spine.

Moving on legs that felt strangely reluctant, she rounded her desk and sat in her chair. She had to be making too much of it, she told herself. The dagger hadn't been a threat, and neither was its disappearance. A prank. Just a stupid prank.

But still her hand trembled as she reached for the card on the flowers. What if it was another empty envelope? The idea that someone might be stalking her turned her uneasiness to a cold chill.

Her fingers were stiff as they lifted the flap and opened the envelope. There was a card inside. All of a sudden she realized she'd been holding her breath. Good grief, she wasn't usually this paranoid. Or paranoid at all for that matter.

Disgusted with herself, she pulled out the card and groaned. It was from Peter Dashay, her would-be suitor. *Congratulations! Dinner tonight? Peter*

She'd been telling him no for six months now, after their one dinner date when she realized she wasn't attracted to him at all and that he wouldn't settle for just being friends. Since then he hovered over her as often as possible, trying to make himself part of her life simply by refusing to go away. She didn't like it, but she didn't want to hurt his feelings. Unfortunately, people as dense as Peter pretty much needed someone to take a pickax to them before they understood.

Vicki popped her head in, smiling. Straight chin-length dark hair framed her face, and her brown eyes were bright.

"Hey, hero lady," she said. "Feeling on top of the world this morning?"

"I was."

Vicki came into the room. Impossibly tiny, barely reaching five feet, she always roused a twinge of envy in Anna's breast. And Anna knew for a fact that she did the same to Vicki. They'd once agreed they'd change bodies in an instant. Vicki wanted desperately to be tall enough to command attention.

"What do you mean, was?" Vicki asked. "You were a megahit."

Anna passed her Peter's card without comment, hoping Vicki would accept that as the complete explanation.

"Oh, man," Vicki said. "That guy is as dense as the Wall of China."

"Yeah."

Vicki passed the card back. "The flowers

are pretty, though. You don't want to throw them away."

"No, but we could put them out at one of the ticket windows."

Vicki giggled. "I'll do it. Listen, I've got a class in fifteen minutes. But I can be back in about an hour and a half if you need me for anything?"

Anna shook her head. "I think it's going to be a slow, quiet day. I need to check out the *Alcantara* exhibit—we're receiving a new shipment today—and I don't expect there are going to be any uproars."

"Oh, that reminds me. Larry said we got a call from the shipper. They'll deliver around two, so I'll be sure to be back by then." Vicki scooped up the flowers and carried them away, taking their perfume with her.

This left Anna alone to contemplate the two business envelopes on her desk, neither of which seemed interesting, and the strange mixture of feelings that had clouded her day. A missing gag dagger and Peter. It really shouldn't bother her at all.

But somehow she knew the day was already going to hell.

A short while later, Anna decided to stroll through the Pocal exhibit. The shipment for the *Alcantara* exhibit wasn't due until two, and she wanted to wait and see what new discoveries had arrived before she started making her plans to improve the display.

Meanwhile, she had a little time to spare

38

and decided to use it productively. She wanted to listen to what the visitors were saying. They would tell her what worked and what didn't.

She skipped the film, which gave a general introduction to the Maya and the jungles in which the relics had been found, and walked past one of the docents, who was offering visitors tape players and headphones.

She'd listened to that tape once, and once was enough. With the information she had provided, a couple of students and professors in the theater department of USF had written the script, and one of the students with a deep, engaging voice had recorded it.

It was a wonderful tape, mostly, telling the story of the discovery of the Mayan relics while providing specific information about the exhibits. Anna loved it, except for the very end.

"Two days after Pocal's tomb was opened, an earthquake struck the area, setting off petroleum fires that leveled two square miles and killed hundreds of people. Was it a natural event? A simple accident of nature? Or did it have something to do with Pocal's Curse ...?"

Once was more than enough.

She slipped through the double doors into the cool dim interior of the exhibit. Wending her way along a narrow path between artfully placed silk-and-plastic foliage, listening to the recorded sounds of birdcalls and distant thunder, she was struck anew by how enchanting this was. In little setbacks to either side, scattered so they didn't overwhelm the jungle feeling, were the artifacts themselves, cased in glass. From time to time there was a bench for visitors to rest on, but mostly the exhibit was designed to keep people moving at a fairly steady pace through the pretend jungle until they emerged in rooms that held the greatest treasures. With a lot of effort, they had tried to paint the walls to look as if they were interior rooms in a pyramid. She still wasn't entirely sure if the effect worked, but it was better than ordinary walls.

But the *pièce de résistance* was the mock-up of the tomb. Along the way she listened to snippets of conversation that indicated people were enjoying the atmosphere, and even the taped account of the discovery. Docents, placed strategically, nodded and smiled as she passed. Several were hard at work giving more detailed information on some of the artifacts to interested visitors.

The tomb replica was at the foot of stairs leading back down to the main floor into an unused storage space. It couldn't come close to mimicking the more than three hundred stairs that had been necessary to reach Pocal's tomb from the top of the original pyramid, but it still managed to give visitors the sensation of being underground.

The first thing she noticed when she stepped into the dim space was that Janine was sitting on one of the benches, her long legs stretched out before her, her hands stuffed into the pockets of her white shorts.

"Something wrong?" Anna asked. There were no other visitors here at the moment.

Janine glanced at her. "No way. I'm admiring our brilliance, which is particularly obvious here. I'm also wondering if I could find a bottle of must to spray around here."

"Must?" Anna was sure she must have misunderstood. "You mean musk?"

"No. I mean must as in musty. What this place needs is to have the scent of old, damp earth and rock."

"True." Anna sat beside her on the bench. "I suppose I could bring in a couple of bags of potting soil…"

"Maybe. But I'm not sure that would do the trick."

"Maybe not. Anyway, we don't want to get in trouble with somebody who gets asthma from molds."

Janine sighed. "I suppose you're right."

"How about a couple pairs of dirty socks?"

Janine looked at her, realized she wasn't serious, and laughed. "Wrong smell."

Anna scanned the room, noting that the sarcophagus, reproduced from a mold provided by the museum in Mexico, looked like real limestone. The guys who had painted it had done a wonderful job. In fact, now that she thought about it, the museum probably ought to throw a party for the theater students who'd helped with all of this, from lighting to scenery, in exchange for credit in their various courses.

"Party," she said aloud. "Remind me, Janine. We should throw a party for all those students who pitched in."

"We should," Janine agreed. "You know, I've

41

been sitting here thinking that if we could make the tomb look this real, maybe we could do the same for the underwater display upstairs."

"Great minds think alike. I'm getting ready to push some ideas on that."

"Want me to bring you some drawings?"

"I'd love it. We can hash it over for a few days, then I can go to work on the directors."

Janine nodded and stood. "I gotta get back to my drawing board. And by the way, if it's not too late, stay away from the *Sentinel* this morning. He praised the exhibit to high heaven, but I get the feeling he's not too fond of you."

"Thanks." Anna lowered her head a moment, wondering what Howell's ax was, then tossed the concern away. Maybe he didn't like his beat, maybe he wanted to be chasing cops around town. Or maybe he just didn't like her because she was a redhead. It wouldn't be the first time.

Sighing, she stood and looked around the tomb once more. Along one wall was a lighted case showing artifacts that had been scattered around the tomb, as if at one time vandals had entered. Then there was the dagger. The most priceless of the artifacts, it stood alone in its own vacuum-sealed, heavily alarmed case. It had been discovered inside the sarcophagus, in Pocal's hands, and now stood beside it on a pedestal, under glass. It winked back at her, cold and deadly, and a little shiver ran along her spine.

Forget it, she told herself. The exhibit was fantastic. All she had to do was ignore the worries that seemed determined to invade her thoughts or run along her nerve endings. Get back to reality.

She heard footsteps coming down the stairs. Visitors. Suddenly she wondered what had happened to the docent who was supposed to be there.

Moments later her question was answered. The docent, a young grad student named Lance Barro, was escorting several people down the stairs, keeping up an interesting patter about the exhibit. He smiled and nodded at Anna and continued talking about the tomb and the artifacts they were about to see.

Satisfied that things couldn't be going any better, Anna headed out. But just as she climbed the first stair on the far side of the exhibit, a glint caught her from the corner of her eye.

Turning with only half her attention, only vaguely wondering what it was because she had never noticed it before, she saw the dagger gleaming in its lighted case. A glint off the glass or something.

But then her heart stood still. Something was wrong. The dagger looked...odd. Ever so slightly discolored. And the corner of something white and flat and very small stuck out from underneath it, something that hadn't been there before. Of that she was absolutely certain.

She hurried over to the case, actually stepping in front of one of the guests who was trying to see it.

Inside the case, looking just as it had when Anna found it last night in her office, was the glass replica. The real jade dagger was gone.

CHAPTER FOUR

Stepping back quickly, she resisted the urge to say anything, even to the docent. Instead she clattered away up the exit stairs.

As soon as she emerged into the bright daylight of the lobby, she hesitated, considering what to do next. If she simply called the campus authorities, Ivar Gregor, the managing director, was apt to be furious with her.

She was, after all, simply the curator. Ivar ran the museum like a general in charge of a small army, coordinating everything, from hiring and firing to making sure all the different teams did their jobs, from the supply people to the shipping people to the security staff. In short, he was the chief executive officer.

And Anna was acutely aware that he was the person who doled out additional people when she needed them, who oversaw her budgets for projects, and who was quite willing to kibbitz her every decision on grounds that it was impractical or out of budget.

He hadn't been too difficult on the Pocal project, but that could change overnight.

She had to tell him first. Sticking her hands into her slacks pockets, she headed down the admin hallway to hunt him up. She passed offices on either side where people toiled with all the paperwork from import licenses to purchase orders to payroll.

Things had certainly changed since her arrival two years ago. The museum, then, had been little more than a few dusty rooms at the back of a classroom building where items were stored. Then the building had opened, and the *Alcantara* exhibit had been set up. First it had been rows of display cases, of little interest to anyone except students and their teachers.

But all that had changed since they had decided to go ahead with the Pocal exhibit and see if they could generate some of their own operating funds, rather than relying on the university, the endowment that had set them up, and the occasional gift from alumni.

Since then, things had kicked into high gear, and Ivar had seemed to thrive with each bit of growth. He'd also become more self-important. More difficult. More of a prick, as Nancy would say.

Ivar was way at the back, his office being the only one on this hallway with a window on the world. He was at his desk, visible through the glass wall that went from ceiling to waist height. He sat at an old mahogany executive desk that he thought gave him more cachet than the fiberboard-and-pressed-wood desks everyone else was using.

Behind him his windows gave a view of the campus: trees, grass, some sidewalks. There weren't many students visible, but the museum was tucked in a relatively isolated location, away from most of the classroom buildings. Florida sun drenched the world.

Anna lifted her hand and knocked, noting that her mouth was dry. Not because she faced Ivar, but because the dagger was gone. In a matter of hours she had gone from the pinnacle to the pits. Her future hung in the balance. And somehow, deep inside, she knew the theft of the dagger was directed at her.

Ivar motioned her to come in and take a seat. A plump man of about sixty, who had only a few wisps of hair remaining, he wasn't inclined to smile easily. From the way he beamed at her, however, she guessed she was the fair-haired child today. Well, that would last only thirty seconds. She waited until he hung up the phone.

"Fantastic," he said. "Meg Allbritten is thrilled with the media coverage." Allbritten was the president of the university, a really charming, pleasant woman. "She says they're thinking about setting up a program to show other university museums how we did this on such a tight budget."

"We had a lot of free grunt labor."

"Well, yes," he agreed. "We integrated some of our teaching programs with hands-on experience. Wonderful idea we had."

It had been hers, but she didn't say so. She was too preoccupied to bother. "Great news, Ivar," she said, entirely too briskly, but she didn't care. "Listen, we've got a serious problem."

"How serious could it be? Everything's going just as it should, like a well-oiled machine."

He was feeling unusually expansive today.

46

It was almost sad to have to ruin his mood. "Ivar. Ivar, listen carefully. You need to call the police."

He looked blankly at her. "Did someone break something?"

"No. Worse. Someone stole the Pocal dagger."

It was horrible to watch his face whiten. No red or purple spots of anger emerged. He didn't spray spittle as he was wont to do when furious. For a minute, he couldn't even speak. "You're joking," he said almost desperately.

"No, I'm not. It's been stolen. We need to call the cops. Then we need to rope off the tomb room and keep people out before all the evidence is destroyed."

"Keep people out?" He was aghast. Then, almost as she decided that shock had turned him into a blithering idiot, he nodded and reached for the phone. "I'll take care of it. Police first, and the security company, then I'll have the guards clear everyone out."

He punched in a number swiftly, then as he waited for an answer, he looked at her. When he spoke, he rocked her to her very toes. "I'm sorry, Anna. This could have been so good for both of us."

Back in her office, waiting for the police while the guards cleared the guests from the exhibit, and ticket-window personnel refunded money, Anna swiveled her chair around and stared out through the blinds at the perfect April day.

47

She understood exactly what Ivar meant, and her stomach churned miserably. Two years ago, just before the new museum building opened, and just before she began working there, there had been a theft. Someone had crept into the chaos of the earliest stages of transition and slipped away with a precious golden mask that had been found with the sunken treasure ship. The mask had been unique, a one-of-a-kind relic of a tribe that had disappeared forever from the earth, a tribe about which almost nothing was known.

Both the university and the museum officials had suffered a great deal of embarrassment over poor security measures. Ivar had been in charge then, too.

Now it had happened again, with the best security in the world. Ivar might well lose his job. And Anna...well, Anna might not find it so easy to locate another. Not for a long time.

The thought that everything she had worked for had been ground to dust under the relentless boot of some crook made her ill.

But not as ill as the loss of the dagger. Nowhere near as ill. The thing was priceless, the inheritance of future generations.

Oh, God, what if the thief had taken other things? She hadn't even thought to look.

Little was as eye-catching as gold, but almost every genuine article in the exhibit was worth a small fortune to unscrupulous collectors. The clay pots, the textiles, the toys carved out of stone for small hands...

Her heart thudded, and her stomach sank

as if she were riding a fast elevator. What if he had taken other things?

And how were they going to explain this to the Mexican museum that had agreed to exchange exhibits? It would be years before any other museum would again consider sharing irreplaceable articles with the Museum of Antiquities.

Ivar was right. They were both dead in the water even if they kept their jobs.

Not that either of them was responsible for security. Dinah Hudson, from HiSecurity, Inc. had overseen that. Her firm wasn't going to be thrilled either. They'd promised to install a state-of-the-art system from the ground up, and it hadn't even peeped when an item was stolen.

Their only hope now was that the police could find the burglar.

The campus police immediately called the Tampa Police Department, which quickly dispatched a couple of cars to the museum, then dumped the call on Clarence Tebbins's desk.

Excitement grabbed him. He'd known something more was going to happen at the museum, and the replica dagger suggested they might be up against a real criminal mastermind. Most criminals were so stupid his job could be a routine yawner, but a criminal like this, one who would go to all the trouble to duplicate a dagger of that intricacy, and thumb his nose at the world by showing the

49

replica first...well, it tickled his fancy more than the cases he was currently working on.

"You need me?" his partner Vance Newman asked. Newman was an average-looking guy with absolutely nothing memorable about him. He was a passable detective, but not up to Tebbins's horsepower, and they both knew it. They also weren't very fond of each other. Newman thought Tebbins was weird, and Tebbins hated it when Newman called him Tebbie.

But he'd learned not to say anything about that. He'd been called Tebbie by his peers ever since third grade, and it had finally dawned on him that the more he objected, the harder his life got. So he'd learned not to say anything at all about it. Besides, anything was better than being called Clarence.

But he was nearly positive that Newman had figured out it bothered him. That would fit with the rest of his character.

"Probably not," he told Newman. "Not for this trip anyway. You go ahead with the Burley case."

"Good enough." Newman looked relieved.

Well, thought Tebbins as he headed out, if he had half a brain himself, he wouldn't want this task. The exhibit came from a museum in Mexico. That meant high-profile media coverage and maybe even some diplomatic kinks. Of course, Newman wouldn't know that. The man was a philistine. His decision wasn't proof of his sanity, merely proof of ignorance. The theft of some dusty old artifact probably sounded boring to him.

But, Tebbins thought with a sense of pleasure, he himself wasn't sane. He was just *good*.

And he wasn't just conceited. He'd cleared more cases than anyone else in the squad. He had a higher conviction rate. He knew it, they knew it. Maybe it would have been better if nobody but the chief had known it.

Well, he was cursed with a great mind and a big ego. And he had no desire to change either of them.

When he arrived at the museum, he crossed the tape boundary, nodded to the cops he knew, and signed in to the building. People were milling all over the lobby, from campus police officers to museum staff. And maybe even some visitors, for all he knew.

"Everyone's a bit upset," Wes Weathers said. He was a moderately tall man with a soft brown moustache and a balding head, and he looked down at Tebbins. A good Tampa cop, Wes had the maturity to keep a lid on things. "I'm going to send them all to their offices."

"Might make things easier. Crime-scene van here yet?"

"On its way. Should be here in about ten minutes."

"Good. For the folks who don't have offices, make them sit up there on the benches."

"Will do."

"Now, what exactly do we have?"

"Somebody managed to steal a jade dagger and replace it with a copy, from inside a vacuum-sealed case. No alarms reported."

"Anything else?"

Weathers shrugged. "So far nobody has noticed anything else."

"Strange kind of burglary. There must be other valuable items around. How many people have been at the exhibit this morning?"

"Lots. The ticket people are counting right now."

"Good job." Tebbins favored him with a smile and headed for Anna Lundgren's office. She had struck him as a take-charge kind of woman, and he was a little surprised she wasn't out here making sure everything was going to her satisfaction. There was, however, an officious-looking guy near the ticket windows, wringing his hands and saying something to the ticket sellers.

Tebbins paused and looked back at Weathers. "Who's that guy by the ticket windows?"

"The managing director of the museum. Ivar Gregor. He's having a cow."

"A Russian cow?"

Weathers laughed behind him.

As he had expected, Anna was in her office. Her chair back was to the door, and she appeared to be staring out the window at palm fronds waving slowly against the sky.

"Good morning, Ms. Lundgren."

She sat up sharply and whirled her chair around, her face pale. "Oh. *You.*"

He smiled and entered the room. "I understand we have a problem."

"This museum certainly does."

"So the dagger was replaced by the replica you showed me last night?"

She nodded, then shook her head. "My God, this is a mess."

"Is anything else missing? Have you walked through and checked carefully?"

"I was walking through this morning before I discovered the dagger. I'm not sure, but I didn't notice anything else."

"Why don't we go check that out right now? Before the techs get here and banish us all to Siberia."

At that she gave him a pale smile. "Siberia actually sounds good right now. It's cold."

"Well, it would be a long way from this situation, I'll grant you. But I prefer the warm weather myself."

"Not I. I'm from Minnesota."

He shivered. "No thank you. I once made the mistake of working for the police department in Syracuse. All I remember about it was the unending nightmare of having to shovel snow and then drive on it. And worse, I don't think I was warm the entire time I was there."

She smiled again. "You get used to it."

"Exactly. You'll get used to it here. It's actually very nice."

She rose, and together they walked toward the exhibit. "Except for hurricanes, tropical storms, huge spiders, and droughts."

It was his turn to chuckle. "We *are* drier than most would think. Except for tropical storms and hurricanes."

She spoke when they reached the door of the exhibit. "Aren't you worried about evidence? Are we going to destroy it?"

"It's my understanding that a great many people have walked through here today already."

"Yes." Her green eyes met his. "You're saying the evidence is already destroyed?"

"Perhaps not all of it. But we're going to walk through exactly as dozens already have. And, I might add, I think that is exactly what our thief intended."

The overhead lighting was turned on in the exhibit, utterly depriving it of all mystery and making it glaringly obvious that this was no trail through a rain forest. The scenery and plants looked fake, and even sometimes shabby. The exhibit cases stood out like sore thumbs.

Anna checked each item as they passed it, shaking her head each time.

"Is the alarm system still on?"

"In the cases, absolutely. There are too many people running around in here right now. Did you enjoy the exhibit, Mr. Tebbins?"

"Very much."

"Do you know much about the Maya?"

"Very little, actually." He paused in front of a tall stone carved with the ornate figure of a man that was at least twice his height. The man's head was facing the left, and he appeared to be wearing flowing feathers on his head and carrying some kind of strange instrument. "Very stylized."

"Most of their art was. My sense from what I've seen was that order was very important to them." She pointed to some small images down the side, all of which appeared to follow the shape of a square with its edges rounded. Inside the suggested squares were various images, many of which seemed to him to be nothing but a conglomeration of lines.

"That's their writing," she said. "Do you see how it all seems to fit a certain shape and size, and how the shape is fully filled in? They were very orderly and precise. But then, they were apparently wonderful astronomers and mathematicians."

He looked at the symbols with even more appreciation.

"Don't tell anyone I said this, but I see strong similarities to Egypt in their art and architecture."

He glanced at her. "What would be wrong in thinking that?"

"Let's just say it bucks mainstream archaeology."

"So buck them." He was pleased when he heard a small laugh escape her. At least she was less upset now. Which meant she'd be more informative. "This thing must weigh a couple of tons."

"The original does, I'm sure. This is a copy, made from a mold of the original. Plastics over foam. Easier to ship, less likely to break."

He was disappointed to discover the stela wasn't real. Which was a strange reaction since he knew perfectly well that many things in the exhibit were replicas. "Why do you use so many replicas?"

"Because so many items are too fragile to

ship. Or so unique and extraordinary that under most circumstances no one wants to risk the loss. And unfortunately, we've apparently become an example of the worst that can happen."

He didn't voice his agreement, deciding it was more diplomatic to keep it to himself.

They resumed walking while she inspected the cases. "Are you in charge of the investigation?"

"At present, yes."

She glanced at him. "What would change?"

"Oh, you never know when someone higher up might want to take over. Have you told the Mexican museum what's happened?"

"Not yet. Unfortunately, we won't be able to keep it a secret for long. Someone from Mexico is expected to arrive in Tampa tomorrow."

He nodded, although he personally thought this was a complication he would rather not have. Next it would be someone from the State Department concerned about relations with Mexico.

Then he put all that from his mind and focused himself on that most delightful of all things in life: a mystery.

They passed through the rest of the exhibit, and Anna pronounced everything else in order. In the burial chamber, now brightly lighted, she checked out the other artifacts and made the same pronouncement.

"He only took the dagger."

"Interesting. There must be other valuable items in the exhibit."

She looked surprised. "Of course. There are gold and silver objects, and the pottery…and the textiles would fetch a pretty price, too."

"Then why only the dagger? What's special about it?"

"Well, it's a fine example; it was found buried with an ancient king… It might be the most valuable item in the exhibit."

"Yes, but that's not what I'm driving at. If there are other valuable items here, why not take all of them? Apart from value, what's special about the dagger?"

"It's unique," she said.

"Okay. Is anything else here unique?"

"A number of things." Her brow furrowed in thought. "I see what you mean."

"So what else is there?"

She stood looking at him, her hands clenching at her sides. "Well," she said in a voice heavy with reluctance, "there's the curse."

CHAPTER FIVE

The silence filling the tomb chamber after Anna's last words seemed to linger coldly in the air. Tebbins turned them over in his mind, savoring the possibilities, feeling a distinct thrill. The curse was, of course, mentioned in the exhibit, but he hadn't thought of that as a motivator. All of a sudden he felt like Sherlock Holmes.

He opened his mouth to ask Anna to explain in more depth, but at that moment the techs arrived. He had to deal with them first.

"This room," he told them, "has been visited by dozens of people already this morning. And until we're ready to open the display case, we can't look for anything there. Focus on it and the area around it, though."

Then he took Anna's arm. She was looking pale and unhappy, he noted. "Let's go to your office. We need to talk."

Three minutes later they were in her office. He noted that she immediately headed for her chair, making herself safe behind her desk. He obliged her by sitting so she wouldn't feel threatened. Why did this woman feel so insecure? Was she actually *afraid* of the curse? He tucked the interesting possibility away for future consideration.

"Tell me about the curse," he said.

Her lips tightened. "You already know about it. It was covered in the presentation last night."

He shook his head. "That was a superficial explanation. I want to know what *you* know about it. The stuff that wasn't included for public presentation."

She sighed and leaned forward, resting her elbows on her desk and toying with a paper clip. "There's really not much to it. Honestly. It's based entirely on a Mayan legend which says that the jaguar god would kill those who trespassed."

"What about the dagger?"

"That's also myth. The locals apparently warned the archaeologists that there was a powerful dagger with the head of the jaguar on it in the sarcophagus itself, and it must not be disturbed. They warned that their fathers had told them that any who disturbed this artifact would be cursed unto the second generation to die by fire in the jaws of the jaguar. Legend further holds that someone tried to rob the tomb many years ago and was killed by a gout of fire that rose up from the earth. And the locals apparently went to some trouble to put the dagger back."

"Pretty," Tebbins remarked. "So, did this legend turn up before or after the archaeologists found the dagger?"

"Before. At least that's what I hear. But who can say for sure?"

"The archaeologists."

She shook her head. "They're dead. Two were killed in the earthquake that devastated the region, and the third died in an auto accident a couple of months later."

Tebbins's eyebrows rose. This was growing more interesting by the minute. "So how in the world did anyone get the dagger?"

"It had already been taken out, along with a bunch of other artifacts."

"But no one else has died because of it," Tebbins said. "So the curse is ineffectual now."

Anna sighed and tossed the paper clip across the desk. "I don't know."

"Why not?"

"Because the museum in Mexico hasn't

allowed anyone to handle the dagger since it was recovered. They say it's out of respect for the beliefs of the indigenous peoples. They might have been persuaded by the earthquake and fire, though, coming as it did on the heels of the discovery."

Tebbins smiled. He was a man of intellect, but he was still very human. He understood the almost subliminal effects of such things. "It's a good story. So, sometime after the tomb was opened and the dagger removed, there was an earthquake. How many did it kill? A few hundred?"

Surprising him, she rose from her chair and went to stand with her back to him, looking out the window.

"It was worse than that," she said presently.

He waited a moment, but she seemed to have nothing more to offer. "Well, the part about the second generation being cursed might put this case in a whole new light."

"I doubt it," she said, her voice almost steely.

"Who was the guard on duty during the night?"

She waved a hand. "I'm not sure. You'd have to check with Ivar. He handles all of that."

"I'll do that. I suppose it's the same with the security people?"

"Yes. I'm just the curator. I worry about the exhibits and how everything is presented."

He looked at her back and wondered what secrets she was concealing. She had access to the artifact, she was the person who found the replica dagger, it had disappeared from her

60

desk... Containing a sigh, he mentally wrote her down as the first suspect in the crime.

Gil Garcia was still at the scene, keeping an eye on the techs, making suggestions...although there weren't very many he could make. Checking the windows for illicit entry or egress—as if that wasn't obvious—and so on. He felt like a fifth wheel.

Cripes, he thought, there isn't anything visible to go on. No signs of struggle. No signs of drug use, other than what was in the living room. Not so much as a knocked-over lamp, a tilted picture, a pillow cushion in the wrong place. The neighbors hadn't seen or heard anything unusual. No window had been jimmied, no lock disturbed...

He loved it. Finally, he decided he couldn't do anything more and should go down to the station to talk to Carole Efrem. It was amazing how much people actually knew that they didn't realize they knew unless you questioned them carefully enough. And at the moment, she was looking like his only lead.

He opened the door, ready to step out into the unusually hot April day, when the phone started ringing. He turned, considering answering it, and saw something at eye level.

The doorframe was a little cracked and splintering, and there were some green fibers clinging to it. Green fibers the same color as the dead man's uniform, found crumpled on the floor of the closet. Too high to have come off his shoulders.

61

"Hey, Les?" he called to the tech who was still going over the couch area.

"Yeah?"

The phone kept ringing.

"There's some fiber here on the door-frame. See if it matches the vic's uniform."

"Will do."

The phone was still ringing. Annoyed and now curious—most callers didn't wait through so many rings—he decided to answer it, since the cop who was supposed to had disappeared into another room.

Grabbing for it, heedless of the fingerprint powder that was all over it, he lifted the receiver to his ear. "Hello?"

"Hi, this is Billie Sue at the Museum of Antiquities. May I speak to Mr. Malacek?"

"I'm sorry," Gil said. "That won't be possible."

"Then could I leave a message? It's urgent."

"It won't matter," Gil answered. "Mr. Malacek is dead."

"Oh!" He heard the shock on the other end of the phone. "Oh, dear! Look, could you please stay on the line? There's a detective here who'll want to know that."

Gil felt the first real smile of the day begin to tug at his mouth. A detective? The plot thickened.

A few moments later, a reedy male voice was on the line. "This is Detective Clarence Tebbins of the Tampa Police Department. To whom am I speaking?"

To *whom*? God, one of those. He was tempted to hand back a Lily Tomlin line but decided to skip it. If this Tebbins was a prick, he'd squeal on him to his bosses. "This is Detective Gil Garcia," he replied. "St. Pete Homicide."

He had the pleasure of listening to a silent line for a few moments as Tebbins absorbed that information. Score one.

Tebbins spoke. "Homicide? The plot thickens. Well, Detective, as soon as you can get away from the scene, we need to speak."

"I'd dearly love to know why."

"I'm sure you would. Suffice it to say, there was a major burglary at the Museum of Antiquities while Mr. Malacek was on duty last night."

"Ahh," said Gil, who felt his heart kick. "Great news. I was looking for a lead."

"So was I. Where and when?"

Gil glanced over his shoulder. The medical examiner had already taken the corpse, the techs were almost done.

"I need to question Malacek's girlfriend," he told Tebbins. "Can you get away?"

"I'm waiting for the security company to arrive. It's important, so I'm afraid I can't. But I would like to know what the girlfriend says."

And Gil wanted to know what had been stolen. How big the case was. And what might have cost Eddy Malacek his life. Important questions every one.

"Well," he said, "there's no point in duplicating. I'll question the girl. Where will I find you in about two hours?"

"I'll be here at the museum. I don't expect to quit early tonight."

63

"Not until pigs fly."

"Or roosters sleep through dawn."

Gil suddenly thought of his partner Seamus, with whom he'd traded just such lines for years. "I wish my partner weren't on vacation," he heard himself say.

"And I'm glad mine's not here," was the dry answer. "Two hours, here?"

"About that. I'll see you then."

Carole Efrem had nothing to add. She sniffled and teared her way through the questioning, using up a whole box of tissues, painting a picture of two students working their way through graduate school, who planned to marry someday, when they could afford it. Students who had so little money that they never used air-conditioning, which meant that determining the time of death was going to get real chancy. The body had been warm when he'd arrived on the scene, but so had the house. And the lack of air-conditioning was no clue to anything at all.

After an hour he had little to show for his time except a list of Malacek's closest acquaintances, some of whom Carole knew by first name only. He was sure he'd be able to locate them anyway. One friend would lead to another.

But he wasn't feeling hopeless anymore by the time he got onto I-275 and headed across the bay to the university. There'd been a burglary while Eddy was on duty, which provided a credible motive for murder. And made for a much more interesting case. He felt the bit settle between his teeth.

Then he remembered Trina, and wondered what she was up to. He should have swung by home, but he was already approaching the Howard Frankland Bridge, and turning around would now cost him at least forty minutes. Breaking his own rule, he pulled his cell phone out of his pocket and autodialed his home number.

The machine picked up.

Natch. She wasn't home. When she was home alone, she always made the phone by the second ring, fearful of missing a call from her friends. When he was there she always politely asked if he wanted to get it. And when she was out, she always turned on the machine.

Damn. He cut the call and tossed the phone on the seat beside him. Dollars to doughnuts she'd gone to the beach with that boy. She just couldn't understand why he had a problem with a fifteen-year-old girl racketing around in a car with a sixteen-year-old boy. Never mind that he thought the kid was a slug. Most boys that age were unimpressive. But the kid didn't have much experience behind the wheel, and on average Florida drivers were some of the worst in the world.

First you had your old folks who quite sensibly slowed way down, but occasionally didn't seem to see too well. Then you had your aggressive drivers who took it personally if anyone got between them and doing eighty in a forty-five-mile-per-hour zone. People who zigzagged, cut you off, wouldn't let you change lanes, rear-ended you when you slowed down...

The list was endless. He often surmised part of the problem came from having so many people from all over the world who brought their distinctive driving styles with them. Mostly he considered it a problem of simple courtesy and patience. For every poor driver there were at least ten who drove in a rage.

And she was out there among them.

Speaking of which...a fuel tanker pulled in front of him, forcing him to jam on the brakes to avoid having the front end of his car torn off. Too bad it was out of his jurisdiction. The Howard Frankland Bridge often reminded him of the Indy 500, everyone jockeying to be first at the highest possible speed.

Thirty minutes later, on the edge of some road rage himself, he pulled into a parking space in front of the Museum of Antiquities. Yellow tape cordoned off the area around the building, and he displayed his badge to get past it.

He stepped into a spacious lobby with a two-story ceiling and noted the number of cops milling around in blue uniforms. Big doings. This wasn't about some office machine missing.

One of the cops approached him, and he flashed his badge again. "I'm here to see Detective Tebbins."

Moments later he was ushered into an office that had apparently been commandeered by the Tampa police. Detective Tebbins rose to greet him, and Gil's first thought was *Oh, my God.*

It wasn't only that Tebbins was a small man; Gil was accustomed, at six-two, to looking down at a majority of people. Tebbins scraped somewhere around five-five or five-six, yet it wasn't his stature or his almost dainty hands and feet.

It was his moustache, black, long, and waxed into curls on either side of his mouth. It was his bow tie, an outrageous Stuart plaid. It was his suit, which looked like something lifted from the Edwardian era. *Hercule Poirot? Sherlock Holmes?*

Gil had met deluded cops before but this... On the other hand, Tebbins couldn't be really deluded and still hold his current position.

"How was the drive over?" Tebbins asked sociably enough.

"It gets more miserable every year. Even when most of the tourists are gone."

"I've noticed." Tebbins's eyes were sharp, intense. "Have a seat. So you have a body I was hoping to find alive."

"Apparently so. What happened here?"

"Theft of the central artifact in the exhibit." He rounded the desk and sat, steepling his fingers in a contemplative pose.

Gil followed suit, taking the chair facing him and crossing his legs loosely. "What was it?"

"A jade-and-gold dagger with a jaguar's head topping the hilt." He opened a manila file folder and pulled out a brochure. "This tells about the exhibit. The missing piece is featured on the inside."

Gil unfolded it, and his eyes immediately landed on the dagger. "Pretty piece. Probably worth a fortune."

"So are other things in the exhibit. This was the only piece taken."

Gil looked up. "I smell a rat."

"Or three-day-old cod." Tebbins smiled faintly. "What's more, the dagger was carefully replaced with a replica. After the criminologists finish up, and the security-system designer gets here, we're going to open the case and find out what's *under* the dagger. Looks like the corner of an envelope."

Gil nodded. "Was there anything special about this piece?"

Tebbins nodded. "One thing. It's cursed."

"Cursed." Gil repeated the word stonily. "Hoo boy. Don't let that get into the papers."

"It already has. It was part of the hype for the exhibit."

Then Gil remembered. Pieces clicked into place. "Got it. I remember now. I wasn't especially paying attention when I first heard about this exhibit, but yeah, there was a buzz about something spooky." He looked down at the picture again. "Witches? A coven? A warlock? Or just somebody who has a thing about daggers?"

"Or somebody who got stopped before he could finish."

Gil shook his head slowly. "No. I don't think so. It sounds too careful, especially the replica."

Tebbins beamed. "Exactly. We have a criminal mastermind here."

Gil's head jerked up and he stared at Tebbins. *A criminal mastermind?* "We don't know that. Most criminals are reasonably stupid."

"True. Which makes them boring. Trust me, this one is *not* boring. What about the guard? Malacek. What happened to him?"

"Death by apparent overdose. However, he was left-handed, but stuck himself in the left arm."

Tebbins's eyes gleamed. "So, an act of stupidity."

"Whose? Malacek or the murderer?"

"The murderer of course." Tebbins waved an airy hand, then twisted one end of his moustache around his finger. "So now we have to wonder if Malacek participated and was killed afterward, or whether he was an innocent victim."

"Brilliant observation, Watson," Gil said drily.

"Not Watson. That was last month. This month, I'm Poirot. Next month, who knows? And pardon me, you don't look a thing like Holmes."

Gil couldn't resist. "I thought the curtain rang down."

"I rang it back up."

Which, now that he thought about it, gave Gil a qualm. In *Curtain,* Agatha Christie had turned Hercule Poirot into a killer who died in the last scene. The final line in the book was something like *The curtain rings down.* He had a moment of unease, wondering about how far Tebbins planned to carry the charade. But Tebbins was already moving on.

Tebbins let go of his moustache and leaned

forward. "I suspect we'll both find our answers at the same place. Shall we cooperate?"

"Sure." Although he was dreading it. A man who was looking for a *criminal mastermind* might miss simple things that were right under his nose—or his moustache.

"And what did the girlfriend have to say?" Tebbins inquired.

"Very little. He didn't do drugs, he hated them. They both worked hard and planned to get married when they finished school. Pretty ordinary story."

"What about time of death?"

Gil shook his head. "Nothing official yet. The body was still warm when I got there, but they never used air-conditioning. The place was pretty stuffy, all the windows closed, and the morning sun had already heated it up pretty well. The M.E. might be able to work out something more accurate, but you know how that goes." As a rule, time of death could usually only be established within a few hours.

Tebbins nodded, once again twirling his moustache. "Well, he's on the security tape, making the shift change at 8 A.M. What time was he found?"

"Approximately 9:30 A.M."

"So. He was here at eight. Dead by nine-thirty. Beautiful."

Gil lifted a brow. "Beautiful?"

"Of course! Surely you see the meticulous planning. The guard..." He checked his notes. "Malacek. I need to remember that. Malacek probably assisted the theft in some fashion, but had to be here for the shift change, and had to appear at appropriate times on the surveillance tapes. So, they had to wait for him at his home and kill him before his girlfriend got there. Meticulous."

Gil had the distinct feeling that Tebbins was searching for something that wasn't there. "Not meticulous," he said bluntly. "The girlfriend was in Melbourne visiting her father. She came home a day early."

Tebbins waved his hand grandly. "Still meticulous. The girlfriend's lucky she didn't come home yesterday. Or too early this morning."

"Not meticulous," Gil said again. "The killer didn't bother to learn that Malacek was left-handed."

That took a bit of the wind from Tebbins's sails. He frowned. "True."

"And that's good."

It was Tebbins's turn to raise his eyebrows. "How so?"

"The more mistakes he makes, the likelier we are to catch him."

"True."

"Besides, I've worked on cases involving meticulous murderers before. Unfortunately, they all turn out to be serial killers. So if you don't mind, I'd really rather this guy not be meticulous."

"Dismiss meticulous," Tebbins said, smoothing his moustache as if he were smoothing his ruffled feathers. "Not meticulous. But still brilliant."

"I'll withhold judgment on that."

71

Tebbins smiled. "As you wish. Still, he managed to carry off the heist without setting off the alarms, made sure that his traces would be well covered by visitors to the exhibit before anyone noticed what had happened, and killed the only witness before anyone got to him. He even made sure the videotape would be normal by having the guard remain to the end of his shift. He appears to have thought of everything."

"Nobody thinks of everything. How did he bypass the alarms?"

"We're still waiting for the security specialist. He should be here shortly."

"What about video surveillance of the dagger? Didn't that show anything?"

"There isn't any." Tebbins raised his hand as Gil started to object. "I know, I know. It sounds insane. But the idea was that with all the redundant security systems in effect at night throughout the exhibit the cameras aren't needed. So they kick on only when an alarm is triggered. No alarm, no pictures."

"Damn."

A tall redheaded woman appeared in the doorway just at that moment and both Tebbins and Garcia immediately rose.

"Detective Tebbins? The security specialist is here. Do you want to meet here or in the conference room?"

"The conference room, please. Anna, this is Detective Gil Garcia from the St. Petersburg Police. Apparently the guard, Eddy Malacek, was murdered this morning."

"Eddy?" Anna paled, and her green eyes

became huge in her face. A beautiful woman, Garcia thought. Absolutely stunning. Slender, with chiseled cheekbones and hair so bright he almost wanted to warm his hands on it. Too bad she was involved in the case.

"Yes, Eddy," Tebbins said, then turned to Gil. "Anna Lundgren is the head curator of the museum. She's the one who discovered the theft."

Gil regarded her with renewed interest. What was she doing, carrying messages like a secretary then? Or maybe the whole museum was just messed up today. Probably, with all the people being questioned. "Did you know Eddy?" he asked her.

"Yes." She shook her head and wrapped her arms around herself as if she were suddenly cold. "Not personally. It's just that...while we were constructing the exhibit he volunteered a lot of hours to help with that, in addition to his work. He was so nice and ready to pitch in."

Gil felt his eyes slide toward Tebbins, and saw the same thought there. "What exactly did he help with?"

"Oh, moving things, painting scenery. Just about anything we needed. He has...had such a lovely girlfriend. She helped, too." Her wide sad eyes met Gil's. "What happened? Why was he killed?"

"We don't know yet."

"Oh, my God. Is Carole all right?"

Gil nodded. "Safe. About what you'd expect otherwise."

"My God," she murmured again, and to Gil

73

it seemed her gaze turned inward to some painful memory of her own. But whatever sorrow she'd been contemplating suddenly gave way to another thought. She looked at Gil. "Do you think it had something to do with this theft?"

"So it seems," Tebbins answered. "And there you have it, Ms. Lundgren. A death associated with the curse."

Something flickered on her face, something wounded and angry. "I don't believe in curses."

"Apparently," Tebbins said, "someone does."

CHAPTER SIX

The conference room was just off the main lobby, easily accessible for use by persons who were not regular employees of the museum. Windowless, it still felt airy and light, with track lighting and potted tropical plants. The centerpiece was a conference table large enough to seat eighteen comfortably.

Dinah Hudson, the expert from HiSecurity, was a small woman of about thirty who wore her black hair cropped close and apparently scorned contact lenses in favor of wire-framed glasses. She was dressed in khaki cargo pants and a black tank top that advertised a whipcord build. The purpose of the pants was soon obvious as she began to pull various things out of her pockets: pen, pad, informational booklets that she passed around. For the schematics, though, she resorted to a long round blueprint case.

She spread the schematics out on the table. Only Tebbins appeared to know anything about what he was looking at, and Gil strongly suspected it was a pretense. A master electrician could probably trace those things for days before he figured out exactly how it worked.

"Why don't I just give a brief overview," Dinah said. "Then you can ask me questions."

Tebbins and Gil both agreed. Anna looked as if she wished she could be excused.

"Basically," Dinah said, "no security system is foolproof. It's a deterrent, a way to make it as supremely difficult as possible for a thief, but it's not foolproof. What we want from the system is threefold."

She took advantage of the whiteboard on an easel nearby and began to write in green.

"One. Deterrence. Two, sufficient redundancy so it's not as easy to knock out completely as human guards. And three, to alert us that something is happening so that a swift response can be made."

She looked around, as if seeking questions, but none were forthcoming.

"Okay," she continued, putting down the marking pen and returning to the table, "what we have here is a near impossibility. I'm not saying *it is* impossible—very little is—but it's still a near impossibility. Since you called, I've been trying to figure out how this could have happened, and I honestly don't know."

"It might help," said Gil, "if you explained how the system is supposed to work. Just an overall view, for now."

"Well." Dinah looked down for a moment. "Where to begin."

"At the beginning," suggested Tebbins drily. "Which alarms malfunctioned?"

"All of them, apparently." She pulled out a chair and sat. "Something sure went haywire. As soon as I was notified what happened, I checked the data readouts from last night. We get a continuous feed from the alarm systems here, and I'm sorry to tell you there was no interruption of any of the systems recorded. We'd have known if a wire was cut, power turned off. Even key entries are automatically logged. There were none."

Gil spoke. "Someone with a key could turn off the system?"

"Yes. Parts of it anyway."

"That explains a lot."

"I wish it did," Dinah said. "Let me explain."

Tebbins spoke, waving his hand with exaggerated courtesy. "By all means."

"We installed a video-surveillance system and a motion-detector system. Either one of these can be switched off. It's necessary to be able to switch off the motion detectors so that people can get into the exhibit. Obviously."

"Quite," said Tebbins.

"Theoretically there's a control on who's allowed to have the keys. They're supposed to be carefully tracked. It is, however, possible that someone with some skill could duplicate these keys."

"Do the security guards have access to the keys?" Gil asked.

"I presume so, but I don't know for sure. Anna?"

Anna, who had been listening silently with her hands folded on the table, gave a small shrug. "I really don't know, Dinah. I assume they must have, because after we worked late, someone turned on the system. Ivar would be the one to ask."

"They probably do," Dinah decided. "The motion detectors are the least of it anyway. As for the video system, it *can* be switched off, but doing so is more difficult. As I understand it, the procedures in place require that only one person have access to the recording room, and that person changes the tapes once every three days. Otherwise, the auto changer just pops in a new cassette."

Gil made a note on his pad. "How much data do you lose on the regular changeovers?"

"Rarely more than a couple of minutes on each camera."

"And what about the automatic changes?"

"Maybe a minute, max."

Gil looked at Tebbins. "What about this morning?"

Tebbins shrugged. "The videotape filming the dagger was changed around 12:30 A.M. and again at 8:30 A.M. About thirty seconds of static, then everything was normal."

"Thirty seconds isn't long enough."

"Nope."

"There's more," said Dinah. "And quite honestly, if you hadn't assured me the dagger was gone, I'd think it was a hoax. Because he *couldn't* have gotten to the dagger."

Gil's interest perked. "I thought you said no system is infallible."

"Well, it's not, but this one comes as close as it can."

Nearly ten minutes later they were back in the tomb mock-up. The overhead lights were still on, making the set look less than real. Dinah went over to the tall case holding the dagger. "Is it okay to touch it now?"

Tebbins looked at the criminologist, who was standing to one side. "Sure," the guy said. "It's been dusted and checked."

"Did you find anything?

"Some threads, a couple of hairs. And a whole bunch of smudged prints. Looks like the visitors can't resist touching the glass."

The hairs and cloth were possibly useful, thought Gil, for tying the perp to the scene, but not for actually finding him.

"So," said Tebbins, tugging on his moustache, "what is so difficult about this?"

Dinah actually smiled, as if she felt proud. "This is the beauty of it. We not only have a disturbance sensor that cannot *ever* be switched off without causing an alarm, but we have a continuously refreshed vacuum seal. If anything raises the pressure even a little, the alarm sounds. And it cannot be turned off.

Any power drop, disconnection, et cetera, will send alarms to our data stations, and sound alarms in here. So…it's damn near impossible to remove anything from the display cases. In fact, if this hadn't happened, I'd've bet my future earnings that nobody could do it."

Gil stepped closer to the case. "What exactly do you mean by a disturbance sensor?"

She tapped the case with a fingernail. "There's a sensor under the dagger. If the item is removed, it sends an alarm."

Anna was staring at the case as if it held a snake, Gil noticed. He wondered what was bothering her, other than the fact that she was probably going to suffer from the fallout over the theft; to him it certainly looked like more was troubling her.

"Let's open it," Tebbins said.

Gil's attention snapped back to the display case. That white corner sticking out from beneath the dagger had him intrigued. A thief and murderer who left messages. Inside a fierce delight bloomed in him. Those who left messages were generally fools who sooner or later tripped themselves up.

He glanced again at Anna, who was now tight-lipped. Behind her the fake wall looked tacky in the bright lighting.

Dinah Hudson had a two-way radio clipped to her belt, and she used it now to contact her office. "We're opening the display case," she said into it. "Station J-3. Ignore the alarm. Call Woody and tell him to silence the audibles after four seconds. I want these folks to hear them. Thanks, Suzi."

Dinah clipped the radio to the waist of her pants and looked at Anna. "Do you have the keys?"

Anna nodded. Stepping forward, she pulled a key out of each pocket and started to lean toward the case. Tebbins stopped her.

"Wait a minute," he said, and turned to the criminologist. "Did you check these locks?"

"No external sign of tampering," he answered. "I didn't want to go any further because of the alarms."

"Okay. Well, you'll have more to check out in a minute."

"Yes, sir."

Tebbins turned to Anna. "Go ahead, Ms. Lundgren."

She inserted each of the keys into the locks, and turned them both at the same time, one clockwise and one counterclockwise.

Gil spoke. "What if somebody turns them the wrong way? Do you get an alarm?"

Dinah shook her head. "No need. They just won't open. But wait and see what happens next."

Reaching out, Dinah lifted the clear cover from the case. Almost the instant it parted from the stand below, a shrieking, deafening alarm began to whoop. Gil winced, and Anna covered her ears. After four seconds, it was silenced.

For a moment no one said anything, as if shocked by both the noise and the sudden silence.

"That's the vacuum-pressure alarm," Dinah said finally. "You can see it's functioning.

The same thing would have happened if someone had cracked the case. Which is polycarbonate, by the way. Harder to break than glass."

Leaning forward, she surveyed the setup. "There are two pressure sensors, here and here. Redundancy, like I said. Underneath, in the case, is the vacuum pump. If it fails for any reason, the alarm will go off immediately, even if the pressure in the case hasn't dropped."

Tebbins spoke. "How sensitive is the sensor?"

"We had to allow a range of variation because of the way the pumps work and because no vacuum is perfect. Within a certain range of pressure rise, the sensor merely notifies the pump to kick on. However, if the rise is too sudden, the alarm will sound. If someone opened the case in some way, the pump would kick on, of course, but the pressure would rise precipitously, causing the alarm to go off."

"Hmmm," said Tebbins thoughtfully, twisting his moustache. Then he signaled the criminologist. "Lift the dagger, please."

"Wait," Dinah said, and spoke into her radio again. "There, we won't have the alarm this time."

"Thank God," Tebbins said with feeling.

The tech stepped forward. Wearing rubber gloves, he used a pair of tongs to lift the dagger. Holding it upright, he showed it to Tebbins.

"Ms. Lundgren?" Tebbins said. "That *is* the dagger that was on your desk last night?"

On her desk? Gil was suddenly full of questions and very irritated that this wasn't his case.

What if Tebbins didn't tell him everything? Already something had been withheld. Although in fairness, they hadn't had much time to cover every detail.

When Anna didn't answer, Gil glanced at her, and found her staring at the small white envelope that was folded in half on the stand where the dagger had been lying. She looked horrified.

"Anna?" he said.

She jerked and looked at him. Apparently the sound of her first name had caught her attention more than *Ms. Lundgren*. "What?" she said, sounding shaky.

"The dagger," Tebbins said. "Is this the same dagger?"

Anna edged around until she was closer to the glass blade and gleaming hilt with a stylized jaguar head at the top. "Yes," she said after a few moments. "It's the same one. And look how the envelope's been slit with a letter opener. I'm sure it's empty, and I'm sure it's the same envelope you opened last night."

Tebbins, Gil, and Anna were in the conference room. The April day had turned dark with thunderclouds, but the room insulated them. And Anna was pacing up and down, frightened and annoyed.

"Tell me this isn't aimed at me," she demanded. "Tell me I'm wrong to feel like I'm being stalked."

Tebbins took a break from twirling his moustache to spread his hands. "I can't."

Gil was fed up. "What the hell aren't you telling me, Tebbins? I know I'm an observer here, but we agreed to cooperate."

Tebbins waved his hand, a theatrical gesture that Gil was already coming to loathe. "My apologies. Last night at the preopening gala for the exhibit, Ms. Lundgren went to her office to get her notes for her speech. There she found a box addressed to her. Naturally, she opened it, and inside was the same dagger we just removed from the case."

"And the envelope?"

"The same envelope, which had no card in it, I might add. Just an envelope with her name on it."

"I suppose there's no hope of fingerprints."

"Probably not. However," Tebbins added, "when I opened the envelope last night, I took care not to touch it. So perhaps..."

Gil stiffened. "*You* were here last night?"

Tebbins gave a deep shrug. "I attended with my aunt, who is a museum benefactor."

"And just happened to be there when Ms. Lundgren found the dagger?"

"I heard her cry out."

"Ahh." Suspicions were blooming in the back of Gil's brain faster than weeds on a poorly kept lawn.

Tebbins, as if he knew it, merely smiled.

"All right, all right," Anna said. "There's something more important right now, to me at least. *Am I being stalked?*"

Tebbins lifted his brow. "One can't say for sure."

"Of course not." Anna threw up a hand. "You

83

know, I felt pretty uneasy last night, the way that thing turned up on my desk and then disappeared. But right now…" She shook her head and wrapped her arms around her waist. "I don't like this."

She sighed, then lifted her head. "I'm sorry. The important thing is, of course, the theft of the dagger. It's going to make this museum look bad, and it's certainly going to make it more difficult to get visiting displays in the future."

Gil spoke. "Will it affect your employment?"

"It might. I mean, I'm not in any way responsible for security, but…" She shrugged. "It won't look good regardless."

"Crap does roll downhill, doesn't it?"

The corners of her mouth lifted slightly. "*Someone* has to take the blame."

"Whatever happened to the buck being passed up the chain?"

Tebbins answered. "The devaluation of the buck."

Gil had to grin. Even Anna managed a smile.

"All right," said Tebbins. "With regard to the stalking question, I'm afraid, Ms. Lundgren, that you do somehow appear to be targeted by the thief. He wants you to know that." He looked at Gil as if for confirmation.

Gil nodded slowly. "At the very least he wants your attention."

"I agree," said Tebbins. He tugged at his moustache, inadvertently straightening it. At once he began to wrap it around his finger, restoring the curl. "Now... I heard something last night about your parents being involved in the discovery of the Pocal tomb?"

Anna shook her head impatiently. "Involved is too strong a word. My father was an engineer. He built oil pipelines all around the world. One of his crews stumbled upon the Mayan city where Pocal's tomb was discovered while they were clearing the forest for the pipeline to pass through. My father merely notified the authorities, as he was required to do, then began work on rerouting the pipeline so as not to disturb the ruins. That's not exactly involvement."

"But," said Tebbins, "I heard he was killed."

Anna's tone was exasperated. "Damn that Reed Howell. I keep telling him it was an earthquake. Earthquakes happen all the time in that region. Why does he keep trying to turn it into a story about that curse?"

"Because," Gil said sardonically, "it sells papers. So what's your version?"

She pulled out a chair at long last and sat down.

"It's really quite simple. His crew found the ruins while clearing the pipeline route. My father reported it. Everybody makes a big deal out of it, but about four days after the dagger was found and shipped out to a museum where it could be properly cared for, a devastating earthquake took place. Unfortunately, the earthquake tore open a section of the pipeline that was being tested, and natural gas ignited. I don't know the whole sequence of events, but the refinery exploded and leveled an area of two square miles, killing nearly three thousand people."

Gil whistled.

"It was terrible," Anna said. "Just terrible. But if you look at the facts, you'll see that it was unfortunate that a set of circumstances joined together to cause a massive blast. It was an *accident,* nothing more."

To Gil it seemed that she didn't quite believe that herself, but he didn't want to press her on the issue. Not yet, anyway. He was in a delicate jurisdictional situation, and despite his and Tebbins's agreement to share, that didn't mean Tebbins would be happy if Gil just stepped in and started acting like the detective in charge.

"Doesn't seem like a very well designed curse," Tebbins remarked.

"No," Gil agreed. "Rather a broad brush to tar a few trespassers with."

Surprising him, Anna actually laughed. A brief, weak laugh, but it reached her eyes.

"Exactly," she said. "The local legend is that trespassers and those who handle the dagger will suffer the wrath of the jaguar god into the second generation. But...an awful lot of people died who had nothing to do with the tomb's desecration."

The second generation. The words struck Gil, and he tucked them away for future consideration.

Anna glanced at her watch. "I'm late. We're getting a new shipment for the exhibit upstairs, and it must have arrived a while ago. I need to go check."

Excusing herself, she walked out. But her head was not held as high as it had been.

"So," Tebbins said to Gil, "we have a curse."

Gil nodded, keeping his thoughts to himself, because something else had occurred to him, something very nasty.

"It gives one an interesting view of the mind of this thief and murderer, if the curse plays a part."

"It certainly does."

"Of course," Tebbins said, "the curse may have nothing to do with it at all. We may be dealing with something as simple as one of Ms. Lundgren's angry former suitors."

"Or," said Gil reluctantly, "we may be dealing with a young woman who lost her father in a terrible accident that many blamed on a curse. A young woman who's been forced to deal with the artifact that supposedly bears the curse."

Tebbins beamed. "Great minds think alike! Of course she is a suspect. The dagger appearing and disappearing from her desk last night makes her a suspect."

Anna left the museum under a low, dark sky with lightning forking from cloud to cloud. The streets were still soaked from the earlier downpour, and rivers ran along the gutters.

Her stomach was queasy; it had been queasy all day, ever since she had discovered the theft. Worse, the back of her neck crawled with the apprehension that she was being watched and stalked.

Was he behind her now in a car, following her home? The fear was strong enough that for several minutes she considered dining out in some busy restaurant. But that wouldn't solve the entire problem, because she'd still need to go home. And the later she went there, the harder it was going to be to make herself go inside.

The clouds were hanging even lower by the time she pulled into the driveway outside the snug little house she rented in Temple Terrace, not far from the university. The wind had ripped dead and dying leaves from the overhanging trees, and scattered them over the driveway. Rainwater dripped with a lonely sound from the roof.

And for the first time she noticed just how far away the neighboring houses were.

Coming from Minnesota and a small town, the first thing she had noticed here was how small many of the houses were, and how close together. But right now that "close together" looked like a huge distance. Would they be able to hear her if she screamed?

She hesitated again, then told herself not to be a ninny. If this guy was really after *her*, he wasn't going to do something so quickly after the robbery. No, he wanted to torment her first.

She climbed out of the car and locked it, then walked to the front door with trepidation, half-expecting to see something waiting for her on the stoop. Maybe another artifact, maybe…oh, something awful. Something sickening.

But there was nothing. She was being too paranoid. Shoving the key in the lock with trembling hands, she scolded herself until she was able to turn the key and push the door open.

The first thing she saw was the back of the swivel recliner. Had she left it that way? She usually liked it to face the window. Reaching out, she flipped on a light.

And saw, propped on the ottoman, denim-clad legs and cowboy boots.

CHAPTER SEVEN

Gil pulled into his driveway at dusk. The rain that was soaking Tampa had stopped by the time he crossed the bridge, and his yard was still as dry as a bone. The lights were on in the house, though, and he figured he was about to discover what Trina had been up to all day.

Part of him didn't even want to bother. He knew what was coming, and he just plain didn't want to deal with it. A couple of hours of sleep didn't hack it, especially when dealing with a teenage daughter. Besides, his head was clogged with swirling impressions of the day's events and the people involved. If he didn't spend some time organizing his thoughts, he was never going to sleep tonight.

But then he kicked himself for being a chicken. There was no way on earth Trina could give him half the trouble of some of the punks he'd dealt with in his job. No way.

Sighing, he climbed out of his car and listened to the breeze ruffle the trees and palms. He loved this time of night. What he'd really like to do was go grab a beer and sit on his screened lanai for a while, listening to night sounds.

Fat chance.

He took a moment to collect himself and order himself into a better mood. Inside, the house smelled of delicious things again, and he decided that one of these days he was going to tell her that good, home-cooked food might make him happy but it didn't turn him into a fool. On the other hand, why disabuse her of that notion? She was cooking some great stuff...

The thought actually made him grin as he dumped his jacket over the back of a chair and entered the kitchen, greeting his daughter. Instead of getting the too-bright smile and chipper voice he expected, he got a glare.

"You're late," Trina said accusingly.

Refrigerator door open, beer bottle in hand, Gil looked at her. "I said hi, how are you doing. It would be nice if you responded in kind."

"Hihowareyoudoing, and why didn't you call?"

She was sunburned, he noted. How many times did he have to tell her what the sun could do to her skin? But the thought barely skimmed his mind as he realized he wasn't in for a snow job.

"What's wrong, honey?"

"Everything!"

Which wasn't too helpful. *Everything* could be just that her favorite shorts had a stain she couldn't get out. He stood a minute, letting a sense of parental helplessness roll over him, then he waded in.

Crossing the room, he put an arm around her shoulders. "What's everything?"

"Everything!"

He smothered a sigh and considered retreating to the table and sipping his beer while he waited for details to bubble out. Something else suggested that would be foolhardy.

"So talk to me," he said. "I've got willing ears."

But instead she tugged away from him. "You won't understand. You'll tell me none of it is that important. And besides, you don't like Jamie anyway."

He found himself hoping she and Jamie had broken up, then kicked himself mentally for wishing his daughter unhappy. Cripes, there was never a right response with a kid. "You and Jamie fight?"

"Yeah. Go sit down. Your dinner's probably ruined. I was trying to keep it warm."

He obeyed, deciding he was only going to get the story when she was ready to tell him.

Out of the oven she pulled a foil-covered plate. After ripping the foil from it, she placed it in front of him. Two pork chops, breaded and baked, a mound of somewhat overcooked broccoli, and a baked potato that had shrunk during the wait.

"It looks really good," he said.

"It's ruined." She sat across from him. "You should tell me when you're going to be late."

"I did. Check the machine. I probably called fifteen times today."

At last a response. She flushed, turning even redder than her sunburn.

"So..." He chose his words with care. "Did you make it to the beach?"

"Did I forget to mention where I was going?" At least she had the courtesy to avert her eyes.

"I guess so. I assume it was the beach. You're pretty sunburned."

She sighed, then wailed, "Everything sucks, Dad!"

"It usually does at your age. But it's kinda hard to commiserate when I don't know what's going on."

"Jamie was so nasty! I got upset because we were supposed to go to the mall for a couple of hours to meet the gang, but he took me to the beach anyway, and I know you didn't want me going down there alone with him..."

He nodded. "Not without asking first."

"That's what I told him, but he wouldn't listen. So we got down to the beach, and I was mad, and he started picking on me for being such a baby, and I got even madder and told him to take me home..."

She stopped and wiped her eyes. "He wouldn't. So I got a ride with a friend."

"But where were you? Honey, you were gone all day. Did something else happen?"

She hesitated, her gaze slipping away again. Gil had to step down on his impatience. "Honey?"

She sniffled.

"Trina?"

"Well..." Her voice trembled. "There was this other guy there I know from school. And Jamie was being so nasty..."

"Just exactly how was Jamie being nasty?"

"He was kicking sand at me and throwing it in my eyes and threatening to hit me if I didn't grow up."

"Jesus." Gil suddenly had a vision of his gun in his holster. He banished it immediately, but that couldn't stop his anger from rising. "Go on."

"So...well, I knew this other guy, and he said he'd take me home, and I said okay, which made Jamie madder."

Gil nodded, feeling his jaw clench.

"So Randy—that's the other guy, he's a football player at school—he and Jamie slugged it out. Jamie started it."

Which didn't surprise Gil.

"Anyway, Randy knocked Jamie down, and then we ran to his car and drove away. Randy said we ought to drive around a while because Jamie was going to be pissed and might go to the house, so I said okay, and I didn't have any sunscreen, and he has a convertible, so I got burned...and anyway..."

"Take a breath, honey, it'll be easier."

She nodded and took a couple of shaky

93

gulps. "Around three he brought me home, and Jamie was waiting, and I was scared, so we drove away before he saw us. But finally Randy had to get home and I had him drop me off in Clearwater to catch a bus. I figured you'd be here by the time I got home..."

"But I wasn't. Why didn't you call me?"

"What's the point? You're always in the middle of something! You had a murder case. Louise told me you were in Tampa. What were you going to do?"

Her voice had been rising again, and she burst into tears anew. "Jamie...Jamie wasn't here when I got home. He probably figured you'd be home any minute. But I've been so scared..."

Ignoring his untouched plate, he reached across the table and took her hand. "I'm sorry, honey. That's awful. And if you'd called me directly I'd have found a way to come for you, or I'd have had someone else come for you, understand?"

"Mom hates it when I call her at work. She says her boss gets mad."

"I won't hate it if you call. That's why I gave you my cell-phone number. So you can *always* reach me. Anytime."

She nodded and sniffled again. "Eat your dinner."

"In a minute. Trina, we need to talk about Jamie."

"No! You hate him. He just got mad, Dad. Everybody gets mad."

"Then why the hell were you so afraid?"

She shrugged. "I don't like it when people get mad at me."

94

"Well, you sure as hell don't hide from me when I get mad. Nor do you hesitate to make me mad."

"That's different."

"That's my point," Gil said forcefully. "It shouldn't be any different with your friends. You shouldn't have to be afraid."

"We'll make up," she said.

He saw the shutters closing behind her eyes. She wouldn't hear another word on the subject, no matter how he flapped his jaws. She was *in love.*

And those were two of the stupidest, most dangerous words in the English language.

"For gosh sakes, cut out that caterwauling!"

Anna's mouth snapped shut and she stared into the face of her identical twin sister Nancy. "What the hell are you doing here? Why didn't you call?"

"Because I wanted the hell out of Austin."

"What did you do? Rob a bank?"

"Actually, my girlfriend dumped me a couple of weeks ago. So I finally decided it was time to get away for a while."

Regaining control of her limbs, Anna shut the door behind her and locked it. Then she looked at her beloved sister, who looked exactly like her, except for her choice of Western clothes.

Then both of them spoke at the same instant, and said the same thing. "When did you get your hair cut?"

Then, laughing, they fell into each other's arms and hugged until their ribs hurt.

"Two months ago," Anna said when she could catch her breath.

"Me, too," Nancy answered. Now they both sported smooth, shoulder-length bobs.

But Nancy noticed something else. "You look about as bad as I feel. What happened? Some boyfriend dump you? I didn't even know you had a boyfriend."

"I didn't and don't. No, there was a theft at the museum last night. A priceless Mayan artifact was stolen."

"Oh, God." Nancy sat on a barstool at the kitchen breakfast bar and watched as her sister started a pot of tea. Tea was an indispensable part of their heart-to-heart conversations. "You must be really upset. I know how much this exhibit means to you."

Anna pretended to shrug it off. "I'm not responsible for security, thank goodness." She didn't mention the other, darker thoughts that were plaguing her. She didn't want Nancy worrying. "And what about you?"

"Oh." Nancy shrugged as if it didn't matter. "I told you. Peggy dumped me."

"After two years?"

"Well, look at heterosexual marriages."

"True. You must be devastated."

Nancy shrugged again. "I don't know yet. Right now I'm hopping mad, and I figured I'd better get away before I did something stupid. You know, like getting even? Then I decided to just let her new girlfriend discover it all on her own. Peggy's a pig. She never cleans up after herself. She cheated on me three times that I know of. She drinks too much, and I figure she's going to have a problem before long."

"And you miss this?"

Nancy's eyes reddened. "Yeah. I was kind of in love with her." She gave a shaky laugh. "I knew you were going to say 'I told you so.'"

"Aw, Nancy..." Anna didn't quite know what to say. She wasn't a hundred percent comfortable with her sister's sexual orientation, but she still ached for her loss, even if she had been trying to warn Nancy for a year that Peggy was trouble.

"Doesn't matter. I'm better off now." Which sounded like bravado. "So, as a result, you get to enjoy my company for two weeks. Aren't you thrilled?"

"Actually, I am." It couldn't have come at a better time. Though she didn't want to expose her sister to any danger, right then the last thing on earth that Anna wanted was to be living alone. "I'm so glad to see you." And she could see that her sister desperately wanted to get away from the subject of Peggy.

"Yeah." Nancy gave her a bright smile. "Same here. Hey, I bet you got to meet a lot of cops today. Any gorgeous ones?"

"For you or me?" Anna asked.

"You, of course. I don't wanna get tangled up with someone who lives half a continent away."

"Well, there was this gorgeous detective, but he's from St. Petersburg."

"Heck, that's only a hop away."

Anna laughed again, but shook her head as she put the teapot on the counter between them, then went to get cups. "He's on a case, I'm part of the case."

"Yeah. Bummer. So, this was the Pocal exhibit that was hit, right? The one Dad found?"

"Dad didn't exactly find it, Nance."

Nancy screwed up her face. "Okay, okay. Be nitpicky. But it's the same one, right?"

"Yeah, the same."

"Cool. You finally get to see all the stuff." She swiveled around on the stool, and looked straight at Anna. "But...don't you feel uneasy?"

She did, but Anna wasn't about to admit it. She'd made it her lifelong goal not to be fanciful like her mother, her aunt, and her sister. Nancy might *think* she was a realist with her job of programming, but she worked on machines that had names like Icarus and Gandalf, and on weekends she played *Dungeons & Dragons*. She read science fiction and fantasy faster than publishers could supply her addiction, and she knew most of the technical specifications of the *Enterprise*. Not the shuttle, but the fictional one.

All of that added to Nancy's cuteness and appeal, making her seem far livelier than her twin, but...sometimes Anna seriously doubted her sister's practicality.

And even now, when they were both adult women with successful careers, Anna wasn't about to admit she shared some of that fancifulness.

"No," she said finally.

"Braaaaaaa," said Nancy, making the buzzer sound for a wrong answer. "Took too long to answer, Annie."

"Oh, cut it out."

"No, I won't. Part of the reason I decided now would be a good time to shake the Austin dust off my boots was because of the Pocal exhibit. You think I don't want to see what our dad died for?"

"Nance, they didn't die *for* that stuff. It was an *earthquake*."

"Yeah. Okay. It was an earthquake." Nancy cocked her head to one side, her green eyes intent. "The problem with you is that you won't let magic into your life."

"Magic? Whatever for?"

"I dunno. Maybe because it makes life more interesting." Reaching out, Nancy picked up the teapot and poured for them both. Aromatic green tea filled the cups, and she sniffed appreciatively. "You buy the good stuff. Yummy. I'm stuck with the supermarket stuff."

"Why?"

Nancy shrugged. "Peggy kind of left me...poorer than I was."

"Oh, man." Anna didn't know whether to shake her sister or hug her. "How'd she do that?"

"She didn't do it. *I* did. I gave her a credit card and bought her a new car. Nobody to blame but me." Her eyes were growing red-rimmed again.

Anna reached out and squeezed her sister's shoulder. "I'm sorry. I'm so sorry, Nance."

"Live and learn. You're right about one thing. I tend to jump in with both feet without checking the water depth first. I'll survive. I just need to be careful for a while."

"I'm still sorry."

Nancy shrugged, but couldn't quite conceal her pain. Anna ached for her.

"But," said Nancy after a moment, "let's not get too far from the subject *you're* trying to avoid. It's much more interesting than *my* least-favorite topic. Dad's dead. Earthquake or curse, what difference does it make? I'd kind of like to believe it wasn't just a nasty accident for no reason at all."

"I'd rather *not* believe that."

Nancy picked up her mug and looked over the rim at her. "How'd you get to be so different?"

"I think it was some kind of compensation. *Somebody* had to be practical and down-to-earth in that house."

Nancy's eyes grew dreamy. "I think that's why Dad loved Mom, you know. Because she *wasn't* practical. I think she was an escape from all that engineering he did."

"Maybe so." Anna looked down at her own mug, watching as a small tendril of steam rose from it. "But...magic is a useless thing to think about. It doesn't serve any purpose."

"Maybe not. All I know is you take after Dad. He was always solid, reliable, and down to earth. Maybe you just wanted to be like him."

"Maybe."

"And I still think the curse might have had something to do with it. I don't know if I could stand working with that stuff. I mean, I want to see it, but I don't want to touch it."

Anna shrugged. "I wouldn't be afraid to. But...nobody *did* touch it. As far as I know, anyway. We made a big deal out of it as part of the hype for the exhibit."

"Did Dad ever touch any of it?"

"I'm not sure. He might have. Then maybe not. Why would he? He didn't have anything to do with the archaeologists."

"So maybe the curse doesn't only affect people who actually touch the stuff."

The thought gave Anna a distinct chill. "Nancy..."

"Okay, okay." Nancy laughed. "I'll stop. I'm just teasing."

But it wasn't a kind of teasing Anna found comfortable, especially not now. Not when she might be the target of a crazy stalker.

Slowly, she turned her head and looked toward the curtained windows. They suddenly seemed poor protection against the night outside.

Later that evening, Gil sat in the recliner in the living room while Trina showered and got ready for bed. He dozed a little, but mostly he turned over the day's events, from Trina to the murder to the museum, and most of all to Clarence Tebbins.

They were after a wily thief and murderer all right, but Tebbins worried him almost as much. The man was not quite...right, for lack of a better word. And his presence last night when the dagger was found...it was more of a coincidence than Gil could easily accept. In his job, coincidence was something to be treated first with suspicion.

And his suspicions were abounding. Sighing, he finally got out of his recliner and went to get a legal pad to scribble notes on. Trina was still banging around in the bathroom, opening and closing doors. As he returned to his chair he heard her blow-dryer come on.

Okay. The guard. Eddy Malacek. According to Tebbins, the overnight video cameras showed nothing unusual. They even showed Malacek leaving at a few minutes after eight, at shift changeover, when the new guard arrived.

Ergo, Malacek had to have been involved in the burglary somehow. And he had to have been killed after he got home, a drive of nearly an hour even at optimal times. So, say around nine.

Neighbors claimed to have noticed nothing unusual, but he wasn't sure he trusted that. Neighbors often didn't notice much, or even pay attention to minor things, like when someone's car was home. But assuming they were right, and Eddy had come home at the usual time, then someone must have been waiting for him.

Gil made notes to question the neighbors a little more closely.

Tomorrow he needed to check out some of Eddy's friends, find out if they'd noticed anything unusual. Or if he'd said anything strange in the days before the burglary.

But Eddy wasn't looking as interesting as he had that morning. Not since Gil had spoken with Tebbins and Anna and learned some of the details of the burglary.

One, no alarms.

Two, nothing on videotape.

Three, the motion detectors hadn't even been turned off.

Then there was the problem of the dagger replica. It had turned up on Anna's desk, then had disappeared sometime during the evening while the museum was full of guests. Tebbins had witnessed it.

That bothered him. All of it bothered him. Any way he looked at it, it seemed to point a finger at either Tebbins or Anna.

The crime itself suggested an insider. Someone who knew how things worked, and had at least an acquaintance with the security system. He supposed that put Dinah Hudson on the list of suspects, too, and however many of her associates.

He tensed in his chair and found himself suddenly wondering how he could have been so stupid. Picking up the phone, he dialed Clarence Tebbins's home number across the bay. He was rewarded with voice mail, the universal prerecorded voice of Personal Secretary, telling him to leave a message.

"Tebbins, it's Garcia. I thought of something. Give me a call."

Then he hung up, thinking about how much he hated Personal Secretary. At least in the days of the old answering machines, people often picked up during a message when they wanted to talk to you. These days, with the phone company doing the job, you couldn't even break in on the message once it had transferred to voice mail.

But Tebbins didn't disappoint him. The return call came after only two minutes.

"It's Tebbins," said the rather high, nasal voice. "I'm sitting here sipping cognac and thinking over the day."

The image immediately brought to Gil's mind a dark, nineteenth-century library with a fire burning beneath an ornately carved mantel. Great for television, horrible for Florida. "I'm sitting here swigging a diet soft drink in my recliner, waiting for my daughter to get out of the shower so I can lay down some new rules about her boyfriend."

After an instant, Tebbins's ratchety laugh reached his ear. "Daughters and boyfriends. I've been spared."

"You don't know how lucky you are," Gil said drily.

"But you've apparently been thinking while you were waiting?"

"Of course. When the day comes I learn to turn off my mind, I might actually consider spending a week on vacation."

"I use my vacations for thinking. Oh, yes." Tebbins sounded quite pleased with himself. "There's nothing quite like being stuck on a Caribbean beach for a week to get your mind working. Sheer boredom does wonders."

"I'll pass."

"So, you said you thought of something?"

"Yes. We've been focusing on the guard who was murdered this morning. Has anyone looked at the guard who relieved him?"

"Only a little so far. He was on the videotape and nothing was disturbed. And he was only there an hour before most of the staff came in. Of course, there were others there before that. One can see him letting them into the building between eight-thirty and nine."

"Hmm. And someone verified that he did indeed let those folks in this morning?"

"I believe so. If memory serves, there were at least three people who confirmed he let them in before the doors opened. We have their names."

"Okay." Gil was disappointed, but something still niggled at him. "There's something wrong with the video-tapes, you know."

"There must be. I have the lab reviewing them."

"And Eddy Malacek may have been killed only because he caught on to something."

"Of course. Or his death may indeed have been an overdose."

Swiftly Gil reviewed the morning's investigation. "He was murdered. Right after he got home."

"Well, I'll not deny it was probably related. It's a rather large coincidence otherwise."

"And I'm still concerned about the relief guard. Can we question him tomorrow?" He hated having to ask, but it wasn't his jurisdiction, something that he figured was going to scald him more than once before all was said and done.

"I'll arrange it," Tebbins said. "But it's pretty slim. He already said he came in like he always did, and we can account for his actions during the critical hour."

"What about after nine? The exhibit doesn't open to the public until ten."

"He was there on the front desk, and the best alibi he has is that you can see the visitors beginning to arrive in large numbers to buy their tickets. But yes, let's talk to him. When?"

"When he finishes his shift tomorrow. I need to go out and question some of Malacek's friends in the morning."

"Fair enough. I'll set it up." Tebbins paused. "Any thoughts about Anna Lundgren?"

"Yeah," Gil said, as something seemed to come instinctively clear. "She's too damn obvious, and too smart to be that obvious."

"Or smart enough to look too obvious," said Tebbins.

God, thought Gil, dealing with this guy was going to be *fun*. He was going to add potential twists and turns to every avenue while he looked for his "mastermind."

"Maybe," he said after a moment. "For what it's worth, my gut says no."

"Ahh, your gut talks to you," said Tebbins.

Gil shifted in his chair, feeling a surge of impatience. "Call it cop intuition then."

"I prefer the brain. It thinks so much more clearly than the gut."

He heard the amusement in Tebbins's voice, but it didn't much appease him. Right now he'd give anything to have his partner back from vacation.

"Something is rotten," said Gil.

"Well, yes, and not only in Denmark."

Almost in spite of himself, Gil smiled. Tebbins didn't quite pick up the ball and run with it, but he at least was in the ballpark answering Gil's reference.

"Okay," Gil said, "we'll talk tomorrow."

"Certainly." Tebbins didn't sound at all irritated that Gil was firmly horning in on his investigation. Give him marks for that.

After he hung up, Gil leaned back in his recliner. From the sounds, he gathered that his daughter was about to exit the bathroom, which meant that the postponed confrontation about Jamie couldn't be postponed any longer.

But for the few minutes he had left, he found himself wondering why he was so reluctant to consider Anna as a suspect, and so ready to consider Tebbins.

The answers he got didn't please him at all.

Outside Anna's house in the deep darkness, the watcher stood within the embrace of a tall azalea, following the shadows of two women cast against the drawn curtains. He'd seen Anna come home, but he hadn't noticed the other woman arrive. Had she already been there? Or had he somehow missed her appearance?

Either notion disturbed him, and for a while he was annoyed by the idea that his careful plan might be going awry. But then he reminded himself that it wasn't yet time. He didn't need to get to Anna tonight. She didn't yet understand her role in the drama, and until she did he couldn't touch her.

No, what he needed to pay attention to,

now that the first stage was complete, was the second act, wherein the message would be made clear to her and others. But mostly to her, because she was the centerpiece.

Nevertheless, he stood in the bush a while longer, savoring his victory of the previous night, and anticipating victories to come, as he drew the noose ever tighter around Anna.

He felt pulled to her, attached to her, he realized suddenly. He didn't want to leave, though he had nothing else to do there. He just wanted to stand and watch her shadow move against the curtains.

But of course he felt attached to her, he reminded himself. They were joined by the curse, locked now in a battle to the death.

It was time to go, he told himself sternly. The longer he stood there, the more likely it was that someone would spot him and call the police.

Just then lightning, absent for hours, resumed its display, arching overhead. The crackle of thunder was deafening and served as a warning.

Until he finished his task, the paw of the jaguar god might reach down and snatch him. And standing in the branches of a bush beneath a large tree was a stupid thing to be doing even when he wasn't under a curse.

After scuffing his footprints in the wet grass and soil, he spared one last glance for Anna's windows, then melted away into the night, like the jaguar he served.

CHAPTER EIGHT

Anna spent a thoroughly miserable morning showing the representative of the Mexican museum through the exhibit. He was not a happy man in any language. While he thoroughly approved of the staging, he couldn't stop complaining about the theft of the dagger, even after Dinah Hudson, hurriedly called in, had explained yet again the security systems.

"In Mexico," he said again and again, "we don't have these problems."

Surprisingly, the police had reopened the museum to the public. She had thought they would want to keep the public out for at least a while longer, but apparently they felt they had collected all the evidence they could. Even more surprisingly, the number of visitors had soared, their interest apparently caught by the robbery.

Around lunchtime, when she turned Señor Cuestas over to Ivar, who looked as if he were swallowing a whole bottle of cod liver oil, she found the lobby packed with winding lines and people waiting for their time to begin touring the exhibit. Three ticket windows were open instead of the two they'd had on opening day.

Anna found herself hoping the interest would last through the rest of the run.

Then she spied Gil Garcia standing in the

line with a girl of about fifteen. The young woman was beautiful, with long inky hair and snapping dark eyes very like Gil's. She was also painfully pink with sunburn, and from the way she moved Anna suspected her tank top and white shorts were irritating it.

Anna started toward her office, then thought better of it. Walking over, she said, "Hi. Going to the exhibit?"

Gil smiled at her. "My daughter is. She's getting bored hanging out while I work, and I thought she'd enjoy this."

The girl's eyes looked doubtful.

"Well, it's a great exhibit," she said cheerfully. "But you don't need a ticket. Listen, my sister's already up there waiting for her walk-through. Why doesn't your daughter go through with her? Nancy's a lot of fun. Kinda crazy, but nice crazy."

Gil's daughter brightened a bit. Apparently she'd thought going through the exhibit alone would be boring. "Dad?" she said hopefully.

"Sure," Gil said after a moment. "What's your sister look like?"

"You can't miss her," Anna said with a laugh. "She's my identical twin, except she's in cowboy drag."

That brightened the girl's face even more.

"She's from Austin," Anna explained. "It's in her bones now."

"Oh, I'm sorry," Gil said, suddenly recalling himself. "This is my daughter, Trina. Trina, this is Ms. Lundgren. She's the museum curator."

That didn't exactly seem to impress Trina favorably. Amused, Anna said, "My sister's a computer geek. Go ahead and tease her about *Star Trek*. Or *Lord of the Rings.*"

Trina giggled at that.

Reaching into her pocket, Anna pulled out one of the guest passes she still had left. "Here you go. Just tell Nancy I sent you. Or, if you want, I'll introduce you myself."

"It's okay," Trina said. "Just as long as she doesn't mind?"

"She'll be delighted."

Trina walked away, and Gil turned to look at Anna. "Thank you. That was very nice. So you have a twin sister?"

"Yes. She arrived unexpectedly last night. But she does that a lot. I'll start thinking about her, and she'll call or she'll just show up."

"I've heard that about twins."

Anna smiled. "It's true about us, at least. Except my radar must have been screwed up the last few weeks. I had no idea she'd broken up with her...S.O."

"So she came to get away?"

"Partly. And partly to see the exhibit."

"Because of your father?"

Reluctantly, she nodded. "I keep telling her, and everyone else, that Dad didn't find Pocal's tomb. One of his crews did. He may have gone to look at the site before calling for archaeologists, but he certainly didn't find it. Unfortunately, Nancy seems as determined as many other people to link the earthquake to the discovery."

"The human mind seems to run that way. Listen, can we go to your office for a few minutes? I'd like to ask you about a few things."

"Sure."

They started walking toward her office, working their way through the growing crowds of visitors.

Gil spoke. "Looks like it's going to be a successful exhibit."

"I hope so. The theft was bad enough. It would be awful if the museum lost its shirt over the exhibit, too." She shook her head. "I just spent all morning listening to how this doesn't happen in Mexico." She glanced at him. "The representative of the museum there is visiting today."

"That must have been fun."

"Absolutely delightful. I can't say as I blame him. But this doesn't happen all that often *anywhere*."

"Wasn't there a theft here two years ago?"

Anna flushed. "Well, yes. I hadn't started here then, so I can't tell you much about it."

"Some mask or something," he remarked. "I recalled it yesterday, and checked it out. One of a kind, I understand."

"Yes." She stopped and faced him. "Are you insinuating something about this museum?"

He shook his head. "Only that it's had a run of bad luck."

"Why do I think you don't believe in runs of bad luck?"

"Oh, I do," he said, surprising her with a smile. "I'm as superstitious as the next guy."

He touched her arm briefly, and found his thoughts straying from business to forbidden places.

And looking into her eyes, he saw his reaction answered. Oh, hell, he thought, this isn't going to help at all.

The watcher was keeping one eye on Anna and Garcia, and another down the hallway where he had sent Tebbins. *Now,* he decided. It had to be now.

He'd been waiting for an opportune moment to put the envelope that was in his pocket on Anna's desk. A moment when someone else might be implicated in the theft. And implicating Tebbins would be choice.

Because Tebbins frightened him. The man, for all he looked like a deluded jerk, was actually very intelligent. This morning the watcher had had the unpleasant experience of being questioned by Tebbins about the night of the benefactors' party. The questions had seemed innocuous, even casual, but the watcher had noted how sharp Tebbins's eyes were, and how he seemed to weigh and retain every single word he heard.

The man was a threat. If he got too close to the truth too fast, the entire plan would go awry.

But now, if the watcher moved fast enough, he could torpedo Tebbins in the most appealing way.

Five minutes earlier, Tebbins had asked the watcher if he knew where he could get a copy of the guest list for the party the night before last. The watcher had opened his mouth to say that Ivar Gregor would have it, as would some of the secretaries, but then the new idea had come to him in an instant.

"Ms. Lundgren has one on her bulletin board," the watcher had answered promptly.

"Really. Well, I don't suppose she'll mind if I make a copy of it."

Anna still hadn't emerged from the exhibit where she was giving that Mexican guy the tour, although she would come out any minute, the watcher had known. But that St. Pete detective was over in the ticket line, too, and if the watcher knew anything about Anna, it was that she would stop and speak with him, and maybe offer him a pass. She was like that.

He loved her generosity, and always had. But just then it was going to aid him.

Unfortunately, she started heading toward her office with the detective too soon. Glancing down the hallway again, the watcher saw that Tebbins was at last emerging from Anna's office with the sheet of paper in his hand.

Could he possibly get down to Anna's office and plant the envelope before she and the detective would see him in the hallway? *Hurry up!* he willed Tebbins. The last thing on earth the watcher wanted was to pass Tebbins in that hallway. Tebbins was too bright.

But then Anna and the homicide dick paused and were looking at each other oddly. And Tebbins slipped into the copier room three doors down from Anna's office.

The watcher took off. Walking as swiftly as he dared across the lobby, he disappeared into the hallway. His feet, shod with shoes that had been carefully chosen, barely made a sound on the hall floor as he quick-walked down it.

If anyone stopped him or saw him, he would say he was going to the bathroom. A perfect cover.

But no one came out of an office or down the hall. Glancing quickly around, he darted into Anna's office and placed the envelope on the end of her desk beneath the corkboard on the wall. Then, slipping out, he hid himself in the alcove once more.

Sitting there he waited, peeling the rubber cement off his fingertips. Someone had mentioned that trick to him years ago, about painting your fingertips with rubber cement to avoid leaving fingerprints. It seemed like it would work, but it was also damned uncomfortable.

Amusing himself, he rolled the stuff up into little balls and scattered them in the corner. He heard Anna and Garcia come down the hallway, talking casually. Where was Tebbins? How long did it take a man to make a copy? He'd been hoping that Anna would find Tebbins in her office, putting the list back.

But still no Tebbins. The watcher sighed and peeled more rubber cement off his middle finger. Damn, the thing he most hated about this was all the waiting.

That and the ever-present possibility of making a slip.

Anna and Gil made their way to her office. She didn't much feel like sitting down, though, and instead leaned back against the ledge under the wide window. She was too wired, she realized. Between the theft and the visit by Señor Cuestas, she was wound tightly as a spring. Folding her arms almost self-consciously—since he had given her that look in the lobby, she'd been feeling as awkward as if a camera were watching her every move—she looked at Gil, who had sat in one of the chairs facing her desk. He had made her aware of her body in a way she hadn't been for a long time, and she wasn't sure she appreciated that.

"Okay," she said when he didn't speak. "What did you want to talk to me about?" She almost thought he looked reluctant.

"About," he said slowly, reaching into his pocket and pulling out a strip of newsprint, "your family ties with the exhibit."

"I told you..."

He shook his head. "Anna, read this. Unless you read the *Sentinel* this morning."

"I stopped subscribing when that weasel Reed Howell started bugging me." She looked at the newsprint with distaste.

"Take it and read it," he insisted. "You need to know because it's going to make your life uncomfortable for a while."

"I already know how he was pushing the curse angle. It's like he hated me for using it, but he couldn't get away from the whole idea. It fascinated him in some ugly way."

"Apparently so. But this is about more than a curse."

Full of disgust, Anna reached for the clipping and after a moment forced herself to read it.

It started the way she expected, mentioning the discovery of Pocal's tomb, the earthquake and fire. Then it segued into local legend, insinuating that the curse might have played a part. So far so ordinary.

But then the article touched on Anna personally. Not only did it mention that her father had been involved in the finding of the tomb, however remotely, but it suggested that the theft made Anna a victim of the curse herself...and then went on to mention that her mother had been a witch.

"Good God," she said, her head snapping up and anger pushing in pounding waves through her. "Good God! What a piece of tripe."

"I agree," Gil said gently. "But this is all over the bay area this morning."

"I knew he was after something like that. You'll notice I was never once quoted."

"No, you certainly weren't. Was your mother a witch?"

"Oh, she and my aunt dabbled in Wicca once. Briefly. I don't think it lasted more than a few months. They were both...eccentric. But what does that have to do with anything? Other than that it's a nuisance, and now I'll probably receive some very strange looks from my coworkers. Ivar may even hang his head in dismay, but since he does that a couple of times every day, I'm not exactly worried about it."

Gil smiled. "Ivar annoys you?"

"He's a fussbudget. A complete devotee of bean counting. He is, in fact, quite talented. He can turn any molehill into a mountain in five seconds flat. He'll certainly make Everest out of this."

She felt the corners of her mouth quirk up with a sour smile. "Since I discovered the robbery, all he's been worried about was that having police all over the place would keep visitors away."

But then she shook her head and sighed. "I'm not being very fair to him. He can be a good person, a very good person, when he's not hysterical."

Gil spoke. "Are *you* a witch?"

"Me? Hah. Not in this lifetime."

"Shoot. I was hoping for a cure for what ails my daughter."

"What does ail her?"

"A boyfriend."

"She's suffering from the frog-prince syndrome?"

"That's a good way of describing it." Gil sighed. "Although I think he oinks more than he ribbits."

She chuckled. "Dad's impartial eye, huh? Poor kid. It must be hard to get a date when your dad's a cop."

He looked a little surprised, as if he hadn't considered that before. "Well, you know us

118

cops. We follow in an unmarked car, spy on 'em with video cameras, and knock on the window with a baton anytime they seem to be getting too close."

Another laugh escaped her. "But oh, those handcuffs!"

It was his turn to laugh, and he laughed even harder when Anna realized what she had said, and her cheeks started to burn.

"Okay," he said after a moment. "This is unprofessional. So I'm going to go back to being a dry stick. At least for now."

"Pity." But actually she was relieved. She didn't have time for complications of that sort.

Just then, Peter Dashay walked into her office, doing an imitation of a lowering thundercloud. He was a handsome man, of average height, with a surfer's dark suntan and shaggy sun-bleached hair. At the moment he looked like a sixties throwback, in cutoff denim shorts and a black T-shirt that screamed *Hell's Angels are more FUN*. His students loved him.

"Hi, Peter," Anna said.

Peter didn't respond immediately. He scanned Gil, who was looking mildly interested, and apparently didn't approve of his Latin good looks.

Then he turned to Anna. "I've been popping in and out all morning looking for you. Did you get the flowers?"

"Yes, I did. Thank you. I meant to call, but then I discovered the burglary..." She trailed off, wondering why she felt she had to explain, especially when his question had been anything but courteous.

"Then you got my note. We were supposed to have dinner last night. And where are the flowers?"

Anna put her hands on her hips and simply stared at him. After a few moments, he unpuffed, but only a little.

"First," she said, "once you gave the flowers to me, they became mine to do with as I wished. It's none of your business whether I dumped them in the trash or put them somewhere else."

"Trash?" His eyes bulged. "That was an eighty-dollar bouquet!"

"Which I didn't ask for. Thank you for sending them. But they're still mine to do with as I please."

He resorted to scowling.

"Secondly, I got your note. There was a question mark after 'dinner tonight,' making it a question, one which I didn't answer. Therefore, you should not have assumed it was firm."

"A question mark? I didn't tell that girl to make it a question. Damn it!"

"It would have been a question anyway," Anna said firmly, "because we had never discussed it."

"God, I don't know why I keep trying to please you."

"Neither do I," Anna said. "We're just not suited, Peter."

Peter turned to Gil. "What kind of woman throws away an eighty-dollar bouquet?"

Gil shrugged.

"It's *you,* isn't it," Peter said harshly. "You're the interloper."

Tebbins's voice suddenly issued from behind the obscuring cloud that was Peter, startling them all.

"He isn't an interloper, he's a detective working on the burglary case."

Peter swung around, revealing Tebbins in all his sartorial glory to Anna. He wore a double-breasted blue pinstripe with a wide gray tie. The diamond—or most likely cubic zirconium—stick pin was ostentatious. In his hand he held a few sheets of paper.

"Who are you?" demanded Peter.

"Detective Clarence Tebbins, Tampa PD. And this is Detective Gil Garcia, St. Pete Homicide."

"Homicide?" Peter seemed to catch only the one word. Reaching for the one vacant chair, he sat. "My God, who was killed?"

"One of the guards," Tebbins said. "What do you know about that?"

"Me?" Peter practically squeaked.

Tebbins smiled, an almost sharklike expression that surprised Anna, for she hadn't considered him capable of anything except looking ridiculous and being bright. "Yes, you," he said. "You spend a lot of time with Ms. Lundgren?"

"Uh..." Peter looked wildly at Anna. "Actually...uh...no. Not for weeks."

"Hmm. But you sent her flowers? An *eighty-dollar* bouquet?"

"I was just congratulating her on the exhibit!"

"I see." Tebbins sounded as if he did *not* see. "Did you know Edward Malacek?"

Peter whitened. "Eddy Malacek? He's in one

of my graduate seminars. If it's the same one. Why? Is he in trouble?"

Gil spoke. "He's dead."

"Oh, my God!"

Gil spoke again. "How well did you know him?"

"As well as I know any of my graduate students. Occasionally we socialize as a group. I see all of them quite a bit. Know something of their personal lives. But I'm their mentor, not their buddy."

"Hmm." Tebbins nodded knowingly.

"Do you know anything about his playing *Dungeons & Dragons*?"

"Oh, he mentioned it. I've talked with the students about it a few times. A lot of them like it." Peter seemed to be regaining his confidence. "But what would that have to do with his death?"

"Maybe nothing," Gil said.

Anna was beginning to feel sorry for Peter. He'd come to her office in high dudgeon over the flowers and the dinner. And maybe he had a right to; it was an expensive bouquet after all. If she hadn't gotten caught up in the burglary, she would have called him to thank him for the flowers and to decline the dinner invitation. But he hadn't received even that bare courtesy from her, and now he was being grilled by a couple of cops who seemed awfully suspicious of him.

But Peter was not without his resources. "Well, I guess I've come at an awkward time." He rose from his chair and faced Anna. "I'll call you later."

Anna didn't want to further embarrass him by telling him to forget about it, but the last thing she wanted was to talk to him. So she didn't respond at all.

Pausing on the way out, Peter gave the two detectives a significant look. "Take care of my girl."

His girl? Anna had to resist the urge to throw a foot-stomping hissy fit as he disappeared.

Tebbins and Gil exchanged looks.

"A veritable brass-plated boor," Gil remarked.

"The south end of a mule," Tebbins replied.

Gil looked at Anna. "What's the story with this guy, and what's his name?"

"Peter Dashay." Pulling out her chair, she sat at her desk. "I don't see what business it is of yours."

"Wrong," said Gil flatly.

"Exceedingly wrong," Tebbins agreed.

"You two are starting to sound like the Bobbsey Twins."

"Anna," Gil said firmly, "answer the question."

"Not until you tell me why you're interested."

Tebbins drummed his fingers impatiently on the side of his thigh. He was still standing by the doorway, papers in hand. "Should I?" he asked Gil. "Or will you?"

"Oh, let me."

"Most certainly."

Gil's dark eyes, now harder, fixed on Anna again. "Essentially, anyone with a potential ax to grind against you or this museum is of interest to us."

Anna felt something inside her shrinking. Since Nancy's arrival, she'd managed to forget the notion that someone might be stalking her. All of a sudden it was staring her in the face again.

"Peter doesn't have an ax," she said finally. "We had dinner together once. Just once. I didn't think we'd suit, and I told him so."

"But he's still hanging around?"

"Every now and then."

"He seemed awfully insistent today."

She shrugged. "That's why I didn't think we'd make a good match. He seemed to consider one dinner a lifetime commitment."

Tebbins and Gil exchanged looks. "How long ago was that? The dinner I mean?"

"Three, maybe four months. I don't remember exactly."

"Tell me about him," Gil prompted, pulling a pad out of his pocket.

Tebbins started to follow suit, but realized he was still holding papers. "Oh!" he said. "Here, this one's yours." He passed one of the papers to Anna. "I took it off your bulletin board to make a copy of it."

She nodded, accepted the paper, and turned to pin it back up. It was then she saw the small white envelope propped against the wall beneath the corkboard.

"Oh, my God," she whispered as her heart slammed. "Oh, my God."

"What is it?" the two men asked at once.

"An envelope...just like the other one..." She turned, feeling the blood drain from her face, and looked from Gil to Tebbins and back. "It wasn't here this morning!"

"Don't touch it," Tebbins said swiftly. He dropped the other papers he was holding on to the desk and felt around in his pockets. "Damn, I don't have any gloves."

"I do," Gil said, reaching into his trousers pocket. "A homicide prerequisite."

"A prerequisite for my line, too," Tebbins said flatly. "I carry a gross of them in my car." Pulling them on, he reached past Anna for the envelope. "It looks the same."

"But it's addressed differently," Anna said. She had noticed that first thing, and the difference made her feel creepy. Before she had been *Ms. Lundgren.* This time she was *Anna.* And it made that creep, whoever he was, feel entirely too close.

"I see that," Tebbins remarked as he held the envelope by the corners. "Let's take a look inside, shall we?"

Gil reached into his other pocket and pulled out an evidence bag. "Here, put the envelope in this."

Tebbins thanked him, then proceeded to use Anna's letter opener once again to slice the envelope and tease it open.

"Ah," he said after a moment, "we appear to have a newspaper story here."

Anna felt herself freezing inside, turning icy with fear. If it was the article from that morning's *Sentinel,* what would it mean? That this person had more knowledge of her? Or that this person had been feeding information to the press. Intimate information that was hard to discover, such as the fact that her mother had dabbled in Wicca many years ago? How closely watched was she?

Impatience seized her as she watched the meticulous care with which Tebbins eased the clipping out of the envelope, the seemingly endless space of time it took him to make sure there was nothing else in there, and then the laborious eternity that passed while he used the letter opener to carefully unfold the article.

"It appears," said Tebbins as he worked, "to be an old AP article about the earthquake in Mexico."

The temperature in Anna's chest seemed to lower even more. Her hands felt so cold that they were nearly numb.

Then Tebbins flipped over the last fold and the top of the article appeared. And scrawled across it in bright red ink was the word: CURSED!!!

CHAPTER NINE

A slight bit of overkill," Tebbins said as he looked down at the article.

"The word or the story?" Gil asked. His mind was ranging over a number of things, not the least of them that Tebbins had been in this office earlier when Anna wasn't here. So, perhaps, had Peter.

Tebbins moved aside so Gil could read. "It's pretty factual," Gil said after a few minutes.

"Yes. But the word scrawled across the top is overkill."

"Perhaps," Gil said, angling his head to look at it, as if he were a connoisseur viewing a piece of art. In fact, he thought Tebbins was making too much of it. The thief and possible murderer had a message to get across, and there was no reason he should be subtle about it.

"Well," Gil said, as Tebbins slipped the article into the evidence bag, "we know one thing for certain now."

Anna, as pale as if she'd seen a ghost, looked at him. "What's that?" she asked, her voice uncertain.

"Actually we know two things," Gil corrected himself. "We know that he's tying the curse into this."

Tebbins nodded. "Quite. And the other?"

"That Ms. Lundgren is the focus."

Anna's voice rose a bit. "Focus? What do you mean by focus?"

"I mean that he's directing this action at you. Probably to frighten you."

"Well, he's succeeding!"

Gil didn't doubt he was. If there was a *he*. He looked at Tebbins and saw a hint of his own doubts reflected there. Anna could be doing this herself, to direct attention away from her, to make herself appear a victim when she was instead a perpetrator.

But if so, she was doing an exceptionally good job of looking frightened.

Hell, this whole thing was getting wacky beyond belief. "You know," he announced, "this is beginning to stretch my credulity."

"Why?" Tebbins and Anna both said at once, Tebbins curiously and Anna irritatedly.

"Well, a thief would take the dagger and run. He has in his possession a priceless artifact he could sell to some collector for a fortune. In that context, even the fake dagger being presented the night before could just signal an arrogant thief with a bit of the prankster in him."

"Yes," agreed Tebbins, as if he savored the thought.

"But to hang around afterward and continue delivering his little messages? No. That's nuts. Everything he does increases his likelihood of being caught."

Anna sagged. "Don't tell me a nut is after me."

"I don't know," Gil said frankly. "But I can guarantee you one thing. Whatever his purpose is, he's only just begun."

Gil and Tebbins adjourned to the conference room, which the museum had offered to let them use as long as it wasn't reserved for another group.

Gil spoke first. "What do you think?"

Tebbins smiled and rubbed his hands together. "I think I like this case."

Gil snorted. "The criminal mastermind again?"

"Absolutely. Someone with a mission. So much more interesting than the usual dope-addict-steals-to-support-his-habit, don't you think?"

Gil, who had sometimes found it quite challenging to identify and locate some of those dope addicts, didn't agree. "Depends on the addict," he said.

Tebbins's eyes sparkled. "Perhaps. But how many addicts return to lay clues?"

Gil had to admit he couldn't remember a one. Sometimes they came back to watch the police investigation, but as a rule they simply stayed away. "That doesn't make him a mastermind."

"No, it merely indicates that he *thinks* he is one." Tebbins's smile broadened. "So, he is sending us messages."

Gil shook his head. "He's sending messages to Anna."

Tebbins threw up his hands. "Where is the excitement in sending *her* messages? No, he is certain the messages are reaching *us*."

More theatrics, thought Gil. "Why don't you just call him Moriarty?"

"Because I am not Holmes!" Tebbins spoke as if that should be intuitively obvious to the meanest intelligence. "Unless you want to be Watson?"

"I'll pass. There's no way on earth I'm going to get involved in your delusion."

"Delusion?" Tebbins frowned, tipping his head back so that he could look down his nose, except the effect was ruined because Gil was so much taller. Tebbins wound up frowning at the knot in Gil's tie. "Why did you have to be so tall?"

"I guess nature fucked up."

"I wouldn't go to that extreme."

"Why not? You go to extremes in everything else."

Tebbins's grin returned. "In short, I'm a jackass. We agree. So, to get back to the problem at hand..."

Gil couldn't believe the guy. He needed to be on the stage. "Yes, why don't you describe the problem at hand."

"Thank you, I will." Tebbins cleared his throat. "First, we have an impossible burglary."

Gil shook his head. "It happened. Therefore, it is not impossible."

"Precisely." Tebbins beamed at him as if he were a brilliant student. "Are you sure you don't want to be Watson?"

"If I'd had to work with Sherlock Holmes, I'd probably have killed him before the first week was out. Keep that in mind."

"Tsk, latent hostility."

"There's nothing latent about it. Get on with it, Hercule."

"My pleasure." Tebbins was enjoying himself hugely, and in spite of himself, Gil was, too.

"All right," Tebbins continued. "We have the impossible-but-not-impossible burglary."

Gil wondered if he'd ever known anyone else who actually spoke with hyphens in his sentences. He couldn't recall. "Right. Clearly the videotapes must have been tampered with somehow."

"Yes. And the lab will discover how."

"Maybe."

Tebbins pursed his lips. "My dubious sidekick. Also, the motion detectors had to be tampered with. And there we have an even more serious problem than the videos."

Gil agreed. Pulling out a chair, he sat at the conference table. If he had to watch Tebbins pace like a whirling dervish, which Tebbins had just begun to do, he could at least do it from the comfort of a chair. "That bugs me. It suggests tampering with the hardware. You've got the security people checking that out, right?"

"I didn't even have to ask. They're more distressed about this than the museum, if that's possible. Their business is on the line. Bad publicity, you know."

Gil could have figured that out on his own, but he refrained from saying so. Something about Tebbins was beginning to remind him of a lawyer in a courtroom.

"Then, of course," Tebbins continued, "we have the supposedly tamperproof display case." The sparkle was coming back into his eyes, and he rubbed his hands together again as he cornered the table at about sixty-five miles per hour.

Gil wondered if he was going to get dizzy. "That," he said, "really bothers me."

"What? The display-case conundrum?"

"No, your pacing. I've never been locked up with a whirling dervish before."

131

"A new experience then," Tebbins replied placidly. "Enjoy the adventure."

Gil barely resisted rolling his eyes. "Look, we already know all of this. Basically what we have to do is reverse-engineer the crime."

The other man's eyebrows lifted. "I've never heard anyone put it that way before, reverse-engineer. So we are engineers."

Gil wouldn't go quite that far. "No, we're cops. And cops—good cops—examine the scene and work backward to discover how it's done."

"Exactly. Which makes us reverse engineers. I rather like that title."

He would, Gil thought. "Let's move on."

"Certainly. Impatience, thy name is Garcia."

"Redundancy, thy name is Tebbins."

Suddenly they were both grinning at each other.

"Point taken," Tebbins said after a moment.

"I'm not being impatient," Gil said. "it's just that the security people are in a better position to discover the actual means of the theft. So are the criminologists. What we need are clues that will lead us to the perp. And right now we don't know a hell of a lot."

Tebbins nodded, and finally came to rest in a chair. "It could be Anna Lundgren. She's certainly in a position to do all of it. For example, that fake dagger in the case may not be the same one I saw on her desk. And we have only her word for the fact that it is."

Gil nodded. "I agree. That thought crossed my mind at about two o'clock this morning.

So if she stole the dagger before it was placed in the case, who would know?"

"And it might have been a second replica on her desk."

But Gil didn't like that idea, not when he thought of Anna's frightened green eyes or her pale, delicate face. *Whoa,* he told himself. Not good. "It could have been," he forced himself to say. But even so, he wasn't prepared to stop there. "There *is,* however, a small flaw with that theory."

"Yes?"

"You heard her cry out when she found it. You said so. Why would she have cried out? She couldn't be certain anyone would hear her—not in the midst of the party that was going on. It would have made more sense for her to 'discover' it the next morning, when other employees in the hallway would have heard her, if that's what she wanted."

"Hmm." Tebbins started stroking his moustache again. "I see your point, although it would have made it harder to claim it was the same dagger in the case. But possibly she could have pretended to discover it earlier in the day, before the party, when other employees were about."

"Same difference."

"However, there are also the notes. The first one, the opened, empty envelope, which she claimed was beneath the dagger in the display case. Once again we have only her word that it was the same envelope."

Gil nodded. "And she certainly could have placed the envelope she found on her desk a

133

little while ago. But then, so could Peter. And so could you."

Tebbins smiled. "I'm being set up, you know."

"Conceivably." He didn't add that he wasn't about to dismiss Tebbins as a suspect.

"Oh, come off it," Tebbins said, letting go of his moustache. "I took the liberty of standing in your shoes last evening."

"Really? I hope you don't have athlete's foot."

"Not recently. No, I stood in your shoes last evening, asking myself what I would think if I were you. A quite useful exercise. I discovered that I would be suspicious of my appearance on the scene when Anna found the dagger. After all, events held for museum patrons are rarely attended by cops, who can't afford to make such donations. I can explain that."

"Be my guest."

"My aunt is a museum patron. She's in her late sixties, filthy rich thanks to her late husband, and fancies herself a patron of all civilized pursuits, largely because she thinks the world belongs to philistines who need to be educated. She frequently calls on me to escort her to these functions. And I don't usually mind it, unless she's decided that some auto mechanic who has welded together car parts into an amorphous blob is the next Picasso."

Gil had to laugh. "I've seen those."

"I tend to prefer more realistic art. Hence my aunt considers me one of the philistines. But *that's* why I was present at the party."

It was a good explanation. But that may have all been part of a master plan from a man who dreamed of mastermind criminals. "Okay," he said, as if he accepted it.

"Our criminal then took advantage of my unexpected presence that night, and decided to slip yet another envelope onto Anna's desk when I might have been responsible for it."

"Possible."

"Not only possible, but likely, if one assumes the thief isn't Anna. He would, after all, like to tease us, like to make his point, and most definitely direct our attention away from him. Or her. Because Anna could have put that envelope there for exactly the same reason. To make herself look like a victim while pointing a finger elsewhere."

"Of course." He didn't like it, but he knew it was possible. "So, what's the motive, Tebbins?"

"Apart from possessing a priceless artifact?"

Gil nodded. "The curse seems to have become central."

"Well, that again would lead back to Anna. She's been quite definite about not believing in it. Using it in that message could be misdirection."

"Possibly. On the other hand, the perp might not know that and might be trying to scare her witless with it. Or, he might be trying to convince her the curse is real."

"And maybe," Tebbins added, "the curse *is* real."

Gil gave Tebbins a sidelong look that made

the man shrug. "One never knows. I don't believe in such things myself, but that doesn't mean I might not be astonished one day. I'm willing to believe in the possibility of miracles."

So was Gil. He'd even had a few in his life. The birth of his daughter. His marriage before his wife had gotten so bitter about his job. Those were the kinds of miracles he was prepared to believe in. "That aside," he said after a moment, "there has to be a motive for wanting Anna to believe in the curse."

"Maybe he just gets his jollies by terrifying her."

That could be. Gil had certainly known enough creeps in his life who enjoyed such things. There were times when he thought that movies and video games were breeding such people. What was it the Denver police chief had said back in the early eighties? That the quantity of violence hadn't changed, but the quality of it had. At the time the chief had held that movies affected the types of crimes that were committed, and he had cited statistics about how the murder rate in Denver hadn't changed in years, but the type of crimes had: More women were victims, and there was more mutilation and torture.

So yes, there were creeps like that on the streets, for whatever reason. But somehow that didn't quite fit. That newspaper clipping had felt more like a message. And he was beginning to get seriously worried about Anna.

"You're going to question Peter Dashay?"

Tebbins nodded. "But not immediately. I

want to do some background on him first. And I don't want to make him skittish."

Gil nodded.

"Any reports from your labs on the Malacek kid?"

"Not yet. They're doing the autopsy tomorrow. Toxicology won't be back for days or weeks, depending on how detailed we decide to get."

"Of course, of course." Tebbins for a moment looked pained, as if he resented having to rely on technology. But of course he would. Poirot had never needed a lab, nor had Holmes.

Yeah, the modern world sucked, Gil thought, and as his thoughts strayed back to his daughter and her boyfriend, he decided that it just sucked more with every passing day. A million years ago he could have gone after that fucking boy with a club.

Twenty minutes later, Gil met his daughter in the lobby. Seeing Anna's twin gave him a momentary start. The women were as alike as peas in a pod, maybe more so, except for clothing.

"Dad," Trina said, smiling for the first time since yesterday morning, "Nancy says we have to come over for dinner tonight with her and Anna."

Gil paused to shake Nancy's hand, which gave him an opportunity to consider the pros and cons of the invitation. On the one hand, he shouldn't socialize with a suspect. On the other he could always put it down to checking out the suspect's home without getting a warrant. Which he didn't have grounds for anyway.

Nancy looked him right in the eye. "So you're the gorgeous cop Anna mentioned."

Gil felt his face heat as Trina and Nancy started to laugh. Now this, he thought, is a good reason not to have dinner there tonight. Who wanted to be thrown in close quarters with three teasing, giggling women. Although Anna didn't seem like much of a teaser.

"Can we, Dad?" Trina asked, getting back to more important matters.

Gil looked at his daughter's bright, hopeful face, and didn't have the heart to say no. "Sure," he said. "It sounds like fun."

But in fact, it sounded like more trouble brewing.

CHAPTER TEN

Anna often worked late at the museum, using the quiet time to finish up her paperwork when she wouldn't be disturbed by meetings or the necessity of keeping up with the exhibit upstairs. But that evening, as people departed and the building became quieter and quieter, she realized she was nervous.

Actually more than nervous. She was becoming afraid. Someone who would go to all the trouble to put that dagger and the envelope on her desk probably had something more heinous in mind than a simple theft.

Cursed.

The word scrawled across the top of the news clipping had frightened her more than she wanted anyone to know. It wasn't just a commentary on the earthquake and fire, it was a threat. Or a warning. And she didn't like either possibility.

Go home. A voice in her head spoke the words commandingly, and she stood up at once to start packing her briefcase. Not that she was going to get any work done at home, not with Gil and his daughter coming for dinner.

Whatever had possessed Nancy to do that? Some misguided notion of matchmaking, probably. She was surprised that Gil had accepted, because she'd seen the occasional flicker of doubt in his eyes when he looked at her. He considered her a suspect.

God, what an irony.

The phone on her desk rang, and she looked at it, unwilling to answer it. What if it was the thief, calling to torment her?

Too paranoid, she told herself firmly. She couldn't let this turn her into the kind of person who saw a threat under every rock. Still, reaching for the receiver felt like reaching for a snake.

"Anna Lundgren," she said, her voice not as crisp as usual.

"Anna, it's Ivar. Come to my office for a few minutes, will you?"

"Sure." Relief hit her. The worst that was going to happen was Ivar was going to bitch and moan. She could handle that.

Out in the lobby, she saw a couple of the docents speaking to the last handful of visitors who were getting ready to depart. No evening hours for the public tonight. The doors would be closed by seven.

She nodded to the docents, Lance Barro and Will Henderson, as she passed. They nodded and smiled back. Both of them were helpful volunteers who had put in some long hours in preparing the exhibit from the very earliest stages. They'd both done carpentry and painting, and even helped with the wiring. More than a dozen other students had been equally helpful. It was one of the nice things about a museum on a university campus.

But as she turned into the administrative corridor, something dark seemed to settle over her. Everybody on this end was gone, having checked out by five-thirty. Closed doors and dark glass looked at her from everywhere. And her neck began to prickle.

Helplessly, she swung around and looked behind her. Nothing. Nothing except silence and the vaguely echoing sounds from the lobby. She wished Ivar's office wasn't all the way at the back. But how else could he have his status window?

The question made her feel a little lighter, and the dread receded somewhat. No big deal. She'd walked this corridor at least a thousand times, both busy and empty.

Ivar's door, just around a corner, stood

open. He was sitting behind his desk with his head in his hands. Oh, great, Anna thought. It was going to be one of *those* discussions.

"Ivar?"

He didn't raise his head. "I managed to convince the Mexicans not to pull out the exhibit."

"Congratulations."

"I also managed to convince the president of the university that two thefts in two years didn't mean our security is lax."

She sat facing him across the desk. "No, it doesn't."

"Exactly. I told her we hired the best security company available. One approved by the insurance company. It's not our fault they fucked up."

Ivar didn't usually swear, at least not when he was on the job. Anna felt a twinge of sympathy for him. "It was a rough day."

"You don't know the half of it." He finally raised his head. "Cuestas was practically chewing the furniture."

"I can hardly blame him. That dagger is irreplaceable."

"Be that as it may, we didn't set out to have it stolen. And you're very lucky you weren't employed here when the mask was stolen two years ago. My God, I've been accused of practically everything."

"I'm sorry."

He stood up and began pacing with his hands clasped behind him, reminding Anna suddenly of Napoleon. "And what the hell was that scene in the lobby?"

"What scene?"

"Didn't you see? Your boyfriend took the flowers from the ticket desk."

"Oh my God." Anna sighed. "He's not my boyfriend, by the way."

"*He* seems to think he is. The woman at the window... Beatrice I think it was...said he couldn't have them because you'd given them to her. He said he'd given them to *you,* and he was taking them back. The two of them stood there tugging on the damn vase while the guests stood around laughing. I thought about calling the police, but the police were already here, and they didn't do a thing about it."

"Oh, boy."

"Cuestas saw the whole thing. I thought he was going to have a stroke. The man demanded, actually *demanded,* to know if I was running a lunatic asylum."

Anna struggled to keep a straight face. "He seems to have a remarkable command of English."

"Actually I have a fair command of Spanish. Thank God. Nobody else seemed to understand him. I hope. Oh, God, I hope. What if *that* turns up in the papers in the morning?"

It suddenly struck Anna that she was on the edge of hysteria. Her moods were cycling too fast: One moment she was frightened, the next she wanted to laugh at something Ivar said, and now she wanted to throw a temper tantrum. And she couldn't quite stop herself.

"Too bad," she said, with an unusual lack of sympathy.

"Too bad?" he repeated disbelievingly.

"*Too bad?* Is that all you can say? Do you have any idea how ridiculous that will make the museum look?"

"No more ridiculous than ballyhooing some ludicrous curse."

"Anna!" He looked shocked. "You know how essential it is to catch the public imagination for something like this. My God, the cost of this exhibit—we'll be in terrible financial straits if we don't get enough traffic."

"I know that as well as anyone. I explained that to the board, didn't I? I came up with at least three different ways to promote the exhibit that *didn't* involve the curse, didn't I? I even pointed out how *unscientific* it would be to use a curse for promotion, but no one was worried about looking ridiculous then, were they?"

"Anna, I realize you're personally involved..." But he was shrinking in his chair, looking as if he wanted to crawl under his desk.

"You're right, I'm personally involved. And you know why you know that? Because I was stupid enough to explain to the board about the nightmares I'd had for years after my father was killed, and how *used* I would feel if we promo-ed the curse."

"I remember," Ivar said, at least making an effort to look sympathetic.

"Well, apparently someone else on the board did, too, because I have been absolutely *hounded* by Reed Howell with his insinuating questions. Some jerk flapped his or her jaws, and that man is raking up my father's death on a regular basis."

"I saw his story."

"Ah, but that's not the end of it, Ivar. Because now someone is using that curse to stalk me."

Ivar looked stunned. "To stalk you?"

"To stalk me."

"I know about the replica dagger."

"Well, there's more than that. Today someone put an envelope on my desk. Just guess what was inside it."

Ivar spread his hands helplessly.

"An old AP newspaper clipping about my father's death. Across the top of it in red someone wrote *cursed*."

Ivar looked appalled. "My God!"

Anna, abruptly running out of both steam and anger, sank back in her chair.

"That's cruel," Ivar said. "Unthinkably cruel." He jumped up and started pacing along the windows. "I can't imagine what kind of person would do something like that. What a horrible joke."

"I don't think it's a joke." Anna sighed wearily.

Ivar halted to look at her. "No." Apparently he couldn't accept the possibilities that flitted across his mind. "But...did you tell the police about it?"

"They were there when I found it."

He grew indignant. "They didn't offer you protection?"

"Why would they? I'm a suspect."

"They told you that?"

"No. But I can see it. I can feel it."

He came around his desk and touched his

hand lightly to her shoulder. "We're *all* suspects at the moment, which only means that these brilliant detectives don't have any idea where to look. Well, if they won't protect you, I will. You come stay with Mary and me."

Anna's throat tightened, and she once again realized how alone she must be feeling, that an offer like that could bring her to the edge of tears.

Her life these past couple of years had been sterile, except for her job and occasional visits with Nancy. Since completing her graduate program, she had been utterly focused on her job, on making a name for herself, nurturing dreams of bigger and better positions at bigger and better museums. She dated occasionally, but nothing clicked, most likely because she didn't really *want* anything to click at this stage. She had a few friends she saw from time to time, but otherwise her life revolved around this museum and its exhibits. Which meant that expressions of concern and sympathy from other people were few and far between.

Her reserves were frighteningly low.

"I'll call Mary," Ivar said.

"Ivar, no. Thank you so much for your offer, but I'm not alone. My sister is visiting, and she's staying with me."

He nodded and retreated to the safety of his citadel behind his desk. Seated again, he pushed a few stacks of paper around, reorganized a few paper clips, and tucked a pen into his drawer. "Well," he said presently. "Well."

That seemed to be about all she was capable of saying, too, so she remained silent.

"This is too much," he said. "Entirely too much. I can't even think what to do about it. The police don't seem to have any brilliant ideas, the university and museum have egg all over their faces, the Mexicans will probably never do business with us again, and now you're being stalked."

He rubbed his chin, drummed his fingers on the desk, and sighed. "Why do I have the feeling that none of this would have happened if we hadn't mentioned the curse?"

"I don't know. Maybe because it wouldn't have been so irresistible to some twisted mind except for my personal association with the Pocal find? That's all I can think of."

He nodded. "That may well be. Well, first thing in the morning I'm going to call the police and insist they keep an eye on you. This is beyond enough. Even the meanest intelligence can see the threat to you in what's been happening."

"But no one's tried to harm me, Ivar." It was true, and scared or not she prided herself on thinking clearly. "All they're trying to do is taunt me." *Or frighten me.*

"Maybe so. But that could change at any moment."

His words were still ringing in her ears as she drove home. *That could change at any moment.* Yes, it could. But she honestly didn't want to think about that. Besides, there were other reasons this creep could be doing this to her. More likely reasons. It was almost too much to comprehend that someone could harbor an intent to harm her. More likely it was a taunt from the thief, who was proud of the burglary. Or just a sick joke.

But the darker possibility was nibbling at the edge of her consciousness like a rat.

She pulled into her driveway behind Nancy's little rental car, and spent a few moments behind the wheel, letting the air-conditioning blow over her and chill her. Sometimes in this hot muggy state, it just felt good to be cold. Her Minnesota blood, she supposed, but whatever, it felt good. As if the heat created some kind of constant irritant that she noticed only when it was absent. And it was unusually hot for April. Ten degrees above normal, all week.

Last year when Nancy had visited, they'd both agreed they missed the cold. Austin was hotter than Tampa, but not as humid, and in August they were both sick of the battering heat. So after dark one night, giggling at their own silliness, they'd turned the thermostat way down, finally managing to bring the temperature to about sixty-five. Then they'd built a small fire in the fireplace Anna so rarely had occasion to use, made a bowl of popcorn, and snuggled under blankets on the couch, laughing and talking until the wee hours.

Anna smiled, remembering how much fun it had been. Her house, sitting on a shady lot on a quiet street, looked inviting when she remembered that. When she didn't remember the stalker.

Her fingers, still holding the wheel, had begun to feel icy. Time to go in. Nancy would be there, so it wasn't as if she was going into an empty house. And the sun was still up, though it could no longer really penetrate the shadows beneath the trees. For the first time, she honestly wished she'd rented a place with a sun-drenched lot.

Sighing, she switched off the ignition, grabbed her briefcase, and climbed out, locking her white Prizm behind her. She was just about to unlock her front door when it swung open, and Nancy greeted her. She was wearing shorts and a T-shirt, and Anna's striped bib apron.

"Hey," her sister said. "I was wondering where you were."

"Ivar wanted to talk."

Nancy stepped back, opening the door wider. "Poor you." She'd heard plenty about Ivar at various times.

The door closed behind Anna, and suddenly she felt safe. It was a wonderful feeling. The doors were locked, the windows were locked, and Nancy was with her. Uneasiness fell away, leaving her feeling pounds lighter.

"Actually," Anna said, following Nancy into the kitchen, and putting her briefcase on the bar, "he wanted to dump. I think I surprised him."

"How's that?"

"He wound up being the dumpee."

Nancy laughed. "Good for you. It's time it was his turn. What did you dump about?"

But Anna didn't want to rehash it. She didn't want to bring all of that into this house. It seemed sacrilegious somehow to invite those shadows in. "Oh, I had a few complaints of my own. Nothing spectacular. What's for dinner?"

"I'm using your grill. Marinated steak, zucchini, and crookneck squash with cheddar-mashed potatoes."

"Man, that sounds good. I'm starved. Need any help?"

"Sure. Or you can just relax. I can make this blindfolded. It's easier than it sounds."

"When did you become a gourmet chef?"

"When I discovered that Peggy's culinary expertise was limited to McDonald's and Taco Bell."

Anna quickly searched her sister's face, but found nothing there except genuine good humor. "Is that what it took to teach you to cook?"

"Believe it. You know how I used to hate it."

"Yeah, I remember. Every time it was your turn to cook you promised to wash dishes for a week if I'd fill in."

Nancy grinned. "It worked pretty well, too."

"Until I figured there weren't enough days in a lifetime to cover washing dishes for a week in exchange for cooking."

Nancy laughed. "Well, okay, it worked for a while."

"Yup. By the time I figured it out, you owed me twenty years of dishwashing. You still haven't paid up."

"Hey, we don't live together anymore. What's a girl to do?"

"I could pack up the dishes and send them to you in Austin to wash."

"Well, with UPS taking anywhere from seven to ten days, you'd need a lot of dishes."

"Nah. I'll express them overnight. You send them back the same day. I'd only need two sets."

"In your dreams, Annie. In your dreams."

It felt so good to be joking with her sister this way again. Anna slid onto one of the barstools and watched as Nancy sliced zucchini and squash lengthwise. "When are they coming?"

"About seven. Gil had to go back to the station first."

That was Nancy, Anna thought wistfully. In just a very short time she could make friends with almost anyone. Anna had always been shyer and more reserved. As a consequence, when they were children, Nancy had made friends for both of them.

"That kid Trina," Nancy said. "She's neat. Reminds me of myself at that age. That's my next goal in life, you know. To have kids."

"I haven't even gotten to the point of thinking about it."

Nancy looked up from her slicing. "That's because you think marriage is part of the equation. You need a man. I just need a sperm donor."

"Isn't that what all men are?"

Nancy went off into a peal of laughter, and after a moment Anna joined her. But it was true; Nancy was right. Anna wasn't even going to consider children until she had a stable marriage. A major difference in outlook.

"Well," said Nancy, "we've got a potential donor coming tonight. And from the look of it, he produces good children."

Anna flushed. "Cut it out, Nance. I don't have time for that stuff. Besides, he's investigating me along with everyone else. I'm surprised he agreed to come to dinner."

"I'm not. I saw the way he looked at you."

"Oh great. That's going to make me really comfortable this evening. Why don't you hang a sign out front. Something like, 'My sister's available.'"

"Hey, I didn't say anything to him. Well, not much."

Anna reached across the counter and picked up a piece of squash to throw at her sister. Nancy ducked.

"Tsk," her sister said. "Violence now. Maybe I'll ask him to handcuff you."

That warmed Anna's cheeks even more. "Don't."

"I'm just pointing out that he has some very interesting equipment. Handcuffs. Leg restraints." She leered. "I'll bet he's strong, too."

"Do you want zucchini down the back of your shirt?"

"Not if you want to eat tonight."

"You're twisted, you know."

Nancy grinned. "And you love it. Think how dull your life would be without me. I keep you on your toes. Maybe I should take Trina out somewhere after dinner, leave the two of you alone."

"Will you stop it?" But almost in spite of herself, Anna was starting to laugh. Nancy's outrageousness always made her smile.

"See?" Nancy said. "You love it. Now go change into something sexy, like that nun's habit in the back of your closet. I'm sure it covers you well enough."

Anna stuck out her tongue and slid off the stool. "Just don't talk like this tonight."

"Why not?"

"Because I'll kill you."

"Right. Let me put that on the menu. Dessert: Nancy Lundgren, stuffed with zucchini, sprinkled lightly with sugar..."

Laughing, Anna went to her bedroom to change.

Changing turned into taking a quick shower, too. Something about the Florida climate, she thought as she scrubbed. She could shower in the morning, spend most of the day in an air-conditioned building, but just the few trips across a parking lot could leave her feeling unclean by day's end.

Feeling fresh again, she changed into some white-gauze slacks and a green-cotton polo shirt. Let Nancy say what she would.

But Nancy didn't say anything at all because Gil and Trina had just arrived. The girl was looking a little shy, and Gil was looking as if he was having some serious second thoughts about being there. Nancy took care of Trina's doubts instantly, dragooning her into helping in the kitchen. Anna considered various forms of retaliation as she and Gil stood looking at each other in the living room.

Finally Anna spoke. "Nancy's really taken with Trina."

He smiled. "Most people are."

"Can I get you something to drink?"

"Ice water would be wonderful."

She guessed he was still on duty. The realization didn't make her feel any more comfortable.

"I never drink when I'm going to be driving," he offered, as if he guessed what she was thinking.

"Wise choice."

"The voice of experience. I've seen too much of what happens when people combine alcohol and a motor vehicle."

Something flitted across his face then, and he shifted as if uncomfortable. "I'm sorry. That sounded like a cop, didn't it?"

"You *are* a cop."

He shrugged. "My ex-wife hated it."

Anna was surprised. "Why?"

"She said she didn't want me to bring the job home with me. She wanted a normal life."

"Umm..." Anna hesitated, then decided to just plunge ahead. "It seems to me that a job is part of a normal life. But I'll make you a deal. You can talk like a cop if I can talk like a curator."

That brought out his absolutely dazzling smile. Anna took a moment to reflect on how that must charm people he was questioning.

153

She went to the kitchen to get his drink and found Nancy and Trina chatting happily as they brushed some kind of dressing over the quartered vegetables. They didn't seem much interested in talking to her, so she popped the top off a chilled bottle of water, dumped ice into two glasses, and filled them.

Back in the living room, she found Gil standing before her built-in bookshelves, admiring the little treasures she'd collected over the years that were scattered among the hundreds of books she'd also collected.

"Are these real?" he asked her.

"I'm afraid not." She passed him his water. "Owning antiquities like these is illegal, so I buy copies. It's a cottage industry in Latin America, and some of the reproductions are so good they'd almost pass for the real thing."

"But not to a trained eye." He looked right at her, and she felt he was fishing for something.

"No," she agreed. "Not to a trained eye."

"Doesn't that bother you?"

"Why would it? I know what they are. I just enjoy their beauty. I can see the real things in museums when I want to."

He nodded and moved a little farther down the bookcase, checking out book spines. "Quite a collection."

"Mostly related to my job and my areas of interest. I have to keep current."

"We all do." He spent another couple of minutes looking at titles. Anna sat in a wing chair and waited quietly. She always appreciated someone else's interest in books.

Besides, she was getting a nice view of a very good pair of legs revealed by khaki shorts. And his polo shirt advertised a flat stomach, too.

But apparently he had something else in mind. "Nancy's gay," he remarked. "Are you gay, too?"

Anna had a few hot buttons, and that was one of them. Without stopping to consider the dangers of angering a cop who was investigating her, one who probably thought she was guilty of theft and even murder, she spoke. Her voice was as thin and sharp as a finely honed blade. "Why? Are you afraid we'll pollute your daughter?"

He turned to look at her. "If I was afraid of that, I wouldn't be here at all. Besides, I know the difference between a pedophile and a homosexual."

"Then why did you ask? It's none of your damn business."

"Well," he said bluntly, "it is. I was wondering if I could stop sweating."

"Sweating?" Anger gave way to confusion.

"Sweating," he repeated, and gave her a bold once-over with his eyes that clarified his meaning beyond any doubt.

Anna felt his look like an electric shock. Her breathing stopped, and she was sure her heart almost did, too. It had been a long time since she had felt such a reaction, and even though this was the worst time possible, and the worst man possible, she couldn't stop the feeling.

After a moment she found her voice. "Keep sweating," she said.

He apparently read her response correctly, because he smiled. Then he laughed heartily. And all the tension went out of the room like the helium from a punctured balloon.

When he stopped laughing, he turned serious. "You know this is bad timing."

"I know, you're investigating me, too. Well, investigate away. You won't find anything. I've never even had a speeding ticket."

"No sense of adventure, huh?"

It was the same accusation Nancy frequently leveled at her, but somehow this time it didn't sting. Maybe because she was feeling adventurous for a change.

"Maybe after we clear this up," he said. "And you know? I never meant to say that. Tape my lips shut."

"You couldn't eat. But I'll pretend I didn't hear you."

"Thanks."

But she knew she wasn't going to forget, not when he'd filled her with a wonderful glow. All of a sudden she felt attractive. Beautiful even. A veritable Helen of Troy. No way was she going to relinquish that; it came too rarely in life, if at all.

But she felt easier with him now. He wasn't just an adversary who might be helping to build a case with her; he was a man who was interested in her. A normal, familiar thing. An identifiable role to play. It was so welcome after days of playing out a scenario that had no known parameters.

Nancy was right; she wasn't adventurous at all.

They ate indoors, all of them agreeing it was just too humid to eat on the lanai. Trina wanted to hear all about Austin, so Nancy regaled her for a while with tales of cowboys and rodeos as if Austin weren't a thoroughly modern city. Apparently it was just what Trina wanted to hear.

"We never go anywhere," Trina said toward the end of the meal.

"What are you talking about?" Gil asked. "We go lots of places."

She screwed up her face. "In *Florida*."

"Ahh," he said. "Just Florida. Vacation paradise. The place that hosts three-quarters of the world's Canadians for the winter every year. The place that is crawling with tourists from all over the world. The place other people pay small fortunes just to visit."

Trina wrinkled her nose at him. "It's not the same."

"Hmm." He pretended to think seriously about it. "So I guess I should ditch the plan to spend a week in Orlando with you in July?"

"Orlando?" Her face lit up. "We haven't been there in a long time."

"I know. I figured Disney World, Universal Studios, and Sea World are missing us."

Her eyes started sparkling. "Daddy, really?"

"It was the plan."

"Oh, wow! We can do Epcot this time?"

"I promise."

Nancy looked at Anna. "I don't know about you, but I think I'm going to die of envy. Of course, *you* probably want to go visit some dusty museum."

"Actually, I was thinking about taking a cruise to Merida. Visiting some ruins."

Nancy shook her head. "I knew ruins had to get into it somewhere." She turned to Gil. "Just a warning. Nothing makes my sister happier than the relics of dead civilizations. You might want to ride a roller coaster, but she wants to climb a pyramid. In a jungle."

"Hey, I get on roller coasters, too," Anna protested. "I rode the Kumba at Busch Gardens."

"After I dragged you kicking and screaming into the car."

Trina giggled. Gil was grinning. Nancy looked at him. "Don't say I didn't warn you."

"Actually," he said, "I wouldn't mind climbing some pyramids myself. And I like museums."

"The exhibit today was neat," Trina allowed. "Anna, Nancy said you designed all that yourself."

"Well, I had the overall concept. But it took a lot of people to refine it and carry it out."

"Well, it was cool. I especially liked going down into the tomb. It was so *creepy*. Too bad the dagger wasn't there, though."

And there it was again, Anna thought, lying on the table among them, dark and ugly. Shadowing them.

Trina looked around. "Did I say something wrong?"

"No, of course not," Anna hastened to assure her, managing a smile. "Thank you for your compliments."

But the darkness remained. And when Gil and Trina departed an hour later, they didn't take it with them.

On the drive home, Trina chattered cheerfully about the day. Gil needed only one ear to attend her. The rest of his mind was busy thinking about Anna. So she collected replicas of things she could never possess. She had seemed to be okay with that fact, but the detective in him was suspicious enough to wonder.

Someone with Anna's interests, who also had a strong acquisitive streak, might be tempted. Given that the dagger was associated with her father's death, she might be even more tempted. Hell, she'd been the initial thrust behind the whole exhibit. Maybe all of this was to get her hands on something she coveted, something that had a personal connection for her. Maybe she'd even had help. Maybe her accomplice was a murderer.

He didn't want to think that, but even though he was strongly attracted to her, he couldn't forget who he was. He'd sacrificed a lot in his life to be a good cop, and he wasn't about to mess that up by allowing himself to be misled by a little lust.

"Anna and Nancy are really neat," Trina announced. "Even if Anna's a little stodgy."

"Stodgy?" He glanced at her. "Stodgy" was the last word that came to his mind to describe Anna. She had unusual interests, yes, but that didn't make her stodgy.

"Oh, you know," Trina said. "Like a parent."

"Oh." As far as he was concerned, that was a recommendation. "We need to have a talk, Trina."

She sighed, that world-weary sigh of a teenager who knew what was coming and figured she could write the lecture herself. "I don't want to talk about Jamie."

"Maybe not, but *I* do."

"Dad..."

"Just listen to me. I have to work tomorrow, and I'm not going to spend the day wondering what kind of trouble you're getting into."

She folded her arms, and frowned, the picture of someone who wasn't going to really hear a word. So he decided not to pull any punches.

"Jamie is abusive," he said flatly. "He took you where you didn't want to go, he refused to bring you home, and when you argued with him he kicked sand at you and threatened to hit you. That is abuse."

"You cops," she said bitterly. "You're all so paranoid."

That had come directly out of her mother's mouth. He'd lost count of the times he'd heard the woman say that over the years. "I'm not paranoid. But I've been around the block enough times to know what's what. And *you have not.*"

She glared at him. He could feel the heat without looking.

"Jamie is history," he said flatly. "He's gone. If you don't listen to me and something else happens, I'm going to get a restraining order to keep him away from you. And if he lays so much as one finger on you in anger, I'll lock him away for a long time."

"Fine," she said angrily. "I'll see him after I go home anyway. Mom doesn't hate him."

"You will not."

"Yes I will, and you can't stop me. You don't have custody, Mom does!"

He refrained from telling her that didn't matter. In fact, he was trying to clamp down on himself. How many times did he have to learn that laying down the law to a child her age never worked?

But Trina hadn't finished. As they pulled into the driveway in stony silence, she burst out, "You cops are awful! You push people around all the time like you own the world!"

She ran into the house ahead of him and slammed the door hard enough to rattle the windows. And Gil started kicking himself in the butt. God, would he never learn?

"He's sweet on you," Nancy announced later. They'd sat around drinking tea together since their guests departed, but neither of them had much to say.

"No he's not," Anna said. She looked at the clock. "Time for bed."

Nancy sighed. "Annie, it was a burglary. You didn't do it. They'll figure that out. But there's no point ruining every minute of your life from now until they do by brooding about it."

Nancy didn't know about the envelope on

161

her desk. Regardless, it wasn't the first time they'd failed to see eye to eye. Nancy lived far more in the moment than Anna, who had a tendency to look far enough down the road to see consequences. A tendency, perhaps, to worry too much.

"It doesn't matter, Nance," she said finally. "He's working on a case I'm involved in. Nothing can come of it."

"Yeah, right. Cases end, and Gil is still a man who's looking at you like candy in a candy-store window."

"Damn it, Nance, I don't want to be candy for some guy. Plenty of guys think I'm candy. I want something more than that."

"Ever the dreamer," Nancy commented.

"And you aren't? Come off it."

Nancy smiled. "But you have to start at the candy stage, Annie. That's where it all begins. They start salivating, and then they start unwrapping. That's when they get to know the real you."

Anna couldn't think of a comeback, and that irritated her. But it irritated her every time her sister started trying to change her. They might be identical in appearance, startlingly so, but their personalities were very different. Nancy just didn't seem able to accept that. She was always pushing Anna one way or another, almost like their mother.

"I'm sorry, Nance. I'm the person I am, and you're just going to have to accept that."

Nancy's smile faded. "Of course you are. I'm sorry. I didn't mean…"

"Yes you did, but it's okay. I'm used to it.

You and Mom and Auntie have always wondered if I was some kind of changeling." She managed a small smile. "I supposed I'm lucky we're twins. Otherwise, they'd have been convinced some fairy put me under a cabbage leaf."

Nancy grew patently concerned. "Annie..."

"It's okay. We'll both feel better in the morning. I'm off to bed."

Then she escaped before her sister could try to smooth things over in a way that would only wind up coming around to the same things. Anna wasn't adventurous enough, Anna was too straitlaced, Anna was too practical, too quiet, too anything except eccentric the way they were. She was used to it.

In her room, she pulled out a light cotton sleep shirt and changed into it.

It had been a long day, she thought. Exhaustion had been building like a storm on the horizon, growing heavier and darker since the very first thing when Señor Cuestas had arrived. Not that she could blame him for being annoyed and demanding. In his shoes, she'd probably have been every bit as difficult.

Then there had been the clipping with the scrawled message. The instant it popped into her mind, she shied away from it. It might, she thought, just be someone's bad idea of a practical joke. It might have no direct link to the person who had taken the dagger and killed Eddy Malacek. But she couldn't quite believe that, so she refused to think about it.

She needed to sleep. She needed to hide in dreams before she picked up her worries again. There was no point being anxious tonight; she couldn't do a damn thing about any of it.

Sighing, shivering as a draft from the air conditioner snaked over her skin, she leaned down and pulled her covers back.

And froze.

"Oh, my God," she whispered helplessly. "Oh, my God!"

There on her sheets, gleaming evilly in the lamplight, was the dagger.

CHAPTER ELEVEN

Temple Terrace cops milled around in the house, talking in low voices. Her bedroom had been invaded by a crowd of strangers. Anna sat on the couch, huddled beneath a comforter, and Nancy sat beside her, with an arm around her shoulders.

Tebbins was there, too, called in once the Temple Terrace police realized this was related to a Tampa case. He was dressed meticulously as always in one of his outdated suits with a red bow tie. He seemed to be everywhere, talking to everyone in a low voice.

Part of Anna wished she could hear what he was saying. The rest of her seemed to be in shock, a place that was cold and dark, where her thoughts hung in suspended animation. She was past feeling anything at all. It was as if her essence had shrunk until she was nothing but a tiny pinprick, a mote floating in the darkest reaches of the universe.

If she shrank enough, perhaps she could cease to be.

Tebbins joined them, pulling the Boston rocker over so he could face Anna. "Can you answer some questions now?"

She nodded, but moving her head was difficult, as if she were controlling it by marionette strings from far away. The movement was jerky, unfamiliar.

"I can answer most of them," Nancy said protectively. "We left the house together at eight-thirty this morning. I hung around the museum until I could get into the exhibit. I left about two, did some shopping, got back here around four. Anna pulled in at about six-thirty."

"So no one was home between eight-thirty and four?"

Nancy nodded. "About that. We had guests for dinner. Anna showered and changed right before they arrived, while I was preparing the food. They left at about nine-thirty, we sat around drinking tea until... I guess it was eleven or so. Then Anna went into her room, and the next thing I knew she was screaming."

Tebbins nodded, making notes.

"But I already told them all of this," Nancy said.

"Different police departments." Tebbins smiled, twisted his moustache, and leaned back.

"But how did it happen?" Nancy demanded. "The house was locked when we left, and it was locked when I got home. Nothing was disturbed." She glanced at Anna. "Well, nothing, apparently, except Anna's bed."

Tebbins looked at Anna. "There's a broken latch on one of the windows in your room. Do you know anything about that?"

Anna felt her heart skip. Oh, God, she was starting to come back. She didn't want to come back, not now. Not yet. Maybe not ever.

"It... I noticed it was broken last week. I meant to get it fixed..." Her voice trailed off.

Tebbins nodded. "Well, that's probably how it happened. Do you have any idea how the latch got broken?"

"No." She stirred herself mentally, trying to focus more on what he needed from her, trying to help him catch the creep before anything else happened. "The piece that swivels was missing. It kind of bothered me, because I couldn't find it on the floor. But nothing else was missing and...well, I used to keep a wastebasket there, and I wasn't sure when it popped off."

Tebbins twisted his moustache. "You keep that window closed and locked all the time?"

"Yes. It's in the back, and it's my bedroom..." She shivered suddenly and felt Nancy's arm tighten around her.

"Wise of you." Tebbins took some time to scribble on his notepad. He then looked at Nancy. "You can account for your whereabouts after you left the museum?"

"Jesus." Nancy stiffened, then shook her head. "You bet your sweet bippy I can. You want to see the receipts from my shopping? I'll bet they all have the time and dates on them."

"If you please."

"Damn," Nancy muttered, rising from the couch. "What kind of jerk thinks I'd do something like this to my *sister*?"

Tebbins answered. "The kind of jerk who's seen too much of what family members can do to each other."

Anna sprang to her sister's defense. "Nancy wouldn't *ever* do something like this to me."

"That's what they all say."

Anna decided she didn't like Tebbins at all. Then she remembered that he was the only thing that stood between her and the snake who was tormenting her. It didn't help much to realize that her only potential savior was hateful.

She was starting to come back, starting to awaken again to the enormity of what had happened, and she clung to her hatred of Tebbins, nursing it in the hopes it would grow big enough to blot out everything else. Instead, it shrank, giving way to terror and despair. By the time Nancy returned with her receipts, Anna was shaking.

While Tebbins examined the receipts, Nancy sat beside Anna again and put her arm around her. "It's going to be okay," Nancy said. "We're not going to stay here. We're going to find a nice hotel. Someplace he can't find you."

Terror gave way to anger, snapping before

the force of it. "A hotel? Are you crazy, Nance? He could get in and out of there a lot easier than he can get in here. And he could find us. All he has to do is follow me from work!"

Nancy appeared taken aback. "I didn't think of that."

"You never think more than two minutes ahead."

"Jeez, Annie..."

But Anna didn't feel apologetic. Her life was in danger, and nobody seemed to have any useful suggestions. Tebbins was sitting there looking like he thought she'd done all of this to herself, and she was sure Gil thought the same thing, especially considering how he'd looked at her collection of replicas. She was alone, and she had never been more frightened in her life. Anger was the only antidote.

A man in a Temple Terrace uniform came over to them, carrying the dagger in a plastic bag. "No prints," he said.

Tebbins took it and looked at it. Then he held it out to Anna. "Is this the real dagger?"

She didn't want to look at it. Revulsion filled her, and she had the wild fancy that she could feel the evil emanating from it. But she forced her eyes to settle on it, forced herself to reach for it. Cold seemed to leap from it along her arm, as if its maker had filled it with part of his ugly soul.

She made herself turn it over, made herself examine its lines. "No," she said finally. "It's a replica. Better than the last. Maybe because he has the original to work from now."

"You're sure?"

"I'm positive. The blade is glass, not jade, and it isn't honed exactly right. See these chips?" She pointed to them with her thumbnail. "They weren't on the original."

"And the hilt?"

"Much better. He must have made a mold and poured it. But he didn't electroplate this one. Maybe not enough time, I don't know. He used some leafing, rubbed it on. But it's not perfect. You can see small places where he was careless."

Tebbins nodded. "Where would he get the leafing?"

Nancy spoke. "You can get it in some hobby shops. I've used it on some of my Warhammer pieces. I suppose knowing that makes me guilty, right?"

Tebbins merely glanced at her.

Anna gave Tebbins the dagger back, dumping it hurriedly into his hands, then shrank back under her blankets. Alone. She was alone. Not even Nancy could help her with this one.

It was nearly four by the time Tebbins returned to his home. He retreated at once to the library, the room which he had decorated to suit his turn-of-the-century personality. The walls were lined with books, the floor was covered with a copy of a worn oriental rug—a policeman's budget didn't run to the real thing—and a massive mahogany-stained desk dominated. He switched on the green-shaded banker's lamp and settled into his comfortable leather chair behind the desk.

He treated himself to a moment to admire his setting, reminding himself he'd kill the property value if he carried his taste throughout the house. People in Florida seemed to prefer light colors, light wood, and rattan and wicker. He himself vastly preferred the style of the heyday of the British Empire.

But he indulged himself for only a few moments. Heedless of the hour, he picked up the phone and called Gil Garcia.

He got dumped into Gil's voice mail twice before he called the pager number. He knew what he was doing. The eight rings would have roused Gil, and now the buzzing or beeping of his pager would bring him to full alert. Moments later his phone rang. He picked up the receiver but before he could say a word, Gil was speaking, his voice thick and disgruntled.

"Garcia," he said. "And this had better be damn good. If you've checked a clock recently, you'll notice you only had to wait a few hours until dawn."

"It's good."

There was a rustling from the other end of the phone, and Tebbins could easily imagine Gil propping himself against pillows and pulling the sheets up. "Talk. Before I roll over and go back to sleep."

Tebbins smiled into the phone. "Now, you wouldn't want to be left out, would you?"

"It happens to be *your* case unless you've found out something about Malacek's murder."

"It's *our* case. No escaping it. Bound by trouble and duty. Anna pulled down her bedcovers tonight and found another replica dagger."

He savored the silence from the other end of the phone. He'd already learned that it wasn't easy to surprise Gil.

"Is she okay?"

The question interested Tebbins. Apparently Gil's focus was a little different from his own. That could cause problems. "Scared but fine," he said.

"Did you put protection on her?"

"I have a car sitting across the street."

"Good. But it's not enough."

"It's all I can get. You don't need me to explain that to you."

"He's going to kill her."

"We don't know that. What we *do* know is that someone's doing enough to keep us hopping without giving us any clues."

"I beg to differ. The curse is the clue."

"Not a very good one. Practically every man, woman, and child in the bay area has heard about it. Any one of them could have decided to do this."

"Not every one of them has the skill or expertise. Tomorrow I want to talk to the security people again. I'm not happy with the 'it's impossible' view of this theft. I also want to know who's been feeding information to Reed Howell. Because there's no way he should have associated Anna with the curse, other than through her work. Where did he find out all that stuff?"

"*He's* not going to tell you. He's a reporter."

"I have my ways." Gil was silent for a few

seconds. "All of Eddy Malacek's friends are saying the same thing. Nothing about his behavior was unusual. He didn't do drugs. He came to the D&D game on Tuesday evening the way he always did, and left around ten-thirty to go get ready for work. However."

Tebbins waited, then prompted him. "However what?"

"However... I talked to one of his friends after I got home tonight. The dungeonmaster of the group. He said Eddy mentioned before he left that he hoped one of the guys at work would bring cappuccino again."

"What guy?" Tebbins's mind spun into overdrive. "Malacek was supposed to be there alone."

"Right. Nobody else was on duty. But apparently some of the employees work late at the museum. My source didn't know who Eddy was talking about, didn't think Eddy mentioned the name. He just had the impression that the person occasionally brought a Thermos of cappuccino and shared it with Eddy."

"Christ. I've got to review all those video-tapes."

"I was going to suggest that in the morning. We need to go back a couple of weeks and see if we can pick that up."

Tebbins nodded, then remembered Gil couldn't see him. "Right. First thing. How long were you going to keep this under your hat?"

"Till morning. I actually have some respect for the average police officer's need for sleep."

Tebbins chuckled. Then he winced as he

twisted his moustache too hard and pulled one of the hairs. He needed to shave the damn thing off but was reluctant to do so until this case was closed. It was some kind of superstition that had surprised him with its sudden appearance. "How's the toxicology?"

"We're on it. I told you, it'll be a couple of weeks. Oh, hell, I forgot. I've got the autopsy in the morning. Well, have fun with the videos."

"Thanks a bunch. Get your ass back to sleep."

"My ass is still soundly asleep, thank you. It's the rest of me that's awake now."

"Well, we've got a break now."

"Yeah, a veritable hole in the dike."

"Maybe even a floodgate."

"I wish. Shut up and go to bed, Tebbins. If I have to work with you, I'd prefer it if your brain were functioning."

Gil didn't take his own advice. Shortly after hanging up, he sighed and climbed out of bed. At the doorway, the memory of his daughter caught him, and he paused to pull on some shorts and a T-shirt. It wouldn't do to have her wake up and find her father padding around the house naked, the way he was wont to do when she wasn't there.

In the kitchen he started a pot of coffee then hunted around in the freezer for some of those sausage-and-biscuit things he kept on hand for emergency breakfasts. Oh, hell, that he kept on hand for most breakfasts.

Why lie to himself? Cooking for one was a chore he avoided at all costs, including his health. He practically felt like a saint when he went to a restaurant and told them to replace the fries with steamed broccoli or a salad.

This morning, before he went to the M.E.'s office, he had to try to straighten things out with Trina. He just wished he knew how. Then he wished his mother was still alive, because she'd always been full of wise advice about child rearing. Then he wished his father was still alive, too, because Hector Garcia would have sat right there at that table with a mug of coffee and told him to get his head out of his ass.

So, they weren't there anymore, but he could still hear their voices.

"You know, Gil," Betty would have said, "teenagers think they're grown up. They like to make their own decisions. You just have to gently guide her. She's a bright child. She'll figure it out on her own."

And Hector would have said, "Damn it, son, that Anna Lundgren is a suspect. What are you trying to do? Lose your job?"

Yeah. Gil filled a mug with steaming thick brew and sat at the table. Then he remembered the sausage and biscuit he hadn't found. Muttering under his breath, he returned to the freezer and hunted until he found the package beneath a heap of other stuff that Trina had wanted to buy and still hadn't touched: frozen lasagne, a box of ice-cream sandwiches, and a few frozen dinners.

Thinking about it, he realized that probably said a lot about the way she was eating at home. Those were her favorite foods.

Hell, he needed to get his butt in gear and cook dinner for the two of them himself. He was no chef, but he could manage better than TV dinners. The problem was, his job often didn't allow him to be home at such a crucial time of day.

Another one of the things his ex had hated.

With his hot biscuit in hand he returned to the table and his coffee. His mind was doing the flea thing, he realized, hopping everywhere except to his major concern: the dagger in Anna's bed.

He wondered if she was sleeping. Probably not. She'd be too frightened, too wound up. He hoped Nancy was making her feel safer. He glanced at the phone, thought about calling, then told himself not to be such an asshole. It was okay to like her—he'd liked suspects before—but it was not okay to get involved.

It was all too neat and tidy, the whole case. Too neat. Anna finds the first replica, Anna discovers the theft, Anna finds the second note, Anna finds the second replica. It was too damn much.

Most cops would probably think she was doing it all herself to point the finger in another direction, playing the victim when in fact she was the perpetrator.

It might be so. He was willing to allow that. He couldn't quite get past all those replicas on her shelves. When he added that to the fact that her father may have been a victim of the curse, he could come up with all kinds of motivations for her. Motive, means, and opportunity, the cops' creed for identifying perps.

In Anna's case, two plus two was definitely equalling four.

But he didn't buy it. What he bought was that the perp had a very different motive than simply acquiring a priceless antiquity. A thief who wanted to do that would have called it done as soon as he rubbed out Eddy Malacek, and would have vanished into whatever hole he'd crawled out of.

Nor was the burglar taunting the cops. Tebbins would, of course, consider that a high probability, since he figured they were up against a mastermind. Unfortunately for Tebbins's hopes, the case wasn't a James Bond movie and masterminds were smart enough not to return to the scene of the crime and sprinkle additional clues by taunting the cops. Unless, of course, they were cops or cop wanna-bes themselves—which kept Gil's attention tuned to Tebbins.

Each one of these clues could easily become the giveaway that would reveal the thief's identity. Serial killers were notorious for doing things like that, things to taunt the cops or to get themselves caught. But this wasn't a serial killer, and a mind sharp enough to bypass all those security systems surely realized the pitfalls in returning time and again to leave his messages.

So, this wasn't about the dagger, not directly. It was about Anna, one way or another. And it was most definitely about the curse.

The biscuit sat like lead in his stomach, and the coffee was giving him heartburn. Gil went to the cupboard and got himself a couple of antacids, then switched off the light. He thought better when he paced in the dark.

The curse. He'd better get some people to start researching in the morning. He needed to know how many survivors there had been after the earthquake and the fire at the petroleum refinery. Probably hundreds, even thousands. The task was daunting. But they had to start looking for someone else with a personal involvement, someone besides Anna.

As he passed by the front window, he glanced through the sheers. Across the street a car was parked, a shadowy shape visible only because it was near a streetlight. It wasn't an uncommon sight, except that the car hadn't been there earlier. Something prickled along the base of his skull, and he decided that maybe he'd better check it out.

But as soon as he had the thought, the car sped away.

Ten seconds later, he was gently shaking his daughter.

"Wake up, honey," he said. "We're going to Anna's *now*."

CHAPTER TWELVE

Anna couldn't hold still. Anxiety kept her pacing the house, making her feel as if she wanted to crawl out of her skin. Nancy sat at the table, watching her from bleary eyes, her coffee growing cold in front of her.

"I guess we need to do something ourselves," she said finally.

Anna gave a short laugh. "Yeah, right. What?"

"Hell, I don't know. But there's got to be something we can do. In the meantime, I vote we start doing the twin thing. This guy can't find you if he can't figure out which one of us is which."

"Don't be silly. You'll only put yourself in danger."

Nancy shrugged. "Maybe, maybe not. Maybe I'm already in danger just by being here. I might be in his way."

Anna swung around sharply and looked at her with horror. "Nancy, no! You've got to go home."

Her sister shook her head. "Pointless. Besides, it sounds to me like this is about the curse. If so, he'll be after both of us."

"Oh, God, why did you have to come to visit right now?"

"Fate?" But Nancy suddenly looked haunted. "Or the curse," she suggested in a hushed voice.

"Curses aren't real." But Anna's voice lacked its usual vehemence on the subject. Maybe curses were real, all right. And maybe they sometimes needed human agents. Her skin started crawling again, and she resumed her rapid pacing.

"You want to know something," Nancy said. "I don't believe in them either. But now I'm starting to wonder."

Anna didn't even want to think about it, but the possibility was stalking her, too.

Just then, there was a knock on the front door. Both of them froze. The knock sounded again.

"I'll get it," Nancy said.

"Not alone you won't." Anna went with her to the front door. Nancy looked out the peephole.

"It's a cop," she said, and unlocked the dead bolt.

Standing on the stoop was a young Temple Terrace policeman. He looked embarrassed.

"Hi, I'm Officer Richter, the guy who's been sitting in the car across the street. Sorry to bother you ladies, but I saw you were still up. Could I use your bathroom?"

"Of course," Anna said, trying to hide her reluctance to let a stranger in, even a cop.

"It must be hard to sit out there for hours," Nancy remarked, trying to sound friendly.

"It's tough," he admitted with a shy smile. "Especially this time of night. I'm having trouble staying awake."

At last there was something Anna could

actually do that would be useful. "Let me make you some coffee, Officer. It's the least I can do."

"Thanks. That'd be really great." He gave them another shy smile and followed Nancy's directions to the bath.

Anna was almost disappointed when she realized the coffee was already made. Nancy had poured one small cup for herself, and there were still eight cups left in the carafe on the warmer.

Oh, well. She pulled out an insulated bottle she rarely used and filled it.

Nancy came up beside her and asked in a voice barely above a whisper, "Do you suppose he's for real?"

"Probably."

"Maybe we just let the killer inside."

"Don't. Don't even suggest it."

"But he could've done in the real cop..."

"Nancy, please." Anna found herself hating this paranoia, hating the way it was twisting her world out of shape, making her suspicious of everyone and everything. "If he *did* kill the cop, what was there to keep him out anyway?"

"True." Nancy became silent just as Richter came out of the bathroom.

Anna called to him. "How do you like your coffee?"

He came to the kitchen doorway. "Black is fine, ma'am, thank you. I really do appreciate this."

"It's no problem." Summoning a tired smile, she handed him the bottle. "Enjoy."

"I will," he promised, holding up the Thermos. "Just let me put this out in the cruiser and take another walk around the house. If you hear anything, don't worry. It'll be me."

He left and Nancy bolted the door behind him. "Whew," she said. "I'm glad that didn't turn into a big mistake."

So was Anna, but she didn't admit it. She *did* however wonder why she'd opened the door to him in the first place. She couldn't trust anybody now. Not anybody.

She peered out the window, watching Richter cross the street. He paused for a moment and tipped his chin toward his shoulder. The radio, Anna realized. After a moment he seemed to speak, then put the bottle on the hood of his car, adjusted his belt and came back in their direction, disappearing around the corner of the house.

"He's walking around now," she said, dropping the curtain back into place. "He's for real."

"Thank God." Nancy returned to the table and took a sip of her coffee, then made a face. "Damn, that's cold!"

"Let me make you some more."

"I don't think my stomach could handle it. I don't know about you, but my eyes are full of sand, and my stomach's burning something fierce."

"I'm too wound up," Anna said. "I don't think I'll ever sleep again."

"You will," Nancy said darkly. "That's the problem. No matter how hard you fight it, eventually you fall asleep anyway."

Anna shuddered. She didn't want to think about how vulnerable that would make her.

Gil made record time on the drive across the bay and Tampa to Temple Terrace. From time to time his daughter stirred herself enough to say, a bit crabbily, "Dad, please slow down. Mom would have a fit if she knew how fast you're driving."

"I'm a cop. I can drive fast."

"Yeah, right." She hunched back into her *the world's gone crazy and I don't want to be here* pose. A while later she groused, "I don't understand why we have to go see Anna and Nancy at five in the morning. They'll be mad when you wake them up."

He hadn't told her about what Anna found, didn't want her worrying needlessly. On the other hand, he hadn't dared leave her home alone, not after seeing that car. Christ, it just kept getting better and better.

"I have a feeling," he said finally.

Her tone was acid. "A cop feeling, I suppose."

She'd gotten that one from her mother, too. "Yeah, a cop feeling. It happens, and when it does, I don't ignore it."

She huffed. Attitude, he reminded himself. It was just a teen attitude, heightened by her mother.

It was just past five when they reached Anna's house. Pulling up along the curb, he switched off the ignition and looked across the street at the patrol car. The cop was sitting at the wheel, a little slouched as if he'd been trying to find a comfortable position. He didn't get out of the car to come check on them though.

Smart, Gil decided. He was probably radioing about their arrival, getting another car here.

"Wait here, Trina. I need to go talk to that officer for a minute."

She sent him one of her patented looks. Gil ignored it and climbed out, auto-locking the doors behind him. He strolled across the street toward the cruiser, keeping his hands in plain view. Much to his consternation, the cop inside didn't react in any way.

When he reached the window and peered in, he saw a young uniform sitting with a plastic cup of coffee on his lap, an open Thermos bottle beside him on the passenger seat. He rapped on the window but got no response. The door was locked. The engine still purred in park.

He rapped harder, still no response, and his heart slammed into overdrive.

Running back across the street, he tapped on his daughter's window. She powered it down a couple of notches. "Something's wrong," he told her. "Stay right here, keep the windows rolled up and the door locked." He passed her his c-phone after making sure it was on. "If there's any trouble, call 9-1-1, okay?"

"Okay." She suddenly didn't look as belligerent. In fact, she looked like a scared little girl.

"It's okay, honey. As soon as I know Anna and Nancy are all right, I'll come for you."

She nodded.

"Now roll up the window."

He waited until it was fully closed, then ran up the walk to Anna's front door. There he banged on it with the heel of his fist, a sound loud enough to wake the dead.

Moments later, Anna opened the door looking exhausted and frightened. At least he thought it was Anna. There was something in her eyes he recognized. But the moment she spoke, he was sure. Anna's voice was softer than her sister's. "Gil, what..."

"Are you and Nancy okay?"

"Fine. Nancy's on the back porch smoking a cigarette, but we're fine. What..."

"The cop who's been watching you isn't responding. Can I bring Trina in? I don't want to leave her in the car."

"Of course."

He ran back to his car and Trina practically tumbled out into his arms. He took the cell phone from her and tucked it into his pocket, then led her up the sidewalk, promising her it was going to be all right. Anna drew her inside and wrapped an arm around her.

"I'm going to check around outside the house. Lock up until I get back."

"Should I call for help?"

"Yes."

She nodded and closed the door on him. He waited until he heard the dead bolt slide into place.

Then he headed around the house with his gun drawn.

The shadows beneath the trees were dark,

darker than the night. The little bit of illumination from the streetlights cast eerie shadows, turning them into horrific shapes. All he could hear were the loud screeches of tiny tree frogs. As he approached they fell silent.

He reached the backyard swiftly, and saw a shadow on the porch. He froze, leveling his gun at it, then saw the cherry tip of a burning cigarette.

Just at that moment, the back door opened. "Nancy," Anna said sharply, "get inside right now."

The shadow moved, stepping into the light falling through the door. Nancy. She said something, but he didn't hear what it was as the door closed behind her.

He took another step forward. Just then he heard movement from the bushes behind the next house over. Just a muffled sound. He started for it, then heard a crash and the thud of running feet.

Shit!

Holding his gun, he gave chase.

Jackson Fisher stared at the gauges again and tapped the one on the right. The needle finally flickered to life. This was the part of the world most people never saw, he liked to think. The grunt work behind all of their lofty ambitions, business meetings, assignations, and the dreams that died like a fluffed nine iron over the pond on six. His job was neither simple nor glamorous. His job was to make sure the sprinkler systems at the Temple

Terrace Country Club functioned normally. When all was well, life was grand. All was not well, and life was not grand. But assuming the gauges weren't broken—again—he was ready to power up the system again.

Not too bad, he thought with a sense of pride, considering the mess he'd been called in to deal with at midnight. By some act of fate one of the watering lines had burst, causing a pressure drop that had sounded an alarm and shut the system down. It had done its job, designed to avoid the waste of hundreds of gallons of water, and the destruction of parts of the course.

So okay. He'd been called in by the night watchman, had finally hunted up the problem, and single-handedly repaired the line. He was quite proud of that.

But fate wasn't done with him. No, of course not. Jackson believed that troubles came in threes, and this night had borne out his superstition. Sure enough, he got the line repaired, patched the hole in the ground as best he could without turf, then had turned the system on again.

Lo and behold, he no sooner got the cycle running again at where it had shut down, than the pressure fell. A half dozen heads blew.

Now that was a puzzlement to him, because he took good care of his system. He cleaned the heads frequently, checked them for cracks, and made sure they were securely fastened to the line. Apparently they had gremlins tonight.

So he'd tromped out, looking for the blown

heads with a flashlight. They weren't too hard to find; water under pressure dug holes in the ground with amazing speed. Unfortunately, some big holes had been dug on the fairways. He'd filled the holes with sand, but the 6:00 A.M. early birds weren't going to be happy.

But Jackson wasn't worried about them. His personal pride was on the line, and he vowed he and the groundskeeper would get them fixed by eight. What annoyed him was that the gauges weren't working right either. All the regions were showing low pressure. Problem three.

"You planning to turn that on anytime soon, Jax?" The groundskeeper was breathing down his neck.

Jax. Everyone wanted to abbreviate his name. But he was rather proud of it. He'd been named for Jackson Pollock, and he doubted anyone had ever called the famous painter "Jax." Still, it beat the other plays on words he so often heard, most of which mated his name with that of a donkey. "Almost up to pressure," he said.

"I can't keep them waiting forever, Jax. If I don't get the mowers out there, people will be complaining about fuzzy greens at dawn."

"And if I don't get this damn system working, people will be complaining about burnt greens by noon. So we both have work to do."

Nancy, holding back the sheers over the patio doors, peered out into the night. "My God," she said. "He's chasing something. He just ran for the neighbors' yard."

"Which neighbor?" Anna was holding the telephone, punching in 9-1-1. Trina huddled on one of the stools, her eyes huge and frightened.

Nancy pointed. "Thataway."

The dispatcher's voice filled Anna's ear. Speaking as quickly and clearly as she could—or hoped she was—she explained the situation.

"There's a detective from St. Pete chasing him," she finished. "He just took off at a dead run toward the east."

"Are you sure the prowler's a man?" the dispatcher asked.

"No. I haven't seen him."

"What about the officer in the car?" the dispatcher asked. "What's wrong with him?"

"I don't know! Detective Garcia said he couldn't wake him. That's why he was out checking around the house, and now he's chasing someone and he needs help!"

"I understand that, ma'am. Units are on the way. He's running toward the golf course?"

"I don't know that. I just know he took off in an easterly direction."

"Keep the line open, ma'am. Don't hang up until I tell you to, all right?"

"Okay. Okay." Phone glued to her ear, Anna gripped the edge of the counter.

Nancy came away from the doors and slid onto a stool beside Trina. "He's going to be okay, sweetie," she said. "Your dad's a good cop."

Trina nodded, but she looked as if she didn't believe it.

Anna came around the counter and put her arm around Trina. The girl immediately leaned into her and hugged her around the waist.

And the darkness outside seemed to be pressing inward, trying to find a way in.

Pipes in the pump room pinged as air flushed through the line. Out there, through that window, everything was lush, green, and manicured. In here, Jackson thought, the odor of old coffee and stale cigarettes mixed with rust. But in here was what made out there possible. Line three was still low, and he opened the valve a bit more. The pings and pops came more rapidly. The needle climbed. And, so far, there were none of the flickers he'd been watching and fighting all night. Flickers as leaks sprang hither and yon and farther yon. His hands ached from twisting wrenches. But he felt a satisfaction in the ache. It was a workingman's ache. He watched the needles rise.

Three blocks and six privacy fences away, Gil was cursing his topsiders, wishing he'd donned his jogging shoes. Every now and then he needed to stop, to listen, to figure out where his prey was. The idiot wasn't worried about being silent, apparently, but he was keeping a good distance ahead. Never had Gil seen more of him than a vague shadow a house or two away.

Pressing the cell phone to his ear with his left hand wasn't helping either. Sweat was making him sticky and slick, and the phone kept trying to get away from him. His heart was pounding both from adrenaline and from running, and sometimes it sounded louder than the night sounds around him.

He was still waiting for a patch to the Temple Terrace police. It hadn't been that long, not in real time, but it felt like a lifetime.

There! A thud as feet hit the ground hard. The suspect had gone over another privacy fence.

He'd turned. Just as Gil was becoming convinced the guy was headed in a beeline for a particular place, the idiot turned. Shit. What was going on here?

Coming to a corner, Gil turned in the direction of the sound and headed up a north-bound street. A zigzag maybe? Staying on the street, he ran faster, hoping to catch up while shrubbery and fencing slowed the guy he was pursuing.

And wouldn't it beat all hell if he was chasing some ordinary prowler?

There was a crackle on his cell phone, and a tinny voice spoke to him.

"This is Corporal Vinzano, Detective. I'm heading up the search team. Where are you and where is the suspect?"

"I'm heading north on..." Shit, he didn't know the streets here. "Give me a minute. There's a street sign ahead. I'm on the street, the suspect is running north through the backyards. Or was a minute ago."

"We're on our way. Get to that sign, will you."

As if he wasn't trying. Gil gave himself another push, speeding up. The sign wasn't under a streetlight, though, and he couldn't read it until he was on it. He repeated the street names into the telephone.

"We'll be there in three minutes," Vinzano told him. "He's still headed north?"

"When last seen. Give me a minute."

But the night offered no clues. Except for sounds of insects and his own heavy breathing, there might have been nothing alive. "He's gone to ground," he said into the phone.

And he was starting to get angry. He knew it was an adrenaline response, and he tried to stomp it down, but at that moment, with blisters stinging on his feet, his body drenched with sweat, his lungs protesting from dragging in huge gulps of air so humid that it was almost like breathing water, he was pissed.

Across the street from him, there was a wall of thick growth, palmettos and palms, oaks and scrub pines. Overgrown with vines, it looked impenetrable. A great hiding place.

Reining in his anger, Gil crossed the street, looking for somewhere a person could get into that growth, looking for something that appeared disturbed, listening all the while for the sound of running feet.

It was dark, too damn dark, to see much, and he wished vainly for the flashlight in his car. Dawn hadn't even started to lighten the sky yet.

Then he saw the hole ahead. Big. Big enough for several people to walk through. Quickening his jog, he headed for it and discovered an asphalt footpath and bike path. There. He had to have gone there.

But now he needed to slow down. The suspect could have gone off the path anywhere, could be hiding behind any bush, tree or palmetto in the shadows. He might be armed.

A new surge of adrenaline filled him as he started down the path. Dew was dripping from branches and fronds with a gentle plopping that sounded almost like a soft rain. The frogs and insects were quiet, sensing an invader.

The suspect was nearby, somewhere. Gil felt the awareness seep through every bone of his body. Moving cautiously, he tried to keep to the deeper shadows beside the path as he scanned for anything that didn't seem right.

Which was ridiculous because nothing seemed right at that moment. Everything was a murky threat.

A sound. He turned toward it, thought he saw a palmetto frond shake.

Christ. Gun at ready, he stuffed his cell phone into his pocket, then gripped the butt with both hands, moving slowly toward the palmettos.

Then, just as he sensed that something was behind him, he was struck hard at the back of his head. The world swirled, went black, filling with stars.

"I've got to get out there, Jax. I can't hold them anymore."

"Go ahead," Jackson said. "Not my problem if you get wet. I'll have them up in about sixty seconds."

"I'll tell the drivers to carry umbrellas."

The next thing Gil knew, he was lying face-down on the path, his chin stinging like fire. He could hear running feet down the path. Struggling, feeling a little disoriented, Gil shoved himself up onto his hands and knees. He still had his gun. It was the first thing he looked for. Then he felt the sticky warmth at the base of his skull.

Jesus! The footsteps were fading into the distance as he stared at the rock that had been used to club him. Jesus.

Feeling a little woozy, he struggled to his feet. He could still hear the running footsteps, fainter now, and he forced himself to take off after them on legs that felt a bit wobbly. He was going to catch that son of a bitch if he did it with his dying breath.

Speaking into his cell phone, he updated Vinzano, who assured him the team was close.

"Are you okay?" Vinzano asked.

"Yeah. I'm fine." He wasn't, quite, but his head was steadily clearing. "You got somebody at the Lundgren house?"

"A couple of cars will be there in a few moments."

"Thanks."

The curving path was leading him through a swamp, over narrow wooden bridges. At least that was some surety the suspect hadn't leapt off to the side again. But every now and then, echoing off the trunks of aged trees, he heard the footsteps. The guy was still ahead of him.

The path suddenly opened onto a road. Across from him were large, expensive homes. The reek of money was as strong as the stink of rotting vegetation from the swamp behind him.

And no sign of his assailant.

The sky was lightening at last, a grayness that seemed to be creeping out of the east. At the moment there wasn't much of an improvement over the darkness, but he could see wisps of fog, rising over the yards across from him.

Then he saw the footprints, a clear path in the dew.

I've got you, sucker, he thought with a savage sense of triumph. He took off again, following the footprints like a lighted highway, past tropical gardens, across manicured lawns and onto a golf course fairway.

The guy was heading west. Gil alerted Vinzano and kept running, following the yellow-brick road.

Engines were loud now. Too loud for cars. What were they doing, bringing in the National Guard?

They were going to get this guy. Part of Gil was already relishing the look on the suspect's face when they nabbed him. The night was brightening ahead of him, as if lights were coming on. The cops?

Rounding a copse of trees, he stopped dead, and felt his heart sink. The mowers were out, a bank of them running side by side in a wedge formation, cutting away the very footprints he was following, masking any sound the suspect might make.

He stood there, holding his phone, watching the mowers chew up the footprints, knowing they had already cut away all the ones behind them.

He clapped his phone to his ear. "Vinzano?"

"Yeah?"

"He's on the golf course somewhere. I was following his footprints in the dew. But you know what?"

"What?"

"The mowers just cut them away."

"Have no fear, partner. We've got the chopper up. If he moves, we'll see him."

Jackson switched the automatic sprinklers to manual and pushed the switch. The gauges held. Finally. Maybe it wasn't such a bad night after all. Maybe it'd be a good day, at least.

The mowers moved closer, drowning out any possibility Gil could use the phone. As they passed him, they looked at him with astonishment. Well, he must look really cool, he thought, a guy in shorts, topsiders and a polo, holding a phone in one hand and a gun in the other. He didn't think it was his imagination when they seemed to speed up to get past him. Behind them lay perfectly trimmed swaths of grass that revealed nothing except their wheel prints.

Overhead, its engines drowned by the sound of the mowers, he saw a police helicopter against the predawn sky. Its flood lamps came on, and the search began in earnest.

There. Two hundred yards away, a shadow darted. Far too distant for Gil to catch him. But he could tell the search team where to look. "Vinzano," he yelled into the phone.

Then with a hiss and a spitting that alerted him but didn't give him time to do anything, the sprinklers along the fairway turned on.

Drenching him. Killing his phone. Turning the last of his night into hell.

He just hoped they weren't pumping reclaimed water.

CHAPTER THIRTEEN

Two police cars sat in front of Anna's house. Another officer had settled on her back deck. The officer who'd been asleep in his car had been taken away in an ambulance. The sun was up, promising another hot, bright day.

But even daylight didn't ease Anna's fear. Someone had done something to the cop who was supposed to be protecting her and Anna, and Gil had torn off into the night after him. And Gil still wasn't back.

Trina was curled at one edge of the couch, wrapped in a blanket, looking fearful and exhausted. Anna's heart went out to her, and as she so often had during the past few hours, she sat beside the girl and hugged her.

"I wish Dad would come back," Trina said.

"Me too. But I'm sure they would have told us if he'd been hurt. He's probably just talking and working with them. Maybe they caught the bad guy." She wished she believed it, but deep in her heart she knew it wasn't so.

She was afraid for Gil, too, but she was trying desperately to hide the fear from Trina.

"My mom always hated him being a cop," Trina said, her chin trembling. "Always. She said he was going to get killed."

"Well, he hasn't been killed yet, and if you ask me, the longer he's a cop, the safer he is."

Trina raised questioning eyes. "Why?"

"Because he has more experience. He knows how to avoid getting hurt."

That seemed to soothe Trina, but it didn't soothe Anna at all. Gil had gone tearing off into the night after a killer. Nobody was safe under those circumstances.

Nancy, who was sprawled on the recliner and had been heard snoring gently from time to time, stirred. "He'll be here soon," she told Trina. "You'll see."

"How do you know that?"

"I'm a witch. Ask Anna."

Trina started to smile, then looked at Anna. "Really?"

"Sure, she keeps her broom in the laundry room. It only works on Halloween, though."

A little chuckle escaped Trina. "You guys are crazy."

"Totally," Nancy agreed. "Well, *I* am anyway. Anna's always trying to pretend she's sane."

"Next to you," Anna retorted, "anyone would look sane."

Nancy spread her arms. "That's why the world needs people like me. So everyone can look at me, pat their own backs, and think, 'Thank goodness I'm not like her.'"

Trina chuckled again, making an effort.

Anna spoke, "Do you have any brothers or sisters, Trina?"

"Not yet. I think Mom's pregnant, though. She keeps barfing in the morning."

"Wouldn't she tell you?"

"Not yet. She and Andrew aren't married yet." Trina shrugged. "I'm not supposed to know they're having sex."

"Ahh." Anna looked at Nancy who shrugged. "I gather you *do* know."

"Sure. I don't need a crystal ball. I guess she's afraid I might get the wrong idea. Anyway, they've been dating for a couple of years, and now they're suddenly talking about having a quiet wedding. Like my dad says, two plus two equals four."

Anna had the feeling that not much slipped by this girl. "What about your boyfriend? What's he like?"

Trina frowned. "I don't know. I used to think he was so cool, but... I don't know. He was kind of mean to me the other day, and now Dad says I can't see him anymore."

"That must have been some *mean*."

Trina shrugged. "He was just mad. People get mad sometimes."

"Well, sure," Anna said, suddenly feeling helpless. "As long as he doesn't hit you or anything."

"He didn't! He just kicked sand at me."

Anna and Nancy exchanged looks. Anna could tell she wasn't the only one who didn't think that was the full story.

Nancy spoke. "Well, much as it pains me to admit it, sometimes older heads *are* wiser heads. And getting hit by someone you love kind of changes your mind and heart forever."

Anna's heart skipped, and she stared at her sister, wondering if Peggy had hit her.

"But he didn't hit me," Trina argued. "Not even once."

Anna knew all the warning signs of domestic abuse, and her head was full of them, starting with the fact that it often began with threats of violence, direct or indirect, such as kicking sand or throwing things. But she refrained from saying so because she had no right to counsel Gil's daughter. And Gil appeared to have his head screwed on straight about the boyfriend.

The front door opened, causing all of them to start. Clarence Tebbins poked his head in, and said, "Knock, knock."

Anna didn't know if she was glad to see him or not. It felt like aeons ago that he walked out that door, and yet it seemed too recently. He irritated her.

"Come in," she said.

He closed the door behind him and walked farther into the living room. "You've had quite a night, I hear." Then his gaze settled on Trina. "And who is this lovely young lady?"

"Gil's daughter," Anna said. "Trina Garcia. Trina, this is Detective Tebbins."

Tebbins's eyebrows lifted, but he leaned forward in a simulation of a courtly bow. "A pleasure, Miss Garcia."

"Hi," Trina said in a subdued voice. "Is my dad okay?"

"Alive and well," Tebbins answered. "He'll be here soon."

Trina sagged with relief, and Anna would have done the same, only she refused to reveal that much to Tebbins. He was already sticking his nose too far into her life.

"What about the cop who was watching outside?" Anna asked him.

"He's going to be all right. Apparently he was drugged, but he's waking up now."

"Drugged?" All the fear slammed back into Anna's heart. "My God..." Drugged. So easy to do. Her stomach knotted painfully, and she wondered if she would dare eat or drink again. "How?"

"We're working on that." Tebbins pointed to the rocker. "May I?"

"Please."

He sat, looking from one to the other of them. Nancy had brought the recliner up a bit and stared back at him from reddened eyes. "You have to do something, Tebbins," she told him flatly. "My sister and I both need some sleep."

"We're going to strengthen the surveillance," he said placidly.

"Oh, gee, thanks," Nancy answered sarcastically. "Be still my beating heart."

Tebbins's expression didn't change. "I could put you both in protective custody, but I doubt you'd sleep any better in the jail."

Jail. With overwhelming certainty, Anna realized that Tebbins would actually like to do that. He honestly believed she was behind all this.

"Jail!" Nancy slammed the footrest down and leaned forward. "If that isn't just perfect. Put the *victims* in the slammer."

Tebbins shrugged. Nancy scowled at him. "How about *solving* the crime?"

"We're working on it."

"Do you have any idea what it feels like to *us*? What it feels like to Anna? She's had someone break into her house to leave a terrifying message, someone who's willing to drug a cop to get to her."

"Nancy..." Anna wanted her to stop. It wasn't going to help anything to repeat what Tebbins already knew, and it certainly wasn't something Trina needed to hear.

Nancy looked at her, then seemed to reconsider. "Jerks," she muttered.

Tebbins began twirling one end of his moustache again, but didn't reply to Nancy's outburst. Silence fell over the room, thick and heavy.

The door opened again, and Gil stepped inside. Trina leapt up from the couch, crying his name, and ran toward him. His arms welcomed her into a bear hug.

His legs were scratched, Anna noted. And his chin. The navy blue polo shirt he'd been wearing earlier had been exchanged for a blue hospital scrub shirt. When he lifted Trina off her feet and swung her around, Anna saw that the lower back of his head had been shaved and a gauze bandage covered it.

"What happened to you?" she demanded.

"Four stitches," he replied easily enough. "A case of stupidity."

"Daddy..."

"I'm fine, sweetie. Just fine. My worst problem is a couple of big blisters."

That's when Anna noticed the bandages on his heels.

"Wrong shoes," Gil said cheerfully enough. "Don't pursue a suspect in topsiders." He looked down at his daughter. "Make a note of that."

Her face had brightened. "Yes, Daddy."

"Didn't catch him, unfortunately," Gil said. "He had an advantage: He knew where he was going." Then he stuffed his hand into his pocket and pulled out a couple of white balls. "It wasn't a total waste. I picked up two perfectly good Titleists. I guess they're worth the price of a drowned cell phone."

He winked at them, and Anna started laughing. She couldn't help it. It was as if the tension of the night past needed to spill out somehow, and that was it. Trina started giggling, too, and even Nancy finally joined in.

Only Tebbins remained silent and unmoved.

"I need to get Trina home," Gil said. He and Tebbins were standing in the front yard. Trina was already in the car, with the motor and air-conditioning running, playing with the radio. Faint sounds of *whump-whump* came through the closed windows.

Tebbins looked up at him, stabbing a finger at his chest. "What the hell were you doing, bringing your daughter along and leaving her with a suspect? Hell, what were you doing coming over here at five in the morning?"

"Well, I had a bad feeling. And I wasn't going to leave my daughter alone in the house, especially after a car that was parked out front took off the instant I saw it."

"What?" Tebbins frowned.

"I think maybe it was her boyfriend. They had a fight, and he threatened her."

"Damn." Tebbins shook his head. "Sometimes I can't stand the human race anymore. Sometimes I think the solitude of a desert island might actually be preferable."

"Yeah, me too. Job hazard. Anyway, I couldn't leave her at home. And suspect or not, Anna wasn't going to do anything to my daughter."

"I guess not. It'd be too obvious."

"But," Gil reminded him, "I chased a suspect. There was someone outside. Ergo, Anna didn't do it."

"I'm not so sure about that. We need to talk. Now."

Gil looked at his daughter again. "That's just a wee bit difficult right now."

"I can't believe you're carting her around with you on the job."

"What am I supposed to do? Leave her to the mercies of that creep she's dating? And her mother's away on a trip, so it's not like I can just hand her back."

"And they thought women were going to be a problem in police work because of kids." Tebbins snorted. "The real problem is divorce."

Gil didn't bother to answer. He didn't like having his judgment called into question when he was doing the best he could to deal with a difficult situation. Right now he had two equally high priorities: catch a bad guy and protect his daughter from harm.

"Hell," said Tebbins, sighing. "Let's go to my place. She can play video games while we talk."

"You have kids?"

"No. I don't even have an ex-wife."

Interesting, thought Gil. Somewhere deep inside him a grin was born as he considered the rather surprising image of Clarence Tebbins playing video games.

The watcher waited until most of the police had left, hiding himself behind tall thatches of pampas grass across the street. He had to be careful not to brush the grass too hard because it sliced like a razor. He already had a thin cut on one arm.

He was still exhausted and frightened from

the close call when Garcia had chased him. Angry that his plan had been blown apart by that man's unexpected appearance. Angry that, for a while, the jaguar god had abandoned him.

But he had not been abandoned, he reminded himself. What had happened on the golf course had saved him, and he had no doubt that the god was behind it, protecting him until he could finish carrying out the curse.

But he also reflected on the possibility that he wasn't doing it correctly. The appearance of Anna's twin sister had spurred him, making him speed matters up.

He hadn't known about the twin, but now that he did it seemed perfectly obvious that he would have to kill them both to satisfy the curse. They were, after all, both the children of the man who had caused the desecration of Pocal's tomb.

But he had moved too quickly, fearing that the sister would go back home, wherever that was, before he could act.

He had thought, when the cop left the coffee on the hood of his car, that the perfect opportunity had arisen. It had been easy, so easy, to slip out of his hiding place and pour the drug into the bottle. It had seemed like a blessing on him, a sign that this was the time.

Apparently not. Just when he'd been creeping toward the back porch after the woman who was standing out back smoking, the cop had arrived.

And now there were two cop cars parked out front, making any action on his part virtually impossible.

But he would find a way around it. The jaguar would give him the opportunity.

Sighing, he slipped out of the bushes into a backyard, then began to walk home, looking like any other soul out for an early-morning stroll. He needed to think some more. To revise his plan.

The jaguar wouldn't bless it until it was right.

Tebbins had an extensive collection of games for his system, most of them bang-bang shoot-'em-ups. None of which Gil wanted his daughter to play. But Trina eventually settled on some innocuous game involving a lizard and a marked absence of loaded guns and dead bodies. Satisfied, he left her to play and went into the kitchen.

Tebbins had his jacket off and his sleeves rolled up and was busy making some kind of omelet loaded with peppers, onions, and sausage. A fresh pot of coffee had just finished brewing.

"Help yourself to the coffee," Tebbins said. "Cups are in the cupboard right above the pot. There's some cream in the fridge, and the sugar bowl's on the table."

"Thanks. I take mine black." He found a cup and filled it. "So what did you want to tell me?"

"Thermos bottles."

"Thermos bottles?"

"Thermos bottles," Tebbins said flatly. "Remember what you told me about the guard telling his friend that he hoped somebody brought cappuccino that night?"

"Yeah."

"Richter, the cop who was drugged, says Anna gave him a Thermos bottle of coffee."

"Christ." Gil felt his stomach sink.

"That alone is enough to arrest her if we find the coffee was drugged."

"But I chased that guy!"

Tebbins didn't say anything for a moment as he carefully folded the eggs in the pan. "It could have been a run-of-the-mill prowler."

Every cell in Gil's body rebelled. "It doesn't fit," he said finally. "It doesn't fit. The shape is wrong. Christ, Tebbins, why would she be doing this? There was no *reason* to drug the cop. No reason at all."

"Maybe not." Tebbins sighed. "Motive is a problem, I admit. But you've been around as long as I have, and you know there often isn't any *logical* reason for what people do. Maybe she has some kind of psychological glitch. Maybe she gets a thrill from it."

"But she's not faking her terror."

"Maybe not. Maybe she believes in the curse and is terrified of having the dagger in her possession. Maybe all she's trying to do is point the finger away from herself."

"Well, that won't add up with Richter's drugging," Gil said forcefully. "No way. She as good as put a sign on herself by giving him that coffee."

"And maybe she wants to be caught. It wouldn't be the first time."

No, it wouldn't. Gil didn't even try to deny that. "Maybe the perp's setting her up."

Tebbins thought about that while he carefully lifted the fluffy omelet onto a serving dish. "Could be," he said finally. "Could be. If so, he's succeeding, because she's in deep trouble now."

"What are you doing?" Nancy asked.

Anna was rooting around in her laundry room cum storage room like a madwoman, shoving things carelessly aside as she searched. "I'm going to make sure that bastard can't get in my house ever again!"

Nancy leaned against the doorframe and folded her arms. "The window latches *are* kind of old."

"Old? They're ancient! Every one of them is a little loose. Damn it, where is it?"

"Have your landlord fix them."

"Harvey? You're kidding, right? Or have you forgotten I finally had to go to the health department when the sewer line broke?"

"Yeah." Nancy sighed. "I guess I did forget. Look, Annie, you're just making a mess here. Tell me what you want, and I'll look for it."

Anna threw a scrub brush and it hit the wall with a satisfying *smack*.

"Okay, okay," Nancy said. "I'll just shut up."

"You don't have to shut up. But that s.o.b. isn't going to find it as easy to get in here again if I have to nail the damn windows shut."

Nancy refrained from pointing out that nailing aluminum frames might be difficult. And expensive. Harvey would make her replace every single one of them.

"Damn it!" Anna swore again. "Damn, damn, damn, where are you, you sucker?"

"What exactly are you looking for?"

"A thick strip of aluminum." She kicked a bucket aside.

Nancy scanned the room. "You mean this?" Reaching across to a nearby shelf, she lifted a two-inch-wide, two-foot-long aluminum strip with screw holes in it.

Anna turned. "That's it. Where did you find it?"

"On that shelf."

"Shit." Anna took it from her, grabbed a hammer out of the open toolbox, and headed for the bedroom.

Nancy followed, watching as Anna placed the aluminum on the sash next to the lock, and began to hammer it under the catch. And with every blow of the hammer, Anna spoke.

"You. Are. Not. Going. To. Get. In. Here. Again. You. Bastard."

Then it was done. Nancy sauntered over and looked at it. "Looks good, Annie." She tried to tug the strip from under the latch, but it wouldn't budge.

"Let's try to open the window," Anna said, tossing the hammer on the bed.

Even with the two of them exerting full strength, the window stayed firmly closed.

"So," said Nancy, "are you going to get strips for all the windows?"

"No." Anna picked up the hammer and marched past her.

Nancy once again followed, this time into the kitchen, where Anna dropped the hammer onto the counter and yanked the yellow pages out of the drawer under the bar. She flipped pages impatiently and finally stopped to run her finger down some listings. A moment later she picked up the phone and punched in some digits.

"Yes," she said a few seconds later. "I want to install a home security system, and I want to do it today. I'm being stalked."

It took three calls, but she eventually found a company that was willing to rush the installation for an additional charge. When she hung up the phone, she was pale and shaking.

"I've had enough, Nance," she said. "I have had *enough*!"

"I can understand that. I'm not real happy about this myself. Look, just sit down and try to calm down, Annie. We need to keep clear heads."

"Oh, my head is perfectly clear. After they install the alarm, I'm getting pepper spray and a cell phone. And maybe a gun."

"No."

Anna shook her head and stared at her sister. "No?"

"No gun. Annie, you don't know anything about guns. You don't know how to use one to protect yourself. You bring a gun into this house and all you might be doing is arming this scuzbucket with a deadly weapon. At least talk to Gil about it first."

"Gil?" Anna laughed bitterly. "Sorry, Nance,

he and Tebbins think I drugged that officer with the coffee. It was all over Tebbins's face."

Nancy couldn't deny that. "But they haven't arrested you."

"Don't hold your breath. If I live long enough, I'm going to have this whole thing pinned on me. See those surveillance cars out there? They're here as much to keep me from disappearing as to protect me."

Anna sagged as her anger deserted her, and she went to sit at the table with her head in her hands. "This guy is ruining my life."

"It seems that way." Nancy went to sit beside her. When she placed her hand on Anna's shoulder, she felt the shudder of tears pass through her. "Aw, sis..."

"I'm okay. I'm okay."

But it sounded like a cry of desperation. Nancy didn't blame her. Life was going to hell like a roller coaster on a downward rush. "You're not going to work today," Nancy said. "You can't. I'm calling your boss."

"No! I'm not going to spend the rest of my life locked inside my house."

Nancy put her hands on her hips and gave her a stern look. "Just what are your other options, Annie? To wind up dead?"

CHAPTER FOURTEEN

Twenty minutes later, Ivar was on the doorstep, arguing with a cop about whether he should be allowed to see Anna. Nancy, overhearing the commotion, opened the door and peered out.

"Oh, he's okay," she said to the cop. "Anna's boss from the museum."

Ivar, his dignity wounded, brushed himself off pointedly and stepped into the house. "Cretins," he muttered. "Nancy? You're Nancy, right?"

"Right." It didn't bother her that few people could tell them apart. She'd had a lifetime to get used to it. "Anna's in the kitchen. She's not doing well."

"I should think not!" Ivar followed her to the kitchen and dining area.

Anna looked up, took one look at him, and said, "Oh, God."

Ivar ignored her reaction. "It's beyond enough," he said, pulling out a chair and plopping into it. "Do you have any coffee?"

Nancy had the urge to laugh hysterically but quelled it. "Are you sure you want to drink my coffee? Tebbins thinks we drugged the cop who was on duty out front last night."

"Didn't I say they were cretins? Of course I'll drink your coffee."

"Well, it's nice that someone believes in Anna."

"Of course I believe in Anna! I've worked with her for nearly two years. *I* was the one who recommended she be named head curator."

Anna lifted her head from her hands. Her eyes were reddened and exhausted. "Thanks, Ivar."

"Yeah," Nancy agreed. "I'll make that coffee now."

Ivar looked at Anna. "You poor dear. Nancy told me what happened last night. You must be beside yourself."

"Actually," Nancy said as she measured coffee into the filter, "she's about ready to kill someone."

"Oh, dear." He reached out and patted Anna's hand. "You don't want to do that. Let the police do it. They have a license to kill. Believe me, you don't want all that messiness."

"Messiness?" Anna laughed bitterly. "Just what state do you think my life is in right now?"

"I know what state it'll be in if you shoot someone. You'll be in jail, dealing with lawyers—I can't imagine a worse fate than that, you know! Lawyers and the press. They'll be calling you terrible names, dressing you in that awful jailhouse orange—it wouldn't do a thing for that gorgeous hair of yours."

"Oh, man," Nancy muttered, rolling her eyes. Ivar ignored her.

"What's more," Ivar continued, "you'd be facing the death penalty. How is *that* going to improve your situation?"

"Ivar," Anna began, but he silenced her with a wave of his hand.

"I can see it now," he said, getting wound up. "Your picture all over the front page, day after day, with the title 'spree killer' attached. Your attorneys, moving to have you declared insane because you've been driven crazy by your obsession with the curse that killed your father."

"Ivar..."

"The jury, handpicked from the best of the Bible Belt because they're willing to sentence you to death, listening to the claims that you've lost your mind. Deciding it's obvious that you've been possessed by some Mayan devil and that you deserve to die. I'd get up on the stand and defend you as a hapless victim, but no one would listen to me." He leaned toward Anna, confiding, "No one *ever* listens to me."

"Ivar..."

"They'd drag you out of the courtroom in handcuffs. I'd be weeping, and it would be on the six o'clock news, and everyone, my wife included, would be wondering if we'd had an affair, or if I was involved somehow in the crimes. I'd be ruined, your sister would be devastated..."

"Ivar, enough! It would be self-defense!"

He looked at her. "Really," he said in a calm voice. "Only if they find the real villain first, my dear. Otherwise, you're going to be blamed for all of it, and your stalker is going to be considered a victim."

Anna fell silent, looking at him from hollow eyes. Nancy muttered, "God."

Ivar smiled. "I knew you'd see reason. Is that coffee ready yet?"

Nancy poured him a cup and practically slammed it on the table in front of him. She shoved the sugar bowl and creamer toward him, and he had to catch them to keep them from going off the edge of the table.

"What did I do?" he asked plaintively.

Nancy put the heels of her hands on the table and leaned toward him. "I wouldn't have thought it was possible to make this situation look any more hopeless."

"Really?" He dumped two heaping teaspoons of sugar into his coffee. "As long as there's breath, there's hope you know. These cops may be cretins—I certainly think so, judging by the way they seem to be floundering around—but at least they haven't arrested you yet. Which means they don't have a good enough case. As long as the possibility exists in their minds that you're *not* the thief and killer, they'll keep looking."

"And I could be dead by the time they find him," Anna said bitterly.

"Now, now, let's not exaggerate. They may be overly muscled cretins but they *do* know their jobs."

"We hope," Anna said.

"Oh, come off it," Nancy protested. "I don't especially care what Tebbins might be thinking because I know Garcia doesn't believe you're guilty, Anna."

Anna shook her head. "What are you? A mind reader?"

"I'm a face reader. Tebbins can point the finger at you all he wants, but Gil thinks you're innocent."

Ivar elevated one brow. "Do I detect the scent of romance?"

Nancy threw a dish towel at him, which he caught neatly in midair.

"Ah," he said with satisfaction. "I thought so."

Nancy looked at her sister. "That settles it," she said. "You *are* cursed."

Anna fell asleep finally on the couch. Nancy spread a colorful ripple afghan over her, pausing a moment to remember the hours their mother had spent crocheting it. The colors were garish, suiting their mother's temperament. Nancy loved hers, an exact duplicate, but supposed the colors annoyed Anna, whose tastes were far more subdued.

Nancy was tired, too, but she hadn't expended her adrenaline yet in a burst of outrage the way Anna had. Funny how the wacky sister had been the more reserved of the two all day.

Though she never would have admitted it to Anna, Nancy was beginning to feel caged and trapped. Just the mere idea that she couldn't go out and run around was having an annoying psychological impact on her.

She understood that she couldn't leave Anna alone; that would be foolhardy. But she still resented the hell out of their confinement.

A peep out the curtains told her the cops were still there. Leaning on one of the cars, they were chatting with each other. She wondered what the neighbors must be thinking, and some of the ideas that occurred to her made her mouth twitch with a grin.

But her good humor, one of her strong points, didn't endure very long. She looked over at her sleeping sister and wondered how the hell they were going to get out of this mess.

Come Monday, Anna would go back to work. Nancy knew her sister too well to believe otherwise. Besides, despite all the craziness their mom and aunt had surrounded them with, they'd both been taught a strong work ethic.

What then? Anna should be safe at the museum, Nancy decided. Too many people around for anything to happen. But she shouldn't come home alone, no matter what. Or go to work alone. Which meant Nancy would be her self-designated escort.

That was fine by Nancy. What wasn't fine by Nancy was the realization that she herself would have to be alone all day, wandering around a mostly strange city by herself, or sitting in this house watching the hours tick by. After their discussion during the night about how Nancy might also now be targeted, the prospects weren't appealing.

But neither was the idea of sitting around the museum all day. Anna might be able to find things for her to do, but they wouldn't be the kinds of things that appealed to her.

It wasn't that she wasn't willing to do necessary scutwork. She'd been doing it as needed all her life. But she preferred things which entertained her. Things having to do with computers.

Computers. The thought sizzled through her brain, capturing her attention. The "impossible" theft had to involve software somewhere in the system. Everything involved software these days. And programmers were notorious for leaving "back doors."

Then there was hacking. A really good hacker could break into almost any system. A moderately good hacker could get into most. Nancy had done a bit of that in her younger, wilder days and knew just how easy it could be. Any computer attached to the outside world could be hacked.

And she was willing to bet the security system was attached to the outside world. It had to be.

Excitement began to throb in her. It took all the resolve she had not to wake Anna and demand they go to the museum immediately. It wouldn't matter even if they did, though, because they'd need the cooperation of the security company.

Damn, she couldn't wait until Monday. Not when every minute might be bringing them closer to death. Finally she went to the phone in the kitchen. Tucked behind it were two business cards, one for Tebbins and one for Gil. It took her no more than a split second to decided which one she trusted more. She called Gil.

The postmortem showed no injuries to Eddy Malacek other than the needle hole in his left arm, and a couple of small contusions that might have come from bumping into anything. He hadn't been beaten, hadn't struggled or fought to defend himself.

"Death by overdose," the M.E. said as he pulled the sheet back up over the body.

Gil nodded. "That's what I expected. What I'm wondering is whether he was drugged with something beforehand."

"We won't know until we get the tox reports. But don't worry, I'm not going to give a final ruling until then. If he *was* drugged, it's anybody's guess how. His stomach was empty."

"Coffee?"

The M.E. shrugged. "Maybe. If it was given hours before his death."

Which was entirely possible, Gil thought as he strode out into the day's rising heat.

Pulling out his cell phone, he called home. Trina answered sleepily.

"I'll be home in about thirty minutes," he told her.

Her answer was almost resentful. "I'm not going anywhere."

Great. She was going to go back to her mother on Sunday mad at him. From experience he knew what that meant. His ex would probably make him sweat for his next visitation. He was getting used to it though. The woman would give him hell, but she wouldn't keep Trina from him. She had too many other things she wanted to do with her weekends, things that didn't involve dragging a teenager around with her. Or even having one at home.

Gil, in his odd moments of resentment, just wished she'd up and marry that turkey she was dating. He'd save a load on alimony. On the other hand, he didn't feel too good about Trina having a stepfather. He didn't like the idea of another man playing dad to his only child. It galled him.

But worse were his feelings about stepfathers in general. Some of them were good, but he'd answered too many domestic violence calls that had involved some man beating on his wife's kids.

His ex would tell him he was being paranoid. Maybe she was right, but he had good reasons for it.

He'd tried to find out how Trina felt about the guy, but she just shrugged. Teenage pretense; she cared but didn't want anyone to know it.

Was that normal? He'd certainly seen it in enough of the kids he dealt with on the street, but they were often abused, angry, and sullen. Was this just the age, or had someone taught Trina that expressing her feelings was an emotionally dangerous thing to do?

He had no way of knowing. For all his complaints about his ex, he knew she loved their daughter. Haphazardly at times, but it was still real love.

And he had never, ever, in his wildest imaginings, dreamed how difficult it could be to be a weekend parent.

Oh, well.

When he got home, Trina had apparently gone back to bed. He used the opportunity to take a shower and wash the smells from the night and from the autopsy off himself. Off course, he had to wear a plastic shower cap over his head to protect the stitches, so the job was anything but thorough. When he stepped out, he was sure he still didn't smell very good.

He thought about trying to cadge a nap, but when he emerged from the bedroom he discovered his pager was beeping. Checking the phone, he found he had a message on his voice mail, too. No rest for the weary, he grumbled to himself.

He called the station and discovered he had a message to call Nancy Lundgren; it was urgent.

What now? Instead of feeling worry, he felt annoyance. It was Tebbins's case on that side of the bay. He couldn't do a damn thing over there except call Tebbins anyway. Not that he could blame Nancy or Anna for not wanting to. After all, Tebbins might *think* he had the great stone face, but the truth was, the man's expressions gave away every thought in his head. The women would have to be stupid not to realize Anna was a prime suspect.

The thought gave him another unpleasant jolt. He wasn't being completely objective, and he knew it. Nor was he happy about it. In fact, he was second-guessing his every reaction to this case, and Tebbins's reactions, too.

Anna was even beginning to invade his dreams at night, and that annoyed him no end. It wasn't that he didn't occasionally dream about his cases. Naturally he did. But he didn't dream about them the way he was dreaming about Anna.

Annoyed with himself, he picked up the

phone and called Nancy back. She picked up as soon as it started ringing.

"It's Gil," he said, recognizing her voice. "What's up?"

"It's a back door," Nancy said.

"What? Someone's at your back door?"

"No, no." She sighed. "Sorry, I've been thinking about it so much that I'm in the middle of my thoughts. Have you ever heard of back doors in software engineering?"

"Uh...no."

"Well, programmers, and sometimes hardware designers, often leave them. Sometimes they have legitimate reasons for doing so, and sometimes it's a just a proprietary feeling, a sense of getting away with something. Anyway, the purpose is to give them easy access to the system."

"So what are you saying?"

"I'm saying someone could have used a back door to bypass the alarm system."

"Damn," said Gil. The sluggish wheels in his brain began whirring up to top speed. "Why wouldn't the security people mention the possibility?"

"Maybe because they don't know it's there," said Nancy. "Or maybe because they don't want anyone *else* to know it's there."

Dinah Hudson, Gil thought. She'd be in a prime position to know how to circumvent the system. They hadn't really looked at her because she had a long track record with her company, and the track record was good. Besides, she was a paperwork designer, not an actual programmer or technician.

But, he thought, she could have left a hole somewhere in the plans. Maybe. He couldn't imagine that her work wasn't reviewed. "How do we find it?" he asked Nancy.

"Well, you could ask the security company but..."

"But they might not want to find it."

"Or you could ask me," she said. "I'm pretty damn good with this stuff. But we'll need at least some cooperation from the security company."

"I'll arrange it," said Gil.

"Great, but I won't be able to get started before this evening," said Nancy. "Anna's having a security system installed here, too. I doubt they'll be done before late afternoon."

"Well, I won't be able to get anything set up that fast, I'm sure. I'll give you a call."

Tebbins's reaction was different. "How convenient," he said from his cell phone. The sounds of traffic could be heard. "Anna has a sister who can break into the security system, a sister who just manages to turn up unexpectedly within a few hours of the theft."

"I didn't say Nancy could break into the system. All I said was she thinks she might be able to find a back door. Why in the hell would she offer if she was responsible for the break-in to begin with?"

Tebbins chuckled. "Come off it, Garcia. Maybe she just wants to wow us. Some criminals need the applause."

Gil refrained from answering by clenching his jaw.

"Okay, I'm up for it," Tebbins said after a couple of moments. "Maybe she'll trip herself up."

When Gil disconnected, he tried to tell himself that Tebbins's attitude was a good check on his own. But that didn't mean that he liked it.

The security technicians finished installing the alarm system in Anna's house by six-thirty. They ran a test, setting off the siren a couple of times. Anna was certain it could be heard all the way to the other end of the block. The cops watching the house were bored and curious, so they hung around watching the process.

It wasn't perfect, though. "It's not completely foolproof," the technician admitted as he explained the functioning. "Someone has to open a door or window to set off the alarm. Breaking a window won't do it."

"We'd hear that anyway," Anna said. "What about the phone line being cut?"

"That'll set it off. If you lose all voltage on your phone line, your system will go off and we'll get an alarm on our end, too. We dispatch the police immediately, in that case."

Anna was satisfied. It was better than nothing. She wrote a large check that meant she was going to have to dip into her savings by the end of the month, and saw the men off.

"Feel better?" Nancy asked.

"No way." Marching into the kitchen, Anna pulled Tebbins's card off the phone and called his number, leaving a message for him. He was back to her in five minutes.

"What's going on?" he asked. "More daggers? Another prowler? Two sleeping cops out front?"

"I'm in no mood for your warped sense of humor."

"Too bad." He sighed. "I guess that means nothing major has happened. What's up?"

"I want to know exactly what's going on with this case."

He hesitated, and Anna was acutely aware of it. He didn't want to talk to her about it. The anger that had been simmering in her all day erupted again.

"Look, Clarence," she said.

"Call me Tebbins. Call me Tebbie—which I hate—but absolutely do *not* call me Clarence."

Anna pulled back from the phone a little bit, wondering how this guy's brain worked. "Fine. Tebbins. I want to know what's happening. And I'm entitled to know because I'm the victim."

He sighed. "You're also a prime suspect."

"I still have a right to know what you're doing. And if you won't tell me, I'm going to find someone who can make you tell me. I'm a prisoner in my own house, for God's sake. I've had to install an alarm system. I'm in fear for my life. And if you had enough to arrest me, you would have already done so. So I want a report."

He was silent for a few seconds. Then he said, "Tell you what. I'm in the middle of making dinner. Hang on for an hour or so, and I'll come over and talk with you."

"Thank you," Anna said with dignity, and hung up.

"Whew," Nancy said. "Are you sure you want to annoy that guy?"

"He's annoying *me*. And I have had enough. If this jackass can't find the creep, I'm going to do it."

Nancy grinned. "Mm-mm, girl. Now you're talking."

It was nearly dusk. The watcher, quite brilliantly he thought, was coming slowly down the sidewalk, wearing shorts and a tank top, and bouncing a basketball. He took his time about it, pretending to be involved in practicing various moves. It gave him a thrill to know he was approaching the police who were supposed to catch him.

His palms grew a little sweaty, and he paused to wipe them on his shorts. Nobody was paying him any attention. But then they rarely did. They were going to be sorry for not having noticed him all these months.

But as soon as he had the thought, he felt creepy. This wasn't about him. This was about protecting himself from the curse.

Feeling suddenly queasy, he sat down using the basketball for a seat. Pretending to tie his shoe, he bent over and fiddled with the laces.

Like a piercing ray of light in the darkness of his mind, a question struck him: What the hell was he doing?

The moment of clarity chilled him to his very bones, and left him feeling weak. His head sagged to his knees as he sought the strength to continue doing what he knew to be necessary.

He had spent most of his childhood in Mexico, although he wasn't Mexican. His father, an American, had worked in management for various petroleum enterprises and had made a good life for himself in Mexico. They had a gracious home, a maid, a gardener, and a cook who were locals. They were always a little apart...except for their son who, having grown up speaking colloquial Spanish even better than he spoke English, had naturally become steeped in local culture and belief, thus fitting in far more naturally.

It had been a good time for the watcher. He had many friends whose mothers treated him as if he were another member of the family. He'd run freely on village streets, under the watchful eyes of neighbors, safer than he could possibly have realized.

Until the discovery of Pocal's tomb when he was twelve. Then the days had darkened with low-voiced conversations among the parents of his friends, conversations that he and the other boys were not supposed to hear.

But he and his friends heard them and talked about them among themselves. The curse. The adults were afraid, and wondered what ill would befall the American consultants and the archaeologists who had desecrated the tomb. Talk centered around illnesses and even plagues, and the adults feared a plague might sicken them, too, even though they weren't directly involved. They worried more that their children would suffer because the legend said the curse struck unto the second generation.

These were people who went to Christian churches and celebrated Christian holidays in a way that harkened back to their Mayan roots, roots to which they clung closely. For many, the Christian god was just one of many gods.

The boys' heads filled with these tales, and the watcher was no different. In his heart he was as much Mayan as any of them. Fear darkened even the brightest summer days.

Then the explosion. The watcher had been taking a bath in the luxurious tub with running water that was something of a marvel locally. It was a huge cast-iron tub with clawed feet, the likes of which he'd only seen in movies since.

He had felt the rumbling, and had known it was an earthquake as he watched the water slosh wildly in the tub, nearly jumping out onto the asphalt-tiled floor. He heard his mother scream. Then came a huge rumble that turned the world topsy-turvy. The last thing he remembered was the feeling that he was flying.

When they found him, he was under the overturned tub, dehydrated and scared almost witless. His home was gone, his parents were gone, and the entire village was burned to the ground. He wasn't supposed to see as they carried him out, but he did. He saw the grotesquely twisted and burned bodies of the people who had been his friends and protectors.

He had never forgotten, and even after he was shipped back to the States to live with an aunt and uncle, he had felt the curse hovering over him, waiting for the moment to strike.

Then, like an answer from the jaguar god, he had learned that Anna's father had been on the pipeline team that had found Pocal's tomb. In an instant, it had become perfectly clear to him. He must offer her heart to appease the jaguar god.

"Are you okay, buddy?"

Startled, he lifted his head and found one of the cops who were watching Anna's house staring down at him.

For an instant he was rattled, almost panicked. Then, as if some blessing came down from on high, the answer was there.

"I think I'm a little dehydrated. Tough game."

The cop nodded. "Want me to call an ambulance?"

"I think I can make it home." The watcher managed a shrug. "I forgot to take my Gatorade with me."

"Hang on a minute. I've got some bottled water in the car."

That sense of pleasant thrill came back to the watcher. It was a sign, he thought. A good sign. He was doing the right thing. And he was invincible.

The cop gave him a liter bottle of water, chilled from an ice chest in the trunk. "Drink it before you try to go home," he said to the watcher.

"Thanks, I really appreciate it."

"No problem, buddy."

Which was how the watcher came to be sitting in plain sight, with an unobstructed view of Anna's house when Tebbins pulled up.

Sipping his water, he watched as Tebbins approached the cops. They talked about him, he knew, because Tebbins and the cop both looked his way. But Tebbins apparently accepted the explanation and recrossed the street to go into Anna's house.

He put his head down quickly when Anna opened the door, not wanting her to notice and recognize him. Although she probably wouldn't. He was one of those unmemorable people, which had always galled him, but now it was a great advantage. Out of context, she probably wouldn't even think he was familiar.

The water was gone, and he no longer had an excuse to linger. Standing, he picked up the ball and continued his walk down the street. This time he didn't dribble the ball or pretend to practice any fancy moves. As he passed the cops, he nodded to the guy who'd given him the water. "Thanks a bunch," he called out.

The cop waved, then went back to his conversation with the other officer.

Invisible. He was invisible. A fierce joy began to fill him, along with a sense of power.

Too bad he was going to have to kill Anna. He liked her. He admired her. But that was part of the price he would have to pay.

He was just rounding the corner, escaping the gaze of the cops, when it struck him that maybe he wasn't worrying enough about Tebbins and the St. Pete cop. He'd figured that Anna would be one of their top suspects by now, but maybe she wasn't. Because if she was, what was Garcia doing having dinner with her, and what was Tebbins doing visiting her on a Friday evening?

A prickle of fear filled him. He might have to do something about those cops, too.

CHAPTER FIFTEEN

Tebbins always had a sense of disorientation upon first sight of the Lundgren sisters. They were so much alike at a glance that it always threw him. After a few minutes he could tell who was who by their differences in voice and expression, but it always baffled him at first. He'd known identical twins before, but none so alike that he wasn't able to fix on some landscape feature, such as a small mole, to tell them apart.

Anna and Nancy didn't have any such helpful markings. It had been easy the first day, when their taste in clothing had set them clearly apart, but sitting here now in identical khaki shorts and matching royal blue halter tops, they might have been duplicate photocopies.

Until he realized that Anna was looking irri-

231

tably at him, and Nancy was looking eagerly at him, sort of like a wolf eyeing a juicy piece of meat. Neither of their expressions made him any more comfortable.

"Do you two always dress alike?" he asked.

Nancy answered. "Only this week. I'm trying to make it harder for a killer to identify my sister—which I wouldn't have to do if you were doing *your* job."

"I *am* doing my job."

"No, you're not," Anna said firmly. "Your mind is already made up. You think I did it. Or that Nancy did it. Or that we both did it together. What you *don't* think is that someone else is doing this."

He gave her a grumpy look and tugged hard on his moustache. "Now you claim to read minds?"

"It's not hard. You've stopped doing any investigating at the museum, you're not checking out the security system any further. Therefore, you think you already know who, and all you have to do is wait until you catch me red-handed somehow and I'll explain the how of it. But you're wrong, Tebbins. I didn't do it. So why the hell aren't you checking out the *hows* anymore?"

"We are."

"Yeah, right." She settled back in her chair and regarded him disapprovingly. "Why don't you tell me exactly what you're doing?"

"I can't. It would compromise an ongoing investigation."

"Sure." She compressed her lips. "Let me

guess. You're doing background checks galore, which won't tell you a damn thing except who took a joyride in high school and who has a shoplifting record. Unless, of course, you stumble on someone who's been charged with robbing a museum before."

"That's routine…"

"Right. Routine. What I'm concerned about is the nonroutine things you're not doing."

"I can't discuss that. Except, of course, we're going to give Nancy a chance to look for this back door she told Garcia about."

"Cool beans," Nancy said. "When?"

"Sunday. The security company needs that long to set it up with the techs."

Nancy frowned. "And maybe hide the evidence."

"Trust me," Tebbins said, "we're making sure they don't have access to the system."

"Except over the phone line." Nancy slapped her hand on the arm of the sofa. "Brilliant, Watson."

Tebbins sighed. "Holmes never said that, you know."

"Really?" Nancy rolled her eyes.

Tebbins twisted one end of his moustache around a finger. "There's a lot to be done in a case like this. We can't do it all at once. Nor can we afford to rush ahead in ways that might cost us important information. You ladies will just have to be patient."

Anna spoke. "Have you even reviewed the surveillance tapes from the night of the robbery?"

"Certainly we have. And we haven't discovered any anomalies. Unfortunately, there are some gaps."

"Gaps?" Anna leaned forward.

"As I'm sure you know, there is no surveillance in any of the offices, bathrooms, or the break room, and none in the hallways in the office areas."

"Major oversight," Nancy muttered.

"Actually not," Anna answered, turning to her sister. "It was explained when we put in the system. People refuse to work in places where they feel they're being constantly watched, and they won't eat in the presence of cameras. So..."

"Cripes," Nancy sighed.

"Exactly," Tebbins said. "So we have the problem of the guard disappearing a number of times during his shift. We also have the problem of the surveillance cameras in the exhibit showing that no one entered all night."

Anna threw up a hand. "Then obviously they were doctored."

"Obviously," Tebbins said drily. "Another so-called impossibility. We're still trying to figure out how it was done. Maybe Nancy can show us."

Nancy looked at her sister. "I don't like the way he said that."

"Me neither."

Tebbins shrugged. "Right now everyone is suspect."

"But mostly me," Anna said. "And I'm supposed to feel safe because you have two cars parked in front of my house. It didn't make me safe last night, did it?"

"Actually, it makes you a lot safer. Not even you could persuade those officers to accept any coffee."

Anna jumped up from her chair. "See, that's exactly what I mean! This weirdo could come along and shoot them both, but I'm safe because I can't give them coffee. Like I drugged the cop last night. Like I would be so stupid!"

Tebbins offered only a shrug and a quiet smile almost masked by playing with his moustache. Jeez, Anna thought, he really does work that prop for all it's worth. The quiet staring contest continued for almost a full minute before Tebbins finally spoke. "What would *you* have me do?"

"I think it's obvious," Anna said, aware that the color was rising in her cheeks. She began ticking off points on her fingers. "It had to have been an inside job. Someone who was familiar with the exhibit and the security. Someone who could move around the museum, anywhere, at any time of day, without anyone paying much attention. Someone everyone thinks they know and thinks they can trust. That's who you're looking for."

"You've just described yourself pretty well," Tebbins said mildly.

"Is intellectual myopia part of police training," Nancy cut in, "or did you come by that naturally?"

Tebbins huffed. Actually *huffed*, Anna thought. She was reminded of the Labrador retriever her aunt had owned. Tebbins had made the exact huff she'd heard so often when the dog had been shooed out from under the table or off the sofa. A huff of polite disgust, as if to say "I ought to be above such indignities."

Which was very close to the truth of what Tebbins was thinking. There were many insults he could endure in good grace. He'd never been handsome, and he knew it. He'd always been a bit of an oddball, and he'd known that too. For him, retreat had come in the intricate intellectual puzzles found in the true crime and mystery books he'd read endlessly until he reached the point where he could sniff out the killer long before the hero was even on the right track. He'd become a cop because it seemed to be the one profession that took advantage of a skill he had fostered and developed through countless hours of childhood and adolescent escape reading murder mysteries. And which he'd fostered further with years of real-world experience, often spent working alongside and sometimes for the very kinds of jocks and "Big Men On Campus" he'd so studiously avoided in his youth.

He'd put up with their squad-room antics, their inability to understand him, their brash mannerisms, because the job gave him an opportunity to put to good use one defining feature of his identity: He *was not* intellectually myopic. He could wander around a case and watch the vectors of motive, means, and opportunity coalesce almost as if they physically materialized from the ether.

And that, he realized with an uneasy clarity, had not happened in this case. Nancy's barb cut close to the bone not only because it flew in the face of everything he liked to believe about himself, but also, he realized, because it was true. Lacking those almost tangible psychic signposts that normally guided him—what others called intuition but he thought of as the hallmark of genius—he *was* walking down the path of least resistance.

He huffed again, this time at himself, and more forcefully because of that. He reached deep inside for something that would pass for a conciliatory smile. "Shall we dispense with the insults and focus on the case?"

"I suppose we could," Anna said. "If you could manage to stop insulting my sister and me by treating us like prime suspects in the robbery of an exhibit I worked for eighteen months to put together, and the murder of a bright young man whom I liked."

He opened his hands. "It's not personal, Ms. Lundgren. It's the job."

Nancy let out a bitter laugh. "It's not personal. I love that one. That's what the mob killers tell their victims in the movies. 'It's not personal, Mr. Rigatoni. It's just business.'" She fixed him with a glare. "Well, Tebbins, it's personal to us."

He nodded. "I can see where it would be. Were I in your shoes, I'm sure I'd be equally uncomfortable. So... I ask again. What would *you* have me do?"

"There can't be that many people at the museum who have all of the right connections to pull this off," Nancy argued. "But I'm sure there are more than just Anna."

Anna nodded. "That's true. I mean, they've all been through the exhibit at one time or another, probably. But knowing enough to come and go without a trace...that means someone who worked on the security, or who was at least around when it was being installed. That ought to narrow the field some."

Tebbins nodded again, and busied himself with his moustache for a moment. "Can you get me a list of the people who were working at the museum when the security was installed?"

"Sure," Anna said. "But of course, I'll be on the list."

"So you will," he said. "So you will."

Anna shrugged. "Just as long as I'm not the only one on the list. You can rule out Ivar right from the top. That man couldn't tell a circuit from linguine. But there are the security people, too, Tebbins. Dinah and her techs. They'd be the best people to bypass their own system."

He wagged his finger at her. "See? You underestimate me. We're already looking into that very closely. The problem there is motive."

Nancy shifted impatiently. "Why? There's a lot of money involved."

"To be sure." Sitting back in his chair, he smiled. "But you see, there is a major difficulty with money as a motivator in this case."

"Why?" Nancy threw up her hands. "A quarter of a mil is a quarter of a mil."

But Anna shook her head. "No, Nance, he's right. That dagger is very identifiable. It's a one of a kind. If the thief was after money, he'd have been smarter to help himself to the gold artifacts. He could at least melt them down."

"Exactly," Tebbins said, beaming at her as if she were a bright pupil. "Very few thieves would have the connections to fence an article of that kind. So, we are looking for someone who is acquisitive, or someone who is in the employ of a collector—or someone who isn't interested in the money at all."

Anna sighed. "Why do I have the feeling I fit at least one of those categories."

"Actually," said Tebbins, "you fit all of them. You could be a collector." He glanced toward the replicas on her shelf. "After all, I have only your word for it that those items on your book case aren't real."

"Jeez." Anna nearly groaned the word. "You know, you could take those to any antiquarian who specializes in MesoAmerican artifacts and verify that they're replicas. Help yourself. Pack them up and take them."

"I just might. Then, of course, being in the museum business, you probably have a great many contacts that could put you in touch with a collector."

"Not that I'm aware of."

He shrugged. "I have only your word for that. And finally, my dear Ms. Lundgren, you have a personal interest in the dagger."

Anna looked at her sister. "I think I'd arrest me, too."

"Well, I wouldn't," Nancy said stoutly. "It's just too absurd. Why in the world would you have told the board about your personal connection with the dagger if you were planning to steal it? You're smarter than that, Anna. You wouldn't have mentioned our dad to anyone. You certainly wouldn't have told enough people that it wound up in the papers."

Tebbins leaned forward. "You told the board about your father? Why?"

"Because I was trying to keep them from ballyhooing the curse in the promotions. First of all, I didn't think that would be scientific. But mostly, well..." She flushed. "I didn't want all that raked up again."

"Hmm." He stroked his moustache thoughtfully.

"I guess I was stupid," Anna said sadly. "Someone sure ran to the press with the story."

"Someone who means you no good, I'm sure," her sister said darkly. "What about that person?" she demanded of Tebbins. "Maybe the thief just wanted to ruin Anna."

"We're looking at that, too," Tebbins said. Reaching into his breast pocket, he pulled out a pad. "There's a certain person...ah, here it is...Peter Dashay. I understand he created a scene in the lobby the day after the theft."

"Peter?" Anna almost laughed. "The thought of him skulking around in the middle of the night to rob a museum... God, that's hysterical."

"Why?" asked Tebbins. "He seems very angry with you."

She shrugged. "His male pride is wounded."

"That could be enough, with some men."

Anna shook her head. "I don't think so, not

him. He's got a touch of the petty tyrant, but otherwise he's a wuss."

"You gotta watch those wusses," Nancy said. "They're the ones who can go off on you."

Tebbins didn't comment. He just made a note on his pad. "Is there anyone else who might have a grudge against you?"

"Oh, probably," Anna answered. "But I don't know who. Nobody's been overt about it."

"Well then." He put his notebook away. "Get me that list of people who were at the museum when the security system was installed. People who maybe hung around more than average, who asked a lot of questions. We're also getting ready to interview all the employees one more time."

"Why?" Nancy asked.

"Because they're no longer shocked by the burglary and death. Because they've had some time to think about it, and some of them might have begun to remember little things that seemed out of place."

"He's not so dumb," Nancy remarked after Tebbins left.

"No," Anna agreed. "But he's still tightening the noose around me."

Sunday morning, Gil returned Trina to her mother. It was always a wrenching experience for him, like cutting out part of his own heart. After five years he ought to be used to it, but he was beginning to think he never would be.

The hug she gave him was stiff, reluctant. She was still mad at him about Jamie, he supposed, but he wasn't prepared to back down, and he didn't know any other way to smooth things over.

Rina, his ex, regarded him with disapproval after Trina had gone inside. "Well," she said, "it looks like you put on another sterling show of fatherhood this week."

Irritation surged in him. As far as Rina was concerned, he could do no right. "I did," he said flatly. "I told her I don't want her seeing Jamie anymore."

"Bright," she answered sarcastically. "We'll have our very own version of the Montagues and Capulets."

He shook his head, feeling the old exasperation return as if it had never waned. "I want to talk to you about that."

She looked to the heavens, as if seeking patience. "You know, Gil, you have to stop filtering everything in the world through that cop lens of yours. Your daughter's fifteen, and she's going to date whether you like it or not."

"I know that. But I'd be a neglectful parent if I didn't step in when my daughter's boyfriend refused to bring her home, kicked sand at her in a fit of rage, and threatened to hit her. She had to come home with someone else."

Something in Rina's face flickered, temporarily obliterating her impatient expression. Guilt? Was he seeing guilt? Was her boyfriend treating *her* this way? Or had she known of previous instances of Jamie treating their daughter this way? "He hasn't done this kind of thing before, has he?" Gil asked.

"No. No. Look, I'll talk to her about it, okay?"

"It's going to take more than talking. She's refusing to listen to sense. She keeps apologizing for him, saying he's just mad. But they're not kids in a sandbox anymore, Rina."

"I know," said Rina. Her face closing, she turned away without saying good-bye and marched into her house.

In his car, Gil had to resist the urge to slam his fist on the dashboard. Parenting by remote control was impos-sible.

He worried about his daughter all the way across the bay, but as soon as he reached the museum, he had to put it on hold. That was considerably easier to do when he saw Anna in the lobby.

She looked great in a green pantsuit. He felt again that pull, that awareness that made him want to stand taller and puff out his chest a bit. That made him want to smile. He forced it down.

Nancy was there, too, wearing shorts and a gray T-shirt with a cowboy hat and boots. Very Texan, he supposed. Or very Nancy.

He greeted them both, then asked, "Where is everybody?"

"I don't know," Anna said. "But it's only a few minutes past ten."

"Fifteen to be precise," Nancy remarked. "I guess everyone is on mañana time."

"We're waiting for Tebbins and the security people, right?"

The women nodded at him.

"When does the exhibit open for the day?"

"At noon," Anna answered.

"So nobody's around right now?"

"Just the guard," Anna said, with a nod in the direction of the security booth, which was next to the ticket windows.

"But the front doors are unlocked."

"I guess he figures since we're waiting for an invasion of cops and security people, we're okay."

That bothered Gil. He would have thought ordinary security procedures would have dictated otherwise. "Excuse me for a moment?"

"Sure."

He felt her gaze on him as he walked over to the glassed-in security room and flashed his badge through the window.

The guard called to come on in. So even the booth wasn't locked. Thoughtfully, he rapped on the window as he entered and realized it was bulletproof. Bulletproof glass, but the door was open. Brilliant.

Inside, he smiled at the guard who was sitting in a wheeled gray office chair before a two-tiered bank of large TV monitors, each split into four pictures. At his elbow was a large foam cup of coffee. He was wearing the gray uniform of a well-known security guard company, and carried a pistol in a holster on his belt, along with a large key ring. The man himself was middle-aged, balding, and a bit paunchy.

"What can I do for you, Officer?" the guard asked. His nameplate announced that he was J. Wiggins.

"I was just wondering about what you do in here all day. And how you manage to stay awake."

"Pull up a stool."

Gil did so, sitting a few feet away and scanning all the screens. "Does it ever get overwhelming to watch all these monitors?"

"Nah. It's busier during the day, obviously, but mostly you just have to keep an eye out for something unusual. So I don't really *look* at them, if you know what I mean. I just kind of sit here and scan until something grabs my attention."

"How often does that happen?"

"Oh, maybe a couple dozen times a day now that the Maya exhibit's so busy. Mostly it's just kids acting up in front of the monitors. Sometimes it's couples having a quarrel." He shook his head and grinned. "Sometimes I wish we had audio."

"I bet you do."

"Reminds me of the *Honeymooners*." The guard swiveled his chair a bit and began pointing at the various monitors. "These are on the exhibit upstairs, the one about the sunken galleon. That's not too busy right now because they're rebuilding it since they moved it. Mostly there's someone there only on weekdays or Saturday, and it's people I recognize, staff mainly, and volunteers."

Gil nodded.

"These here are the public places, the upstairs and downstairs lobbies, the ticket booth. Over here is the outside doors, all of 'em, and that one's shipping and receiving.

That gets hectic every now and again. And these over here are the Pocal exhibit. Lots of 'em.''

Gil nodded. "What if you want to see better than this?''

"Oh, that's easy.'' He used a mouse to click on one of the images, and it immediately filled the whole screen. "And see? With this knob here, I can zoom in.'' To demonstrate, he did so with a flourish, bringing the empty dagger case into screen-filling relief. A moment later, he zoomed back to normal view and clicked again, restoring the four-way picture split.

Gil glanced at the lobby monitors and saw Anna and Nancy in two of the images, from different angles. They were together and talking. He imagined with that zoom that he could probably read their lips.

"What about the halls and offices that aren't under surveillance?''

"Well, in the daytime it don't matter much because everybody's here. But when we're closed, I'm supposed to get up every half hour and take a stroll around.''

"So somebody could be in one of the offices and no one would know?''

"I would, sooner or later. I suppose they could hide if they was careful, but...'' He shrugged. "What's the point in hiding? You can't do anything.''

Gil nodded as if he agreed. "Did you know Eddy Malacek?''

"That kid that was killed? Yeah, sorta. I mean, I switched off with him a couple of times, we chatted for five or ten, then we'd part ways.

He seemed nice enough. Pretty reliable, too. He never kept me waiting. I was kinda leery when the company told me the contract required them to hire some students for part-time work, but Eddy was a good egg. Seemed to take it seriously." Wiggins shook his head woefully. "He had big dreams, I guess."

"Big dreams, how?"

"Oh, I just meant him going to graduate school and all. Him and his girlfriend both, he said. Must've wanted to get somewhere real bad."

Then Wiggins laughed. "I wanted to get somewhere, too. Problem was, I didn't look far enough down the road."

"What did you do?" Gil asked, smiling.

"Oh, I was in too much of a hurry. Jumped right into construction from high school. Figured I'd work my way to the top. Made it to site supervisor up in Ohio, then the wife got arthritis pretty bad, and the doc said she'd do better in a warm climate, so down we came. Pay's not as good here."

"So I've heard."

Wiggins nodded sagely. "No unions. It's a right-to-work state." He guffawed. "Right-to-get-fired state, they mean."

"Did you get fired?"

"I wish. Naw, I fell, broke my back in two places. So here I sit, getting older and fatter, and I just don't see getting to the top of my profession." He laughed again. "This *is* the top."

Gil had to laugh with him. But he had another question he wanted to ask, ever since

Wiggins had mentioned that Eddy never kept him waiting.

"So," he said when Wiggins's laughter eased. "Some of these guys keep you waiting, huh?"

He wanted to kick himself almost as soon as he spoke, because Wiggins's face suddenly shuttered.

"No big deal," the guard said flatly. "Sometimes somebody'll get here late. Could happen to any one of us. Traffic, whatever."

"How late?" Gil persisted. He couldn't make it any worse now.

"A few minutes."

"How many? Ten, fifteen?"

"A *few.*"

And that was the end of it. But Gil made a mental note to have Tebbins check more closely on the guard who had relieved Eddy. Something about the way Wiggins had mentioned the tardiness originally suggested that he was bugged by at least one person's lateness. Someone who maybe did it almost all the time.

A flicker of movement in the corner of Gil's eye caught his attention, and he turned to look at the monitors. Nothing. "Is anyone in the building except the four of us?"

Wiggins shook his head. "Just us ducks."

"I thought I saw something move on one of these monitors." He pointed.

"I didn't see anything. These things can be jumpy, you know. Sometimes you get a little glitch and one of the pictures will roll a bit, or flicker. Probably all you saw."

"Maybe." But he was staring at the loading-dock feeds anyway. "Are the exit doors alarmed?"

"All except the front ones, yeah. Doesn't much matter. Nobody can open them from the outside."

"Can the alarms be turned off?"

"Yeah. Naturally. They're code doors."

"Code doors?"

"Fire-code doors. Somebody pushes one of them suckers open, and the fire alarms go off. You gotta be able to silence them. You'd be surprised how many jokers think it's fun to do that."

Actually, Gil wouldn't, but he didn't say so. At that moment the lobby doors opened and Tebbins arrived, trailing Dinah Hudson and two scraggly-looking guys, both carrying laptops, in T-shirts and shorts, one of them pasty pale. It was unusual in Florida to see anyone that pale unless he was sick. You didn't have to sunbathe on the beach to get a tan; all you had to do was walk to your car across a mall parking lot every now and then.

So the guy was a mole. Probably spent his weekdays in a windowless room at the security firm, and the rest of his time glued to computer games.

He rose from his stool. "Thanks for all the help, Mr. Wiggins."

"Sure. Anytime." But the invitation was cautious.

Out in the lobby, the first words out of Tebbins's mouth were an apology. "Sorry we're late," he said. "There was a severe acci-

249

dent on 275, and Dinah and her crew were stuck behind it. They called to let me know they were going to be late." He shrugged. "I checked on it, and I figured they'd be tied up there for a couple of hours. I had to go rescue them."

The pasty guy spoke. "It's kind of cool to have the cops escort you past all those stuck cars." He grinned. "How many times did we get flipped off, Dinah?"

She shrugged. "I wasn't counting. I don't pay attention to that stuff." She waved a hand. "These are my two best techs, Turk and Boomer." Turk was the pale one. "No, that's not their real names but they won't answer to anything else. Turk's the software wiz, and Boomer does the hardware."

Nancy looked the two over. "Why Turk and Boomer?"

Boomer answered. "Because he's a software turkey, and I..." He shrugged. "Let's just say that when I first started, I made a few things go boom."

Turk chortled. "Man, that was totally awesome. We had sparks and smoke-downs going everywhere. I wish I'd brought the marshmallows."

"Ignore them," Dinah said. "Unlike most people, they learn from their mistakes. Give them a problem, and they're bulldogs. Smart bulldogs."

Turk looked at Boomer. "You wanna be bull or dog?"

"You're full of more bull than I am. Me, I'm a hound dog. Just give me the scent, baby."

He tipped his head back and howled like a wolf baying at the moon.

Dinah rolled her eyes, but Anna and Nancy both laughed. Gil and Tebbins exchanged looks but otherwise didn't react.

Dinah looked at the women. "Which one of you is Nancy?"

"I am," Nancy said. With Turk and Boomer in the room, she no longer looked so outrageous in her strange outfit.

"I should have guessed," Dinah said with a small, humorless smile. "I'm going to tell you right now that we don't have any back doors. That's strictly forbidden. It would compromise our systems."

Nancy smiled tightly. "It may be forbidden, but I know my colleagues."

Boomer spoke. "Aww, take it easy, gals. Dinah, you know it's possible. Turk and me set the whole thing up for you, but we're not the only ones who actually work on it. Something could get slipped by us."

Dinah looked disapprovingly at him. "You guys are supposed to prevent that."

"Mostly we do. The guys who work under us know we've got our eyeballs on 'em and their work. But I don't believe in impossibilities. I never have. What about you, Turk?"

"It could happen," Turk said with a shrug. "Not likely, but definitely possible."

"And more possible with a system like this," Boomer observed. "I've been working on it since the theft, and I haven't found anything yet, but this is a customized, complex system. It might have shortfalls we haven't even figured out yet." He looked at Nancy and nearly leered. "A fresh pair of eyes could be useful."

"Eyes are all you're going to get," Nancy said with a toss of her head. "Eyes and my brains."

They moved then to the room that held the brains for the system. Tebbins arched a brow when he found the door unlocked. "Why isn't this room locked?"

"It should be," Dinah said. "But museum personnel have the key, too."

"But it's not necessary, dude," Turk said. "Anybody fiddles with the equipment, we get an alarm."

"Apparently not," Tebbins said drily, motioning everyone in before him.

Gil drew him aside. "I saw something funny on the security monitors just before you arrived. I think I'll take a stroll around."

"Avoid the exhibits. The motion detectors should be on."

"It was from the loading-dock area."

"Want some backup?"

Gil shook his head. "Not necessary. The guard thinks I just saw a screen flicker. He says it happens all the time."

"Okay. Send up a flare if you need me."

As he walked away, Gil heard Turk say, "It could have been solar flares, man. Didn't you hear how they messed up a bunch of radio stations earlier this week?"

"Right," Boomer answered. "Like the guy could count on that."

"Hey, it was just a suggestion."

Shaking his head, Gil moved away, into the silent depths of the museum.

CHAPTER SIXTEEN

Around a corner their voices faded away. Around another corner, and Gil could have believed he was alone in the building.

Except he didn't feel like it. Crazy as it sounded, he had the sense that there was something else present. Or someone else, other than the people in the equipment room and the guard.

The back of his neck started prickling as he moved along silent corridors, and a weight grew between his shoulder blades. Something or someone was aware of him.

He caught the thought, turned it around in his head as he reached the lobby again. *Something?* He'd been in creepy situations before, where he was looking for an armed perp in the dark of some deserted building, but the word *something* had never entered his head.

He wanted to shake his head, brush it off, but he couldn't quite do it. There was something different about the feeling he was getting, and he couldn't quite define it. Something larger than the nastiness of the average murderer or thief.

Reality check time, he told himself. This case

was affecting him in ways he didn't like, and had never experienced before. Take Anna. He'd never been anywhere near this attracted to a suspect before, and certainly not to the extent that she was invading his dreams.

It wasn't that he didn't sometimes become involved. There had been some juveniles he'd really felt for and had tried to help. There'd been some battered spouses he'd gotten really angry for. It wasn't that he didn't give a damn about the people he ran into in the course of his work.

But not like this.

And now weird fancies about *something*? Definitely time for a reality check.

Ignoring the feeling, he marched himself over to the security booth and told Wiggins he was going to the loading dock.

"Hold on just a minute," Wiggins said. "No point in having the motion detectors start screaming."

He reached for the key ring on his belt and pulled it. A retractable cord extended, allowing him to slip a key into a slot. Then he punched a code into his keyboard.

"Okay," he said. "They're off."

"So you have to have both a code and a key?"

"You bet. And they'll call me anyway, asking about the turnoff. Pretty good system, huh?"

Gil nodded, although he had a few doubts about that, for obvious reasons.

"How many people have the key?" He supposed Tebbins had asked that question, but if so, he hadn't passed the information on to Gil.

"Just the desk guard. We hand off at change of shift."

"Nobody else?"

"I suppose the security company does."

"And how do you know the codes?"

"Each guard has his own code. And the different sections of the system are numbered, so it's a combination. A mixed-up combination. Not likely anyone could guess."

Not that it matters, Gil thought. There was no record of a turnoff the night of the robbery.

"Thanks," he said, and headed back into the depths of the building.

Once he got out of the lobby, the feeling started to return. The sense of not being alone. The sense of being watched. There was no one around, though, and nobody could move as fast as he was going without making some noise.

Nobody was following him. But maybe someone was evading him?

He could feel the adrenaline beginning to pump into his blood, heightening his senses, calming his brain. The cold air that trickled down his neck from overhead vents felt like ice. Every shadow seemed darker and more ominous. He could hear the echo of his steps off the walls, even though his shoes were soft-soled.

Reaching under his jacket, he pulled out his gun. Its weight was reassuring in his hand. Only twice in his career had he needed to fire it other than on the shooting range, and he hoped that didn't change now.

The large metal doors marked SHIP-PING/RECEIVING were unlocked. He hadn't asked for a key, and Wiggins hadn't offered him one, which probably meant the doors were kept unlocked most of the time. Which also meant that folks around the museum were relying too damn much on the electronic security. He needed to check into that.

Cautiously he pushed the door open and waited. No sound. Nothing moved. He stepped into the cavernous room and listened to the door swing shut behind him, closing with a thud.

The room was two stories high with a freight elevator that went up to an oversize garage door on the second floor. It smelled of wood, stale sweat, damp concrete, and oil. Stacked everywhere were wooden packing crates and smaller metal shipping containers. The left side of the room had large signs painted on the wall, all of them saying the same thing: RECEIVING.

The right side was labeled SHIPPING, and a smaller cordoned off area was marked EMPTY CONTAINERS. It at once looked both organized and disorganized. He figured there were one, at most two people, who actually knew what was going on in the area to the last detail.

It was also a great hiding place, and his neck was prickling like mad. He could sense someone else's presence the way a dog could scent a trail hours after the animal had passed, and his eyes were noting each and every nook and cranny that could conceal his prey. Or his hunter.

Someone was hiding from him. Someone who was dangerous. Lifting his gun to the ready, he began to move along the stacks of boxes, figuring that when he got close enough, he'd flush his quarry. He mentally cursed the *whiff* of his own jacket against his slacks, certain that if he could hear it, the other presence could, too.

He figured Wiggins was watching him. The guard had probably also figured out that something was going on by the way Gil was moving and holding his gun. Almost as good as a backup.

But part of him was still refusing to believe there was someone in here. What would be the point? Nothing was happening, and nothing *would* happen until tomorrow. With all the surveillance and motion detectors in this room, it just didn't add up. He wouldn't be able to steal anything, or learn anything while hiding around here.

So maybe he wasn't really hiding. Maybe he'd come in just ahead of Gil. Maybe he'd been slipping just ahead as Gil walked through the building.

Why?

The thoughts that occurred to him weren't pleasant. In fact, they began to make him feel as if he were the stalkee rather than the stalker.

Gripping his pistol tighter, he started to check behind crates.

Wiggins, watching from the relative comfort of the security booth, was beginning to think the cop was a crazy man. There couldn't be anyone or anything that moved in that room. Until he'd turned off the motion detectors, nobody could've gotten in or out without setting them off. Hell, two weeks ago a *mouse* had set the damn things off. It wasn't supposed to be able to, of course, but apparently the rodent had done something just so, and had interrupted the beam just enough.

That had been a bit of fun.

But today? No. Not possible.

So why the hell was that cop creeping around like he was sure someone was in the room? Maybe because he was?

The idea unsettled Wiggins, who began to think about what he maybe ought to do. Get more help? Go help the guy himself? But he wasn't supposed to leave his station except on his regular checks, and the rest of the day guards weren't due in for another twenty minutes.

But that sounded like overkill anyway. There was nobody in that room except the cop, and just because he was skulking around like he thought there was didn't mean it was time to call in the Marines.

So he sat there watching and feeling his own uneasiness grow.

Anna, who'd been hovering in the background while her sister talked of arcane things such as subroutines and objects with Turk and Boomer, felt herself growing more and more nervous.

"What's taking Gil so long?" she finally asked Tebbins.

He glanced at his watch. "I don't know. I'll give him another five, then go looking."

"Maybe I'll go talk to the guard."

Tebbins hesitated. "You sure you want to be walking those corridors alone? There's no surveillance on them."

She was simultaneously aware that it might well be foolhardy to wander around and equally aware that if anything at all happened, she wanted to be under Tebbins's eagle eye so he couldn't blame her for it.

But her thoughts kept straying to Gil.

"You know," Tebbins murmured to her, "I never asked you what scenario this guy might be playing out if he really believes in the curse."

A shiver passed down her spine. Only through strenuous effort had she managed to keep herself focused on the theft as a theft, and the links to the curse as some kind of taunting. She really did *not* want to believe that someone out there believed in the curse and was using it in some twisted way. "I don't know," she said finally. "I guess it would depend on how he saw his own role."

"Such as?"

"I don't know. Maybe as an avenger?"

"For the tomb desecration?"

"Maybe. Or maybe just because we have the dagger here. Maybe he thinks we're desecrating it by putting it on display."

"Hmm. What else?"

She shrugged. "Beats me. I suppose, given

the things that have been in the paper, that he might see himself as carrying out the final stages of the curse."

"Final stages?"

"Sure. If this guy figures my father was responsible for the tomb's discovery, he might figure that Nancy and I are cursed, too. Unto the second generation, the legend says. I told you that, didn't I?"

He looked away, watching the three heads bent together over the console, at the stacks of videotapes in the automatic cartridge changers, at Dinah Hudson, who seemed to be viewing the whole process with disapproval, although from time to time she made a suggestion.

"So," he said slowly, "imagine that he thinks the latter. That makes both you and your sister the objects, right?"

"Right." Anna felt a great weight settle in her. "Nance and I have discussed that."

"It would have been nice if you'd discussed it with *me*." His sharp eyes settled on her, and he gave his moustache an almost sensuous stroke.

Her temper flared just a little. "It would be a whole lot easier to discuss things with you if I didn't feel you were twisting everything I say to match your belief in my guilt."

"I don't believe in your guilt. But I'd be a fool to ignore the large number of coincidences and possibilities that seem to hover around you."

"I suppose. Well, you'll have your answer after he cuts out my heart."

Tebbins was plainly shocked. "You don't mean that seriously!"

Anna herself was startled by what she'd just blurted. Not once had she even considered such a thing. It must have popped out of her deepest subconscious. But she didn't want Tebbins to know that. She didn't want him to think her capable of wild statements. "Why not? If this guy is really wrapped up in the curse, there's a chance he believes in the old ways. And if he does, the most appropriate thing he could do would be to cut out our living hearts and make an offering of them."

"Jesus Christ." It was the first time Tebbins had said such a thing—swearing—in her presence, and it conveyed his reaction more adequately than a hundred other words might have.

But Anna didn't want to think about being a human sacrifice. The very notion sickened her and terrified her with its enormity. She couldn't afford to start thinking about that or she'd wind up a gibbering idiot.

"I'm worried about Gil," she said again. "He's been gone way too long."

Wiggins saw it happen. He saw the impossibly huge cat suddenly leap toward Gil, he saw Gil take an instinctive step back. But not far enough.

Gil heard an almost inaudible scrape against wood crating and spun around, gun leveled.

What he saw was a huge cat leaping toward him. It was the biggest damn cat he'd ever seen outside a zoo, ginger in color, with large green eyes. Feral eyes. A second too late, he recognized the terror in them.

As he jumped back, a crate crashed onto him.

Wiggins leapt up from the console, but not before he saw a flash of something else moving. He couldn't make out what it was. It disappeared behind another box too quickly.

Grabbing his radio, he called the campus police for backup. Then he abandoned his post, stopping just long enough to lock the door behind him.

Running past the corridor where the equipment room was, he called out, "Trouble at the loading dock! Cop's been hurt." Then he forced himself to speed up, and wished he were fifteen years younger and thirty pounds lighter.

Tebbins heard the guard's shout. So did all of them. He scanned the startled faces. "You all stay here. Lock the door behind me."

Dinah nodded, but Anna started to follow him as he hurried out of the room.

"Don't be stupid," he said sharply. "You can't help."

She nodded and fell back, but he saw the worry and fear in her eyes.

On his way to Shipping, Tebbins radioed for backup. In five minutes the place would be crawling with cops. None too soon. He drew his gun. It didn't make him feel any safer.

He reached the doors of Shipping almost at the same instant as the guard. Wiggins was winded.

"Damn, I'm outta shape," Wiggins gasped.

"Too much time at a desk," Tebbins said. But the words came out on autopilot. He was thinking about what lay behind those doors, and whether Wiggins would be a help or a hindrance. "What happened?"

"Hell, I don't know. This giant cat leapt out of nowhere at your cop friend, then a huge packing crate fell on him." He paused. "And I think I saw something else moving in there."

Tebbins's mind began to construct scenarios, rapid-fire, one after the other. They all ended at the same place. Gil was hurt, maybe seriously, and if the bad guy was in there, he'd probably use the opportunity to kill Garcia.

"We're going in," Tebbins said. "Unholster your weapon."

Then, hardly were the words out of his mouth when he heard the sound of a huge metal door being raised. A garage door, by the sound of it. *Damn!*

"Don't fire unless you're sure what you're shooting at," he told the guard as he reached for the door and began shoving it open. "Now!"

Gil lay under the packing box, face up, his skin pricked by splinters. The fall had knocked the wind from him, but not for long. The fingers of his right hand still clutched his gun.

Except for minute twitches here and there to test for major injuries, he didn't move. He tried not to breathe, partly so an assailant wouldn't hear him, partly so that he could hear any approach.

There was nothing. He thought he might have heard the padding of paws, but he wasn't sure. He certainly didn't hear any panicked footsteps. What was going on?

Finally, he moved a little, testing to see if he could knock the crate off himself, but found it was too heavy. Lying as he was, he couldn't get the leverage.

He felt about as exposed and helpless as a fly on fly-paper.

Then he heard a loud click, and the sound of the loading door rolling up. A few moments later, another click, the door paused, then began moving again. With a thud, it hit the concrete.

At that instant, another door opened.

"Garcia!" Tebbins shouted.

"I'm okay, but I can't move. I think the guy just slipped out the loading door."

"I'm on it. Stay here, Wiggins. See if you can get that crate off him."

"You got it."

Gil heard Tebbins's remarkably light feet racing across the floor.

"Hey, is *this* the cat?" Tebbins asked.

Then the loading-dock door started rolling again, and Tebbins's footsteps faded away.

The crate moved. Splinters scraped at Gil's

face and his left hand. "Watch it," he said. "I like my skin where it is."

"Sorry, guy. This thing is damn heavy. You sure you don't have any broken bones?"

Gil heard the sound of approaching sirens; backup was arriving. "I don't think so."

"Then maybe we should just wait until the cavalry gets here. Can you breathe okay?"

"Well enough."

"Then we wait," Wiggins said firmly. "It's gonna take more than one old guy with a bad back to get this off of you without turning you into mincemeat."

"Hey, I like mincemeat pie."

Wiggins gave a chuckle. "Not if you're an ingredient."

This is humiliating, Gil thought. Trapped under a crate, unable to be out there with Tebbins hunting for whoever had shoved it down on him. All because a damn cat had startled him. A big cat, unquestionably. But still a cat.

Wiggins spoke, interrupting Gil's self-disgust. "The cat I saw on the monitor was bigger than that tom over there. A lot bigger. Like a panther."

Gil rolled a few frames back in his mind and remembered that insane instant when he'd seen the cat leap toward him. "I don't know," he said. "It was all stretched out. Probably looked bigger that way."

Their discussion ended as the backups began pouring through the door. A minute later, six cops had lifted the crate off Gil without doing any further damage.

Five minutes later, Tebbins returned. "You look great," he told Garcia. "Sort of like a human pincushion."

"Did you spot him?"

Tebbins shook his head. "I didn't see a soul out there. This area of the campus is dead right now, but the university police are still searching. Are you okay?"

"I'm fine."

Tebbins pointed to a large ginger cat that was lying on the floor next to what was probably the garage door control. "There's your cat."

Gil looked at it. "I guess so."

"I'm telling you," said Wiggins, "it ain't the same damn cat. The one I saw was a lot bigger." He spread his arms to indicate the size.

At that moment, the cat reached out a lazy paw and punched the button on the door control. At once the thing began clanging its way down again.

Gil started to laugh. "All that uproar over a damn cat."

Moments later everyone else was laughing with him. All except Wiggins.

Wiggins returned to his post, muttering about strange doings and how he was *damned* if he was ever going to work there alone again.

Gil and Tebbins pretty much ignored him. Neither one of them believed the cat had knocked the crate over; it was too heavy. The question was how someone could have gotten into the room without triggering the motion detectors. They assumed he'd left by way of the garage door when it opened.

"Same problem times two," Tebbins remarked. "I can hardly wait to meet our perp."

"Me too. But for different reasons."

They found a normal-sized door behind boxes on one side of the bay. The arrangement of boxes created a narrow path to it, and there was an opening large enough to accommodate someone trying to open the door. It didn't take long for them to figure out that there was no motion detector on the door.

For good reason. It opened into what appeared to be a blind hallway with several offices, a unisex rest room, and a fire door. Anybody trying to go out that way would trigger the door alarm.

Back in the middle of the room, they stood looking around.

"It must be hard to rely on motion detectors in this room," Gil remarked. "Too much stuff stacked around. So the detectors must all be limited to the doorways."

"It appears so," Tebbins agreed. "And what's this cat doing in here? You'd think people would notice it on the cameras, or that it would trip the alarms occasionally."

"You'd think."

But the answer to that might have been that the cat wasn't supposed to be in the shipping bay. There was a litter box, food, and water in one of the offices.

"So how did it get in *here*?" Tebbins wondered.

"Someone else came in here, and the cat came in with him."

"Obviously. But that leaves the question of how our guy got into those offices without tripping the detectors on the door."

"Do you feel like we're going in circles?"

"Absolutely. Same problem, once again. If we figure out how this guy is evading the motion detectors, we'll have it made."

"If I were you," Gil said, keeping in mind that he was there on sufferance, "I think I'd have the guard turn on the detectors back here right now. Then we see if we can trip them."

"Good idea." Tebbins pulled out his radio and called an officer at the security booth. "Mellors, have the guard in the booth turn on the motion detectors in shipping and receiving again. We're going to see if they work. Let everybody know the alarm is going off."

He hung the radio back on his belt. "Okay. Let's hope it works."

"Actually, I'm hoping they don't work. We might discover his method before he can cover it up again."

"Well, that's what I meant." Tebbins shook his head. "Give me more credit, Garcia. My brain is not one of my shortcomings."

"Did I ever say it was? Besides, I'm the guy who's tangled with this jerk twice already. That's egg on my face, not blood."

Tebbins used two fingers to smooth his

moustache. "I wouldn't say that. But you definitely need to get those splinters removed."

"I will. Later."

Tebbins's radio crackled, and a voice told him the motion detectors were on. Tebbins waved his hand grandly. "You first."

Gil headed for the double doors leading into the corridor, but before he reached them, one of them opened and Anna burst into the room.

"Are you okay, Gil?" she demanded. Then, before he could answer, she turned to Tebbins. "Don't ever leave me locked up like that without information again. I've been out of my mind with worry."

Tebbins looked at Gil. Gil looked at Tebbins. They didn't respond to her.

"I don't hear an alarm," Gil said.

"Nor I."

"Now why do you suppose that is?"

"Oh, if I were feeling grandiose today, it might occur to me that it has something to do with our perp."

"What are you talking about?" Anna demanded.

Gil spoke. "Let's check the loading door."

"Absolutely." Tebbins passed the happy-looking feline on his way, and said, "Open the door, cat."

Much to his and Gil's amazement, the cat pawed at the button, and the door began to rise. Tebbins froze.

"He's trained," Anna said impatiently. "The supervisor taught him the trick. He's been doing it almost since I started here."

"My, my," said Tebbins and continued to the door. "Shouldn't an alarm have gone off when the door opened?"

"We'll have to ask Dinah Hudson," Gil said. "I'd've thought so."

Tebbins stepped out onto the dock, then back into the bay. "Nothing."

"Very interesting," Gil remarked. "Maybe we should check the exhibits, too. But first..."

Tebbins nodded. "We don't leave this room unprotected until we get Hudson and her band of merry men down here to check this out."

Anna spoke. "What in the world is going on? And you have to get those splinters out of your face, Gil. They could get infected."

He turned to her and gingerly smiled. "They can wait a little while. Meanwhile, the motion detectors are on. Did you hear any alarms?"

Her face paled a little, and her eyes widened. "You mean this place is unprotected? My God, we've got a hundred thousand dollars' worth of artifacts in here from the sunken galleon."

"But nothing from the Maya exhibit?"

"No, of course not. That's all in the exhibit..." Her voice trailed off. "Oh, my God, what if the alarms aren't working there?"

She spun on her heel and nearly ran from the room.

"Methinks we lit a fire," Gil remarked. "But she shouldn't be running around in here alone."

"Go after her," Tebbins said. "I can wait for Hudson and the henchmen."

270

Gil paused long enough to arch an inquisitive brow at him. "Do I hear a change of heart?"

"A small shift. A very small shift. She *was*, after all, with *me* when the crate attacked you."

"She was also with her sister when I chased the dweeb all over Temple Terrace. Keep that in mind."

"I keep everything in mind," Tebbins said pleasantly, twisting his moustache. "*Everything*. You'd do well to do the same."

CHAPTER SEVENTEEN

Dweeb. The watcher didn't much like being called that, but he supposed it was better than *creep*. He had more important things on his mind anyway.

He'd screwed up twice, and his life was going to be considerably more difficult. Especially after *this* foul-up. At least after the first one, when Garcia had chased him through Temple Terrace, the cops hadn't been certain that he wasn't just a routine prowler. But this time...this time they'd figured out too much.

And it was his own fault; he knew it. He wasn't one to lay blame elsewhere. When he'd heard the rumor that the cops and security techs would be in today to check for back doors, he'd decided he needed to be there, too. He needed to know just what they were thinking and how close they were to uncovering his methods. Instead of learning, he'd handed them a plum.

And all because he'd had to dismantle the shipping-bay motion detectors so he could hide out without being disturbed by the guards, who sometimes had a penchant for opening all the locked offices and checking them out.

He wasn't a killer. He didn't want to kill any more guards. Eddy Malacek had died only because there was no way around it. Not only had he needed to make sure that Eddy didn't remember anything about that night, he'd also needed to point the finger as far away from himself as he could. Killing Eddy made it look possible that the guard had been involved in the theft, and Eddy wouldn't be around to deny it.

But he didn't want to kill some rent-a-cop who happened to open the wrong office door during the night. So the previous afternoon, he'd slipped into the security equipment room and typed a code into the security program. Characters he'd learned by looking over the shoulder of one of the technicians while they were testing the system.

There had been glitches at the beginning; there always were, the techie had told him. So they had a hidden function that allowed them to disconnect any part of the system while it was still operating. They had to be able to test the functioning system without setting off alarms.

The watcher had made good use of that knowledge, along with the code keys he'd picked up by looking over the tech's shoulder.

But now they were bound to discover how he'd done it. He'd been able to cover his tracks last time, but not this time. And he feared that would bring them closer to him.

God, he'd messed up. Hanging around trying to hear what the security-systems people were up to had only resulted in nearly being caught. But how could he have known that Garcia would get it in his head to come to the loading bay? He must have seen the damn cat on the monitor.

As a result, he'd been forced to move swiftly through the halls, just ahead of his pursuer. He'd thought he would be safe in the bay because everyone thought the motion detectors were on.

Big mistake. And if he didn't figure out something soon, it might prove to be his last mistake.

Gil caught up with Anna as she reached the lobby. "Excuse me, ma'am," he said courteously, "but where do you think you're going?"

"I'm going to check the exhibits. What if something else has been stolen?"

People were beginning to enter the lobby in noticeable numbers, lining up at the ticket windows. Four additional guards were in evidence, and cops were still hanging around here and there.

"Let's go then. But first let me make sure the alarms are off."

Wiggins, who was still grumbling to himself, told Gil that he'd shut off all the motion detectors. The damn place was getting as busy as Grand Central, according to him.

"Okay," Gil told Anna. "Let's check it out."

They headed for the Pocal exhibit.

Turk and Boomer exchanged looks as a Tampa cop told them they needed to go to the loading dock and why.

"Jeeeeeez," Turk said.

"You screwed up, man," Boomer said, shaking his head.

"Like hell I did. *You* and your magic men screwed up."

"Boys," Dinah said warningly. "Boomer, let's check it out."

Gil and Anna passed through the Pocal exhibit in record time. Apparently Anna simply wanted to make sure nothing was missing. She didn't say much, but her face was tight.

They boarded the staff elevator for the second story, and Gil spoke. "I'd almost bet there's nothing gone. This guy isn't after anything else, or he'd have taken it the first night. And nobody else knows the system was down."

"You're probably right," she said, her voice strained. "But I'm the caretaker of these items. I have to know."

When they emerged into the *Alcantara* exhibit, Gil wondered how she was ever going to know. Around the bones of a display in the making there were crates, some opened, some not. A couple of cannons sat in one corner of the huge room. The room was littered with tools, wood, glass, and huge screens in the process of being painted.

There were also the remnants of the previous exhibit, paintings, empty display cases, a couple of large dioramas.

"The really valuable artifacts are in the vault," Anna said.

"Did anyone check that out last week?"

"Of course. Ivar and some of my people did. But no one can get into it at night, Gil. It's a time lock. Anyway, nothing was missing from the inventory."

Still, she walked around the room, as if she expected to find vandalism. After ten minutes, she was apparently satisfied. "Okay," she said. "It's okay. Now, what about the splinters in your face?"

Gil touched a particularly annoying sliver in his cheek. "Do you have a pair of tweezers?"

Boomer arrived at the loading dock with a satchel in hand and Dinah on his heels. Tebbins was waiting with a couple of uniformed policemen.

"Okay," Boomer said, setting his satchel down by the door. "Let's see if he tampered with the circuits."

"Is that possible?" Tebbins asked. "I thought Ms. Hudson said that any interruption would cause an alarm."

Boomer looked at him. "Hey, man, I'd've said nobody could get into that display case. Right now, all bets are off. No stone unturned, and all that crap."

Tebbins held up a hand. "Fine by me. That's what I thought was going on all week."

Dinah frowned. "Of course it has."

Boomer snorted. "Oh, come off it, Dinah. We're limited by our imaginations. After we figure out how this guy did it, I want to hire him."

Dinah surprised Tebbins by smiling faintly. "He does occasionally make sense," she remarked to Tebbins.

"Thank God," he said. "It's time *something* about this case made sense."

"Oh, it makes perfect sense," Boomer remarked, kneeling down to test the current running to the laser that was positioned a foot above the floor. "We're just too stupid to see it. I can hardly wait to meet this guy. He's got this whole system psyched out."

"In what way?" Tebbins asked, not because he hadn't figured it out, but because he kept hoping somebody would say something that would open this whole mess like a can of sardines.

"Well, he figured out the best place to hide. Cameras are damn near useless in here, except to film someone who's actually trying to steal something. You could hide for a long time if you didn't want to take something big out of here. The motion detectors are supposed to prevent that, but if you manage to bypass them, ain't nobody going to look for you nohow. Why? Because we all know nobody could get in without tripping the detectors. Why the hell did that cop come in here anyway?"

"Because," said Tebbins drily, "he saw the cat move."

Anna and Gil went back to her office. She had a pair of tweezers. "I often get splinters when I unpack crates."

"Convenient. What about a mirror?"

"No mirror except in the rest rooms."

He lifted a brow at her. "You don't have one in your purse?"

She shook her head. "Sorry."

"No compact?"

Anna shook her head again. "I don't worry much about makeup."

"I'm in love."

Her startled eyes flew to his face, and a blush heated her cheeks. "What *are* you talking about?"

He gave her his most devastating smile. "My ex used to spend more time looking at herself in her mirror than at me or Trina."

"She can't be all bad. You have a lovely daughter."

"One who isn't speaking to me right now."

"She'll get over it. She's just fifteen."

"Yeah," he said philosophically. "Maybe in ten or twenty years she'll remember my phone number."

In spite of herself, Anna laughed. "Don't be so dramatic."

"I'm just being realistic. Pull the splinters, will you?" He handed her the tweezers.

"I don't want to hurt you."

He shrugged. "Trust me, I want to hurt myself even less than you do. I'm not afraid to admit I'm chicken. Pull away."

"No circuit interruptions," Boomer announced a half hour later. "That means it's Turk's problem. I knew it!" He crowed.

At the other end of the museum, Nancy was scanning the uncompiled lines of code that scrolled slowly up the screen of Turk's laptop. "Hey, what's this routine called 'normalize'? Why isn't it commented?"

Tebbins stopped in Anna's office on his way back to the equipment room. "It's not the hardware," he told Gil. "So it must be the software."

"Nancy was right then," Anna remarked as she tugged another splinter from Gil's face.

"Apparently so." Tebbins leaned over and looked at Gil's face. "You need to go to an emergency room."

"That's what I keep telling him," Anna said. "I can't be sure I'm getting all this stuff out. He's stubborn." She touched the corner of Gil's eye. "Close your eye."

He complied.

"No way," Anna said, tossing down the tweezers. "You've got a splinter that's completely embedded in your eyelid. I'm not messing around with your eyes."

Gil reached up and touched his eyelid. "It's not that bad."

"I guess you don't have any idea how thin your eyelids are. I worked in an optometrist's office when I was in college. Gil, you need a doctor."

"Absolutely," Tebbins agreed. "One of my men will take you over to University Community. Anna, you go with him. For some reason I don't like the idea of you hanging around here today."

Gil groaned. "That'll take hours."

Tebbins cheerfully clapped him on the shoulder. "Buck up. I'll keep you posted."

"Nobody can get to it," Turk said, as Tebbins entered the room behind him. Dinah and Boomer were already there.

"It's here," Nancy insisted. "Somebody can get to it."

"What's going on?" Tebbins asked.

"Oh hell," Turk said, throwing up his hands.

Dinah spoke. "There's a subroutine for bypassing alarms. It's a test routine. It is *not* a back door."

"It's as good as one," Nancy said firmly.

"But nobody can get to it but us good guys," Turk said.

Nancy stabbed a finger at him. "If *anybody* can get to it, a good hacker can."

Tebbins looked at Dinah. "What's going on?"

She sighed. "We have a subroutine in the software for test purposes. We have to be able to check systems without setting off alarms, so it bypasses the alarms while the systems are still functioning. Instead of sending out the alarm signals that get you guys running over here, the computer logs that alarms were triggered. It's a standard test function." She caught Tebbins's suspicious look and continued. "Look, you know the story of the boy who cried 'wolf.' If the alarms go off often enough, people get lazy about responding. This *helps* the security. And it's only on the motion detectors, by the way. Not on the display cases. Those can't be interrupted at all."

"Okay," Tebbins said. "Why is he saying nobody can get to it? Obviously, you folks can."

"Because," said Turk with a wide wave of his arm, "it's on a secret menu."

Nancy snorted. Turk glared at her.

"Listen," he said, turning back to Tebbins. "To get to the menu you have to have a password."

"Big deal," Nancy said. "Hackers get past that all the time."

"Yeah," Turk said, "but there are some other complications."

"Back up," Tebbins said sharply. "Explain to me from square one. Nancy found a subroutine or whatever that allows you to bypass the alarms. Okay. If she could find it, why couldn't anyone else?"

"*She* found it," Turk said, "because she was reading my uncompiled code." He pointed to the screen of the laptop. "See that? It's sort of like a bridge between En-glish and machine language. But it's difficult for even an experienced programmer to read because it's not English. It's a whole bunch of commands, and you have to trace it very carefully to see exactly what it does, and man, you could spend a hell of a long time trying to figure out just parts of this code."

"This is why commenting is used," Nancy interjected. "Comments are like notes, in English, used by programmers to explain what each line or subroutine of the code does."

"Right," said Turk. "But even so, it doesn't matter that this can be read. Because," he said, with a little bit of flourish, "*this* code is not available on the on-site system. All we have on the on-site system is the compiled code. Machine language."

He leaned over the console beside Nancy and typed in a few commands. Moments later the menu disappeared and the screen filled with scrolling lines of ones and zeros.

"That," said Turk, "is all anybody can get here. This is what a program comes down to when it's in a form the machine can read. A jam-packed sequence of instructions that all boil down to telling the computer which flip-flop to turn on, which to turn off...and in what sequence. Beautiful, huh?"

Beautiful wasn't the word Tebbins would have used, and he had to admit it was daunting. "Somebody got around it."

"I know." Turk sighed. "What I'm trying to do is explain to everyone that the bypass routine isn't something anyone can just luck onto. In my opinion, nobody could have figured out this code in the amount of time it's been installed here. *Nobody*."

Dinah nodded. "He's right. Nobody here even knew it existed until this morning. That's part of the security, too. No one in on-site security knows the function exists."

Tebbins stared at the screen. "Someone does."

Turk leaned over and typed in another command. The screen went back to its previous menu function.

"So okay," he said. "We still don't trust that much to chance, humongous though the numbers are against anybody stumbling on it. Nancy found the routine in the uncompiled code, primarily because it looks different. Very few comments, for one thing, and the comment for the subroutine itself is misleading. So say somebody got a hand on the uncompiled code and studied it, like Nancy. She still can't get to the point where she can actually use it."

Nancy looked as if she disagreed, but didn't say anything.

"In the first place," Turk said, "she has to get into this room. Access is limited to employees of my firm, and theoretically only to the museum director. It's supposed to be locked at all times. But assume she manages to get in. She still can't make the on-site system do a damn thing unless she has the proper access code. To get to the so-called public menus, like this one, she needs a seven-digit, alphanumeric, case-sensitive password. What are the odds against that, Boomer?"

Boomer started to pull his calculator off his belt. "I don't remember. Let me calculate it."

"Forget it," said Tebbins. "I get the idea. Astronomical."

"Exactly. And you'd have to get to this menu first if you want to go any further. So that's one astronomical problem. Then, once you get to this menu, you have to know how to get to the secret menu. That entails using this command here..." He pointed to a line which said COMMAND. "You have to type in a specific command like so..." He demonstrated, selecting COMMAND. Immediately the screen switched to black with a single question mark prompt.

"Now you have to know what command to type in. But before I do that, everybody look away, huh? I don't want to have to change all this."

Everyone obliged, except Tebbins, who kept his eye cocked in that direction even though he couldn't see exactly what Turk typed.

"Okay," Turk said. The screen now displayed the prompt: *p?*

"It's asking for the password," he continued. "Another, different seven-digit code, like the first. Another astronomical guess. And on this one, you only get three tries. Do it wrong and it shuts down. And I do mean shuts down. The monitoring functions continue, but nobody can access the machine. We get a hacker alert, and I've got to come out here and restart the system with another code. One nobody else knows. One that's locked up in our safe at the company."

He pulled out one of the task chairs and sat at the computer. "Okay, say our guy lucks on the code. He types it in..." Turk did so, putting a string of seven asterisks on the screen. "Note nobody can read the password over my shoulder."

Another menu popped up. This one was simpler, not at all pretty like the very first one, just a list of numbered words. He highlighted the one that read *9) bpa*.

"That's your bypass routine. I hit Enter and we get this screen." Another question mark appeared. "Here," Turk said, "I have to enter another password, an area designator, and a one or zero for bypass off or on. All concatenated."

He stopped there. "So we're talking about a lot of layers of protection here. First you have to know there's a bypass. Keeping the existence of that routine unknown to anyone except a few people inside the company is the best security there is. Trust me, nobody's going to luck onto it.

"Then it's useless unless you know what it's going to do anyway. But say the guy found out. He knows it's there and that he can shut off the motion detectors region by region. He still has to have three different passwords, he still has to know the command to get to the secret menu, and he's still got to know exactly how to enter the information the routine requires. And he can't just muck around in here without shutting off system access. We made this thing hypersensitive to hackers."

"What about the audit trails?" Nancy asked.

Turk shrugged. "There weren't any from the night of the robbery. We checked the next morning. That's another thing I can't figure out."

"He must have known his access would be logged," Nancy said simply. "So...he deleted the audit file."

"I might be able to restore it," Turk said. "It might still be on here."

"How?" Tebbins asked.

"Deleting a file doesn't erase the memory," Nancy explained. "It just changes the first character of the filename and deletes the keys in the file tree." Tebbins put a hand up in confusion. She took a breath. "Basically, when you delete a file on a computer, the computer just hides it and marks that part of the disk as being available. Sooner or later, it gets overwritten by some other program."

Turk had been typing away while she explained. "Damn, he's good. There ain't shit here. Probably rescrambled the filename so not even the restore function can find it." He looked up at Tebbins. "It's gone, man. Gone gone."

Nancy nodded. "So somebody managed to get the codes. Who knows them?"

"Me and my two assistants," Turk said. "Nobody else. Well, except the safe at the company."

"Then," said Tebbins, "I need to talk to your assistants. Now."

"But," said Turk, reaching for the tattered remains of his dignity, "none of this explains how he got into the display case." He jerked his thumb over his shoulder in Boomer's general direction. "That's *his* problem, man."

The watcher, established once again at a vantage point in the room across the hall, listened. And felt the first trickle of real fear that he might not accomplish his task in time.

Pretending to busy himself with papers, he looked up from time to time as other employees passed the door and hailed him. He was invisible again, protected by the fact that he was supposed to be there. But that offered him little comfort.

He had to act soon.

CHAPTER EIGHTEEN

Anna left her car keys with Nancy in case she needed to get home before Anna returned. Tebbins filled Gil in quickly and promised to let him know the results of the interviews with the technicians.

University Community Hospital was only a few minutes away. Anna expected to wait a long time, as was usual at emergency rooms, but Gil was in treatment ten minutes after he'd checked in. Anna and the Tampa police officer who'd driven them sat in the waiting room alone.

The officer didn't seem inclined to make idle talk. He skimmed magazines one after another and listened from time to time as his radio crackled with messages Anna couldn't even begin to understand.

She gathered he would rather be doing something else.

Well, so would she. Her own life had begun to make her feel claustrophobic. Everywhere she went, she was watched. Her activities were hemmed in to the point of absurdity. The hours of waiting for something, anything, to break seemed to grow longer with each passing minute.

But she wasn't foolish. She wasn't inclined to try to slip her guards or go places where she might be a defenseless target. Her stalker was too good at his game for her to think she'd be safe in a crowd, or that he couldn't find her at the mall or the beach. So she submitted to the constraints.

But that didn't mean she had to like it.

She tossed her magazine aside and began to pace the waiting room. Gil would probably want to go right back to the museum when he got out of the ER. She didn't want to. The place was beginning to feel like a tomb to her. Her own tomb.

In fact, the only good thing she could say about this mess was that she'd met Gil and his daughter. And that didn't amount to much because once this was over she'd never see either one of them again.

So much for looking for the silver lining in the cloud, her mother's favorite axiom.

Gil emerged an hour later looking only slightly the worse for wear. They'd had to take a stitch in his eyelid.

"It's as annoying as hell," he remarked. "I feel it every time I blink. But I'm okay. Do you want to go back to the museum?"

Anna shook her head. "I'd rather go home. I feel like a fifth wheel there. At least at home I have things I can do while I'm being watched."

"Fair enough. I imagine the surveillance team is still there."

"I think so."

"Let's go then. I'll stay with you for a while. Tebbins knows how to reach me."

For some reason the idea frightened her. "That's not necessary. I'm sure you want to go back and see what Tebbins is up to."

Gil shrugged. "Like I said, he knows where to find me."

The two patrol cars were still parked in front of Anna's house. The officers were busy chatting, but they vetted both Gil and Anna before allowing them to approach her house. In turn, the Tampa cop vetted the two Temple Terrace officers before he returned to his other duties.

"See?" she said. "I'm safe. You don't have to baby-sit me."

Standing in the middle of her living room, he looked at her. His dark eyes caught her green ones, holding them. As if by some magic the air around them seemed to thicken. Anna wondered if she had ever felt like this before, as if the very air were pregnant with earth-shaking possibilities. She couldn't even move, for fear she would destroy the moment.

He spoke, almost gently. "What are you afraid of, Anna?"

Under the circumstances, it should have been an absurd question. But she wasn't thinking of those circumstances, and neither was he.

He slipped off his suit jacket and tossed it on the couch. His tie had vanished while he was in the hospital. Anna felt her breath catch, and some part of her recognized that she was being offered something wonderful by a universe that wasn't entirely heartless.

Gil stepped toward her. "I shouldn't feel this way."

She didn't know how to respond. Couldn't have responded even if she did. Because blossoming deep within her was an acute awareness that she wanted him more than anything else in the world at that instant.

"You're a suspect. This could kill my career."

She did speak then, a throaty whisper that seemed to come from elsewhere. "I won't tell."

The smile he gave her sent warmth rushing right to her toes.

Tebbins sat in the conference room, looking across the table at the technician. At the far end sat Dinah Hudson, observing. She had already told the man to cooperate.

But Arnold LaCombe was not someone Tebbins would have hired to shine his shoes. The man might be as good a programmer as

Turk said, but he also had an attitude problem and all the signs of a man on marijuana.

Tebbins was a realist, however. He personally didn't much care if someone smoked pot, any more than he cared if someone had an occasional drink. He himself liked a glass of wine from time to time.

The problem, however, with people who smoked pot, the problem that made them worse than weekend beer drinkers, was that they were doing something illegal. *That*, to Tebbins's way of thinking, said something about their characters.

At that moment, Arnold LaCombe looked like a man who'd been through a lost weekend and was just waking up enough to turn resentful and obstreperous. But Tebbins was perfectly willing to turn the screws.

"I want to know," he said, "if anyone showed unusual interest in the security system while you were working on it."

"What's unusual?" LaCombe said. He slouched back in his chair, wearing a T-shirt and shorts that looked as if he'd slept in them more than once. No, Tebbins thought, I definitely wouldn't hire this man to clean dog droppings from my yard. He must present a very different attitude and appearance to his employers during the week. Turk and Boomer were weird, but they were helpful and earnest.

"Asking questions," Tebbins said.

"Everybody asked questions. This place was crawling with people who asked questions."

Tebbins doubted it. "I mean people who

asked specific questions about the functioning. About the test procedures."

LaCombe shrugged. "I guess. Probably a few. Doesn't mean I answered. I'm not supposed to answer those questions."

"But I still need to know who asked."

"How the hell am I supposed to know? There were a hundred people crawling around this place. You think I cared who they were?"

"But somebody asked you these specific questions."

"I didn't say that. They could have."

Dinah stirred and sighed. "I told you to cooperate, Arnie. I meant it."

"I *am* cooperating. People asked questions. I don't know who they were. I didn't answer any questions I wasn't supposed to."

"That better be true," Tebbins said. "Because if it isn't, you might be charged as an accessory."

That jolted the guy. His already dilated pupils dilated even more. "I'll think about it," he said finally. "Maybe I'll remember something."

"You do that."

LaCombe left the room. Dinah slapped her hand on the table. "Would you believe we do random drug tests? I wonder how he's missed detection."

"Maybe you ought to find out."

She nodded. "Trust me, I'm going to. I swear one thing to you, though. If I'd ever suspected he could be like this, he'd've been long gone. He's gone now."

"Not yet," Tebbins said. "I don't want to discourage him from remembering."

She sighed. "Fair enough. But I'm not keeping him forever. He's a threat to the company."

"What about the next guy?"

"Akeem Wilson. I'm almost afraid to say anything about him after LaCombe."

"Tell me anyway."

"Smart, responsible, reliable. If Turk left, he'd get the promotion."

Wilson was a small man with a big smile that lit up his dark face. In a soft voice, he greeted Tebbins and shook his hand. Unlike the others, he appeared to favor khaki slacks and polo shirts.

"Yes," he said in answer to Tebbins, "a lot of people were interested. Arnie's right about that. But I see what you mean about specific questions. I *did* get those. It was one day early on when we were testing one of the areas we'd just installed. Several people asked how we could do that without setting off the alarms. I told them it was a trade secret."

That caught Tebbins's attention. "So people around the museum knew you could shut down the alarms without turning off the system."

"Well, several seemed to." He rubbed his chin. "One was Mr. Gregor. The managing director, I believe he is. He quite naturally was concerned. At the time they had a number of valuable pieces on the loading dock, and he was concerned that while we ran tests the items might be unprotected. I reassured him, of course. It only seemed proper."

Dinah nodded. "I'd have done the same thing, Akeem."

He smiled at her.

"What about others?" Tebbins asked.

"There were a few." He thought about it. "I seem to remember one of them was a friend of the curator's. A man. He was around a lot, but I don't think she liked him much. I'm also under the impression that he's a teacher, not a museum staffer. Anyway, he was curious about a lot of things. And there was one of the young volunteers. A very helpful type. I think he even helped Boomer with some of the wiring. At any rate, he reminded me of a groupie."

"How much did these people learn?"

"Nothing useful," Akeem said. "Not from me, anyway. The company has a strict policy about that, and I happen to like my job."

Dinah smiled at him.

Tebbins was following another train of thought. "What about LaCombe," he asked. "Would he have told them anything?"

Akeem Wilson visibly hesitated.

"Go on," Dinah said. "You can't make things any worse for him."

"Well," said Akeem after a few seconds, "Arnie does like to show off. I don't know if he said anything he shouldn't have, but sometimes, when I was around, he came awfully close."

When his cell phone rang, Gil was buried deep inside Anna. He ignored the call. In fact, he resented the hell out of it.

What had happened between them had

been explosive. One minute they had been in the living room talking, the next they had been naked in bed together. The impatience between them had been overwhelming, leaving little time for finesse or tenderness. As if they *had* no time. And maybe they didn't.

All he knew was that he was having a few of the most incredible minutes of his life, and nothing else mattered.

Plunging even deeper, he felt the shudder of release pass through her, heard a soft cry that was almost a groan. Deep inside he let go himself, rushing headlong over the precipice.

The phone rang again.

"Damn it," he muttered. He sagged onto her, feeling their sweat-slick skin meet.

"You'd better get that," she said.

Lifting his head, he looked down into her eyes and saw fear. "It's okay," he said, his voice gritty and breathless. "It's okay. I promise. I..."

"Just get the phone," she said, and turned her head away.

She was sorry. And now that his head was clearing, so was he. Not because he hadn't wanted her. Not because it hadn't been stupendous, but because he had crossed a line he never should have crossed.

The answering service on his phone kicked in, and the ringing stopped.

"Anna..."

"It's okay. We're both grown-ups." She looked at him again, her green eyes veiled, and gave him a wan smile. "Wrong time is all."

She was right. Next week, next month..."There'll be a right time," he swore.

She didn't answer.

And the damn phone started ringing again. Sitting up, he went to find it. It was on the living-room floor, mixed up with his pants and his socks.

"Garcia."

"How's your face?" Tebbins asked. His tone suggested he knew Gil's face wasn't the most important thing he could have asked about. The damn cop had probably returned to the museum and reported that he'd left Gil at Anna's house.

"It's fine. What's up?"

"Maybe I should be asking that question. Getting involved with a suspect ranks for stupidity of the year, Garcia."

"Just get on with it, will you?"

"Certainly." Tebbins paused, and Gil could easily imagine him stroking his moustache.

"Okay," Tebbins continued after a pregnant moment, "we have three possibles who were overly interested in the alarm system. Ivar Gregor, Peter Dashay—remember him? Anna's boyfriend."

Gil felt a bubble of anger at the description but ignored it. "And?"

"And some volunteer and part-time employee no one can seem to name. I can't get a hold of either Gregor or Dashay right now, so that's going to have to wait."

"Okay. We can get them tomorrow. But this other guy... Listen, we need to interview the guard who relieved Malacek."

"Because he might be the guy who's always late?" Tebbins hummed one note. "Well, so what? We saw the videotape. The changeover took place. Malacek was alive."

"Excuse me," Gil said, "but the absence of stuff that we *ought* to see on the tapes has me seriously wondering about the stuff that we *do* see."

Tebbins fell silent again, and finally gave a rueful chuckle. "You just made me feel stupid, and I hate that. Unfortunately, you're right. But the lab still hasn't been able to find any evidence of tampering."

"Something was tampered with, and we both know it. I've been thinking about it since I talked with the duty guard earlier, and it occurs to me that it would be easier to replace a whole tape than to diddle with one that was made."

"Good point." Tebbins grew thoughtful. "I'll find out who he is and talk to him. And I think I need to do another personal review of the tapes from that night. Maybe Anna can help identify this part-timer in some locale where he shouldn't be."

"Are you ruling out Gregor and Dashay?"

"Not yet. But I'm more curious about Mr. Invisible, if you get my drift. Okay, get back to whatever you were doing." His tone suggested that he knew perfectly well. "I'll call as soon as I locate the guard."

"Thanks." Gil disconnected and turned to see Anna standing in the bedroom doorway. She was fully clothed. His heart sank.

She spoke. "Time to go back to being cop and suspect," she said coolly.

"Anna..." Once again he stalled on her

name. He wasn't in a position to make wild promises about anything. And he wouldn't be wise to, just yet.

"It's okay," she said again, and smiled slightly. "It's okay."

Then his damn phone rang again. This time, however, the call drove everything else out of his mind. This time the call was from his ex.

"Where the hell have you been?" she demanded. "Trina's run off with Jamie!"

Tebbins spoke to the guard by telephone. His name was Johnny Kews, and he was jovial.

"Sure, I had the shift the morning after the robbery."

"Right. Well, what I want to know is, was Eddy there when you arrived?"

There was a silence. "You saw the tape. Of course he wasn't."

Tebbins felt his ego shrink to the size of a pinprick, and he didn't at all like it. A moment passed before he could even manage to speak calmly. "Why didn't you mention that?"

"What are you accusing me of? You guys had the videotape. You saw what happened. I figured if you needed to know more, you'd ask."

Tebbins had the urge to act like a two-year-old and kick something. He refrained; after all, Hercule Poirot didn't behave like an ass. Of course, Poirot never made a mistake this stupid.

"The videotape shows you arriving ten

minutes late and getting the keys from Malacek."

"Oh, boy." Kews whistled. "The truth of the matter is I was twenty minutes late. Got hung up in traffic. Eddy was gone when I got there. I figured he had to go to class or something and couldn't wait. But everything was fine when I got there. I checked it out. So there didn't seem to be any point telling on the kid. He mighta got fired."

Tebbins suspected Kews was less concerned about Eddy than himself. "So no one else was in the building?"

"Not a living soul."

"You're sure about that?"

"Positive. I checked, Detective. Carefully. I didn't want to have to be explaining myself. I guess I have to explain anyway." He sighed. "I don't know what the tape shows, but I was late, Eddy was gone, and I just about busted a gut checking things out. I have to do that every time I take over anyway, but that morning I was hustling."

"Did anyone arrive between the time you did and eight-thirty?"

"No. Most of the early birds don't start showing up until a few minutes before nine. That morning I didn't see anybody until oh, I guess it was ten till nine."

Which didn't explain how anybody could have gotten into the equipment room to change out videotapes at eight-thirty. Unless he was already there. Which meant Malacek might have been long gone.

We've learned a lot today, Tebbins thought

as he hung up. Including the fact that he could miss what was right under his own nose. He was not going to enjoy telling Garcia about it.

But as much as they had learned, it wasn't enough. He still needed to review the video-tapes.

An hour later Tebbins was back at his desk. He'd had the lab make him duplicates of the tapes he was most interested in: those covering the main lobby during the party, during the night, and the following morning. There were twelve of them in a neatly bundled stack waiting for him. He sighed, imagining the hours of boredom that lay ahead of him.

But there was a file folder on his desk, too, flagged for his immediate attention. He opened it and found the phone records he'd subpoenaed from the phone company: Anna's calls from her home phone and her office for the last month. The secretary, Joyce, had left a Post-it note stuck to the first page.

Take a look at the ones I checked. They're all to museums and antiquities dealers abroad.

Tebbins felt his breath quicken. God, he loved Joyce. Being a secretary hadn't kept her from turning into a wonderful detective in some ways. And what's more, she always took a research job past what was required. Like this one. All he'd requested were the records. She hadn't needed to check out the numbers.

He scanned the numbers, noting that the calls to dealers had been made from Anna's home. She would probably need to call museums from time to time, but *dealers*? From home?

Picking up the phone, he called Gil again, and was a little startled by the snap from the other end of the line.

"What?"

Tebbins held the phone back from his ear, looked at it with distaste, then brought it back. "Tebbins," he barked right back. "We need to talk. Can you get away from Anna?" He had visions of having interrupted Garcia in a delicate position.

"I'm away from Anna. In fact, I'm chasing my runaway daughter. This had better be good."

"Keep chasing. I just wanted you to know that I have Anna's phone records here. She's made more than a dozen calls to foreign antiquities dealers. From her home."

Gil disconnected and tossed his cell phone onto the seat beside him. Antiquities dealers? His stomach, which was already sinking like lead, sank another forty feet. Christ. Oh, Christ.

So the guy he'd chased to the golf course might have been her accomplice, coming to meet her—or just a prowler. The dagger in her bed could have been nothing but misdirection. The mess in the shipping room could have been nothing but a cat and a poorly balanced crate. He could already feel the egg on his face.

300

Fuck it, he told himself. Just find your daughter. You can take care of Anna later.

Rina said the two kids had planned to go to the beach, but she'd told Trina that she forbid her to go to the beach with Jamie. The girl had left that morning before her mother woke up. Her bathing suit was missing.

Gil supposed it was just a teenage act of disobedience, but after what had happened last time with Jamie, he didn't trust that little prick any farther than he could throw him. Maybe not even that far. Jamie would do something to Trina to teach her a lesson for running away from him with another guy. He knew it in his bones. And apparently, so did Rina. Otherwise, she never would have called him.

There was no answer at Jamie's house, so he decided to check the beaches first.

But he did know the make, model, and license number of Jamie's car. Reaching for his phone, he called in the cavalry.

It was his only advantage as a cop. Otherwise, he was just any jerk who made the same stupid mistakes. *Really* stupid mistakes. After five years of avoiding women because he didn't want to be betrayed again, he'd gone and gotten involved with a suspect.

Shit, it was going to be a long day.

Tebbins picked up his phone yet again, and this time called Anna. Her answer was subdued.

"Hello?" she said, her voice heavy with reluctance.

"This is Tebbins," he told her. "I need your help."

She seemed to perk up a little at that. "What can I do?"

"I've got a bunch of videotapes to review, and I want you to help me identify people. Can you lend me a few hours?"

"Sure, I'd be glad to."

"Thanks. I'll send an officer for you. He'll bring you to my house." He'd done that for a specific reason. Bringing her in to the station might tense her up, make her overly cautious. His home would be a much less threatening atmosphere, one that wouldn't make her too wary. "Say, forty-five minutes?"

"I'll be ready."

Things were getting too dangerous, the watcher thought as he followed Tebbins from the station to his home. Too dangerous. He never should have taken the dagger.

But even as he thought that, he understood he'd had no choice. He needed the dagger to perform the sacrifice, and he needed to return it to its rightful place so the curse would end. He knew that.

But events had mushroomed. The police had figured it out before he could make his offering. He'd made a serious misstep by putting the fake dagger in Anna's bed. He'd been so consumed by his need to let her know she was being haunted by the curse that he'd been a fool.

He hadn't thought the police would watch her house after she found the dagger. He'd assumed they would come, check things out, and leave. Instead he'd had to drug a cop so he could approach the house to kill Anna, and had been nearly caught by Garcia. It was enough to make him think events might be conspiring against him.

But that couldn't be, he reminded himself. He had the jaguar god on his side. No, it was just a greater test. He was having to prove himself, was all.

Now they were getting too close. He had to stall them. He'd heard Tebbins say on the phone that he was going to review the tapes, and he had to prevent that. Because all the while he'd been telling himself they wouldn't find him because he'd changed the recordings for the lobby and exhibit cameras covering the time from 12:30 A.M. to 8:30 A.M., he hadn't been able to switch any of the tapes of the lobby from the night before or the morning after.

He'd been able to duplicate tapes of night shifts from the preceding week without any trouble. The problem was, there was no way he could duplicate the lobby tapes from the night of the party. Nor had he been able to change the morning tapes because the robbery had been discovered and the tapes locked down before he could have done so.

He should have picked a different night to rob the place, he realized. Then he could have used duplicate tapes that showed him leaving the night before, which would at least have covered his ass somewhat, even though he couldn't switch to a tape showing him arriving the next morning.

If someone noticed that...

He swore under his breath. Hubris. He'd wanted the splash of committing an impossible crime directly after the party. He'd told himself all those people would be potential suspects, concealing him even better.

But he'd left a great big hole in his own alibi. And if Tebbins noticed...

He had to get Tebbins out of the picture, at least long enough to give him the opportunity to sacrifice Anna, and maybe Nancy.

He had no choice. But he hated having to drag others in. He didn't even want to kill Anna and her sister, but it was the only way he could save his own neck from the curse. Unfortunately, that was now true of Tebbins as well.

The curse had reached out, snaring others. Others whose only sin was to be remotely involved. Just like his own mother and father.

He steeled himself by remembering that he would be saving lives in the long run if he succeeded, the lives of others who would fall under the curse for preventing the dagger's return to the tomb. Hadn't the last week shown it was still reaching out, snaring others in its maw?

But he had to move swiftly.

Tebbins felt pretty good by the time he arrived home. The case was about to break big-time.

He had enough now to knuckle Anna under with some questioning, although at the moment he preferred to wait a little while. She didn't seem in a hurry to go anywhere, and he didn't have a whole lot to go on, at least until the toxicology was back on the coffee she'd given the cop. No, he needed a whole lot more.

And he hoped he might get some of it today.

But first he had to make this look like a social setting. He dug a box of scones out of his pantry and arranged them on a doily-covered plate. He put them on the tea cart next to the elaborate porcelain tea service he'd bought a few years before. The small blue roses had appealed to him.

Boiling the water and heating the milk would have to wait until Anna arrived.

He surveyed his preparations with approval, then checked to make sure his entertainment system was set to run videotapes. All ready.

Humming "Rule Brittania," he went to slip on his smoking jacket.

Anna felt uneasy. She told herself she was being ridiculous, that she was riding in a police car to visit a police officer, but she felt uneasy anyway. Going to Tebbins's house rather than the station bothered her, but she hadn't been able to figure out a good reason to call him back and refuse.

Instead, she sat in the car and remembered how Tebbins had been on the scene almost the instant she found the dagger on her desk. She didn't have any trouble imagining that a detective might be involved in the robbery.

He would certainly have the knowledge and resources. And, if he wanted, access to a great deal of information about the security. Better still, he'd be all but invisible to everyone, including the investigators.

But he can't do anything today, she reminded herself. The cop who was driving her would be there. She was safe. She was just being paranoid.

But her discomfort continued to grow. She wished Nancy were with her, but Nancy had called to say she was going to stop off for a beer with Boomer and Turk before coming home. A fugitive smile curved her mouth as she considered the shock those two guys were going to get if they made a pass at Nance.

But amusement didn't lift her spirits for long. Her anxiety still grew, a feeling of impending doom, as if she were hurtling into the darkness.

Looking at the cop beside her, she knew she was trapped. She just hoped she was with the good guys.

The watcher was hiding behind a vine trellis in a neighbor's yard, keeping an eye on Tebbins's house. He stood near a fire-ant mound and the nasty bugs were getting up inside his pant legs, stinging like mad. He needed to move, but he didn't dare. Not yet. Tebbins was still moving around too much, visible as he passed by windows.

Then the cop car drew up out front. An officer climbed out and came around to the passenger side, opening the door.

Anna! At once a sense of exhilaration and a sense of despair filled him. Two of his targets together. But that other cop…that other cop would be a problem.

Straining, he listened as the front door opened. He heard Tebbins tell the cop to go get himself some lunch.

The watcher felt blessed. The jaguar god had stood by him. Staring after the departing police cruiser, he felt the gun in his pocket and the dagger in the small black bag he carried. He had his weapons. Now he had to find his opportunity.

CHAPTER NINETEEN

Anna's heart sank as Tebbins told the officer to go get himself some supper. He seemed to sense her dismay, although he probably didn't guess the reason for it.

"You'll be safe here," he said. "No one else knows where you are. He can't find you."

But the identity of *he* was the big question,

Anna thought miserably as she allowed herself to be ushered into the living room and seated on a sofa. Tebbins excused himself to make the tea after ascertaining that she did indeed enjoy Earl Grey.

At least he hadn't lied about the videotapes; the cartridges waited on the small table next to the entertainment center, a big bundle of them. So maybe he hadn't lied about anything else.

A short while later, Tebbins returned with the tea cart. The elegance of the service surprised Anna, then she wondered why. Everything about Tebbins was unusual.

"I scalded the pot," he assured her, "and warmed the milk."

"Wonderful." Even though she drank her tea straight and didn't do anything fancy in the making of it, she appreciated the finer points, having heard about them.

"No reason not to do it right." To her relief he took the armchair beside the couch and reached for a delicate cup and saucer. "How do you like yours?"

"Plain please."

"Tsk," he said, a teasing twinkle in his eye. "A bar-barian."

She managed to smile back at him. "I suppose so."

"I hope you like scones." He offered her the plate and waited while she selected one.

"I don't believe I've ever had them." And this was too absurd, she found herself thinking. Just too absurd. She felt as if she'd stepped backward a century in time.

When she was served, he moved the cart aside and went to the stack of tapes. "I'm trying to decide which ones are the most important to look at."

"What are you looking *for*?"

He faced her, sticking one hand in his trouser pocket and twisting his moustache with the other. "One of the people I'm interested in is a part-time employee and volunteer. The thing is, I don't know his name. There are quite a few, aren't there?"

"We do hire a lot of students," Anna agreed. "But Ivar would be better able to tell you how many. I know there have been quite a few, but they come and go."

"How about those who have pretty much been there since you started to implement the exhibit? Maybe even as far back as the point in time where you had to tell the directors about your father."

Anna felt another shiver of apprehension, though she wasn't sure why. Mention of her father's death always disturbed her, but it didn't make her feel this way, as if unseen eyes were boring into her. "Let me think."

But thinking was hard. It was as if her mind didn't want to settle on the subject, but instead hopscotch between all her fears and worries. "Maybe...a dozen," she said finally. "Maybe a few more. I'm not exactly sure. I don't work with them all, and we have so many volunteers also that it's hard to keep track. Really, Tebbins, Ivar could help you more with this."

"Well, I'm primarily interested in whether you'd recognize faces."

She nodded slowly. "I might recognize most of them."

"What I'm especially interested in is whether you noticed someone who came into the museum during the evening of the party but didn't leave. Someone who might well have been there in the morning but isn't seen arriving."

"Oh!" She felt relieved. "I think I can do that. I thought you wanted a whole bunch of names or something."

"As you said, I can get that from Ivar. In fact, I think I may already have it. But right now I'm interested in someone who can identify faces."

"I should be able to do that."

"Excellent." She watched him put in the tape and tried to relax, suspecting that this was going to be a long and boring process. But the feeling of something bad about to happen just grew thicker, as if it were filling the room.

She shifted uneasily on the couch and fought an urge to look over her shoulder. Tebbins turned on his system and pushed in the videotape. Snow filled the screen.

"This is supposedly a lobby tape from the evening before," he said. "Remember, I just want you to get an idea of which employees and volunteers were present. Or if someone was there who shouldn't be."

"Right."

"This tape starts at four-thirty that afternoon," Tebbins said. He returned to his chair.

It was as boring as Anna had anticipated. They watched the snapshot motion of people moving around the lobby, caterers beginning to set up for the evening. "It's not what I expected," she remarked. "These are just photos."

"Right," Tebbins agreed. "To save tape. The computer stores the image about once per second."

Which saved time in the review, Anna realized. After merely twenty minutes, they were watching the caterers whiz around like stars in an early Hollywood film, with jerky movements. That was one relief. At least each tape wasn't going to require an eight-hour review.

That was when they heard the thud from the back of the house.

Tebbins was out of his seat in an instant. A second later he had a gun in his hand. "Stay here," he told Anna.

Stay here? Icy trickles of terror began to run down her spine.

Jeff Ingles drove away from Tebbins's house toward a small restaurant a few blocks away, thinking about a burger or maybe a steak sandwich. He hadn't eaten since breakfast that morning, and his shift had just begun. Damn his kid anyway for showing up at the breakfast table at ten-thirty with his tongue and nipples pierced. That had thrown Roxie, Jeff's wife, into a tizzy that hadn't quit.

Jeff didn't like the piercings. Hell, no. He saw enough of that crap on kids he had to arrest. But he'd long since figured that his own son, Vic, was a few bricks shy of a load anyway. And he'd long since figured out that Vic reacted to authority the way most cats reacted to having their fur rubbed the wrong way. Roxie hadn't come that far. She was still trying to control the kid's every action, and expecting Jeff to play the heavy because he was a cop and wore a gun.

Like Jeff would ever pull his gun on his own kid.

Anyway, the day had gone downhill from there. Roxie wanted to ground Vic until he took the rings out of his nipples and tongue. Which was pretty much impossible. Jeff was well aware that short of turning his house into a prison camp and not even letting Vic out to go to school, they couldn't do that successfully. And he wasn't sure it would make things better anyway. But hell, Roxie was even demanding that Jeff put Vic into the sheriff's boot camp—as if the kid had done something criminal.

Not that Jeff didn't care. But his son was a stupid teenager who was going to do stupid teenage things, and getting those piercings, revolting as they were, was a far cry from the things Jeff worried about, like the kid staying out until two in the morning. Which Vic didn't do.

It would have been nice if Vic had wanted to be a football player, but the kid wanted to be a rock star. Jeff figured it was enough to keep him away from drugs and get him to graduate from high school. So far, both of those plans were on course. The rest of it was just rebellion.

Anyway, the upshot was, getting out of his house late in the afternoon to go to work had come as a reprieve. The problems on the street were easier to deal with than Roxie on a tear. He felt a twinge of sympathy for his son.

He was also suffering some serious hunger pangs, now that he was far enough away from the uproar to feel them. So it was great that Tebbins had told him to go eat.

Except that by the time he was a couple of blocks away, that began to bother Jeff. The woman, Anna Lundgren, was apparently the target of a stalker, which was why Jeff had been asked to escort her. So why had Tebbins told him to leave?

Damn detectives. They forgot that they grew soft sitting at their desks, that their reflexes and street smarts started to fade. They weren't on the firing line every day anymore. Which was okay, as long as they didn't start thinking they were as good as they used to be.

And bringing that woman to Tebbins's home...that bothered Jeff, too. It was irregular.

He thought about it for a few more minutes, but then he was at the restaurant, and that steak sandwich sounded too good to pass up. And Tebbins hadn't given him a specific time to return, so maybe he could actually savor his meal.

Finding Jamie and Trina proved surprisingly easy. Well, not surprisingly, Gil amended, not when he considered the resources he'd called into play. It apparently hadn't occurred to the stupid little prick that Trina's dad had enough friends in local police departments to get help from all the law-enforcement agencies on the beaches, and from the sheriff's department as well. It was unofficial, of course, but it didn't take them an hour to find Jamie's car parked in the public access lot in St. Pete Beach, near the Don Cesar Hotel.

Especially since the little turd had already managed to get himself a parking ticket by not pumping quarters into the meter when it had expired.

Gil made record time getting there from Madeira Beach. He'd started at the north end of the barrier islands, at Clearwater Beach, figuring since he was already near there on his way back from Tampa that it was the logical place to start. He made pretty good time heading south on Gulf Boulevard and giving thanks that tourist season had pretty much wound down.

He found his daughter and her boyfriend in the company of two St. Pete Beach officers that he knew fairly well. Jamie looked sullen and resentful, but much to his amazement, Trina didn't. She started toward him, but one of the cops stopped her.

The other officer, Mel Gasper, drew him

aside. "Listen, Gil," he said. "I want to talk to you about this before you talk to them."

"What happened?"

"That's just it. Nothing we can arrest him for. But frankly, I don't like it. It might just be a prank."

Gil's impatience soared. "Just tell me, Mel."

"He buried her in the sand near the water-line. You know."

"Yeah." Gil clamped down on his impatience. "Okay."

"Well, the thing is, once he had her buried, he told her he wasn't going to dig her out. By the time we found her, a couple of the waves had rolled over her head. She was pretty hysterical."

Gil's jaw clenched, but before he could say anything, Mel gripped his arm. "Don't do anything stupid, buddy. Kids pull pranks all the time. You won't get anywhere with it legally."

Anna watched Tebbins move silently across the living room toward a hallway. When he disappeared from sight, she started to wonder wildly if she should hide.

But it couldn't be anything, she told herself. Nobody would be stupid enough to break into a cop's house. Nobody. Not even her stalker.

Then she heard two gunshots.

315

Gil crossed the parking lot toward his daughter and Jamie. Mel was right beside him. He took some small pleasure in the fact that Jamie backed up a pace when he saw Gil's face.

"Daddy," Trina said tearfully, and moved toward him. He waved her back with his hand. "In a moment. First I have some words for Jamie."

Jamie's face settled into an angry, resentful frown, but he at least showed enough survival instinct to keep his mouth shut.

"Here's how it's gonna be," Gil said to the kid. "You're never going to come anywhere near my daughter again. Because if you do, I'm going to make you sorry. My job won't matter. Nothing will matter. I'll follow you to the ends of the earth."

Jamie tried a sneer. It didn't quite succeed. "You can't do that. It's illegal."

"There's an older law," Gil said, his voice like honed steel. "You hear me? An older law. Fathers protect their daughters. And I won't give a damn about consequences."

Jamie looked at Mel and the other cop. "He threatened me. He can't do that."

"I didn't hear a thing," Mel said. "What about you, Dave?"

"Not a thing."

Jamie searched their faces again, but apparently didn't find them any friendlier than Gil's. Then he turned to Trina. "You're an ugly, fat cow anyway. Run home to Daddy."

Trina burst into tears, but it was her father's arms she threw herself into.

"Time to clean up the beach," Mel remarked.

Dave nodded. "Get out of here, jerk," he said to Jamie. "And don't let me see your face in this town again."

St. Pete Beach was small enough to make that threat real.

Oh, God!

Anna leapt up from the couch and wondered what to do. Run? But she'd be all alone on the street. And what if Tebbins was hurt? She couldn't leave him.

Her heart was galloping like a horse in a quarter-mile heat. Part of her was praying desperately that Tebbins would come back down that hallway and tell her he'd caught an intruder. In broad daylight. Right.

It had to be the stalker. Had to be. Crazy as it sounded, he'd found out where she was. Tebbins must have shot him. But why didn't he come back?

Oh, God, she had to hide. Looking around, she tried to decide where was the best place to go. The thought of tearing out onto the street all alone, where anyone could find her unprotected, chilled her as much as the possibility of what might be going on in the back of the house.

But at least she could *run.*

And leave Tebbins, possibly wounded, to the mercies of whoever was back there.

No.

Gasping air in great gulps, she retraced Tebbins's earlier steps to the kitchen, taking care to make no sound. A knife. It wasn't as good as a gun, but at least it offered some protection. And her pepper spray. On the way by, she pulled it out of her purse.

Call 9-1-1? In the kitchen, she pulled the phone off the hook and let it dangle. She punched in the numbers, knowing someone would be sent to investigate. That was when she realized she didn't hear a dial tone.

Grabbing the handset, she lifted it to her ear. No. No dial tone.

She squeezed her eyes shut for a second, telling herself to calm down, to think. She couldn't leave Tebbins. He might be grievously wounded. She had to go back there and see if she could help him.

Forcing herself to take one quiet step after another, with a butcher knife in one hand and the pepper spray in the other, she left the kitchen cautiously.

Sticking her head out carefully, she peered down the hallway. She couldn't see a thing. Three doors, two on the right and one on the left were open. At the very back was another open door, through which she could see a wooden desk and bookshelves.

She should turn and run. The thought hammered at her with every heartbeat, but awareness of Tebbins's possible state kept her from doing so. She'd never forgive herself if he died because she ran. Never.

She took the first step down the hallway. Whoever it was might be gone. Tebbins might have scared him off with his gun, even if the detective had been shot. Trying to remember what the two reports had sounded like, she thought they might have been different. From different weapons.

So Tebbins could be hurt, and the intruder could even then be running away. Or waiting for Anna to burst out of the house.

True terror was a strange thing. It wasn't like the nerve-stretching uneasiness that sometimes kept her on the edge of her seat for a good movie. Part of her mind, as if stepping back, was amazed at how calm she was. At how aware she was of things that didn't seem important.

Every sound, even her own breathing, was loud now. The softness of the hallway carpeting, which she never would have noticed otherwise, felt like pillows beneath the soles of her shoes. The knife in her hand felt strangely light, as if gravity had disappeared.

At the first door, she paused and listened. Nothing. She was about to step inside and check it out when she heard a groan from down the hall. Tebbins. He *was* hurt.

Tightening her grip on the knife, she moved more quickly. If he was bleeding, every second would count. She had to find him.

The moan had sounded as if it came from the end of the hall, from the room with the desk. Stepping out of her flats, she started tip-toeing that way.

Then she heard a sound behind her.

Whirling, she came face-to-face with a man she knew. In one of his hands was a gun. In the other was the Pocal dagger.

The steak sandwich looked like something out of an ad. Not one of those crummy little things with thinly sliced meat that tasted like cardboard sitting on a hamburger bun, but a genuine slab of steak a quarter-inch thick trickling hot juices all over a fresh hard roll. Heaven.

Jeff dug in, flavor bursting in his mouth, juices trying to run down his chin. His radio, clipped to his belt, crackled with cross talk he attended with only one ear.

He was on his second bite when his heart stopped. Units were being asked to respond to an alarm at Tebbins's address. The security company said the phone line was dead.

Jeff hesitated. He didn't have to go. Others were responding. The steak tasted good and he was starving. It was probably a false alarm, anyway. Most of these home security alerts were.

But he was on duty. Supposed to protect the woman he'd left at Tebbins's house. Swearing silently, he choked down the food in his mouth, tossed twelve bucks on the table, and headed out to his car.

It still wasn't as bad as Roxie on a tear.

He had a gun and the Pocal dagger. She had a butcher knife and pepper spray. They stared at each other, and somewhere behind Anna, Tebbins groaned again.

"Lance," she said, disbelievingly. "Lance." Lance Barro, the pleasant, kind, helpful grad student who had volunteered countless hours at the museum in addition to his work as a part-time docent. Lance Barro, the quiet, inoffensive, reliable workhorse.

But he looked different. Of average height and average looks, he usually almost blended into the background. At that moment he wouldn't have blended into any background. His cat green eyes were hard, hot. Strange. His face was drawn tight, until it looked as if his skin were stretched over the bones beneath.

"Lance," she said again. Some instinct told her to try to reach the likable person buried somewhere inside him, the one hiding behind a predatory veneer. Even as she spoke, though, her brain was calculating methods of escape. It could find none. He stood between her and the doors. And he had a gun.

The realization filled her, and seemed to flip some internal switch. She was going to die. The only question was how.

"Lance?" she said again.

"Anna," he said, almost caressing her name as he spoke it. "You know why I'm here."

She knew then what a mouse felt like when a hawk snatched it from the ground and carried it away. The body might struggle, but the mind and soul were resigned. Far away. Beyond the fear she should be feeling.

"No," she said. It was as if someone else spoke.

"Of course you know," he said almost

gently. "You're the sacrifice. It's the only way to save everyone else."

"Everyone else?"

"It's the curse, Anna. You know that. Your father found the tomb."

Part of her was trying to make sense of what he said, but part of her was still scurrying for ways to escape. Except that gun looked so big, and it was pointed right at her.

"Make it easy on yourself, Anna," Lance said. "Drop the knife. I'll make it as painless as I can."

"Painless?" She repeated the word incredulously. "You're kidding."

He shook his head slightly. "You know I'm not. I need your heart. Your living heart. You can either give it to me, a true sacrifice, one that will make you godlike, or I can shoot you in the leg and take it anyway."

God, she couldn't believe someone was actually saying these things to her. But what she *did* know was that she had to find some way to use what he was saying against him.

She spoke, her hand tightening on the pepper spray. "Only a warrior can be offered."

He shook his head. "You know better than that, Anna. Anyway, the curse demands more."

"But I didn't do anything wrong."

"Neither did I."

"You?" Startled, she almost lost her death grip on the knife.

"My parents and my friends died in the refinery explosion. I almost did, too."

That cast a new light on what he was doing,

one that didn't reassure her at all. Her mouth grew even drier. "I'm sorry. But...hasn't there already been enough death?"

"The curse has to be satisfied. You owe it to the rest of us, Anna. It was your father who caused it all. Drop the knife now, or I'll have to shoot you." He aimed the gun at her legs.

She dropped the knife. It thudded on the carpet beside her. Never in her life before had she felt so defenseless.

Casting about desperately for a means of escape, she tried to buy time. "You're the one who talked to Reed Howell."

"It doesn't matter. I just had to be sure you understood what was happening. You had to have time to prepare yourself."

"Prepare myself?" The gun. She looked at it. He needed her living heart. Maybe he wouldn't dare to shoot her if she moved too quickly for him to take careful aim. He wouldn't dare kill her with the gun.

"For your offering," he said, as if that were intuitively obvious. He was getting impatient. "Come on, Anna. It's your fate. And it's the only way I can save myself and the others."

"What others?"

"All the survivors of the earthquake and explosion."

"But...why are you at risk? You didn't do anything wrong. I didn't do anything wrong."

"It's the curse," he said, as if that explained it all.

Realizing he was trying to save himself, and not just some amorphous "others," galvanized her. He wouldn't dare shoot her.

Drawing a deep breath, she leapt toward him, spraying him in the face with the pepper spray. He howled and stumbled to the side as she shoved past him. A few of the droplets got on her skin, burning like fire. A bit got into her left eye, searing it so badly she couldn't keep it open.

But what she noticed more was the fiery sensation in her left arm, followed by a throbbing that felt almost like a hammerblow.

He had stabbed her.

But she didn't have time to think about that now. She could hear him cursing behind her as she ran down the hall into the living room. He'd be blinded for a few moments, long enough, she promised herself. Long enough.

As she passed, she knocked over lamps and tables, creating an obstacle course to delay him as he stumbled after her.

Reaching the door, she threw back the dead bolt and ran out in the rapidly deepening twilight.

CHAPTER TWENTY

Jeff Ingles rounded the corner onto Tebbins's street in his cruiser and slammed on the brakes as a woman spilled out of a hedge. He felt the rapid-fire jerk of his antilock brakes and the sharp jolt against his seat belt as the

Crown Vic halted. Heard the terrible thud as she fell against the hood of his car.

In awful slow motion, he watched her blood smear over the hood as she sprawled onto the car and slid to the ground. *I was stopped!* a futile voice in his head cried out. *I didn't hit her!* It didn't matter. He watched the face of the woman he'd been assigned to protect disappear below the hood, her bloody hand the last to slip away.

He barked into his radio as he shoved the door open and rounded the fender. She lay on the street, copper hair streaked and matted with a deeper copper, her eyes barely registering him. Her lips moved, and he bent closer, hardly aware that the spurting spray from her arm soaked him. Her lips moved again.

"Tebbins," she whispered.

He clamped his hand down over the wound, pressing with all his might to stop the arterial bleeding, heedless of all the training that warned him not to get blood on himself. Too late, he thought distantly. She might die. Cocking his head, he spoke into the microphone on his shoulder, telling dispatch he needed an ambulance and backup right now. *Now!*

Another cruiser rolled up. "Check the house," Ingles called out. "The assailant may still be inside. Possible officer down."

The officer nodded, drew his gun, and headed for the door, pausing only a moment as more backup arrived. Ingles noted them only from a corner of his eye. His focus was on the woman. "Ma'am, what happened?"

She whispered again. "Tebbins."
And then her eyes closed.

She'd gotten away. The cops had arrived too quickly, and she'd gotten away. He was terrified as he crept through backyards, keeping to the thickest growth, hoping that night's curtain would fall quickly, granting him its protection.

He was terrified that she would die before he took her heart. He was terrified that he had failed his mission. He was terrified the cops would catch him and put an end to his attempts to satisfy the curse.

Lance Barro was more terrified than he had ever been in his life.

Anna knew who he was. If she lived—and he hoped she would because he still had to deal with the curse—she would identify him, making his life impossibly dif-ficult.

Oh, damn, he had screwed up badly. *Badly.* He never, ever should have tried to take Tebbins and Anna at the same time. Where was his brain? What was he thinking?

He should have waited. He should have been more patient. He should have thought things through instead of allowing fear to goad him into acting precipitously. He should have realized that trying to deal with both of them at the same time would only make it more likely that he would fail.

He wondered, if Anna died would Nancy be a sufficient sacrifice? Why not? They were twins. Offering both of their hearts would have been better, but maybe just the one would do. It bothered him, strangely enough, that if Nancy hadn't appeared by happenstance, he might never have known Anna had a twin. If he sacrificed only one of them, would he still satisfy the curse?

Realizing his own thoughts were getting muddied, he hid behind a Dumpster in a darkened parking lot at the rear of a strip mall.

He couldn't go home, but that was okay. He had anticipated the moment, and had emptied everything important from his apartment. He'd known he'd have to go on the run when he was done. So he went on the run a little sooner. No big deal.

But he needed to go to ground for a while. Seriously needed some time to calm down and reassess the entire situation. His whole plan had blown up, and everything he'd done to try to patch it had only seemed to make things worse.

So he'd have to make a new plan. Lull them into a sense of security. Then he would strike.

Feeling better, he went into an electronics store, blending with the people, looking at games he had no intention of buying.

Gil got to the hospital around midnight and found himself faced with Tebbins's partner, a young man named Vance Newman. Newman didn't impress him much.

"They're both in surgery," Newman said. "She's got a severed brachial artery, he's got a chest wound. They think the shot might have nicked his lung."

"Jesus." Gil absorbed the news with more difficulty than he would have imagined. Tebbins...well, he'd thought he didn't particularly care for the man, but apparently he was wrong. Worry squeezed him. And Anna. Thinking of Anna set off an almost intolerable ache deep inside him. "What happened?"

"The way we figure it," Newman said, "is she attacked him."

"*She* attacked *him*?" Gil was stunned.

"That's how it looks. She must've shot him. We found the gun in the hallway."

Gil shook his head. "What about an intruder?"

Newman rolled his eyes. "Yeah, right. They were the only two people there."

"I want to see the scene."

Newman shook his head. "No need. We're handling it."

"I want to see the scene," Gil said, his voice taking on an edge. "Tebbins and I are working on a case together."

Newman looked about to argue, but after a moment gave in. "Sure, why not," he said. "But I'm going with you."

It was like any other crime scene. Yellow tape cordoned off the yard. Bright lights poured out of the inside windows from the floodlights being used by the remaining criminologists. The work was almost done. For now, anyway.

But this one was different for Gil. Because

he'd been to this house before. As a guest. As a colleague. The familiar sight of the crime-scene activity jolted and scraped against the familiar sight of a house he knew.

Markers were scattered on the lawn. A closer look showed that they indicated a blood trail leading to the hedge between Tebbins's house and the neighbor's. Gil followed the trail with his eyes up to the open front door of the house. God, she had been bleeding heavily.

Inside the house there was more blood, and overturned furniture.

The blood trail went down the hallway, but about midway it changed. Instead of the signature arterial spray, it lessened to a thinner trail, as if someone had crawled or dragged himself from the room at the end of the hall to this point.

"This is where we found Tebbins," Newman said. "And the gun and the butcher knife."

Gil nodded, studying the trails, reaching conclusions.

"The way we figure it, she shot him back there in his office. Then she came out this way, probably to look for something. Maybe those videotapes in the living room. She's a suspect in the museum robbery, right?"

"Some think so."

"Well, there must have been something on the tapes to incriminate her, we figure. So she shot him back there, then came out here. Only Tebbins wasn't out. He crawled down the hallway, she heard him, came back, he stabbed her."

Gil nodded slowly. "Where the hell did he get the butcher knife? And where was *his* gun?"

"His gun was in the study where he was shot. It was fired once."

"And the knife?"

Newman shrugged. "Maybe he'd carried it back there for some reason. People use knives for all kinds of things."

"True. But he had a gun. So why didn't he bring it with him instead of a knife?"

Newman shifted uneasily. "He'd been shot. He wasn't thinking clearly."

"Clearly enough to crawl down the hallway."

"Maybe she brought the knife with her when she heard him moving. Maybe she meant it for extra protection."

But she was the one who got stabbed. The scenario bothered Gil, but he was well aware that with a little polishing, it could play out in a courtroom, unless there was a stack of physical evidence to disprove it. And so far the stalker, whoever he was, had been damn good at not leaving useful evidence behind.

"What about signs of forced entry?"

Newman shook his head. "The French doors in the study were unlocked. No sign of forced entry."

"Somebody said a cop almost hit Anna when she ran out of the hedges."

"Yeah." Newman pulled a pad out of his back pocket and consulted it. "Jeff Ingles. He was the one who brought Lundgren here from her house."

"I want to talk to him."

Jeff Ingles was still shaken. Paramedics had doused him all over with hydrogen peroxide and sent him home to shower and change. Roxie, of course, turned her ire from Vic to him. The whole time he showered, she stood outside the stall and ranted about the stupidity of him getting covered with some stranger's blood, and how they weren't going to have sex again for six months until she was sure he hadn't caught anything. By the time he got out of the shower, he actually thought that sounded like a relief. His son Vic, much to his amazement, had decided Jeff was a real hero, and got into it with his mother over whether Jeff had done the noble thing by saving Anna Lundgren's life.

Jeff, who wasn't used to his son considering him anything except a walking, talking squawk box, felt kind of good about that. But he felt pretty bad leaving Vic behind to deal with Roxie. Although Vic seemed less troubled by Roxie's rants than Jeff.

Back at the scene of the crime, he hung around, answering questions, waiting for someone to tell him what he was supposed to do next, other than fill out his reports. He was assigned to the Lundgren woman, but she was in the hospital. Maybe he ought to go down there and keep an eye on her, since he hadn't managed to do a very good job of it earlier. He felt really bad about that.

But just as he was deciding to go call in and

find out what they wanted him to do, just as the crime-scene van was about to finish up, he was called over to talk to a detective from St. Pete.

He recognized Vance Newman, although he'd never worked directly with him. The detective was a newcomer to the area, having come from Orlando about a year ago.

He'd also recognized Garcia, whom he'd seen around the museum.

"So what's the story?" Garcia asked him.

"I was assigned to bring Anna Lundgren to Detective Tebbins's house this evening around six."

"Did anybody explain why?"

"Yes, sir. Detective Tebbins explained that she was a material witness, and he needed her assistance reviewing some videotapes. He also explained that she had been threatened, and that I was to be extremely careful. Which I was. When I delivered Ms. Lundgren to his door, he said that she would be safe with him, and I should go get some supper. Which I did."

Garcia nodded. "And then?"

"While I was eating, I heard about the alarm at Tebbins's house. So I hurried back. I just came around the corner over there when I saw a woman jump out of the hedges and run toward the street. I jammed my brakes on so I wouldn't hit her. Right about the time I stopped, she impacted the hood of my car."

"Impacted?"

The memory was still too vivid in Jeff's mind.

It was a moment before he could continue in a properly detached tone. "Yes, sir. Impacted. I was stopped, and she ran right into me. Hard. Then she sank to the ground. I got out and did what I could to stop her bleeding."

"The woman was Ms. Lundgren?"

Jeff nodded.

"Was she trying to escape?"

Jeff shook his head. "I assume she was trying to escape from an assailant."

"No, I mean, did she try to avoid *you* in any way."

Jeff was surprised. "No, sir. It was obvious she was running out to get help. She came out of the bushes as soon as my car was visible, and she came straight to me. No way was she trying to avoid me."

He noted the way Garcia looked at Vance, but it wasn't his problem. All he wanted was for this damn shift to be over so he could go home. Or maybe go to a motel. All he knew was it was going to be a long time before he forgot the sound of Anna Lundgren running into the hood of his car. Or the sight of her blood in the dusk.

"Forget it," Gil said to Newman. "You can just forget it. You're in too much of a hurry."

Newman flushed angrily. "I don't buy into phantom assailants without proof."

"You've got proof. The phone lines were cut outside. Just when did Lundgren have time to do that? She was being watched constantly by police officers. Are you suggesting that when she arrived here Officer Ingles gave her a few minutes to run around the side of the house, shinny up the tree, and cut the phone? Or that Detective Tebbins let her run around outside while he stayed inside so she could do that?"

Newman frowned. "That's still not enough. There could be another reason the line was severed. An accident of some kind. Or, she could have an accomplice."

The word "accomplice" caused a twinge inside Gil. Nancy? Where *was* Nancy anyway? Then he dismissed the whole idea. Crazy or not, he didn't believe Anna capable of shooting Tebbins.

"There's a problem with this whole idea that Lundgren did this," Gil said after a moment. "Apart from the telephone line."

"I'm listening."

"It's the whole idea that she shot him and didn't run away. Why would she hang around long enough for him to crawl halfway down the hall? And if she did, why didn't she just shoot him again? It's not adding up, Newman. Let me give you my take."

"Go ahead."

"The assailant came in by way of the French doors. Tebbins heard something and went to investigate. He was shot and returned fire once. Anna went to investigate with the only weapon she could find, a butcher knife. She met the assailant halfway down the hallway."

"So why didn't the assailant shoot *her*?"

Good question, Gil thought, staring off into the night. A damn good question. "I guess," he said after a moment, "it's because he needs her living heart."

Nancy never left Anna's bedside from the moment she was moved into a room from recovery. Tebbins, on the other hand, went from recovery to ICU. The prognosis on both of them was good.

"I'm glad to hear it," Nancy said when Gil told her. "I kinda like the little jerk."

"He's not a jerk," Gil said. "Weird, maybe."

"He's a jerk. He knows someone's after my sister but he sent the cop away. In my book, that makes him a jerk."

Gil couldn't rightly argue with her. He let his gaze trail to Anna, who was almost white against the blue sheets, except for the brilliance of her hair. Over the years he'd questioned a lot of people who looked as bad or worse, but they weren't people he cared about.

"Is she waking up at all?"

"In and out, she has spells of moaning. But she hasn't been fully conscious yet. Why?"

"We need to ask if she saw who did it."

"*We?*"

"Detective Newman is outside."

Nancy scowled. "You mean they don't think Anna did it? They're not absolutely convinced that she shot Tebbins and stabbed *herself*? Those cops in the hallway have been looking at her like they'd like to kill her. I get the feeling they think she's a serial killer. First Richter, now Tebbins."

"It *does* look suspicious," Gil said, his voice heavy with reluctance. "You can see that, Nancy."

Her eyes were reddened as they rose to his. "I thought you were on *her* side."

"I am. And that's why I need to ask her if she saw who did it."

Nancy looked down and twisted her fingers together. "What if she doesn't know who it was? I mean, what if she saw someone but can't identify him?"

"Then maybe she can give us enough of a description to go on."

Nancy nodded slowly. "Just make sure those guys outside know that it's as important to keep strangers out of this room as it is to keep Anna and me in here. God!" She shook her head and looked out the window. "As if she could get up and go anywhere on her own right now."

"I'll make sure they know." Walking to Anna's bedside, he took her hand gently and held it. Memories of the afternoon, just a few short hours ago, seemed a long way away now, at once sharp and haunting, and far beyond reach.

They should never have made love. Never. Not just because it violated his professional ethics, but because he sensed that in some way he had wounded them both. He didn't really trust his own judgment now, and she probably felt...used. Taken advantage of by a man who might hold her future in his hands.

It left a sour taste in his mouth.

Too late now. Gathering his thoughts, he

resisted an urge to bend over and kiss her. Instead he let go of her hand, nodded to Nancy, and returned to the hallway.

He wasn't going anywhere, he decided. This might not be his case, but he wasn't going to leave it up to Vance Newman.

Not as long as there was someone out there who wanted to kill Anna.

Gil was on his way to the cafeteria to get some coffee the next morning when his boss called him. Finding a quiet corner, he put the cell phone to his ear. "What's up, Ed?"

Ed Sanchez's voice dripped sarcasm. "And here I thought things would be quiet for a while since Scamus is away on vacation. Now I'm hearing rumbles that you're sticking your nose too far into a Tampa PD case."

"I'm working my own case," Gil said, silently cursing Vance Newman. "The Malacek homicide."

"Last I heard, that was looking like an O.D."

"The toxicology still isn't in. And like I told you, it looks like it's related to the museum robbery."

"Your name is becoming too familiar across the bay. You understand?"

"I understand. I also understand I'm chasing a killer. I don't have to cooperate, I can run my own investigation wherever it leads me."

"Within reason. As long as you're not treading on the toes of other jurisdictions. And you apparently trod somewhere you shouldn't."

Gil sighed, restraining his impatience. "Detective Tebbins suggested we join forces."

"Detective Tebbins, I hear, is now lying unconscious in ICU. That changes the players."

"Same case, same rules."

It was Sanchez's turn to sigh. "Why are you so hot on this? If it really is connected to the museum robbery, they'll catch the perp, and you'll have your man."

"I'm hot on it because they're looking at the wrong suspect. And if they don't start looking in the right direction, someone else could get killed."

"I hear she's pretty."

Damn Newman, Gil thought. Newman must have seen him take Anna's hand last night in her hospital room. "She's also going to be the perp's next victim. I'm staying."

"I could yank you."

"Don't. Don't."

Sanchez was silent for a few moments. "I could propose an M.O.U."

"You could propose it," Gil agreed. A memorandum of understanding—detailing the shared jurisdiction and setting out working arrangements—would put him on the case officially, even in Tampa. What he and Tebbins had done by mutual, informal agreement, he and Newman would do by order of their respective departments. "Of course, TPD might not accept it."

"It's worth a try," Sanchez said. He paused a moment. "Just don't let me hear any more complaints."

Relieved, Gil disconnected and got his

coffee. He had more time. And with any luck at all, Anna would wake up and be able to identify the perp.

Any luck. And it was about damn time they had some.

When he got back up to Anna's floor he found Vance Newman had arrived. The guy looked fresh, as if he'd managed to get a shower and some sleep. He also looked a little surprised to see Gil.

"You still here?" he asked.

"I'm working a murder case, remember? Lundgren's a material witness. My boss is going to write up the M.O.U. I'm sure it'll fly with your boss."

After a moment, Newman shrugged. "Just don't get in the way."

They entered the room together. Nancy was sitting on the edge of her sister's bed, looking exhausted but much happier. "She's waking up," she said. "She spoke to me."

Newman nodded. "I need to ask her a few questions."

"Just don't wear her out. The nurse said she needs to rest. She lost a lot of blood."

"I know." Practiced sympathy. He turned to Anna. "Ms. Lundgren? Ms. Lundgren, do you hear me?"

Anna's eyes fluttered open, sleepy, pain-filled slits.

"Ms. Lundgren? Who stabbed you?"

"Lance Barro."

"Who shot Detective Tebbins?"

"Lance." A tear ran down her cheek. "Tebbins...okay?"

"He's going to be fine," Gil said when Newman didn't answer. "He's going to be just fine."

"Lance," she said groggily. "It was Lance. I liked him..."

"Okay," Nancy said. "That's enough. You've got your name. Now get in gear and find the son of a bitch."

It wasn't that easy. He hadn't shown up for work or classes that morning, and he hadn't been seen around his apartment for several days. By evening, it seemed as if he had disappeared from the planet.

Worse, Gil found as he checked out the man's academic record, Lance Barro very nearly *was* the Invisible Man. The transcripts were real enough, but that was it. None of his graduate program professors seemed to know more than that he was in their classes. His academic advisor recalled talking to the man, but couldn't remember anything about him. The same held for Barro's undergraduate work at the University of Minnesota. He was just a face in the classroom, a name in the grade books.

His trail died at U of M. It was as if he'd invented his identity when he entered college. And had kept it a closely guarded secret. Even his ID photo said nothing about him. A face, neutral and wholly unremarkable, looking into the camera but devoid of any discernible feeling about having to do so. No forced smile. No distracted stare. Nothing.

Lance Barro had practiced hiding for a long, long time. Gil had no illusions about the ease with which someone could disappear, especially in a large, transient, metropolitan jungle like the Tampa Bay area. With the right posture and body language, he could walk through a crowded mall with his picture posted on every door and shop window, and no one would give him a second glance.

Now back at the hospital, looking down at Anna's sleep-softened face, with Nancy curled uncomfortably in a chair across the room and fidgeting in a dream, Gil realized he'd learned more than he'd thought in the seemingly futile day's work. Newman would continue the chase, Gil knew. But they wouldn't find Barro. Somehow, Gil would have to get Barro to come to him.

As he studied the veins visible under Anna's pale skin, Gil knew what that "somehow" would be. And he didn't like it one bit.

CHAPTER TWENTY-ONE

❖❖❖

Five days later, Tebbins was reasserting control of the case from his hospital bed. Newman didn't like it, but Gil was grateful for it. Newman was singularly unimaginative, and while Tebbins could be overly so, his imagination was much more useful than Newman's plodding, prosaic mind that could only see what was right before it.

Anna, her left arm in a sling, and Nancy were also present in Tebbins's room. Nancy had demanded that Newman confiscate some chairs from a couple of empty rooms so that she and Anna could sit against the wall. And when Newman had suggested they had no place there, Anna had gotten fired up.

"I *belong* here," she told Newman icily. "It's *my* heart he wants to cut out, and I have every right to know what you're going to do about it."

"Let her stay," Tebbins said. He still didn't sound quite like his old self. His moustache was gone, having given way at some point during his treatment. His upper lip was pale from lack of sun, almost like a vestige of a moustache.

The head of the bed was raised so he could see them all, but his movements were still languid and an IV inhibited them even more. He looked deflated somehow, as if his essence had been reduced.

But his dark eyes were still sharp, and his tongue equally sharp. "Fill me in," he said to Anna. "Exactly what did he say to you?"

"Basically that he has to offer my living heart in order to put an end to the curse."

"So he *does* believe in the curse."

"Yes, he does. Apparently his family was killed in the refinery explosion in Mexico. Anyway, he seems to think he's trying to save a lot of other lives by taking mine."

"Hardly an original motivation." Tebbins lifted his right arm, the one free of tubes and tape, and attempted to stroke his missing moustache. The movement made him wince. "But still we know very little about him."

"We know *nothing* about him," Gil said. "He's been covering his tracks for a long time. Being as invisible as he could be while still pursuing some kind of life."

"So he's planned this for a long time."

"So it would seem."

"And now we need to draw him out somehow."

Gil couldn't help it; he looked at Anna. Her eyes widened a shade. Then she spoke.

"You need bait," she said. "That's what you're thinking, isn't it?"

He nodded, his heart heavy with reluctance.

Tebbins tutted. "That won't do at all."

Nancy's objection was even more adamant. "There is no way you're going to dangle my sister in front of that sicko like a piece of meat on a hook. No way."

"I quite agree," Gil said. "No way. The problem is...until we catch him, Anna's still the bait on the hook any way you look at it. He's still after her. What we need to do is make it happen in a controlled situation."

"The department will shit a brick," Newman said. "I won't allow it."

Tebbins barely glanced at him. "Be silent unless you've got something to offer other than an objection."

Newman was silent, but he didn't look as if he'd spoken his last.

Gil spoke. "I don't like the idea either. In fact, I *hate* it. I've been trying to find a way around it for four days now. But it remains, we can't find a trace of Barro. Not a trace. He's exactly the kind of guy who could disappear in a crowd and never be seen again. We can't find any frequent contacts or friends he might turn to. No family. No favorite hangouts, other than the museum. Everybody seems to know him but not know him, if you know what I mean. He doesn't even have a girlfriend. Or a boyfriend. It's like he's there but he's not."

Even Newman had to give a reluctant nod to that. "We've checked every avenue. No car, no credit cards. There's been no activity on his bank account since Friday when he withdrew everything except a hundred dollars. He was ready to go into hiding. And he could be anywhere."

"Exactly." Gil looked at Tebbins. "We have to draw him out. Because if we don't, he could stalk Anna for weeks or months. Even years. However long it takes for him to feel safe enough to act again. And we both know we can't guarantee her safety for that long."

Tebbins sighed and closed his eyes.

"Give me another plan," Gil said. "I'll jump at it. The last thing I want is to put these women in jeopardy."

"We're already in jeopardy," Anna said. "I'll do it."

"No." Nancy's tone was sharp. "*I'll* do it. I'm in better shape right now, and I can pass for you without any trouble at all. I can even do your voice."

Gil was ashamed of the relief he felt when Nancy volunteered. Ashamed that Anna meant so much to him that he was more willing to risk her sister. Ashamed because he knew that Anna would be horrified if she even guessed.

Tebbins opened his eyes again. "I don't have another plan," he admitted reluctantly. "And you're right. The Lundgrens are at risk until we catch Barro. However long it takes. If he really believes in the curse, he's not going to drop it just because it got difficult."

"No," Gil agreed. "It started to get difficult the day I chased him. Nothing's been going right for him since."

Tebbins nodded slowly. His right hand moved futilely toward his mouth, but he stopped it mid-movement. "We still need a method of drawing him out," he said. "Bait or no bait, we have to be able to get to him somehow, and convince him to come out of hiding."

"Which means," Gil said, "that we need to use his own beliefs against him. We need to make him think the curse is turning against *him*."

"Yes," said Tebbins, and his dark eyes were suddenly sparkling. "Yes, indeed."

"There's just one problem," Newman said from the corner where he was sulking. "You have to be able to communicate with him. How the hell are you going to do that when you don't know where he is?"

Gil shrugged. "Oh, I think Reed Howell might be just the mouthpiece we need."

"Yes, he would," Anna agreed. "And he owes me, after printing all those insinuating stories about my father."

Newman didn't like the idea. "You can't lie to the press. You'll give the department a black eye."

"Nobody," said Tebbins, "said a word about lying."

"No, we don't want to lie," Gil agreed. "We just need to shade a little." He paced over to the window and looked down at the parking lot, which was falling into the shadow of the building as the sun settled firmly in the west.

"We know he believes in the curse. We know he thinks he's saving himself and others by trying to kill Anna. He spoke of offering her heart and...what was it he said, Anna?"

"There's a belief that the sacrificial victim becomes godlike. It was quite an honor, actually. He seemed to be offering that as an inducement."

"So basically he thinks the gods are on *his* side," Gil said. "What if we convince him otherwise?"

"He'd panic," Anna said flatly. "He's half-panicked now, I think, convinced that if he doesn't offer my heart, the curse will get him."

"So...we convince him the curse wants him, not you."

"Easier said than done."

"I don't know," Tebbins said musingly. "It might not be as difficult as it sounds." Suddenly he smiled. "No, it won't be difficult at all."

Several days later, Anna, Nancy and Gil gathered around Anna's television to watch the

346

evening news. Reed Howell's paper, the *Sentinel*, was owned by a media conglomerate that also owned a local TV station. Reed had wanted the exclusive from Anna, but he'd also demanded some video clips he could use to put a brief story on the evening news before the full story hit the morning paper. Gil and Tebbins had talked it over and agreed. Two swings at Barro were better than none.

They had, however, insisted that Anna not speak on camera, primarily because it wasn't Anna being filmed, but Nancy. Gil had worried that if they gave Barro too good a look at her, he might catch on, and one of the main ideas he wanted to convey was that Anna was having a "miraculous" recovery.

So they watched as Nancy sat at Anna's desk, pretending to work while Howell did a voice-over. At one point the camera zoomed in to show just a small bandage on Nancy's arm.

"It's eerie," Anna said when the segment was over. Nancy clicked off the TV.

"What is?" her sister asked.

"I think of us as being identical until I watch you pretend to be me. It's eerie how much you have to change."

Gil spoke. He was sitting on the couch beside Anna, a fact which everyone had avoided commenting on. "You move very differently. And you have different voices."

Nancy looked at him. "The question is, did I pass?"

"You passed," Gil said firmly. "If he sees it, he'll be sure it's Anna."

Lance saw it. He'd taken a room in a run-down house not too far from campus in a bad neighborhood. Nobody cared who he was or when he came and went. It was enough he'd paid a hundred dollars cash to get the room for a week.

It wasn't much of a room. Roach-ridden, filthy, with bare wood floors that hadn't been cleaned in a lifetime. He crashed on a battered bit of stuffing that had once been a mattress and spent all his time trying to figure out how he was going to get to Anna now.

Finally, frustrated and despairing, he walked to a nearby bar and ordered a beer.

In time to see the evening news.

Anna's face floated before him on the TV at one end of the bar, riveting him. Over the din of the other patrons, he could barely hear Reed Howell's voice talking about how Anna had made a miraculous recovery, and how the police were certain they were close to capturing him. His face, from his university ID card, flashed on the screen, causing him to start, but then he reminded himself that no one would recognize him. Not only was he supremely ordinary-looking, but the photo had never resembled him at all. Nobody turned to look at him.

Reed went on about how Anna was returning to work, that she wasn't afraid because the museum had all kinds of security, and now that the police knew how Barro had beaten it, he

348

wouldn't be able to do so again. And he finished up by saying that while Lance Barro thought he was serving the gods, it was apparent that the gods were on Anna Lundgren's side.

Lance didn't even finish his beer. Shoving himself away from the bar, he got up and hurried out into the warm evening, needing to be as far away as he possibly could.

The gods were on *her* side?

The thought infuriated him. The hubris of it infuriated him. *He* was the servant of the jaguar, not her. He was the one devoting his life and strength to returning the dagger to its rightful place.

But he knew a niggle of fear, too. He had shot Tebbins. He had stabbed Anna. Badly. He'd seen the blood. She couldn't possibly be healed by now, unless divine intervention had assisted her in her recovery. And Tebbins had survived.

Something was very, very wrong. What if Howell was right? What if the gods were on Anna's side? What if Lance had messed up so badly that the jaguar god had withdrawn his favor?

He had to redeem himself, and soon. Very soon. Throughout the night he paced the streets, trying to figure out how to do it. How to do it without failing. Without a single slip.

He couldn't afford to fail again.

Anna absolutely refused to allow Nancy to replace her at the museum.

"For God's sake," Nancy demanded, "why not? You're badly hurt. You don't have the strength to do this."

"I have plenty of strength, and I'll be damned if I let you go into this tiger's mouth in my place."

Nancy waved a dismissing hand. "The place is going to be crawling with cops. He won't be able to breathe without getting caught."

"Exactly," Anna said, looking at her with fiery eyes. "So *I* can do it."

Both Tebbins and Gil had been shunted to the side in this discussion. Tebbins, freshly out of the hospital, was looking rather peaked as he sat in a corner of Anna's living room. Gil was standing near the front window, watching the street as the morning sun brightened it. The two surveillance cars were gone, a calculated risk. The cops were now inside with them. Waiting.

Nobody had slept very well the previous night. The story was in the newspaper that morning, teased on the front page, above the fold. They all figured that if Barro had missed the newscast, he was sure to see the paper.

The question was, where was he going to strike? And when? Everyone, Gil included, felt that he would probably choose to come after Anna at the museum, after closing, when she would stay late, ostensibly to catch up on her work. There would be more opportunities for him to hide himself there, or so he would think. What he wouldn't know was the number of Tampa police officers who would be there, ready to spring on anything that moved.

But the house was a risk, too. One of the sisters would be here, under police guard.

"Both of you," Gil said, "are going to be in jeopardy. I can't make that clear enough. Anna, there's no way you have enough strength yet to put in a full day at the museum and then hang around there this evening. No way."

"Exactly," Nancy said. "Don't be a goose, Anna. I'll go to work for you. At least here you can sleep when you need to and be comfortable."

"Everyone will know it's not me! You don't know my job. You don't know the people."

Tebbins sighed. "She has a point."

"I can go to work late," Anna suggested. "It won't matter. After what I've been through, not even he would expect me to be there on time. So I'll go in late, and work late. He's not going to pull anything in broad daylight anyway, not when there'll be so many people around."

"If you're going to go in late," Nancy said stubbornly, "*I* can do it. I can cover for that long."

Tebbins spoke. "Are you two always so argumentative?"

Neither woman answered him, not that he seemed to expect it.

And the problem still wasn't solved, Gil thought, looking out at the street again. They were on the horns of a very real dilemma, one which, he realized, would have been a whole hell of a lot easier if Anna hadn't had a twin.

"They both go to the museum," he said finally. "There's no other way to do it. From what Anna says of his motivation, he might be after both of them."

"Having both of them together might compound our problems," Tebbins argued. "Not only would we have two people to watch, but he might be put off making his move if he thinks he has to go up against both of them at the same time."

"I know." Gil turned from the window. "But I don't see that we have any choice. The last thing we want to do now is give him two separate targets to go after."

The afternoon shift changeover in security at the museum went off as usual. The only difference was that the men wearing the uniforms of the security contractor were Tampa police officers. Another group of officers trickled in wearing plainclothes, appearing to be museum visitors.

Officers were concealed in the security equipment room, to ensure that Barro didn't get a chance to disrupt the systems. Others were stationed in offices near exterior doors to prevent anyone from coming and going without being seen.

Little by little they sifted into their places of concealment, waiting for the museum to close.

Anna and Nancy holed up in her office. Anna was looking pale but plowed determinedly on through the paperwork on her desk.

Nancy scanned some of Anna's journals, filling the time.

Little by little the museum grew quieter. Outside the windows, night settled over the world. Finally, Anna got up and closed the blinds.

They were locked in for the night.

By midnight Anna was dozing in her chair, and Nancy's nervous pacing had given way to nibbling at hangnails. Gil rubbed his tired eyes. There was nothing more to do tonight except drive everyone to exhaustion. It was time to go home and try again tomorrow.

The problem, he knew, was that this waiting game took a toll on diligence and attentiveness. Time was on Barro's side. With every night that they went through this routine, the human security would weaken.

He shook Anna gently. "I'm going to call it for the night," he said when her eyes focused. "We all need rest."

She nodded sleepily. Even Nancy seemed too drained to object. As they packed up, he picked up his walkie-talkie.

"We're moving. Switch to transit assignments. Nominal overnight watch, so everything looks normal."

Most of the undercover guards headed out to their cars, some going off shift, others preparing to escort Anna and Nancy back to their house.

The new shift, a group of officers pulled from both the Tampa PD and the Sheriff's Department, took their assignments in the lobby. The shift supervisor, a corporal from the TPD, looked with distaste at a rookie the sheriff had sent. Nobody'd even bothered to tell him to wear plainclothes.

"How long you been on the job, son?"

"Six weeks."

The supervisor sighed. "Well, okay, then. You take the equipment room." It was the least troublesome assignment, and the safest place for everyone to stash a rookie. Behind a locked door, he couldn't get into too much trouble.

And Lance Barro, wearing a deputy's uniform, walked into the one room in the museum that he most wanted to enter.

CHAPTER TWENTY-TWO

It was ten o'clock the next night. Anna was sagging over her desk, looking even more exhausted than the night before. Nancy had given up on the journals and was playing solitaire at one end of the desk.

Gil was in danger of pacing a hole in the industrial carpeting. "Who wants coffee?" he asked.

"Coffee?" Anna said.

"Hey, this place is full of cops. You don't imagine we can survive without it. I'll bet there are doughnuts, too."

Anna smiled wearily.

"Sounds good," Nancy said. "Anna?"

Anna nodded. "Thanks."

"How do you like it?"

"Black," the sisters answered in one voice.

"Makes my life easy." He smiled, hoping the expression looked natural. He didn't want them picking up on his nerves. "Lock the door behind me."

He waited in the hallway until he heard the lock *snick* into place. It was a good opportunity to check out the precautions. He found the officer at the front desk, wearing the commercial firm's uniform, sipping coffee and eating a glazed doughnut. "How's it going?"

"A-OK," he answered. "Everyone's where they should be. All the systems are functioning."

But Gil had been stung by those systems once before. "Just keep a good eye on the video. This guy is smart."

The officer nodded. "Will do."

"That coffee any good?"

"Made it myself a little while ago. The urn's full."

Gil made his way back to the break room. An officer in plainclothes was there, filling a half dozen foam cups from the urn, apparently to distribute. There was a box of two dozen doughnuts next to the urn. Gil almost grinned. Didn't that figure?

"Everything okay?" Gil asked.

The officer nodded. "Not a peep, not a move. Nobody's going to get in here tonight."

Gil was hoping somebody would at least try.

He filled three cups for himself and the women, and carried them back to the office on a plastic tray.

Nancy opened the door and let him in. "You know," she said as she took one of the cups, "this is the most boring thing I've ever done."

"Stakeouts usually are."

"The guy must be onto us."

"Maybe." It was a possibility Gil had been turning around in his mind for a while. "We'll deal with that if we have to."

It was amazing, Lance thought, how easy information was to come by. The cops probably thought they'd been secretive about their plans, but he'd overheard enough from conversations to figure out what was happening. They'd set a trap for him. The idea actually thrilled him, put him on his mettle. It would make his triumph all the greater.

And it was so easy to find things out. So easy. People talked, and no one gave a second glance to a trim, youthful deputy sipping coffee and chewing a donut. He thought he'd blown it when he'd been the only one to show up in a uniform, but apparently that had worked in his favor. He'd seen the dismissive look in the cop's eye when he assigned him to the equipment room.

The breaks were coming Lance's way again, and he could nearly smell his victory. The jaguar hadn't forsaken him. Anna was wrong about that.

He'd spent the day above the second floor, in the crawl space where all the service conduits and ducts ran. It had been hot and miserable, but he'd stashed enough water and granola bars before he made his first move to keep himself comfortable.

Now it was night again, and the museum was his. He'd bypassed the alarm systems last night, and no one knew it. No one had any reason to know it. They all appeared to be functioning.

He could go anywhere he wanted. Anywhere at all. And the officer making that pot of coffee... Lance almost rubbed his hands in delight. He'd dumped in the last of the rohypnol he'd bought on the street weeks ago. It would be enough to knock out everyone.

Then they'd all be at his mercy. Every last one of them. And he would get to make a double sacrifice on the altar in the exhibit. Two at once. Surely the jaguar would bless him now.

And the yoke of the curse would be off his shoulders forever.

All he had to do was wait a little longer. Just a little longer.

Anna fell asleep in her chair. She yawned and leaned back and her eyes closed. Gil watched her sleep, feeling pretty tired himself. He glanced at his watch. Another hour or so and he'd call it off for the night. And tomorrow he had to figure out another way of getting at Barro.

He ought to consider that now, but he was feeling too drowsy. He glanced toward Nancy and found she, too, had fallen asleep, curled into a tight ball on the armchair. How did she do that?

With no one to talk to, his mind seemed even more prone to drift. Strange dreamlike images began to float in his brain, and he had to jerk himself awake a couple of times.

This won't do, he told himself. Picking up his radio, he asked the stations to report in.

But no one answered him. Not a single soul replied.

A chilling thought wafted into his consciousness. The coffee. They'd been drugged.

Adrenaline began to pound through him, easing the effects of the drug. Rising, he decided to call for help before he did anything else.

Just then the office door opened and a uniform stepped in.

"What the hell's going on?" Gil asked him, finding it difficult to force the words out. "Nobody's answering the radio."

"They're all asleep," the deputy said.

Then, before Gil even saw it coming, a baton snapped open and cracked him in the side of the head.

It was such a strange dream, Anna thought. A deputy with Lance Barro's face was urging her to come with him. She'd be safe, he assured her. She just had to come with him. She might not have trusted him except that

Nancy was there, too, urging her to come along. But Nancy sounded funny, her words slurred.

But it must be okay, because the deputy was helping her walk, talking in an encouraging voice. Except why did he look like Lance Barro?

They entered the exhibit through the double doors. It was only dimly lit, and Anna's mind struggled with the bizarre images that seemed to pop out of the shadows. The jungle seemed to have thickened, filling with danger, and she wondered if they were somehow in a real jungle. Had she been magically transported across time and space? Or was she just dreaming?

No, she thought dimly, as panic began to rise in her, it was the exhibit. It was. She could tell as dimly lit display cases floated by. And Nancy was still with her, beside her. Stumbling from time to time as if the floor were rough and ragged. She would have stumbled, too, except the deputy kept supporting her.

She looked up at him, smiling, wanting to thank him for his help, but in the strange lighting his face had grown strange, too, like a hardened mask. Who was he?

Then came the steps. She knew where they were now, and that eased some of her panic. The Pocal chamber. They were just in the exhibit. He must think she and Nancy would be safer hiding here.

He let go of her, and she slumped to the floor beside the sarcophagus. Dimly she was aware of the beastly pain in her arm, a hammering throb, but it seemed a long way away. Nancy slumped beside her.

"Nance?" Her sister's name came out thickly. Nancy didn't even look at her.

It was strange, so strange. Then she looked up at the deputy, wondering what they would do next.

When she saw the dagger, she knew.

Gil came to with a jolt. Rolling over, he groaned and stared up at the fluorescent lights on the ceiling. What had happened?

His mouth tasted bad, his head throbbed as if it were being worked over by a pile driver. It was difficult to even focus on the lights.

Where was he? Then he remembered. With a crash, it came back. He'd been drugged. Then he'd been cracked on the side of the head with a baton.

Nancy. Anna! Groaning again, he rolled over and shoved himself to his feet. Oh, God, they were gone!

Reaching for the phone, he dialed 9-1-1.

Lance Barro looked at his two lovely captives and felt a pang for what he was about to do. Even though it was a right and necessary thing that he must do, he couldn't help but feel badly about it.

They were so lovely, the two of them. Like bright candle flames of life, youth, and beauty. But of course, that was why they would make such a perfect offering. Those who were chosen were always young and in their prime. Warriors, as Anna had said, and maidens and youths. Perfect offerings. For centuries the Maya and Aztecs had preserved their world through such offerings. Now he was going to preserve his own, and the worlds of others who had no idea they were under the curse.

He felt good about that, but he felt bad, too. He had always liked Anna, and he supposed he would have liked her sister. Part of him rebelled at what he was about to do.

But that was an important part of the sacrifice, he knew. If it was easy to do, it wouldn't be meaningful.

The rohypnol had been a perfect touch, he thought. In the old days, sacrificial victims had been given hashish to dull their senses. He had simply gone one step further, to ensure that the sacrifice these women were about to make would be flawless. Their cooperation was ensured. As it should be.

But he hesitated still. He didn't know if he could do it. In a moment of lucidity, he wondered if he was capable of cutting out a living human heart. He had read about it, had envisioned it countless times, but now that the moment was at hand, the enormity of his intentions seemed to strike him.

Another test, he told himself. A test of his determination. One he must pass.

He had given careful consideration to the place and manner of his gift. There was a mock-up of an altar in another room of the

361

exhibit, but he had decided the rite would be far more meaningful here, on the replica of Pocal's sarcophagus. It would symbolize—better than anything else he could do—his reconsecration of the desecrated tomb in Mexico.

The only thing that could have been better would have been sacrificing Anna and Nancy in the original tomb. But such was impossible. That had been one difficulty he couldn't see any way to surmount.

But this was good enough. The intent was clear. And after all, rites were symbolic.

They were looking at him, his two lovely captives. Nancy's gaze was vague, almost opaque. As if she were hardly aware of what she was seeing. Anna's gaze was a little sharper, as if her drugged brain were making connections about him and the dagger in his hand. But the rohypnol worked, and she didn't move. Didn't even utter a mewl of protest. It was good.

Encouraged, he decided Nancy should go first. In whatever dim brain Anna had left, he wanted her to understand what was going to happen to her. She needed to understand to make the perfect sacrifice. Watching her sister go first would make her fully aware of her role.

Setting the dagger aside, on top of the case that had once protected it, he bent to help Nancy to her feet.

"Come along," he said, keeping his voice soothing and gentle. "You need to do something for me."

Her eyes barely focused on him, but she

struggled to comply. He needed to help lift her almost as much as he needed to steady her, but at least she wasn't an unconscious weight flopping around. She cooperated as much as she could.

"Up here," he said, keeping his voice gentle. With a little prodding and pushing, he got her up onto the sarcophagus lid, and persuaded her to lie on her back.

"There," he said, feeling suddenly very kind, "you're just going to take a nice nap."

"Nancy..." Anna's whisper reached him, sounding eerie in the stillness of the tomb.

He glanced quickly down at her, but she hadn't moved. Good. The drug was still working. As it should be. If he had needed it to, it would have worked for several hours. But all he needed was a few more minutes. He went to get the dagger.

Tebbins was having a fit of frustration. His wound was keeping him out of the action, away from the museum. He fumed and fussed and listened to his scanner. Nothing, nothing, and it was annoying him no end that this creep, this animal, might be outwitting him. He wouldn't be allowed to sustain this operation much longer. No way. He might get one more night, maybe two, before they'd be all over his ass, demanding that he stop wasting resources.

Then what? A headline in a few days or weeks announcing the mutilation death of Anna Lundgren? The possibility gnawed at him.

But even as he turned these thoughts around in his mind, Tebbins knew he was reaching. There was no great criminal mastermind behind this case, no huge intellect with an army of henchmen. There was simply one deluded man.

The hardest of all to catch.

Then he heard something on the radio that caused him to sit upright. A jolt of pain shot through him, making him grit his teeth, but he ignored it. Thirty seconds later he was on the phone, demanding a cruiser to pick him up immediately.

The world was swimming, as if Gil were on a ship in storm-tossed seas. The floor seemed to cant to one side and then another, forcing him to grip the wall as he stumbled down the hallway toward the lobby.

He didn't know if it was the drug or the blow to the head that was affecting him; he didn't have the energy or clarity of thought to worry about it. His one thought, his one clear thought, was that he had to find Anna. Now.

The lobby was empty, but it wasn't still. It kept heaving on him. He could see the back of the cop sitting at the security station in front of the row of monitors. He called out, but got no answer.

Clinging to the wall, he made his way there. The door was locked. Hammering on it got no response. Drugged. The guy was drugged. The adrenaline in his system surged, warring with the drug, making him suddenly so sick that he nearly doubled over.

No time for this. *Absolutely no time for this.* By sheer effort of will he battered down the nausea and pulled his gun. It seemed to want to stick in his belt holster, but at last it came free. To steady it, he had to put it right against the door lock.

He fired. The sound seemed to echo through the lobby, ringing in his ears. Oh, God, maybe he shouldn't have done that. What if Barro heard it?

But it was too late now. And the security cameras were his only hope of finding Nancy and Anna in time.

Shouldering his way into the room, he pushed the snoring guard aside and leaned over the console. Images danced in front of his eyes, reluctant to resolve into anything useful.

But then his gaze flickered over the screen showing the tomb. All of a sudden everything resolved into stark clarity. Two cameras showed Nancy lying on the sarcophagus as if asleep. Another one picked up a man in a deputy's uniform. He was carrying the dagger.

The adrenaline punch surged over the inhibiting drug. Turning, Gil ran unsteadily toward the door to the exhibit.

Anna saw the dagger. Everything around it was a blur, but she saw the knife itself sharply, clearly as it moved toward her. Her arm, still resting in a sling, twinged with remembered pain. He was going to cut out her heart.

For some reason the thought seemed distantly interesting, not at all frightening. She ought to be frightened. She knew that. But she was paralyzed by an immense indifference. A strange dissociation, as if what were about to happen were going to happen to someone else.

But the dagger moved past her, sparing her. She watched it dreamily, wondering why she had ever been afraid of it, watching as it rose in the air.

Nancy!

A cold wind suddenly froze her heart, sweeping away all the dreaminess. He was going to kill Nancy. And somehow that was far more important than what he did to her.

Turning against the sarcophagus, forcing reluctant muscles to work, she bent over, and with all her might she bit Lance Barro on the Achilles tendon. She half spat, half retched blood and tissue on the floor.

A howl of pain filled the tomb, and the dagger clattered to the floor.

She had to get it. Scrambling as if in molasses, she crawled toward it. She didn't care anymore that it was cursed. She didn't care that her father might have died for it.

All she cared was that it not claim her sister's life.

The jungle closed in around Gil. In searching for the light switches on the panel outside, he somehow managed only to turn on the sound system, filling the exhibit with the roll of distant thunder and the cry of birds.

He heard another cry, far away, muffled by the labyrinthine twists and turns of the exhibit. A cry of pain? God, Anna...

Jungle paths gave way to exhibit rooms, then turned into jungles again. His mind played tricks on him, making the air seem dank and heavy, too hot and humid, filling the shadows with threats. Fake foliage seemed to reach out and try to grab him.

And no matter how fast he moved, it was not fast enough.

Lance lay curled on the floor, howling in pain. Anna, holding the dagger, leaned against the sarcophagus, trying to shake her sister. "Nancy! Nancy, run! You've got to run!"

Nancy groaned, her eyes flickered, but she didn't wake.

Panic was beginning to break through the drug haze, but not enough to make Anna steady on her feet. Shaking her sister, she was dimly aware that tears were running down her cheeks, that Nancy wasn't waking.

And Barrow was turning over, groaning, trying to find his feet.

The dagger. If she took the dagger away, he couldn't hurt her sister. He wouldn't be able to perform his obscene rite.

Turning, she staggered toward the exit stairway, aware that she might have only seconds before he caught her.

It was like a nightmare. No matter how fast she tried to move, it was like moving through mud. The stairs seemed to come no closer.

Oh, God, please help me...

"Can't you go faster?" Tebbins demanded of the patrolman who was driving him to the museum.

The siren was screaming, the lights were flashing, but every intersection was still an impediment, forcing the officer to slow down. Tebbins knew he had no choice. More idiots than he could believe tried to cut in front of speeding emergency vehicles.

But the officer said, "Yes, sir," and floored it. To the next light, where he screeched the brakes and slowed down to make a reasonably safe crossing. Tebbins's teeth ground so hard that his jaws ached.

What the hell had gone wrong up there?

Gil stumbled through yet another corridor of snatching leaves and fake trees, his head throbbing so hard it was nearly blinding him. The labyrinth, which had seemed short and simple enough when he'd been a visitor, tonight seemed to stretch for miles with unexpected twists and turns. Once he got disoriented in a group of exhibit rooms, unable to tell which way he had entered, or which way he needed to continue.

But then he remembered, vaguely, and

plunged ahead, damning the drugs in his system and the blow to the head that was making it worse.

Then, at last, he saw the entrance to the tomb, a dark yawning maw leading downward. God, he hoped he was in time.

Anna struggled up the stairs, feeling as if each one were a mountain. She heard Lance behind her, dragging his foot, groaning, but moving steadily toward her.

She didn't dare look back.

Another step, and another, and finally she reached the exit door. It was closed, locked for the night, and for a few moments she thought the panic bar wouldn't work.

Shoving with all her strength, she at last heard the lock snap open, and the door yielded.

And only a few feet behind her, she heard Lance mumbling, "I'm gonna get you, bitch."

She shoved through the door, staggering into the exit chamber with its seats and guest book. Behind her, she heard the door close on Lance, heard his *hmmph* as it hit him. Then heard it open again as he came through.

He was moving faster, she realized, but she wasn't moving any faster at all. The floor kept trying to reach up for her, and again and again she had to steady herself to keep from tumbling over.

Go! Keep going. Get the dagger away from him. Go.

He was closing on her again as she rounded

the corner and burst onto the mezzanine. On the back of her neck she could almost feel his hot breath.

Vertigo grabbed her unexpectedly as her eyes saw the end of the mezzanine and the far-below cavern of the lobby. She wanted to turn away, but she was unsteady and...

He grabbed her. She felt him grab her injured arm.

A squeal of pain escaped her, and the dagger clattered to the floor as she fell.

Panting wildly, panicking, she began to crawl as best she could with one arm and disobedient legs. Keep going. She had to keep going.

She reached the railing, planning to use it to pull herself back to her feet. But as she turned over to grab it with her one good hand, she saw her nightmare vision.

Lance stood over her, with the dagger in his hands. Raising it. Letting it glitter cruelly in the light.

Gil nearly tumbled down the steps into the burial chamber. It was empty, except for one of the sisters. His heart skipped a beat and he hurried over to her. Nancy.

"Nancy!" He shook her. She groaned and curled up into a ball. No blood. Thank God.

But Anna...

Even in the dim light he could see the dark wet trail leading up the exit stairs. Leaving Nancy, he headed for it, praying he wasn't too late.

⬥ ⬥ ⬥

Tebbins's car slammed to a halt in front of the museum. The seat belt hurt the incision on his chest, for an instant making everything swim.

Other cars were coming. He could hear them. But he couldn't wait.

Reaching across with his good hand, ignoring the shriek of his wound, he unbuckled the belt. "Let's go."

The front door was locked. No one was visible inside except a cop who appeared to be sleeping at the security console.

Then he saw movement up on the mezzanine.

"Shoot the lock out," he told the patrolman beside him. "Now!

The young man obliged, taking it out with two shots. Then the officer shoved the door open, and went in ahead of Tebbins.

Lance Barro stood on the mezzanine, looking down at them, the dagger raised high in his hands.

"Shoot him," Tebbins ordered.

Gil burst through the exhibit exit doors to see Barro standing over Anna, the dagger clutched high above him. Sideways. For an instant Gil doubted his ability to shoot him.

But then there was a shout from below, and a gunshot. Gil heard the ricochet as the bullet struck the steel railing. Barro turned toward Gil.

And Gil, his head suddenly clear, took aim and squeezed the trigger.

His bullet went wide. He was still too unsteady. Barro started to smile.

Gil dropped to one knee, resting his elbow on his thigh to steady his aim.

"You see?" said Barro. "You can't shoot me. The jaguar's protecting me." He lifted the dagger high again.

"Bet on it, you son of a bitch." Gil squeezed the trigger again.

Barro's arms wheeled and he staggered toward the railing. An instant later, he fell over it.

CHAPTER TWENTY-THREE

Ignoring everything else, Gil rushed to Anna's side. Her face was tightened in a grimace of pain, and there was blood on her chin.

"Anna? Anna are you all right?"

"I'm fine...I'm fine...Nancy?"

"She's okay. Sleeping, but okay."

"Oh, God, I bit him. Like some kind of animal..." She rolled onto her good arm and retched with dry heaves.

"It's okay," he said, rubbing her back. "Baby, it's okay. You did what you had to."

Then, leaning closer to the railing, he looked down. Tebbins and the cop were standing on either side of Barro's sprawled body. "Is he gone?"

"Gone," Tebbins said. "Most definitely gone."

Anna caught her breath. "I need to see. I have to see him, Gil. To know..."

He understood. Gently, aware of his own lingering unsteadiness, he helped her to her feet. Slowly, like a pair of drunks, they made their way down the ramp to the floor below. A group of other cops burst in through the front doors, but Gil and Tebbins ignored them.

Tebbins pointed to the body. The tip of the dagger protruded from the center of Barro's back like a bloody jade obelisk.

"Hoist on his own petard," Tebbins said. "Right through the heart." He looked up. "Anna, it seems the gods were looking out for you after all."

One week later, Gil, Anna, and Nancy paced the museum lobby. A discreet sign near the door asked patrons to be patient with repairs. A square of bare floor showed beneath the mezzanine, where the bloodstained carpet had been taken away. Fresh, unpainted spackle covered a bullet hole, high in the wall. The security-booth door had been replaced, but the front doors still bore signs of the violence. The press coverage had been extensive, and a line was already forming outside, ready for the exhibit's reopening.

Anna almost didn't recognize Tebbins when

he shambled through the front door. He actually shambled. Gone were the dapper suit and bowler. His hair was artfully disheveled, and an oversize, rumpled raincoat hung over a plain brown suit. His teeth clenched an unlit cigar.

"Tebbins?" she asked. "Is that you?"

Gil was already laughing, shaking his head, even before Tebbins answered.

"They took away my moustache," he said with a shrug. "Can't do Poirot without the moustache."

"So now you're Columbo," Gil said.

Tebbins patted each pocket of his raincoat before finally fishing around and withdrawing an object wrapped in a wrinkled handkerchief. He pulled back one corner to reveal Pocal's dagger. "You'll be wanting this back, Anna. But not quite yet. It's just procedure, you know. A couple of details are still bothering me." He offered a slightly hunched bow. "Could we look at the crime scene again, ma'am?"

He was playing this new role to the hilt, Anna realized. She smiled. "Sure, Tebbins. Let's go on down."

"It kept nagging at me," Tebbins said as they walked through the exhibit. "How did he get the dagger out of that case? With the vacuum seal and all."

Anna shuddered as they entered the sarcophagus area.

"Are you okay?" Gil answered.

"Fine," she said, hoping her voice carried more conviction than she felt. "I just haven't been back down here since. But I need to get used to it. This is *my* exhibit. Not Lance Barro's."

"I'm sorry about this, ma'am," Tebbins said. "But these details... I like to tie up all the loose strings."

"You want to show off," Gil said with a wry smile. "You've figured out how he did it."

Tebbins opened the glass case. "I woke yesterday scratching at my arm. From where they had the IV in me." He took the cigar from his mouth and touched his fingertips to his forehead. "And that's when it hit me. That's how he did it."

"I don't understand," Nancy said. Anna nodded agreement.

Tebbins squatted and pointed beneath the case. "This vacuum alarm. He had to fool the sensor into thinking the pressure hadn't changed. So he had to keep a vacuum right next to the sensor itself." He looked at the bottom of the case for a moment, then straightened and examined the top surface. "Right here. See it?"

Anna stepped closer. Tebbins's fingertip pointed to the small round hole where the sensor fit into the case. "I don't see anything."

"You gotta look real close," Tebbins said. "It's just a tiny pinprick. Right...there."

"Yeah," Gil said. "But that's barely big enough for a needle."

Tebbins brought his hands together in a slow-motion clap. "Exactly. A needle. Like I said, it was the IV that got me to thinking. If he made a small enough hole, the pressure wouldn't drop enough to trip the alarm because the pump kicks in for small changes. Now look at the sensor opening. See how it looks a little wet? Shiny?"

Anna nodded. "Condensation?"

He shook his head. "Silicone. He took a hypodermic syringe and filled it with silicone. Then he drilled that tiny hole, right next to the sensor. And he injected a bubble of silicone, over the opening. That formed an airtight seal." He looked up. "So the alarm didn't trip when he opened the case. There was still a vacuum next to the sensor."

"But how about the pressure switch?" Gil asked. "How did he take the dagger away without tripping that?"

"Very carefully," Tebbins said. "Like this."

He laid the real dagger so that its blade rested atop the blade of the glass replica, which was still in its place. Then he slowly slid the two daggers over, until the real dagger lay over the switch.

"The pressure on the switch never changed," Tebbins said. "That pressure alarm's on now. He just had to be careful to keep the daggers overlapping, so the weight over the switch at any given moment was the same."

Pocal's dagger now rested exactly where it had been when the exhibit first opened. Tebbins wrapped the other dagger in his handkerchief and looked at Anna. "May I keep this? As a souvenir."

"I certainly don't want it," Anna said.

"Thank you, ma'am," Tebbins said. He

looked back at the case and gave a small nod. Next he replaced the glass cover and switched on the vacuum pump. He nodded again.

"Case closed." Tebbins smiled.

"He really was clever," Nancy said.

"Well, you've got your dagger back," Tebbins said. "I guess I'll be getting back to work." He shuffled toward the exit, paused, and turned. "Oh. Just one more thing."

Now even Anna laughed. He'd obviously been rehearsing that moment.

Tebbins put his fingers to his forehead and looked at Gil. "I'm curious. How soon are you transferring to the Tampa PD?"

"Me? Why would I want to do that?"

Anna smiled at him, lifting her brows. "*I'm* in Tampa."

"Good point," Gil said, his cheeks coloring.

Nancy grinned. "You go, girl."

RACHEL LEE, winner of numerous awards for her best-selling romantic fiction, is the author of Silhouette's #1 miniseries, Conard County. She also writes lighthearted contemporary romances as Sue Civil-Brown. But suspense fiction that zings like a high-tension wire with excitement and passion has become her signature style—and has made her previous Warner book *Before I Sleep* one of the best romantic reads of the year! As *Romantic Times* says, Rachel Lee is "an author to treasure."